To all Julians
and all Daphnes

Triad

三合會

David Gordon Rose

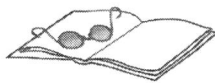

RoseTintedSpecs Imprint

Triad is a work of fiction. Names, characters, places, incidents
and organisations are used ficticiously or were created by the
author. Any resemblance to organisations, events, locales, actual
persons living or dead is coincidental. The central character is a
ficticious master of the art of the *Hwarang* of the ancient Silla
Kingdom of Korea and the generic spelling *Hwarang* or
Hwarangdo is used throughout the book. The name Hwa Rang
Do® was registered in 1968 and is the property of the World
Hwa Rang Do Association. There is no link or intended
association with this modern martial art.

Cover images "Foo Lion, Jasmine Gate, Forbidden City" and
"Star Ferry Pier, Kowloon Side" courtesy of Rose Photo Archive.
Font licensing correct at time of publication.

ISBN 978-0-9544518-2-0

RoseTintedSpecs Imprint
PO Box 209, Whitstable CT5 2WD, United Kingdom
www.rosetintedspecs.com
email: publisher@rosetintedspecs.com

Printed in the USA and UK. Comments on any of our booksare
welcome. Please contact the publisher. British English spelling is
used in this book.

ACKNOWLEDGEMENTS

An author is usually alone with a book to the end. During this time there will be people to thank for their advice, support and superior knowledge, especially with a book laboured over several years. Since this one was actually begun and mostly finished a good while ago I am no longer in touch with many who jollied me along. My thanks still goes out to them.

Most recently I would like to thank those authors and critics of the Authonomy community kind enough to read it and comment, especially those I quote on the first page. Talented writers themselves, they gave me the incentive to publish. There was no excuse for this thriller gathering further dust in my computer.

To my Rose also ...

... and to my mother, Skat, who flicked through the proof copy and said she might read it.

TRIAD – PART ONE

CHAPTER ONE

Maassluis, Holland, Friday 05 July, 1979

"Holy Mother of ..."

Meredith, the DEA officer stumbled over the latrine bucket, cursing. He hadn't expected to see a cage of wooden pallets with two girls in it huddled under a blanket. His flashlight lingered over the sordid scene on the top floor of the waterfront warehouse. He fully expected he and his companion, Julian de Lyon, would find drums of number three heroin, 'Chinese Brown Sugar'.

"That fucking light ..." one of the girls hissed in English.

Julian hushed the girl and the American with some urgency. Meredith turned his flashlight off. Moments earlier the only sound had been lapping water and the occasional cry of a curlew. Vehicles had arrived in the compound below and two Chinese could be heard talking quietly on the stairs.

With the drums offering no cover, Julian forced back one of the pallet's slats and bolted himself and his partner inside the cage with the girls. He caught a glimpse of one of them. Her hair was a mess, her face had the previous week's make-up all over it but her mouth was one of grim determination. She told him her name was Beverley and was about to introduce her companion, when it was Meredith's turn to insist on silence.

The footsteps of the Chinese crossing the concrete floor were light but not furtive. He opened the door and sniggered as the glow from his oil lamp picked out the fine black hair of the younger girl in the cage. When he saw the overturned bucket his leer disappeared. He let out a torrent of abuse in Hong Kong Cantonese, then saw Meredith.

There was a loud crack as Julian drove his arm through the pallet door, making contact with the man's scrawny head. The lamp shattered on the floor and the second Chinese called out nervously in the darkness. Meredith kicked the oil lamp away. There was a report and spurt of flame from the stairway and he returned fire reflexively with his .45.

Julian turned to Beverley whose fingers were in her ears from the explosion of the American's more powerful weapon.

"Have you got shoes?" he asked, smashing the cage door open, this time with a kick.

"They took them away from us," Beverley responded.

"Is she fit?"

Beverley grabbed her friend's wrist and hauled her to her feet.

"She is if you're taking us out of here ..."

Minutes later on a warm July night, Julian, Meredith and the two girls were scrambling along a short quay jutting into the grey waters of the Lek. There were now four vehicles in the compound with Chinese running everywhere. Julian watched Meredith tap his radio, muttering obscenities because it was not transmitting. The American's T-shirt, emblazoned PITTSBURGH 12 might just as well have read AMERICAN AGENT. Clearly, it was not a good night for an investigation.

The quay from which they were to be picked up was a mess of boating paraphernalia; oil drums, frayed hawsers, scrap timber and rusting machinery. Strained voices sounded all about them. It would be a trying few minutes before the launch arrived. There was an upturned skiff on the quay but even if they managed to lower it into the water it would be suicidal venturing out in it. Julian lifted both girls past a bin of scrap steel and settled them behind a stack of concrete sleepers. They had suffered because of their bare feet but not uttered a sound. Beverley did not want to let go of him.

"You're strong, aren't you!" she whispered.

He put a finger to his lips, loosened the cord of his hood and listened. Beyond the noises of their pursuers and lapping of the water below he could just hear the throbbing of diesel engines of the launch riding the turning tide. Meredith indicated he heard it too and Julian flashed the emergency signal. A searchlight from the launch several hundred metres out in the channel locked onto the quay. There was a muffled roar and the craft turned.

A machine gun on the other side of the sleepers began rattling insistently until a grenade from someone on the boat with an M79 silenced it. The girls reeled from the explosion and hail of concrete chips. Meredith was stung in the face. The launch pirouetted in a mass of white froth, thumping the quay broadside on. Crew members bundled the girls below. Julian and Meredith jumped aboard and held fast. The engines throttled open again and they were away.

Julian wiped the spray from his face and looked at the warehouse. A small fire had started in the yard, throwing an orange light and flickering shadows up its massive brick frontage. Car headlights were swinging about. With the sound of explosions and gunfire across the estuary making enough noise to wake up the nearby town, the river police would not be long in coming.

"Christ, that was risky, an M79 ..." Meredith said to one of the crew.

"One of those piss-pot grenades!" the young officer replied, pouring generous measures of Jim Beam into tin mugs.

"Been on the receiving end of one lately?" Julian countered. The three men began chuckling.

After a stiff drink and several minutes of the fresh night air on his face, Julian went below to the cramped quarters. Beverley and her friend, pale and exhausted, were clutching mugs of tea. He made sure they had no immediate problems or needs and reassured them they would be comfortable at the police headquarters in Rotterdam. Someone from the British consulate would see them later in the morning, he said. He didn't mention they would soon be on their way home. That didn't always go down well.

A familiar tale unfolded as Beverley answered his questions. She wasn't telling the truth, saying she had been in Amsterdam for a year as a waitress but he didn't pursue it.

"We'd been in that hole a week," she went on. "There were six of us, then they took the others away. The Chinese and sometimes a Dutchy gave us food every day but didn't seem to know what to do with us. They knew what to do with us at night though, the bastards."

Her voice tailed off but her face took on the determined look Julian had first seen. True grit, he could have called it had he known the expression, although he knew she was from somewhere in the North of England. The other youngster 'Suzy', was clinging silently to her. She was younger, about thirteen years old and looked Hong Kong Chinese. He spoke a few comforting words to her in Cantonese but she did not respond. He asked Beverley how she had got into the situation.

"She was on a cultural visit with friends of her family, she said. A right posh lot they must be. They live in a château near Paris. I call her Suzy. You know, Suzy Wong, because she's from Hong Kong."

She shook her friend's shoulder to no avail. The girl had been alone in the château one evening when two men had walked in to her bedroom. They held a cloth to her face with chloroform, or something, on it. She had only vague

10

recollections of what happened after that.

"She's only eleven, the bastards."

Julian turned his attention to the landing lights of a mooring platform he could see through the porthole.

"Were you friendly with the man who got you into this?"

"He's a Chinese, but not like you. You're only half, aren't you?" she asked, looking up at him. "His name's Johnny, Johnny Wan, I think. I met him a couple of months ago in the club. He's been good to me, giving me money and fags and meals too in his restaurant on the Oude Zijds, by the Town Hall. Until last week, the rat."

A scowl swept across her tired face but the smile soon reappeared and Julian was amazed again at how forgiving people could be. She called out her thanks as she and Suzy were leaving the boat, blowing him a kiss with the words,

"If I were only ten years older ..."

Meredith grinned but thought better about any ribald comment. He didn't know Julian that well.

1/2
Amsterdam, Saturday 06 July

The following evening was also warm and pleasant. Julian stopped on a bridge, adjusted the zipper of his track suit and watched the light playing on the oily surface of the canal. There was a tinkling of glass from a restaurant at the water's edge. People laughed. Plane trees whispered all around. Amsterdam was at its best.

He was not in harmony with this prettiest of cities. Life was good for those enjoying a summer weekend but while two young girls had been brought back from the brink of domestic and sexual slavery, a hundred others would have been drawn in. The trade was remorseless and expanding.

The weekend was not improving. He looked back at the traffic across Rembrandtsplein, his vision of Ann-Marie lingering. She had neither home nor business interests in

Holland, having long accepted the Dutch were too liberal and that an aristocrat would be swallowed whole. Had it been her in the Citroën that passed him in the square? He had hardly seen her in recent months but thought she would be in Paris that weekend for her father's birthday. He should know if his wife had just driven by.

He walked on along the cobbled quay to the Oude Zijds and into an empty restaurant by the Town Hall, squinting in the neon brightness. A tight-faced Chinese youth in a dirty apron viewed him with suspicion. Being part-Western, with dark brown hair and bigger physically than most Chinese, Julian's presence invariably provoked this response. The youth took his order in silence and left a beer unopened by the glass.

Julian stretched his legs under the table. Ross had laid the weekend's operation on him at a ridiculous two hour's notice. This was not what he wanted to hear when about to pitch into Friday rush hour in Brussels.

It was now after eleven at the end of a long day at police headquarters in Amsterdam assisting with interrogation of hard-done-by couriers and surly Chinese without proper identification. He had stayed late only because of the DEA operation and the chance he might pick up some information for the office and make the weekend worthwhile.

He finished a bowl of noodles and contemplated ordering another Tiger beer. It was more than a casual reminder the Singapore triads had taken over the narcotics trade in Amsterdam, pushing out the Hong Kong-based 14K and Wo triads to other cities. He would have to put narcotics and his wife's recent erratic behaviour and periods of disappearance aside. His office's information was that a Dutch cell of one of these Chinese organizations was behind the huge increase in the trafficking of teenagers out of Holland.

Beverley and Suzy were lucky. If they had been abducted for prostitution their breaking-in period could have begun within days in a brothel anywhere between Casablanca and Cape Town. After this would be imprisonment in a stinking room somewhere between Marseilles and Macao servicing anyone who could pay their owner. Their fate could also have been one of sexual entertainment with animals or as victims of torture on film. Whatever it was, they would probably not have survived their teens.

After three years in Europe, Julian felt only bitterness that a tiny under-resourced office of the United Nations, the Committee on Slavery, was the only organisation in Europe making an active stand against a billion-dollar trade. It was a grim tale of impotence and indifference and of collusion and profit to the highest levels of society and government.

It was almost midnight when four Chinese swaggered into the restaurant laughing loudly. They sensed trouble when they saw Julian stand up. One reacted immediately, running into the kitchen and scrambling into the alleyway over rubbish bins, bicycles and empty cardboard boxes. There was only one way out to the canal front and Julian was waiting.

The expensively-dressed Singaporean backed into the shadows. His hair was coiffured like that of the younger men and slightly stiffened by an adoring girlfriend's hair lacquer. A trace of make-up on his face would not have looked out of place in old Bugis Street.

"Johnny Wan ..." Julian said with the faintest of smiles. "You look well, Johnny. The Dutch have been good to you."

Johnny with his lacquer and mascara was wanted for a list of unpleasant activities going back to 1972 in Toronto's Chinatown, when Julian had worked for the Bureau of Narcotics and Dangerous Drugs. More recently his name had been linked with a transport company operating out of

13

Belgium with a sideline in little girls. This meeting could be the break Julian had hoped for that weekend.

A chill went down the Singaporean's spine. He had enough experience of narcotics agents to know he should do as he was told. Julian nodded toward the canal and he acquiesced, his senses straining. The vigorous clacking of *mah-jong* tiles from a room high above them stopped. This should have been followed by their clattering over the table but there was silence. Julian read the signs too. The restaurant fronted a gambling house, controlled no doubt by Johnny's gang, the See Tong. The alert had gone out.

Johnny's companions reappeared on the empty quayside at the entrance to the alley. More of their kin tumbled out of the kitchen at the back end. There were a dozen men around Julian. Cleavers and kitchen knives glinted but it was Johnny who hissed they should not even think about it. He might just walk away from the police station that night.

The Singaporean missed the point. There was a flash of a steel blade and he sank to his knees, astonishment across his face. Someone had decided he was a liability.

Julian's attention turned to the two burly youths nearest him in the gloom of the alley waving knives with more bravado than technique. A double kick sent one of the youths on his back on the blackened, greasy cobbles and the blade through a first-floor window. The only sounds were those of vertebrae cracking and glass breaking. The other attacker Julian gripped at a pressure point above the wrist. The youth went to his knees gasping in pain, looking helplessly at his knife. A *ma hyel* below the elbow induced paralysis and the youth rolled over convulsing.

There was some muttering in the alley and general movement ceased. Julian remained motionless. Indeed, it looked as though he hadn't moved at all. His eyes flashed in the darkness, defying any of them to come closer but it was the insistent sound of a police siren on the other side of the canal that scattered them into the night.

"Talk, Johnny, you're going to die," Julian whispered. Blood was spurting from the Singaporean's chest. "Why do your Brothers kill you?"

Johnny Wan was grinning. No matter how bitter he might have felt in his last moments he would say nothing. Fear of the Brotherhood and of the oaths he had sworn would go with him to his grave.

Julian prompted again, asking if he did not want something better for his wife and child. Johnny, still grinning, could not resist the words,

"Look in your own backyard – "

1/3
Brussels, Monday 08 July

When Julian returned to his apartment in Rue Américaine after another difficult day at the office in Place Madou he was greeted by the pungent odour of his young nephew's enthusiastic cooking. He poured a drink and looked down into a street in shadow with the evening sun warming the chimney pots. Peter had come over to Belgium for his last three vacations from university in England and Julian felt they were getting to know each other. It was unfortunate his nephew's presence that week was inappropriate.

After the incident in the Amsterdam alleyway that left one man dead, Julian submitted a brief report to the head of the city police's Criminal Intelligence Division and took an early flight back to Brussels. Towards dawn, Meredith was murdered in the doorway of his apartment block in the Hague with a single silenced shot. This prompted an altogether more urgent flurry of calls between Brussels and Geneva over this matter. The American was a CIA field man using DEA cover and the US authorities were demanding answers from the Committee on Slavery's parent organisation, the Bureau of Social Affairs.

"O Mighty One, do you desire tea?" Peter asked a second time, smiling engagingly at his uncle standing by the window. Julian declined. Something curry-like was dripping onto the carpet from the wooden spoon his nephew was holding.

"Something to eat, perhaps?"

Knowing he would not be good company that evening, Julian said he would eat in town and Peter should invite over someone more deserving. Peter ignored his uncle's slippery compliment of a meal he was actually preparing for Thérèse and said he had a theory one could test a girl's sexuality by how hot she could eat a curry. Amused by the idea of a controlled experiment, Julian poured another bourbon and asked how his nephew graded his results.

Peter found himself struggling.

"I prostrate myself, O Divine One, for my fatuousness," he said, admitting his evidence was far from conclusive.

Julian walked to the tram stop a little way down the Chaussée de Charleroi, leaving Peter and Thérèse alone. It had taken his nephew a long time to persuade his Continental friend to sample one of his creations. Thérèse was the epitome of Eve of the Sunday school lessons of his childhood. Fair-haired and of slender build she could not have contrasted more with his nephew's current punk look and almost manic concern with physical fitness.

He couldn't help smiling at the young man's nerve and was sure in his own youth in Hong Kong he had been more respectful to young women, to everything. Thinking further, he realised the point would not stand much scrutiny.

On his return later that evening through the silent streets of the old city, Julian regretted not taking up his nephew's offer of dinner. Peter was his only family left in Europe and he should be making every effort to know the young man better. He caught a 32 tram on the boulevard at Porte de Namur and as it trundled south past the end of his road, he realised he was prey yet again to a conflict of interests.

The tram left him alone at the end of the Avenue Louise, in embassy land, where gendarmes patrol with submachine guns. Julian pulled the collar of his coat about his face and began walking back up the avenue. He was in no hurry but was dissatisfied with the evening and irritated at finding himself drawn once again to his wife's empty apartment.

He was not unduly worried about Ann-Marie's current disappearance. *Madame*, as she was known along the tentacles of her family's business empire, did as she pleased and could have been anywhere in the world.

Julian didn't change his mind about going into her town apartment. A dead CIA agent in the Hague, the appearance of Johnny Wan, the sighting of a disappeared wife in Amsterdam and an enquiry into the weekend operation were a set of circumstances he needed to think about. Johnny Wan's last words had concentrated his mind.

The porter in the brilliantly-lit foyer of the marble-clad building on the *rond point Louise* showed him to the penthouse apartment. The living room was as he had left it a couple of weeks earlier. Cushions showed the same creases, ashtrays remained unused. His note was unread and this at least would have been removed by Ann-Marie or her maid.

He found himself again rankled over the artefacts in glass cases. They were arranged such that on a fine evening the last rays of sunshine would fire the bold colours of the Aztec pottery and give a rich redness to the mellowed Inca gold. Even under soft artificial light the collection had a vibrant, pagan power. It delighted Ann-Marie who once said the full ritual of human sacrifice must be one of the most potent events a human being could witness.

It was not the materialistic excess characterizing his wife's family that dominated Julian's thoughts as he returned to the midnight streets. The last time he and Ann-Marie spoke he mentioned something of the Committee on Slavery's work; that a powerful French family could be involved in a spate of highly-organised abductions across Europe. She had displayed an unseemly anger at the suggestion. It had triggered something he feared he would regret.

A few minutes after leaving the apartment he turned into a dimly-lit Rue Américaine and noticed a car ahead of him, creeping, without lights. When the car stopped, he did too. Brussels is a provincial little town settled by nine and asleep by eleven. When the car moved off again Julian broke into a trot. Its two occupants were following someone. The shadowy figure, also running, became visible in Place Leemans. Again the young man stopped, leaning this time against a lamp-post to massage his calves. Julian's thoughts hardened. It was his nephew being followed.

After waiting in the darkness until the car had left the street Julian let himself into his apartment. Peter was in an armchair in the living room. He had run all the way from Thérèse's place after taking her home and had a touch of cramp.

Julian poured a drink for them both and asked if the young woman enjoyed dinner. Peter began relating the evening with a sparkle in his eye until Julian told him he keep his fantasies to himself.

"In fact, young nephew, I have the rest of the week off. We haven't done anything positive together and you've been here two weeks. This will be a good opportunity."

Peter avoided asking what it was a good opportunity for. He did request they go for a spin over the weekend, meaning he wanted to get his hands on his uncle's car.

"I had other things in mind."

"Ominous!" Peter responded, grinning. "Still, it'll serve me right. I didn't do half as much training as I should have last term."

CHAPTER TWO

Brussels, Monday 15 July

Mademoiselle Arameau stared vacantly at the traffic in Place Madou while her boss read the documents she had placed on his desk. He was muttering over another delivery from head office in Geneva. To make matters worse she didn't quite understand his question.

"What is Julian about this morning?" he repeated.

She shifted uncomfortably.

"What appointments does he have, *Mademoiselle* – "

Mlle. Arameau had been Ross McReedy's personal assistant for a week. A French-speaking Belgian, she was uncomfortable with his accent in both French and English. Their office was a feasibility study set up after a 1975 UN resolution and responsible to the Bureau of Social Affairs in Geneva. The job ought to have been a glamorous one but such ideas disappeared as she became familiar with the files. She reminded the director that M. de Lyon had his young nephew with him and he had given him the week off.

"Of course," Ross tutted, "our Number One you think might still have criminal inclinations?"

"This is not what I said," Mlle. Arameau replied, regretting having made any remarks about their senior operative. It seemed obvious head office would be interested in the criminal convictions referred to in Julian's file if there was to be an investigation into the death of the American agent in Amsterdam. A review of methods and working practices of the field men had been requested with Herr Brandt specifically asking for copies of Julian's recent reports.

"It is a suggestion I bear in mind," Ross went on, softening his tone. "If the office in Geneva is to turn this review into a piece of theatre I shall need all the prompting I can get!"

He swivelled in his chair to see a blank look on his young assistant's face but was tired of translating into baby English. At least his last one appreciated his occasional joke.

She was called away to the computer room and Ross sat back mulling over Meredith's death after the weekend operation. The Dutch police and the DEA wanted to interview Julian, of course, but a security review annoyed him. For the second time in a week he found himself flicking through Julian's file.

Julian de Lyon, born 1941, Saigon. Childhood in Vietnam, Korea and Hong Kong to the age of 16. Father French, a veteran of the war against the *Viet Minh* in Indo-China and casualty of the 1954 massacre of the French Expeditionary Forces at Dien Bien Phu. Mother Chinese national, returned to Communist China 1956 ...

He skipped pages until he came to the lines,

Two criminal convictions, prosecution by the British authorities in the North Kowloon Magistrates court, February and March 1957, for threatening behaviour and possession of an offensive weapon. Cautioned for the former and sentenced for the latter to sixty days corrective detention. Sentence reduced for good behaviour ...

Looking across the city to the cathedral the Flemish call Koekelberg, Ross decided the information was old hat. A boisterous teenager with considerable fighting skills wouldn't have come out of the Gorbals, or its Hong Kong equivalent, without ink on his copy book. Julian had also worked for agencies of the American government before joining the UN and would have been vetted many times, his experience as a former triad member perhaps considered a bonus.

Ross was respectful of the professionalism and abilities his Number One brought to the Committee's operations. He was also aware of a darker side to the man many found daunting but which he thought was just the need of a bit of honest family life. His current marriage, or perhaps liaison was a better word, did not provide that.

When his assistant returned with another pile of printouts he suggested brusquely she take it up to their Number Three, Marc Vlaminck. Mlle. Arameau blushed about the extra work but said the DEA regional office in Paris were being very helpful about van Merken Transport. Ross expressed mild interest. He was thinking about head office intentions and about Julian's absence with so much work on the table. But Julian was due time off and was concerned about his wife's well-being. This would give him breathing space.

2/2

After a morning run to the park at the top of Avenue Brugmann, returning through the well-heeled residential areas of Ixelles and Uccle, Julian and his nephew had breakfast before Julian excused himself for things he needed to do in town. Peter always thought of his uncle as having lots to do and wasn't concerned. Term was about to finish for most of the friends he had made in Brussels in the previous two years and he was looking forward to some parties and trips out in Thérèse's old car that was frequently transport to six of them at a time.

Julian walked into town later that morning. He crossed the boulevard by his office and went on to the Grand Place.

The walk took an hour and he welcomed the exercise and time to think. When he reached the bustling old market square he turned down Rue de l'Etuve to the bar opposite the *Manneken Pis*. Raoul, the proprietor, treated Julian to a cognac. Even with such an illustrious neighbour who had been dressed in a commando uniform and black beret that day, Raoul struggled to keep the place open. It was ten o'clock and the bar was empty, though it was a favourite with police from Central Division and Raoul could do Julian the occasional favour.

Julian passed him the registration number of the car that had followed Peter to Rue Américaine the previous Friday evening. He was about to leave when a young Flemish policeman strode in, ordered a beer and drank it in a single draught. He downed another almost immediately and looked at his watch.

"Busy, Artur?" Julian asked.

"Busy ..." he replied in English, running a hand through his hair. "This town is like bloody Chicago."

Julian had been on a daylight raid with Artur in the city before Christmas. The Gang Squad, acting on information from the Committee on Slavery had, without a warrant, smashed their way into the basement of a boutique and released a teenager they found bound and gagged. An abduction business operating in the centre of Brussels had been uncovered.

"Is this why you carry machine guns?"

"You've got nothing to fear," Artur retorted.

"A young friend of mine shouldn't either but was stopped last week by the *Gare du Nord*. Looking at the girls in the windows, I expect."

"We usually search 'long hairs'."

"In broad daylight, with submachine guns?"

Raoul shifted uneasily.

"We do a good service for the public," Artur snapped.

"We carry them for hold-ups and robberies. We were twenty-nine in the Squad in January, now we are twenty-two. With seven friends dead, I shoot first and ask questions later ..."

With this remark the policeman walked out.

"For God's sake!" Raoul hissed. "You soured his beer last time he was here. He doesn't like you because of your family. You know how he hates big nobs around town."

He finished abruptly and laughed.

"On the other hand, he occasionally speaks well of you. Today he is not happy in his job, I would say."

"None of us are wild about him starting his shift full of beer."

Julian decided his week had not started well.

When he called at the bar again the following morning, Raoul poured a Remy under the counter and said he couldn't talk. The bar was full of police changing shifts. Julian sat by the door with the second edition of *Le Soir* and watched the tourists coming up from the Grand Place. The bawdy little figure they were seeking was sporting his Maurice Chevalier outfit, another from his extensive wardrobe of costumes.

When Raoul finally had a moment it was to say it would be a busy day. Julian was about to leave when Artur appeared.

"Mind if I sit here?"

"I'm just leaving, Artur."

"Fuck you, have a beer," he replied, catching the waitress's attention.

"I only drink when I'm working ..."

"Okay, okay! I don't like you either but you wanted some information ..."

The young policeman was pleased with Julian's silence. The girl put a beer and a cognac on the table with the boss's compliments. He shouted across the bar to Raoul,

"Business good, eh? Have one yourself!"

He saw Julian look at his watch and said he would come to the point.

"First, the registration number belongs to a pool car from a shipping firm, van Merken Transport and Shipping. Don't look so surprised. Most of the information you ask Raoul for comes through me and I might need a favour from you sometime."

He took a mouthful of beer.

"I was moody yesterday, I admit. I'd stopped a Lincoln during the night I knew was owned by a High Court judge and thought some stick would do him good. He had some tart in furs with him. Anyway, I gave him a hard time because he didn't have his ID and she actually refused to show me hers! Then when I radioed the chief, that ass-licker told me to apologise for detaining them and ask if I could be of service and escort them somewhere."

"There is no justice, Artur!"

"It wasn't funny. We do a good service – "

The young policeman laughed when he realised he had turned full circle.

"And the point is?" Julian asked.

"I thought I'd tell you, since your committee outfit is interested in van Merken, there's a probable new route for live cargo in and out of Holland that starts near Maassluis. A group of girls were found in a container vessel involved in an accident on that part of the river. And something else. There's another snuff movie they're all watching at headquarters. It was with the group. Vice traced it to Hamburg and are sure they're using amateurs. Girls who've been abducted maybe? Then, you'd know all this."

"You know a lot about our office," Julian responded.

Artur took another swig of Stella.

"My brother works for Rotterdam Criminal Intelligence. We're Dutch you know, not Flemish. He's worked with you. At least, he knows of a guy based in Brussels who's half-

Chinese and has joined them on operations. I've always assumed it's you!"

Julian stood up and nodded his appreciation.

"Well, I'm off to bed," Artur said finally. "God, it's a terrible time of the day to try and sleep. Back on at ten."

He looked thoughtfully at Julian.

"Have a chat with one of van Merken's regular fancy bits, a blonde called Sophie, if you want to know more about that firm. You'll have seen her at the kind of parties you go to. She's often down at the Hyatt. Expensive, I should say."

Julian was interested in a link between van Merken and Chinese criminal activity in Dutch ports. Van Merken Transport and Shipping was a suspected member of a syndicate whose activities now included the abduction of a particular social group of teenagers into a form of prostitution for the more discerning.

So brazen were the syndicate's methods, police forces around Europe had turned part of the Place Madou office of the Committee on Slavery into an operations centre. Ross's budget and the experience of all eight of the Committee's operatives were fully stretched. Interpol were waiting for the final pieces of evidence from Ross that could justify a raid on van Merken's road transport operations. Julian had been working on the file for weeks and on this point alone Ross's reasons for giving him time off must have been important.

Crossing the Grand Place on his way back to his apartment, he was greeted by his nephew, Thérèse and a young woman he remembered meeting at Christmas. Peter was about to introduce Daphne when Julian shook her hand and began,

"A pleasure meeting you again, *Mademoiselle* Daphne."

"How nice, you remembered my name!" Daphne responded, beaming. "We met on this very spot, under

25

Christmas lights but not under festive circumstances."

Daphne was the persistent young teacher who prompted the raid at the boutique where Julian had also met Artur, six months earlier. Two school friends were shopping in Rue Neuve. One went into a *pâtisserie* and the other into the boutique opposite. The girl never came out of the clothes shop and her friend, after searching up and down the street, knew something was wrong. By chance she came across Daphne, their teacher, who ran to police headquarters by the Grand Place and would not leave until something was done.

It was Thérèse who broke up the reunion with a reminder they had things to do in town. If Daphne had not met Peter's uncle before, she had now, she thought. Her cousin was positively glowing.

When Peter got back to the apartment that evening he brought up the subject of their meeting in the Grand Place, filling in gaps about Daphne he thought his uncle might like to hear. Though Daphne was Thérèse's cousin she was more like an older sister, he explained. She was ahead of all of them, studying for her master's degree in economics and computer science. Julian was poring over a map and some papers. Peter, seeing he was making no impression resorted to asking outright what his uncle thought.

"She has the hair colour of a warrior."

"Is that good or bad?" Peter asked after a pause.

"That would depend on whose side she was on!" Julian replied, looking up at his nephew.

Knowing his uncle was as forthcoming as he would be, Peter confessed he was passing on a party invitation from Daphne to her end of academic-year celebration. She was planning a Provençal evening and it was likely to be a memorable one.

"Will the young woman be giving this invitation herself?"

"No," Peter began cautiously, "she ..."

Peter observed his uncle's lips curl into a smile. It was just as well the invitation hadn't actually been declined as he was under threat. Daphne had bombarded him with questions about his uncle that afternoon.

The party invitation was the second Julian received that week. The first was for cocktails in Ghent that Thursday evening. Such a mix of society and business people was the kind of occasion Ann-Marie hosted and attended and some of her stable of social friends would be there. He occasionally made time for such events. This one was celebrating a new business in leisure boating and there was a van Merken connection.

Feeling he and Peter had seen enough of each other for the time being, he decided he would take up the invitation. His nephew had threatened to return that evening with the gang and he knew his presence would not enhance their evening. He changed into a dinner jacket and glancing in the mirror was aware he had smiled little in recent months. The contrast with the youngsters who had called that morning could not have been greater.

Locking his study he went through the basement to the courtyard and stood in the darkness by his car. The buildings around him and the street beyond the archway were quiet. Within minutes he was on the Porte de Halle in heavy traffic. It had been a toss-up between a crowded train to St. Pieter's station in Ghent or late afternoon traffic flowing west on the Ostende motorway.

Soon after Julian's departure, Peter and his friends arrived at the apartment in high spirits after their day out at Ronquières. Here in idyllic countryside not far from Brussels, barges on the Brussels-Mons canal are hauled up and down a hill in tanks in twenty minutes when previously they had to negotiate sixteen locks. Peter was impressed with this monumental piece of engineering at Easter and Thérèse promised she would organise another visit.

Peter set about getting drinks, combining this with a loosening-up routine that made him look rather comic. Well-built, with spiky hair and always cheerful he frequently caused Martine to giggle, though she was kind enough not to say, with a pipe in his mouth he could be *Monsieur* Hulot on holiday.

Daphne called later. Peter let her in and told her she might yet save the evening with the flagon of wine she had carried heroically from her place by the Parc du Cinquantenaire. Daphne knew immediately he and Thérèse had been arguing. She was kneeling by the Hi-Fi, Henri and Martine were in the kitchen sharing a beer in silence and Claude and Michelle were on a sortie to the local shop.

Daphne decided she should tackle Peter and prevent the evening grinding to a halt but was immediately distracted by the apartment. It was her first visit.

"All these oriental things," she began, "and those swords. They are so beautiful."

"Cheery little things, aren't they!" Peter responded. "That one is a Korean Silla sword. Uncle calls it a *bonguk geom*. These two curved ones are Japanese. The longer one is a *tachi* a samurai wore with armour. The shorter is a *katana* for civilian dress. They're Fourteenth Century and as sharp, apparently, as the day they were forged."

"Did you say Fourteenth Century?"

Peter started chuckling. Daphne looked at him.

"Well, it's not funny really," he said, as they took a closer look at the swords in the display cabinet laid over white gravel and partly withdrawn from their scabbards. "This *tachi* was made by Muramasa of Ise. His swords gave their owners reputations as butchers. They're supposed to bring bad luck as well, which is probably why I'm not allowed to touch it. A sword was believed to be the soul of its master and followed his will."

"Deadly but beautiful." Daphne corrected herself. She wasn't sure if it was the music Thérèse was playing or the presence of the man whose apartment this was making her feel strange. Suddenly forgetting her cousin's dislike of the whole subject of martial arts, a major cause of the arguing, she asked Peter if his uncle had sword skills. He had seen him once with them out of the case, Peter replied, describing the display as awesome.

"You and I certainly wouldn't have lasted in the shogunate period in Japan!"

Daphne looked at him again.

"You couldn't be mouthy with a *samurai*. If he was not suited to something and touched the handle of the *tachi*, you went down on your knees. If he withdrew it just one centimetre, you were in deep do do!"

Daphne burst out laughing at his colourful French. He couldn't have learnt it from Thérèse. She asked if he addressed his uncle as *sensei* because he was his teacher.

"I use it as a term of respect, like the Japanese," he replied, glancing now in Thérèse's direction. "With uncle it would be *si fu*, which is about the same, 'father' in Chinese. It's one of lots of titles in their family system of martial arts. There might be one for your actual uncle, if he is your teacher ..."

"*Mon Dieu*, Peter," Thérèse interrupted, finally.

Daphne's look stopped her saying more. She squeezed a sullen-looking Peter and said she was enjoying the music at least. Seeing the words Classical Japanese on the cassette in English she almost hadn't put it on. There was a beautiful, haunting quality to the string and wind ensemble and she wanted a copy.

"Don't get me wrong, I do respect your uncle. I'm just afraid of what he can do and that it's related to killing."

"I don't think it's as simple as that," Daphne responded

coolly. "These societies were, on the one hand barbarous and cruel and on the other, cultured and highly sophisticated. These are the extremes. Martial arts is a philosophy drawn from the whole spectrum. That's right, isn't it, Peter?"

Peter winked at her.

"And there was a rationalisation of this power. There always has been in history."

Thérèse didn't argue beyond telling her cousin not to be so clever. Henri, who played a bit of guitar, didn't help by pitching in that the music was pentatonic and she should have worked that out.

They decided after eating, and drinking a little wine, they would go down to Place de Brouckère and have a laugh at the late-night *kung fu* film. Even Thérèse warmed to the idea but wanted a shower first. Peter found a new towelling gown for her to take up to his room and adjacent shower room and poured himself more wine.

Daphne and Henri were engaged in some good-humoured martial arts posturing of their own. Henri asked Peter if his uncle did any teaching or demonstrations.

"He doesn't seem to be involved in it at all these days, I suppose being in an office and all that. He's shown me simple things but I can't begin to think of the secrets he possesses."

"What do you mean, secrets?" Daphne asked.

"Well, just the way he moves and the advice he comes up with sometimes. And the speed, like with the swords. You'd have to see it to know what I mean. He must be a master of something. My teacher has a high ranking but uncle makes him look like *Sensei Plod*."

"You'd better watch it!" Henri proffered, seeing Daphne lost in thought again. "He might devour little girls for breakfast."

"Do you think I wouldn't be able to cope, Henri?"

She tried to look serious but couldn't help laughing. After

reminding Peter she was relying on his persuasive ability with regard to her Provençal evening she said he must watch his moodiness. Thérèse should not have to put up with it. Peter was suitably humbled.

A light in the attic room jolted the figure in a corresponding room on the other side of the street. After several days in the empty house the man was bored rigid. Now there was activity, seven youngsters. The man put his eye to the camera and couldn't believe his luck. The girl removed her top.

"What a little peach ..."

He moved the F1 a fraction on its tripod and refocused the 1000 millimetre lens. Three shots in quick succession caught her peeling off her vest and her breasts popping out. He broke into a sweat. She fiddled with button and zip on her jeans for a moment and let them fall to the floor, looking idly at something in the room. He squeezed the plunger twice more and put his hand down his trousers.

"Come on, *chérie* ..."

Dutifully the girl slipped the tiny panties down her legs and stepped out of the pile of clothes. He moved the Nikon a fraction again, taking more shots of the naked girl bathed in golden evening light, hardly able to keep his eye against the viewfinder. The sun caught the curve of her abdomen and wispy pubic hair as she twisted slightly. It was almost a bonus she lifted her arms, gathering her blonde hair off her shoulders and pinning it up.

"*Merde*, that's it, keep still ... those nipples ..."

And as he was thinking of easing his erection the girl crossed her arm over her breasts, leaned toward the window and let the blind drop.

"Too late, darling ..." he leered, "... too late."

Julian had no difficulty in locating the cocktail party. It

31

was being staged in an empire-style house in a square known locally as Millionaire's Square. Two hundred people including a cabinet minister, a pop star and media personalities must have been present. Van Merken made a brief appearance. He was renowned for his habilatory elegance and flamboyant manner. Combined with a shock of white hair, steel grey eyes and the attention he was receiving from a pair of aggressive socialites, he could not be missed.

Julian had been in the house half an hour and was about to leave when he crossed paths with someone he had not seen for a while.

"Good evening, Sophie. How is the conspicuous consumer?"

"I am fine, *monsieur*," Sophie countered.

"Still eating two kilos of meat a day?"

"And it's working wonders for my figure!"

Julian knew Sophie from these social occasions, as Artur had supposed. She was a professional escort, an expensive one. Her current favourite topic was Brutus. The idea for a canine bodyguard came one night Julian was walking back to his apartment. Two men outside the service flats in nearby Rue de Facqz were treating her badly and he had intervened. He subsequently discovered an interesting character who liked powerful cars and big dogs.

The man watching them intently came over. He was wearing gold lamé trousers and a black velvet jacket edged in lilac satin. A heavy gold bracelet clinked against the crystal glass of Chivas he held in his fingertips.

"My Darling Sophie," the man began above the noise of the band, planting a kiss on her cheek, "I hope you are not avoiding me."

Sophie introduced Daniel to Julian with a courteous smile but left no opening for conversation. He offered his hand to Julian. It was a true Belgian handshake, limp, though he at least looked Julian in the eye.

"He is amusing," Sophie volunteered when he had gone. "Unfortunately, anything a man wants, any type of deviation, he makes a speciality. With the name-dropping he does – police inspectors, government people, magistrates, royalty even – we call him Pimp to the Establishment. I'm independent enough to stay out of his pocket but I have to make a living and he knows everyone, just everyone."

Sophie fell silent, knowing she had said enough. Julian had watched Daniel earlier in conversation with van Merken and decided to ask Sophie a favour. She listened intently then asked what hat he was wearing that night, though her mischievous smile did not beg an answer. He left the crowded reception room for the relative quiet of the front hallway and was joined minutes later by Daniel.

"The adult entertainment you are interested in is not a problem, *monsieur*," Daniel said, coming straight to the point. "What you need first is a drink and a good show to set you up. You will find both at the club by the Hilton tonight."

He waved his hand discreetly when Julian hinted the usual Brussels' night life was not what he was interested in. Studying Julian's face he went on,

"Tonight's floor show will amuse you, I am sure. A simulated rape."

Julian calculated how little he was known around town and how much he was relying on Sophie's discretion and replied,

"This is more what I had in mind ..."

"Then mention my name at the club after the show. They will fix you up with what you want."

Sophie touched Julian's shoulder in the doorway and asked if she could slip out with him. She was even more pleased he offered to escort her home. He had not seen her car among the other exotic machinery packed into the driveway and parked around the square.

A maid fetched her silk shawl.

"More than ever these days I need professional headaches," she muttered, unsmiling.

The late evening sky was blood red with slivers of orange and flecked with blue. The smell of the countryside came in through the open roof of the car. The flat farmland of West Flanders is not much to look at but Julian found the air fresh compared with the oppressive heat and humidity of the Far East. A frown crossed his forehead, however. Major changes were about to occur.

As they motored around the new intersections into Brussels, passing the huge concrete sculpture signifying a hand open in welcome, Julian was inclined to invite Sophie to dinner. He didn't carry it through. He didn't like to feel it was because he had nothing else to do.

Sophie thanked Julian warmly for the lift home. Her mind having been on similar lines during the drive she decided next time they would have dinner.

CHAPTER THREE

Hamburg, Saturday 20 July

"Now we have agreed to the quantities of numbers two and three for next month," the strident, effeminate voice went on, "I come back to our losses on meat sales."

Four men, a middle-aged German businessman, a German-American and an over-weight Belgian were listening intently to the plump little Chinese gangster, Chu Yuen Muk. They were seated in late morning sunshine at a conference table at the Ballindamm headquarters of a Hamburg dock terminal operating company. Chu's bodyguard, 'the gorilla', was standing by the panelled doors. Hauptmann, the owner of the company which handled containers in several German and Dutch ports, cringed.

"You don't like my expression, Herr Hauptmann?"

Chu understood the heavily-jowled German would rather be having lunch with his family. Then he remembered Hauptmann had no children, just a young wife who liked young men. A grin broke across his face. There was a flicker of a smile from the other two, a creeping discomfort at what the gross little Chinese in his under-sized silk suit was about to say.

"We have all tasted meat. I trust we all like it. Some of us are even married to pieces of meat – "

The gorilla, seeing Hauptmann's fists clench, stepped forward. Hauptmann's command of English did not match Chu's but he understood the insult. The gaunt-faced

German-American, Eric Kolmann, intervened. He suggested they conclude as soon as possible that morning so they might appreciate their wives' cooking and was relieved to see the Chinese smile again.

The idea for the business the syndicate was operating was put to the triad boss a year earlier by Kolmann and an elusive French aristocrat known as 'The Frenchman'. Chu agreed the supply of young girls to a voracious sexual market around Europe was piecemeal and the needs of the more discerning were not being met. The two men presented the Chinese gangster with a plan for the acquisition of suitable females from wealthier families across Europe, those with a higher social status whose young daughters would already have been shown off in public. Dossiers would be prepared and girls could be ordered, procured and delivered within sixty days.

Chu liked the audacity, the exclusive pricing and the idea of a catalogue. They were immediately inundated with enquiries from dealers and agents of the wealthy. With the asking price of the merchandise upwards of $30,000 split five ways, girls were disappearing, money was pouring in and repeat orders growing.

Hauptmann handled the shipping. Eric Kolmann, a Frankfurt-based operator in child prostitution and pornography was the syndicate's agent and the man in possession of the catalogue. The Frenchman and his associates were concerned only with procurement and contacted Kolmann to settle accounts and update the catalogue. The fourth man, the Belgian, Winkel, was in charge of storage, road transportation and security.

Almost as soon as the business began there was wastage, logistical problems and complaints of bruised fruit. There had been disruption by law enforcement agencies and dozens of girls languished in temporary confinement. Dealers in Antwerp, Rotterdam, Hamburg, Nice, Marseilles and Casablanca were the most vocal in their complaints. More worrying for Chu, he had shortly to account to Hong Kong for falls in revenue in this venture from cells he was responsible for across Europe. Triad resources funded the operation.

"So, Herr Hauptmann," Chu began again, "perhaps you can explain these latest losses at Maassluis?"

"It was an extraordinary raid on the warehouse, as I say, Herr Chu," Hauptmann replied grimly. "Two agents, the DEA man and a Committee man from Brussels were in the warehouse when we arrived. The tip-off came too late. The freighter scheduled for picking up that batch of girls was delayed in Marseilles. That is all."

Chu's face tightened.

"Is this your answer? Are we now letting people walk in and take merchandise away? Perhaps you will let us know how you plan to make good these losses?"

"We must be more realistic," Hauptmann went on, gritting his teeth. "With port security, export regulations and extra payments for transshipment we cannot process human cargo as fast as you propose."

"So we hold back while orders pour in? Herr Kolmann's figures show over three thousand to be shipped out of Europe next month to very eager buyers. There is also considerable interest in the Middle East in our white merchandise. The Frenchman talks of thousands more little ladies for the taking yet you think in hundreds. No, Hauptmann, your part of the operation will be put right. We cannot lose a hundred thousand, two hundred thousand dollars a month because there are not enough containers, or a ship might be rumbled. This is beginning to cost us dear."

As Chu spoke he knew he should not be getting so agitated, even if such behaviour was normal for Europeans and Americans. It was new for the triad, working with non-Chinese in this way and he did not like it. They were arrogant, secretive and stupid.

"However," he went on, forcing a smile, "we cannot let lunch go cold over a little disagreement! I suggest two things. We depend less on the routines we use for narcotics and we make it clearer to organisations like the Brussels Committee and Drug Enforcement Agency we mean business."

Hauptmann and Kolmann glanced at each other, unable to believe what the Chinaman was advocating. He appeared to be condoning Winkel's incredibly stupid move after the weekend, the killing of the DEA agent. It had been done without general approval and the meanest intelligence knew such action would end in them facing the might of the United States government.

Winkel spoke for the first time.

"I must advise, Herr Chu," he said smugly, "we now have last weekend's Committee operative under observation. They have eight agents and this one is their senior. It is he who has given us bad publicity several times this year."

"The Chinese agent?" Kolmann asked.

"Part-Chinese, Herr Kolmann."

"Gentlemen, his religion is unimportant," Chu interrupted. "But do nothing, Herr Winkel. We have a surprise planned. Be sure next Sunday to Monday your men are not near the Committee offices or the homes of its operatives. We would not want our friends getting their fingers burnt."

Kolmann, Hauptmann and Winkel remained tight-lipped as they watched the gorilla pick up his boss's briefcase. The few Europeans Chu did business with considered this strange. They did not understand that even Chu, the head of the European Lodge of the 14K triad, had but a small part in a global organisation to which total obedience was the law.

Hauptmann had an idea German efficiency in business, including that of the criminal organisations, paled beside that of the triads. He shared business with several branches of the 14K at ports his company operated in and was more wary of Chu. He knew sentence for triad members stepping out of line could be carried out within hours. But even he had difficulty in understanding Chu did not regard the briefcase as his own, rather it belonged to the 14K.

None of the Europeans around the table knew of the order contained in the briefcase. Chu's bosses in Hong Kong had responded to his report on the operative, Julian de Lyon. Authorisation of assassination came from the highest level, the council in Hong Kong. It was sealed with the chop of the turtle.

"Nothing is to go wrong with the next movement of live cargo out of Rotterdam," Chu said finally at the doorway. "This is a first warning."

Hauptmann waited until the door was closed before slamming his fist on the table. Able to express himself in his own language in his own office for the first time in two hours, he raged,

"That little shit. Who is he pushing around?"

3/2
Brussels, Sunday 21 July

It was almost midday on Sunday when Peter arrived at the new concourse in Place de la Monnaie where the Police Band was about to give a lunch-time concert. He found Daphne without difficulty. She was drinking Campari under a sunshade by the bandstand with Henri, Martine and two others he hadn't met. Thérèse was in Paris for the weekend visiting her stepfather.

Henri introduced his friends and asked Peter if he would like a drink.

"Not that red stuff," Peter replied in French. "It makes my toes curl."

Martine, one of Thérèse's flatmates, stifled a giggle. She long thought Peter's expressions were examples of *humour Anglais* but had learnt it was him. She could understand Thérèse preferring his company rather than the more intense of their friends. Those like Henri, doing politics and sociology.

They soon left Daphne and Peter alone. When Peter voiced his suspicions they had felt obliged to leave, Daphne said it was obvious something was troubling him. He hadn't smiled once and they were just being discrete.

The band began playing and Peter cheered up in the opulence of an open-air café on a fine day surrounded by alcohol, pastries and waiters with white bibs. Daphne too was just perfect, with auburn hair, a wonderful smile and legs up to her armpits. She was also smoking a Gauloise from a yellow packet when everyone else's was blue. He was pleased she and Thérèse were like sisters. Both were nice to look at but Daphne was easier to talk to.

"So, is the problem Thérèse, or your uncle?" Daphne asked.

Since coming over from England he had found his uncle a bit distant and yes, things were strained that morning, he admitted. Finishing their drinks, Daphne suggested they walk down Rue Neuve. She would treat him to a T-shirt and he must tell her what was wrong.

"I thought, as uncle seemed to be in a good humour this morning, we would go for a run. He wanted to see how my *katas* were progressing. You know I was graded black belt in *shoto-kan* earlier in the year? As he rarely shows interest in martial arts, let alone give any tips, I didn't want to pass up the offer.

"We went down to the *marché aux puces*. There are always characters down there and pretty girls on a sunny Sunday! It's interesting how different the stuff is from back home. Brits would never chuck such good stuff."

"Portobello Road and Carnaby Street are top of the list when we come to visit you!" Daphne interrupted, smiling.

"Well, uncle gave me a hard time on the run back up to the apartment."

"What do you mean, running too fast?" Daphne struggled to understand Peter's lapse into English.

"That too and I got cramp. He told me about running through snow and across sand and that I shouldn't be pathetic. More to the point, he said I was insular, made demeaning comments about women, was physically intimidating and it was time I learnt such things are not appropriate in martial arts."

Daphne had pulled out a t-shirt with the word STUD on it but put it back on the rack and asked Peter what point Julian was making.

"He reminded me about my saying last year I wanted to become a serious martial artist and that I would not have it so easy this summer."

"Grim," Daphne muttered.

"I must say, he did tell me some interesting stuff about his early days. He started serious training in the fighting arts when he was ten, in a monastery in the mountains on Jin-do, an island off the southern tip of Korea. When he was older he spent time in Japan too, at the end of a stick, he put it. Apparently, his *sensei* would sit on a horse and guide them twenty kilometres every day around the foothills of Mount Fuji. The *shuvjo*, the stick, he used on those who lagged behind. Once they even ran up Mount Fuji."

Peter went quiet again and Daphne had an idea what was coming.

"Well, when we got back to the apartment he said it was time I did some proper study on the subject and when I questioned this, he actually kicked me."

Daphne's eyes opened wide.

"It's not quite how it sounds. I shouldn't have got cross.

We were sitting at the table talking when I stood up – the intimidating bit – and he kicked me from across the table. I don't know how he did it. I didn't see his foot coming. All I remember is being on the other side of the room on the floor with him whispering in my ear."

"For God's sake, whispering what?" Daphne asked.

Peter winced as he turned towards Daphne.

"His words exactly, were 'understand nephew, I could break your jaw on my knee or fracture vertebrae and invertebral disc, or incapacitate or kill you in a dozen different ways'. He also warned I must control my anger and if attacked, no matter how hard I might have been hit, I must by reflexive action defend myself and not wallow in the possibility of dying."

Among other things he didn't tell Daphne was his uncle strongly advised not to try intimidating him again.

"So what is it you're supposed to be working on?" Daphne asked after a long silence.

"Breathing, getting fitter and keeping my mouth shut, basically. And I've got to find out what it is women fear."

Seeing Peter was shaken, Daphne asked if he needed to put up with any of it. Peter replied he really liked coming over to Belgium. More important, his uncle was the head of what was left of the family. All Daphne could say in reply was he had better gather his wits.

She soon saw there were other things on his mind. An assistant pulled aside the curtain of a cubicle in the boutique to reveal a girl stepping out of her dress. Another was lying on the floor in front of them, struggling to get a pair of jeans over her hips.

"You must keep your mind on your girlfriend!"

"That's proving frustrating," Peter responded with a weak grin. "She's very proper and I like this. But ..."

"Don't you recognise unbruised fruit when you handle it?"

Peter glanced at her.

"Yes, I know, it's man's talk and a bit annoying as we all start off like this! Having said it you will win her, when you prove to yourself you are worth it."

"Now I don't know what to do," Peter responded, barely audible over the music booming around the boutique.

Daphne huffed.

"You can start by warming her up, not rubbing her up the wrong way. I happen to know you're halfway there!"

Peter cheered up immediately, even animating with the tantalising smells of waffles and apple fritters at the top of Rue Neuve. Daphne asked when he would be starting his serious training, in view of his uncle's advice. It wasn't too far to her place, so why didn't she take a tram and he run? She would prepare a proper lunch for him and if he was quicker than expected he could run around the park as well.

"That's blackmail!" Peter remonstrated. "It's easy for girls. You don't have such punishments."

"We have our own forms of punishment Peter, plenty of them. Make no mistake!"

After spending the afternoon with Daphne and the evening with Thérèse, Peter returned to Rue Américaine and was keen to relate part of the day's discussion to his uncle. Julian asked if he had eaten. Peter replied he had not eaten much. He was careful not to say both Daphne and Thérèse had prepared for him the kind of light meal a woman eats. He couldn't think of it in any other way. Julian began the preparation of a larger quantity of rice.

"That's a strange grain!" Peter said, dropping his bag on the kitchen floor.

"Unpolished rice and *riz sauvage*. Not the Chinese way but more wholesome. But go ahead with your discoveries."

"Well, I asked Thérèse how she prepares herself if she has to walk through a dark alley. I asked delicately, of course," he added. "She just looked at me and said women spend a large part of their time avoiding dark alleys. When I asked if she knew how to make a fist, she just burst out laughing. It was amazing, uncle. She had no idea what to do!"

"It is certainly interesting," Julian remarked.

"And another thing. Henri always crosses the street if he sees a girl walking towards him late at night so as not to worry her. And the girls told him he was a gentleman! Well, tomorrow I shall talk more with Daphne."

"Excellent," Julian responded. "Just the person to keep you on your toes."

3/3
Monday 22 July

Julian went in to Place Madou early on Monday morning and was surprised to learn from the porter there was already someone at work upstairs. Though not yet seven o'clock he was not surprised to see Ross's assistant at her desk determined to clear a pile of work before the telephones began ringing.

"Forgive me, Monsieur de Lyon, you are not supposed to be here," Mademoiselle Arameau said uneasily.

"And what else has the Big Boss decreed?"

Julian knew he should not be teasing her. She was turning redder by the second behind her spectacles, torn between saying 'come' and 'go'.

"May I remind you, you have this week off as well. Please telephone if there is something you really need to know."

He asked if Marc had agreed to take the Marseilles operation at the beginning of August. She replied this was so. He also asked her if she would like some coffee. She half-stood, sat again, then regaining her composure reminded Julian more firmly he should not be in the office.

As Julian left, the young woman picked up the 'phone and asked the porter tartly to let her know if there were any more visitors before the offices opened. Julian was not smiling either as he left the building. It was not just an hour or a day of his time. It was time that could have been more precious to a hundred, a thousand others at that same moment.

He bought the morning's newspaper from a stand in Place Madou and caught sight of Marc coming out of the Metro. It had been weeks since they had run into each other. It was Marc who was working on a dossier on the German members of the syndicate, the pornography distributors and now, apparently, the organisation marketing the abducted youngsters.

"I heard rumours you'd been put on holiday, Old Man!" Marc exclaimed, as they stepped into a busy café on the Chaussée de Louvain. "I haven't been able to thank you for standing in for me in Amsterdam."

Marc went on to say the weekend operation in Marseilles was likely to be a dud. An organisation of Algerians had revived an old routine of putting advertisements in South Coast newspapers for girls to work in bars in North Africa at fabulous salaries. The police found it incredible young women were still falling for this trick and had asked for support in locating the embarkation point in Marseilles.

Marc also mentioned the upheaval during the week, with Ross in late every night on what he was sure was a security shake-up. He was sorry about the trouble and a killing. He also knew the American, Meredith.

"I wish I could lose interest and move on," Julian said, hinting only at something he was planning. "I may need your help soon, whether I'm working for the Committee or not."

"Anything, of course," Marc replied cautiously. "I owe you favours enough."

Marc was a Belgian and older than Julian. After thirty years pushing a pen in the *Ministères* his circumstances changed abruptly. His wife died and he realised he had achieved little and aspired to nothing. He abandoned his career in the civil service and contracted himself to the United Nations and active work with the Committee on Slavery. Depression took a hold and it was only a passion for music that kept him going. Feeling his time was yet to come he frequently compared himself with Caesar Franck, who blossomed at the age of sixty-seven with his Symphony in D minor, the first of several great pieces of music.

Julian half-listened to the new leads on Johnny Wan and van Merken amidst the sounds of an espresso machine and murmuring of customers. Only when Marc fell silent awaiting a response did Julian realise it was something he had not wanted to hear.

"You did say 14K, Marc?"

Marc nodded.

"14K it is. Criminal Intelligence in Amsterdam confirmed it yesterday. It's not Johnny Wan's mob, the See Tong, involved in the syndicate. It's a Hong Kong gang whose main European cell is in Amsterdam. They have given us the name of their top man, Chu Yuen Muk. Our *mademoiselle* is doing a profile on him and the triad this morning. It's apparently most unusual they're doing business with Europeans."

Julian had hardly digested this information when Marc also dropped on him news of an article about to be published in *Le Monde* on a rare instance of the 'death of a thousand cuts' in the South of France. The French newspaper were linking it to the 14K triad and had requested information from the Amsterdam police.

It was Marc who brought the meeting to an end. Glancing at his watch he asked Julian if he was not impressed with the early start. A charmer, he called Ross's new assistant, blushing when he saw how the situation must have looked. His parting words were he would keep Julian informed by accident and by design.

Later that morning Julian sat deep in thought in the Grand Place with a mineral water before him. He was hardly aware of the bustle of tourists, shoppers and traffic. The old market square was alive and restless. Flags fluttered, the gilded parapets sparkled with Renaissance splendour. The summer-long assault by an armada of coaches and batteries of camera shutters was under way.

After leaving the office that morning he bought himself membership of the club Daniel recommended. He didn't normally bother with expense claims but kept the receipt for the 100,000 Belgian francs he handed over. A note would come back from accounts querying it. He was already interested in the convoluted conditions of membership regarding 'special evenings' available soon to new members.

It was only a feeling this might edge them a little closer to a fifth syndicate member. None of the four the Committee knew of, including the triad, were connected with wholesale abduction. There had to be a fifth.

Kidnapping is an exacting business and it was almost unreal so many pubescent girls were being abducted with impeccable timing, some even from their home. It was unlike child abuse, where children are violated from an early age, usually by family, shared at abuse parties and introduced into paedophile and torture networks. Physically and psychologically damaged, there was a measure of acceptance of the situation by these unfortunate children.

Julian was wrestling with the ill-considered decisions of his youth in Hong Kong catching up with him when he saw Daphne among the flower stalls. She was walking slowly in his direction between the large striped umbrellas, appraising the profusion of blooms on display across the cobbles. Being brought up in a community guided by superstition and omens good and bad, and curious why this young woman should seem like an old friend, he decided a meeting would be propitious.

"Oh, they're so nice!" she responded, taken aback at being presented with a mixed bouquet of lilies. "No-one has given me flowers for no reason before."

Julian was silent for a moment then suggested she was an excellent reason, compounding the compliment with a Chinese saying: If you have only two pennies left in the world, you should spend one on a loaf of bread and the other on a flower as a reason for living.

She went quiet and he felt it necessary to apologise for making her self-conscious. The sun played on her hair. Her eyes danced, giving everything away, almost.

"I am shy," she said, flashing a smile. "Do you think it suits me?"

"I do," Julian replied, missing her gentle teasing.

"I can't help getting euphoric in company, though it's usually the wine."

"Would you like to join me for a glass now?"

"And why not lunch!" Daphne found herself saying, knowing she was pushing her luck.

Julian was again lost for words.

"I shall learn more about this balance of modesty and forthrightness in you, young lady. It will be a salad for me as I seldom eat during the day."

"Why's that?"

"It's to do with the blood being in the right place at the wrong time," Julian replied. "So I generally eat late, when I'm sure it's safe."

"You're pulling my leg now, aren't you?" Daphne asked cautiously, seeing his brown eyes smiling.

At nine that evening at Ma Campagne, the junction of Avenue Brugmann and the Chaussée de Waterloo, Julian waited for the evening's entertainment in a grimmer mood. He had enjoyed Daphne's company during the afternoon and knew the contrast was likely to know no bounds. A

Lincoln Continental with tinted windows pulled up and the uniformed chauffeur ascertained discreetly Julian was his charge. Julian checked as he got in that the tinted windows and interior partition were not armour plate. The driver apologised over the intercom for the isolation, saying ambiguously the organisation, the club, endeavoured to guarantee the anonymity of its members.

They moved off down the Chaussée de Waterloo and on to the motorway to Liège. The drive took an hour, the last quarter being one of much changing up and down of the automatic gearbox. There was finally the crunch of tyres on gravel.

When the driver opened the door for Julian the outside was as dark as the interior of the car. A château and woodland surrounding it loomed over him. There was no light coming from the building and the only detail discernible was the shape of four distinctive towers against a wild, inky sky. Several other limousines and at least thirty other cars were parked on the drive. They were somewhere in the Ardennes, north of Luxembourg.

Inside, Julian was met with the smell of cigars and mutterings one might expect from an exclusive gentlemen's club. The ground floor was furnished in period Eighteenth-century style. It looked like a private house except for the pornographic film projected on the wall behind a curving marble staircase. In the hallway were twenty-two other men, middle-aged to elderly, seated or standing, conversing with a dozen scantily- but expensively-dressed hostesses. Four young women in skimpy French maid costumes served drinks from silver platters.

The gathering was invited to an upstairs gallery and shown into cubicles around the balustrade. Each cubicle had a window of one-way mirror glass looking over a studio floor that was empty except for a *futon*.

The lighting was dimmed momentarily before growing

brighter as a young girl was pushed into the centre of the studio. Dressed only in white ankle socks and a silk kimono she immediately fell to her knees on the mattress, wrapping the gown tightly around herself. She was fourteen years old, well-developed for her age and very frightened.

Her name was Michi, 'Micky' to her family. Julian knew who she was, having seen a file on her the week before. She was the daughter of a member of a Japanese trade delegation to the EEC. There was considerable embarrassment and a massive search organised after she was abducted, assumed kidnapped from the delegation's hotel in Paris.

Her file was one of hundreds by his desk and he only remembered it because of the press photographs showing daughter and mother enacting the Tea Ceremony at the *Centre Pompidou* during an exhibition of Japanese products.

The girl looked years older now. Her eyes scanned the mirrors, one fist clenched to her mouth.

Several minutes passed, until the words *vien, petit lapin, vien* ... came through the speakers in the cubicle in stereophonic sound. A short, stocky man with greasy hair, stained vest and muddy tracksuit bottoms appeared and knelt close by her. He patted the floor, asking again she come to him. Grinning, he edged towards her on his knees. She drew her legs and arms tightly to her.

Julian was on his way down the staircase when the screaming began, echoing around the elegant house. Catching sight of himself in a large ormolu mirror he adjusted his bow tie. Intervention was not an option on this occasion without planning and back-up. It did not stop him running through appropriate punishment for the forty or fifty people in that house that night. He hoped, for their sake, no-one crossed his path before he reached the door.

He was chauffeured back to Brussels on a pleasant

50

moonlit evening and bid a *bonsoir* by the driver at Ma Campagne. This was a disgusting exhibition, he decided, a blatant kidnapping of a child whose picture had featured in a national newspaper the week before. Tacit approval from many in the audience would be needed for such a show to take place and the girl remain in captivity. Sophie's assessment of Daniel as Pimp to the Establishment flitted around his head.

There were no cabs in the rank at the top of Rue Africaine. Several people were waiting, laughing and happy after a pleasant evening out. There are one or two good restaurants and several bars near the top of Avenue Brugmann. It was nearing the end of July and the promise of fine weather for the summer holidays.

CHAPTER FOUR

Brussels, Monday 29 July

It was almost dawn on Monday when Julian and Peter left Daphne's Provençal evening at her apartment in Etterbeek. Peter was a little tipsy and reluctant to throw away the straw in his pockets. Julian had also drunk some wine and the pair of them crossed the cobblestones of a deserted la Chasse singing as quietly as they could. The Avenue d'Auderghem, its tram lines gleaming under white lamplight stretched silently toward Place Schuman and the Berlaymont building. In Place Flagey some twenty minutes later the early morning air was sobering Peter up. He was quieter and looking forward to his bed.

Julian's mind was on other things. They had been followed from the railway bridge, down the winding Rue de la Brasserie. Place Flagey was deserted except for two cars on the other side of the lake with their engines running. There was plenty of opportunity for an encounter but whoever it was following were holding off.

As they crossed the open square with its fairground silent and under wraps, Peter saw the cars and mumbled there was a lot of traffic about for the time of night. They quickened their pace up the hill towards the Avenue Louise. Turning into Rue Américaine Julian counted a third vehicle and decided it was time his nephew understood the situation. He knew now they were being led.

"You may have to use your fighting skills, nephew," he

said quietly. "Three cars, seven people. I don't know what's going on but if we have to fight, every blow must count."

Peter glanced up and down the street and got the message.

At Place Leemans there were now two cars behind them and two men standing casually in the roadway ahead. T-shirts and jeans were normal enough on a summer night, iron bars were not. Peter was about to suggest they took one each when his uncle broke into a trot. The two men backed away smartly. Peter, with every confidence with his uncle leading, was game for a fight until he saw in the pre-dawn gloom what they were up against. There were nine or ten men around them, between cars, on door steps and behind trees.

"Crowded, eh ..." he heard his uncle mutter.

Peter heard someone come up behind him, ducked beneath the metal bar swung at his head and sent his attacker staggering into the road with a blow to the solar plexus. Almost at the same instant his uncle took the heavy bar out of the man's hand, sent him further on his way with the gentlest of kicks to the backside and flicked the bar with devastating accuracy at the next figure approaching them.

Peter gaped at the effect. The bar bounced off the man's head and embedded itself in a car door. He dropped like a nine-pin. Peter was not surprised there was no further movement towards them.

Within sight of the apartment, Peter thought they might just make it to the courtyard. To Julian, it was too easy. There had been no attempt to take them on, even with superior odds. They were being funnelled to the apartment, or courtyard. He saw what he was looking for at the end of the street, a man holding a device with an aerial. He pushed Peter between the *poubelles* on the corner, told him to stay put and melted into the alleyway.

Three of the longest seconds of Peter's life passed. He stood up with a view to following his uncle, was amazed at seeing him return, almost flying, then found himself on the other side of the street, winded, coughing and deafened by the loudest bang he had ever heard. A pall of acrid white smoke hung over that end of the street. The street was suddenly empty of people and quiet again except for someone's burglar alarm and a last piece of glass falling to the street.

Julian had rolled under a car and saw his nephew float across the street with the rubbish bins. The fireball had followed him out of the alleyway with a deep boom, a red and orange ball expanding into an intense white cloud. Flames flickered gently in the courtyard. The stench of burning paint and rubber hung over them.

Peter got up stiffly, rubbing his eyes and looked nervously around. The bonnet of a red car lay in the street.

"The car ... they blew up your car ..."

"Not mine, nephew," Julian replied, brushing himself down. "Mine is in for a service. This one the garage kindly loaned ..."

4/2

Almost immediately they were inside the apartment the telephone rang. Peter took the call. It was Mlle. Arameau warning that the Committee's offices and two other operatives' homes had been fire-bombed in the past two hours. All operatives were to be vigilant until it was clear what was going on. Julian was checking the concierge and her husband were unhurt. Their ground floor apartment was badly damaged.

A mobile *Gendarmerie* unit was still in Rue Américaine at 08.30 when the post was delivered. Julian had been questioned for two hours about the blast and was not in the mood for the postman's banter, or for the single letter from Paris. Though there were no Chinese in the street during the attack, the note made it clear they were involved, as was his wife. Its one line, in her hand and underlined several times read SUFFER THE NIGHT OF THE LONG KNIVES.

The distraction of his car being returned by the garage and the mechanics' fascination with the wreck he was handing back eased Julian away from such a note from Ann-Marie. He needed to work faster to put together the pieces of the syndicate and perhaps his wife's well-being. He scanned the day's *Le Monde* before turning his attention to his nephew coming down the stairs. Peter would have to leave that morning.

"Great party," Peter said, managing a grin. "Some finale!"

Julian fetched the brew he had prepared for his nephew's hangover and lack of sleep and went into his study to telephone *Le Monde's* offices in Paris. He exchanged pleasantries with Pierre, an old acquaintance now a sub-editor in France's most solid newspaper and asked him about an article he had been expecting all week on the Marseilles gangland killing.

"Ah, yes. We did request some information from your office in Brussels then decided last night to hold off on both story and pictures. I suppose I'm not surprised to hear from you," Pierre replied.

"It was a Chinese killing?"

"Absolutely. The Corsican families deny such barbarism. There were, or are, Chinese down in Marseilles who did not like the victim."

"And your editor sees fit not to mention any of this?"

"The pictures are appalling," Pierre replied guardedly. "It's our suggestion it was a 'death by a myriad of swords'. Police experts are still studying the photographs."

"Do they know which triad?"

"It's somewhere in the notes, 14K, I think."

Julian now had two good reasons for wanting to see details of the suppressed item. He was concerned about Marc and the Committee's imminent operation in Marseilles.

"Could we meet today?"

"Certainly. I finish at about one o'clock and would like to get away quickly. My holiday, you understand. You know where we are, Rue des Italiens. Meet me in the bar opposite despatch, *le Pub Haussman.*"

"At one," Julian confirmed.

Returning to the breakfast table he made Peter finish the China Light, despite his complaining the lavender in it made it smell like the Zaryl Scaldyl works on the Ostende-Brussels motorway. He asked if a trip to Paris might fit into his vacation.

"Wow, Paris!" Peter responded less than convincingly, even though it would be his first. "But I was going back down to Daphne's place. Thérèse will be there. I'm dying to tell them what happened here."

"Perhaps they would like to come? We can pick them up in half an hour … overnight bags would be a good idea."

"Wow!" Peter exclaimed once more, heading for the 'phone.

"And nephew, don't mention this morning's incident for the moment."

Julian breathed more easily at Peter's compliance. They had probably been followed to and from Daphne's apartment and she might also be safer away from Brussels for a few days.

The three youngsters piled out of the car beside the *Café de la Paix* in Paris, windswept and exhilarated after an open-topped 300-kilometre ride from Brussels. Peter stood staring at the green and gilt-roofed *Opéra* presiding over the square. Thérèse was pleased to be back in the city she grew up in and it was left to Daphne to arrange where they should meet up, as Julian had calls to make. The gendarme striding toward them on the bus lane began throwing his weight unexpectedly at the irate driver of a tourist coach behind them and Daphne wondered if Julian's luck might also save him being booked by an *aubergine*. Only when he pulled out into the traffic did she notice the *Corps Diplomatique* plate on the car.

He joined them later in Place Beaubourg, finding them in earnest debate about the architecture of the new arts centre that overpowers the old square. He thought it was like a giant adventure playground and insisted they spend the rest of the day showing Peter more of the things that make Paris a truly gracious city.

Their final stop that Monday evening was a Vietnamese restaurant in Place Maubert Julian had visited with Ann-Marie. The proprietor remembered Julian spoke Vietnamese and the foursome were welcomed as old friends.

Thérèse and Daphne groaned as they sat down, not believing how much they had seen in an afternoon. Looking at Peter, Thérèse said it was a pity they had missed the *Juillet Quatorze* fireworks and hoped they would make the next. He missed the implication of the invitation and Daphne grimaced at seeing her friend hurt. He compounded his insensitivity by saying he was running the distance they had walked that day, every morning in Brussels.

"And I can't think of a better way of spending the evening than with a nice meal and lots of wine ..."

Three pairs of eyes watched him.

"Would last night's hangover bounce around your head if I hit it?" Thérèse asked in a distinctly unfriendly tone, relenting when a happily-grinning waiter popped the first of the evening's bottles at precisely the wrong moment.

"Well, my young friends, I must put some suggestions to you," Julian began.

The table was covered with empty porcelain bowls, the smell of mint lingered. The food had been good. Daphne even tried an imported *33* lager so she could tell her father it was still being brewed in Ho Chi Minh City.

"As none of us are dressed for any serious night life we can return to Brussels tonight ..." which was met with more groans, "... or stop-over to see what a new day tempts us with!"

There were broad smiles all round.

"That's decided. Are there any requests?"

"More sightseeing is fine by me," Peter said.

"And if it's hot like this again, I'd also like to swim."

Daphne's suggestion was approved unanimously.

"I don't have a costume," Thérèse said.

"Neither do I, but these men have seen girls in their knickers before!"

Thérèse lowered her eyes blushing but couldn't help smiling.

"Then I have the answer. As the *piscines* here may not appreciate such overt innocence we shall drive down to the *Côtes d'Azure* for a couple of days and do all these things!"

There was a spontaneous cheer. Peter brought up the subject of money. Julian said he would foot the bill. There was a louder cheer now inviting attention to the group. Julian resolved not to order any more wine but minutes later could think of no real reason why they shouldn't open one last bottle.

At dawn, after a second restless night and in a different mood from the evening, Julian was speaking to Mlle. Arameau from a 'phone booth in a hotel in Montmartre. She listened to his suggestion there could be imminent danger down in Marseilles and connected him directly with Ross at his home.

Ross agreed tetchily a couple of days on the South Coast was not a bad idea as Marc was on his own. He was irritated Julian had not called sooner with the operation having been brought forward because of the national holiday. There was no word from Geneva but he wanted Julian back in the office on Thursday afternoon for a concentration of minds on the fire-bombing.

Julian made hotel reservations in Cannes and was lost to his thoughts. After seeing Pierre he had called briefly at his wife's family château at Meaux, outside Paris. The housekeeper reaffirmed how worried she was. They had not seen Ann-Marie for seven weeks. She had not even attended her father's seventieth birthday. Julian said he would appreciate any news despite what her father may have ordered.

He was still experiencing discomfort over the photographs in Pierre's file. The victim was a Chinese, the hirer of an expensive Mercedes found nearby but an otherwise lowly employee of Eurocargo, a dock terminal operating company in Hamburg the Committee suspected was involved with the syndicate. Its head office confirmed the man had reported sick and had no idea why he was so far from Hamburg. Julian told Ross the victim could have been one of Marc's contacts and the reason they had been recently successful in preventing girls being shipped out from there.

The unpublishable pictures of the bloated, lacerated corpse turned Pierre's stomach and made Julian uneasy. Seeing a human being strapped to a table and cut with a range of surgical knives, beginning with swift and precise incisions into the toes and working up the body, avoiding arteries while making sure the victim retained consciousness, was an experience relegated to a darker side of Julian's conscience.

This 'death of a thousand cuts' is one of a gentle draining of blood preventing shock, inducing euphoria and ensuring complete immobility until the final release of the cutting of the throat, or of burial with the heart pumping gently. The memory of the victim's desperate breathing, the fear across his face and his blood dripping from the table forming rivulets across the floor had troubled Julian since he was fifteen years old.

Facing Daphne smiling radiantly as he stepped out of the telephone booth caught him completely off-guard.

"I've been sitting on the steps of *Sacré-Cœur* this last hour," she said excitedly, kissing his cheeks. "A priest opened the doors at sun-up and I've had *Christ glorifié* watching my back and the sun warming my front. And I came across a Picasso museum! It's so kind of you to treat us to a hotel up here. It's now my favourite spot in all Paris!"

"I hope your good fortune might one day rub off on me," he said smiling. "I've only ever strolled here at night, on my own."

He asked if she had eaten breakfast.

"No, but the cafés at both ends of Place du Tertre are open, if you were thinking of a walk as well!"

She put her arm through his and matched his strides, humming the *Marseillaise*. Both he and Peter were very tired for some reason, Julian especially. She and Thérèse would be doing well if they could cheer them up again over the next couple of days.

It wasn't until days later Daphne realised the significance of Julian's words.

Cannes, Wednesday 31 July

Late the following evening, after their first full day in Cannes, Julian sat alone on the terrace of the Montfleury Hotel overlooking tennis courts, palm trees and a bay below, alive with the lights of numerous yachts. Over a last drink he was thinking about Daphne saying he needn't continue playing nursemaid as they had enjoyed their splash in the sea in bikinis they had bought. She was pleased he enjoyed her party but Paris, the *Côtes d'Azure*, the hotel, was far too generous an exchange.

He was about to go to his room when Peter asked if he could join him.

"Thérèse and I rowed, again," he began glumly. He declined a glass of chilled white wine saying he'd probably had one too many beers. "It was the usual thing, *sensei*. People don't understand that martial arts could one day save their life."

"It is a problem," Julian replied, "with the Japanese being such barbarians ..."

Peter grinned briefly, realising how foolish he sounded.

"But how do people cope with situations like the one the other morning without knowing something about fighting?"

"You did well there but situations differ and people do cope. Move on in your head to other things."

There was a long silence before Peter admitted he shouldn't argue with Thérèse. He had been warned. He had told her she was the sort of girl who, if she had a small dog and was attacked, would be more concerned about the safety of the dog.

"Or child," Julian said. "You miss the point, nephew. Is it possible Thérèse sees something more gentle in you but cannot resolve her feelings because you persist with this machismo?"

Peter picked at the soft bark of one of the palm trees leaning over the terrace. His uncle's words, like Daphne's, sounded good and he would think about them.

"She was in a terrific mood this evening."

"And you thought she might be receptive to your amorous advances!"

Peter nodded.

"You're not learning very quickly, are you?" Julian grinned.

"I do appreciate these bits of wisdom you lay on me!"

"Don't take them too seriously, nephew. Occasionally I realise I've only just understood it myself!"

"Like 'the more you know, the more you realise you don't know'?"

"Along with 'the older you get, the wiser you think you are.'"

Julian put his glass down.

"Time to hit the sack, I think. The prettier among us have been asleep for a while. There could be something in this!"

Peter chuckled. First, he would write a note of contrition and a little poem to Thérèse and slip it under the girls' door.

4/3
Thursday 01 August

It was five when the telephone rang at Julian's bedside. He peered behind the heavy curtains at a pale and bloodshot blue sky and picked up the receiver.

"These early morning conversations are becoming a habit, *mademoiselle*."

"I apologise," Mlle. Arameau responded curtly. "I am glad you haven't left. I know you were returning to Brussels today. We have just received information from the French police. *Monsieur* Vlaminck is in a clinic just outside Marseilles. He was found in an alley an hour ago. The boss would be very grateful if you could get over to the *Douane* control in Marseilles and report on this er, mess, as soon as possible."

She added clumsily he could put in for expenses for the journey.

Julian scribbled a note and left it at his sleeping nephew's bedside. He was not pleased his door was unlocked. His mental processes sharpened further in the morning air when his car pulled up in front of him. There was no excuse for him having allowed it to be driven up by one of the hotel staff.

He was on his way to Marseilles within minutes of the call. The sky was blue, the *péage* deserted. The Ferrari sang.

"We do not expect him to regain consciousness, *monsieur*," the doctor began, "though you are welcome to wait."

Julian ignored the detective sitting in a corner of the room reading an Asterix comic and looked closely at Marc's blue and swollen face. His head, upper trunk and hand were swathed in bandages. He was a sick man.

"It surprises us your colleague lives. He was hit, or rather battered with great force. The injuries to his ears puzzle us too. There is also the question of the finger. It was surgically removed."

Julian did not react. He read the report on Marc's condition and suggested the bruising around the ears and rupturing of the capillaries of the auditory canals was caused by a cupped-hand strike on the head. The doctor raised an eyebrow. Julian did not comment further. The double kick with ball or heel of the foot to Marc's solar plexus damaged spleen and pancreas. The assault was intended to stun, then kill through massive haemorrhage.

Julian touched Marc's hand. The others watched in silence. If they didn't know exactly what was going on they could feel the energy generated. He then had a sharp exchange with the detective who asked of his interest in the 'body'.

Julian was sorry it was Marc. He should have stayed with the cut and thrust of the civil service. Ross recently admitted he had begun reserving potentially dangerous operations for his Number One but hadn't been concerned about this exchange with Marc.

The operation was to have been one of observation in advance of a bigger raid planned for the end of August, when abduction of the flotsam of teenage girls who drift across Europe is at its peak. Julian decided he could do no more and should return to Cannes.

On leaving the clinic his thoughts were interrupted by a

young man stepping into the lift with him. He apologised for the intrusion, introduced himself as a journalist from the local paper and asked if the one found in the alleyway that morning was a colleague. Julian said he had nothing of interest to offer.

"Please believe me, *monsieur*, when I say I'm here unofficially. My editor knows nothing of this. It is slaving, with a Chinese connection I'm interested in."

"Are you not being rather imprudent?" Julian asked. The journalist began perspiring even though the clinic was efficiently air-conditioned.

"It's just, I discovered your colleague is United Nations. And you are, well, part-Chinese. I was really hoping you might be able to help me with some of the goings-on down here even the bigger papers are silent about. A Chinese cut into little pieces last week, for example?"

The doors opened on the ground floor. Julian glanced at his watch.

"We might be able to exchange some information."

"Then perhaps we could have a beer?"

"I'll buy you breakfast."

The young journalist suddenly couldn't believe his luck.

Julian drank a bowl of coffee in a café off the Canabière and listened to the gangling young man, Jean-Phillipe, telling his interest in slaving began when he was a musician in a local band in the early Seventies. It was nothing exciting he stressed, just cafés and smaller clubs and dreams of the Big Time. Four years on it was still a purple satin costume backing cabaret and playing boring bossa novas and he knew he was going nowhere.

He explained there were always girls interested in the band and one in particular, a Spanish girl named Blanca, he liked. But one day she vanished and he wondered if her talk of hundreds of girls disappearing, girls like herself who drifted along the coast following the musicians but allowing themselves to be picked up by anyone when they had run out of money, could have been true.

He got a job as a cub reporter on the local paper and became even more interested in Blanca's disappearance when put on a story of two society girls invited to a party on a yacht in Cannes being found drugged, dumped and in a sorry state a few days later down the coast.

The man also related the story of the twenty-six women answering an advertisement in his newspaper four years earlier for well-paid jobs in North Africa as waitresses and barmaids. They arrived at an address in old Marseilles and were locked in. No subtlety in that one. They were to be abducted en masse and were lucky a boyfriend had checked up on the lateness of one of the women that evening.

The journalist would have talked all morning if Julian had not stopped him. There were thousands of such case files in his own office in Brussels, with an estimated 10,000 French girls disappearing each year. Lucrative jobs for young women on the Riviera ending with their export to Africa and South America; employment and dancing contracts in exotic locations, with the youngsters' money running out and passports held back and being forced into prostitution; picture slavery, job slavery, domestic slavery, paedophilia. The stories were monotonously repetitive.

Julian asked Jean-Phillipe finally what brought him out so early in the morning.

"Boredom. Not being married," came the reply. "This was a tip from a friend who works at the police station. Your colleague apparently said two words my friend thought were interesting, 'Chinese girl'."

Julian raised an eyebrow.

"Yes, it is strange. Something about his girlfriend, maybe. That's what I was supposed to be interested in."

He shrugged his shoulders and said most of his file on the Chinese was like this and he should have followed the

American. He saw Julian's surprise and perked up again.

"Yes, there was an American from the consulate at the station when my friend 'phoned but he wasn't interested in your colleague. He was concerned about the body found nearby at the same time, dead from a bullet wound. There was some whispering it was CIA because of the speed with which they took the body away. Anyway, who knows. If I had followed that lead it would probably still have been the wrong horse."

Julian walked by the *Bureau de Poste* on his way back to the car, having no intention of calling at Marc's control. Everything had fallen into place. A second American agent had been shot dead, again by one of his own, Julian suspected. A ritual death had taken place and an assassination attempted. It was his name on the list, not Marc's. If he hadn't swapped the Marseilles operation with Marc he may have been able to nip this in the bud.

It was imperative he return to Cannes, to his nephew and two friends. Somewhere along the coast was a 14K group including a Red Pole, the Incense Master, his assistant and 'the Butcher' whose trademark was a severed finger. His past was now staring him in the face.

4/4

"There was a fight. We knew nothing, *monsieur* – "

Julian brushed aside the hotel manager's embarrassment. Daphne's note explained she and Thérèse had found Peter on the bathroom floor.

He followed Daphne's directions to the clinic on the outskirts of Cannes and was there within minutes. She caught him in the foyer and told him Peter had a broken arm, cracked ribs a punctured lung and seriously wounded pride. He asked if she and Thérèse were managing but didn't need the reply. She had a grip on the situation and he was impressed.

"Well, young nephew. I hope you're feeling better than you look," he said at Peter's bedside.

"If my lips move, I'm alive ..."

There was another pause before he also whispered,

"She was tiny, *sensei*, but Christ, she hit hard. 'De Lyon?' she asked. I blocked her first kick but my forearm fractured and she kicked me to the bathroom."

The anaesthetic was wearing off and he was gasping between sentences.

"I saw stars but locked the door. She just walked through it. I remember her elbow above my neck. If Thérèse hadn't screamed my name ..."

A nurse signalled the end of the conversation.

Thérèse gave Julian a cold and silent stare. She made it clear Peter's fighting skills had done him no good at all, that it was his fault for influencing Peter and that he had brought this on him. The look conveyed it all. Daphne quickly made some suggestions but found Thérèse would not be told what to do.

"We heard noises and saw Peter's door was open. I was afraid," Daphne said, walking with Julian to the car. She had never seen Thérèse so angry and requested they go for a drive. Thérèse wanted to stay with Peter.

"The first pages of Genet's *Journal* made sense suddenly when we saw the woman. You know, the bit about extreme violence showing in some people. But it wasn't violence I felt, it was evil. Poor Thérèse. She screamed and cowered behind me. The woman and a Chinese guy walked calmly past us. The woman was petite, as Peter said, smaller even than Thérèse but we both felt the evil."

Half an hour later they were seated under a sun shade outside a café in a village in the mountains about forty kilometres inland. It was cooler than along the coast. The men had begun an evening's *pétanque* under the plane trees in the village square.

Daphne was listening carefully to Julian telling her about his job and occasional incidents on assignments. He did not explain why a professional killer was involved in this one. He said the attack on Peter was a mistake and was meant to be a warning to him. She did not press him, however. She was more worried about her cousin.

Thérèse was gentler toward Julian when they returned and said she would like to stay at the clinic for the few days Peter would be confined to bed. She thanked Julian for the offer of his car but said she could not contemplate driving them back to Brussels. He arranged for bills to be sent on to him and gave Thérèse money for expenses. He also asked Peter if he should let his mother know what had happened but Peter said there was no need to worry her.

Though strapped up and half-asleep he was more like his old self. All they needed, he muttered, was a dog called Timmy and they could be the Famous Five. He was disappointed none of them understood but would explain when his tongue was working better.

It was midnight when Julian set out with Daphne on their return to Brussels. He was already a day late for meetings and asked if she was up to a journey of thirteen hundred kilometres in one go. With stops they would be back mid-afternoon. She was absolutely fine, she said, about keeping him company and would try and stay awake. Thankfully she had a bedroom to return to. With the rush to get to Paris, Martine had volunteered to stay on after the party and finish clearing up.

She spent some time talking to Julian about fear and violence and attitudes toward it. Paradoxically she cheered up. Her lack of awareness of such things was apparent and made her realise she still wandered around most of the time in a dream.

Julian also spoke about his brother – Peter's father – and

Peter's interest in the martial arts. His father had been getting into a cab in Orchard Road in Singapore when two thugs intent on robbing the cabbie decided he was in the way and stabbed him. That was seven years before and it was a sad irony he was the member of the family with no interest in such things.

Peter began self-defence classes after this, though his mother had not encouraged it. Being a quarter Chinese he also regarded martial arts as a link to his oriental roots. The local club happened to be a Japanese style. It may also have been his way of coping with his father's death. With reasons like these Daphne's heart went out to Peter and his dilemma over Thérèse's obstinacy. She would talk to her about it as soon as possible.

The car purred on up the RN past Lyon in the early hours. Traffic was continuous in the opposite direction and tiring on the eyes. The August exodus was under way and Julian was grateful he was not alone. Daphne alternated between periods of garrulousness and silence. She was still having trouble understanding why big strong Peter had not been a match for a woman much smaller than him. She closed her eyes as Julian began a folk story.

"It's a tale about a boy whose father was a master calligrapher at the Emperor's court," he began. "The boy also displayed a talent with brush and ink and when he was fourteen it was considered his talent could soon be greater than his father's.

"At the age of sixteen," Julian went on, "the boy won a scholarship and was proud to show his father the character for the goose he had drawn as part of the examination. His father pointed out respectfully his son had forgotten the double point and picking up the brush he completed the character.

"Now perhaps a little too pleased, the boy called his mother to look at the finished work. Admiring the competence in her young son's work she said, 'this is a piece you can be proud of. But I am obliged to say, with respect, only the double point is worthy of comparison with your father's work ...'"

"That was lovely," Daphne murmured. She had snuggled up to Julian as much as the car would allow. Such stories have their origins in Hindu mythology, she heard him say. Chinese gods are deified mortals, the stories largely happy ones in idyllic settings.

She made a mental note to read more. She would tell him a story as well, something from German folklore but first she would shut her eyes for a minute.

CHAPTER FIVE

Brussels, Friday 02 August

On their return, Daphne went straight to bed and Julian to Place Madou, straight into a brain-storming session with all but one of the Committee's operatives. The normal office routine was unaffected by the holiday period and fire-bombing. All rooms had been refurbished with only the smell of fresh paint indicating anything had happened.

During the evening he prepared a report on the incident in Marseilles before grabbing a few hours sleep. He returned to Place Madou early the following morning. Despite it being a Saturday, Ross was there waiting. Mlle. Arameau was in also, sorting the post.

"I am sure you'll be pleased to hear," Ross said, taking the report, "Marc's condition is now stable."

Julian nodded.

"I'm glad you were in the area, though Brandt does not share my feelings. He has expressed regret but is also asking we 'restrain ourselves in our actions where the safety of our hosts and integrity of their work is concerned'. He was not thrilled about the fire-bomb incident either."

Julian was not in a mood that could be called humorous and decided not to exacerbate the situation. They heard Mlle. Arameau gasp in the next office. She was staring at the bloody contents of the package from Marseilles. Ross too, stood stock still when he saw the severed finger, complete with wedding ring.

"Is the warning of what we are up against clear now?" Julian asked coldly. "My finger should have been in the package. Instead it is Marc's and my nephew is also injured and in a clinic in Marseilles. Tell Brandt I am not interested in Swiss office protocol. We must have his support, or my work with the Committee is finished."

Later that same day an American Army major whose booming voice Ross knew well over the telephone, entered a conference room at the NATO base at SHAPE. He was Major George Cummings and he was clutching to his chest a dossier on recent activities of the Committee on Slavery. It included personnel files and a report on the Marseilles operation. He didn't feel an hour's delay too bad considering the haste with which a weekend meeting had been called by their high-powered visitor from Bonn.

The visitor had a reputation for irascibility. He was Major 'Johnny' Walker, head of CIA, Section II, Europe. The recent involvement of the Committee with the deaths of CIA agents in Amsterdam and Marseilles was a key item for discussion. Cummings was not surprised at Walker's visit as Section II are concerned with such internal matters.

Also in conference were senior officers involved with the DEA/CIA investigations into narcotics entering Europe from Communist countries. This was the second item for consideration as it was during investigations into this problem, agents had been killed.

Major Walker acknowledged Cummings' 'good evening' and asked if the Committee's director had been co-operative.

"McReedy himself brought the dossier over this afternoon and we had a chat. He was certainly not enthralled about a security check on his golden boy."

Walker glowered.

"Their head office has told them nothing, Major. He shouldn't know anything of this."

"He is rather a canny Scot – "

" – so were my ancestors. It is not a question of divine right, it's what they see and hear around them. We are concerned with security here?"

Cummings did not reply.

"Okay, lieutenant, let's have it."

Walker's aide, lieutenant Jones, speed-read the first pages of the report outlining the working goals of the Committee on Slavery to those in the room. When he came to the type-written sections he began to read.

"Well, gentlemen," he concluded, "the Committee has provided us with a little more on the Amsterdam business last month in which Agent Meredith was killed. There is also a patchy report on Marseilles, as their man is hospitalized, under curious circumstances, it seems. There's confirmation this operative swapped with de Lyon a week ago but no reference to Agent Johnson's death in the old town of Marseilles. They have provided files on the operatives involved and there's a non-committal statement from this Julian de Lyon gook ..."

"Gook, lieutenant?" Walker interrupted the lighting of a cigar.

"Well, Sir, he is half-Chinese."

"Lieutenant, less personal comment – "

The young man apologised, clearing his throat and was about to continue when Walker interrupted again.

"Am I hearing things? De Lyon swapped but was still down in Marseilles?"

The lieutenant confirmed this was so. Walker pursed his lips then waved the young man on.

"Beginning with the de Lyon file, it appears he entered the Customs Bureau in 1971. His first employment in the West and the first with Uncle Sam ..."

Walker looked up. The lieutenant went on hastily,

"... after graduation from Tokyo and Stanford

universities. He took a Masters at the latter in Far-Eastern Studies. The Customs Bureau took him on as a special adviser on narcotics movement out of the Triangle. He moved with them from New York to Washington in 1972 but transferred to the BNDD. They requested his transfer, apparently, because of his martial arts skills.

"That was at the time Nixon increased their budget for overseas work, Sir. As de Lyon was good on undercover work, they wanted him in their Manila office. After a couple of years in the Far East he joined UNFDAC, then UNICEF and is currently in Brussels on a five-year contract with the Bureau of Social Affairs."

The lieutenant scanned the rest of the report picking out items of relevance to the meeting. Walker sat back and asked,

"What office was he with in the BNDD?"

"The Strategic Intelligence Office, Sir. He worked for eighteen months on their Special Reports of the refining and trafficking operations in the Triangle."

"And how old was he when he signed with the Customs Bureau?"

"Twenty-eight, Sir."

"God-damn old for a graduate?"

Walker turned to the others for comment. They decided the circumstances of his arrival in Japan needed further clarification. They also pondered the item detailing de Lyon's criminal convictions in Hong Kong and decided there was nothing significant there, except he would not have been getting into trouble on his own.

"Okay, lieutenant," Walker said finally, "I want a full brief on the circumstances of him entering university in Japan. Ask Hong Kong how big the triad was – the 14K, you say – wherever it was in Hong Kong he lived in the middle Fifties and just how high he rose. If his name and the 14K's are mentioned anywhere in the same sentence in the last twenty years I want to know. When it comes to the family thing, the

Mafia have nothing on those little bastards. We'll find out who is helping who around here."

The lieutenant made notes.

"And find out why he was in Marseilles – and I don't want to hear he was on vacation. Get the surveillance team on him in Brussels. Someone's creaming it, getting East European smack into Germany but he can't do it on his own. With two agents to his credit, agents about to expose him, we're looking for an expert. De Lyon sure fits the bill."

5/2

Daphne got an unexpected note from Julian a few days after they returned from the South of France. It was an invitation to see what the *Ommegang*, the Flemish Festival in Brussels, had to offer that morning and she took care over her appearance. He was in a good humour and she found him much more relaxed than the previous week. He telephoned the clinic in Cannes every day and reported Thérèse was fine and they would be leaving at the weekend.

He also presented her with a box of Godiva chocolates from their shop in the Grand Place to thank her for keeping him company on the drive back to Brussels. She had stayed awake most of the time making sure he drank plenty of water and ate. She had also massaged him regularly from his neck to his hands.

While they were walking through the crowds in the centre of town a sudden brilliant idea came to her. He had mentioned he would be in Germany shortly and she asked if Peter might be better off in Wiesbaden, at her uncle and aunt's summer house when discharged from the clinic. She had just been telling him her parents spent most of the summer at the house. Thérèse was a favourite niece and they all wanted to meet Peter. The peace and quiet of the forests would surely also be perfect for convalescing.

"Is it possible," she began carefully, "if I went too, you

could come and visit when you finish what you're doing in Germany and I could get a lift back with you?"

Julian thought for a moment. It would be an ideal way of keeping Peter away from Brussels. The apartment was being watched and he had yet to ascertain by whom. The alternative was sending him back to England.

"I was planning on taking the car," he replied deftly.

Daphne's eyes lit up.

"Oh, you would really like my parents. My mother can be a bit strange, like brushing the Siamese cat with a Mason Pearson brush but you'd really warm to her!"

"I don't know my itinerary until this afternoon," he said with a little smile "but I would be pleased to take up your invitation. Peter too, I'm sure."

Daphne beamed. She knew it would be a big step forward if she could draw him in to her family, even only for one day.

"You'll like my father too. We lived in Vietnam after the *Légionnaires* left and he knows South-East Asia well. I was born in Saigon."

"What a coincidence!" Julian replied. "It's also my birthplace, a little before you. So that's why you wanted to try the lager in Paris?"

"Well, hardly. I was only there till I was two!"

"Was your father a *Légionnaire*?"

"He was an engineer with a company fighting the *Viet Minh*. He stayed on after that big battle in 1954. One of only a few survivors, as I understand it."

"Dien Bien Phu?" Julian asked, surprised once again. They stopped in the shadow of the *Bourse*, in one of the narrow streets leading out of the Grand Place. He drew Daphne closer so she would not be swept away by the festival crowds.

"Yes," she replied and asked what was wrong.

His father also fought at Dien Bien Phu with the

Expeditionary Forces but did not survive. Daphne fell silent, thinking how amazing it was that her father might have known his. She would 'phone Wiesbaden straight away and tell her father about their conversation and new guests.

She was about to ask about Saigon when the *Hôtel de Ville* clock struck one o'clock and Julian apologised for having to abandon her. He was late for the Hamburg briefing. Daphne insisted she didn't mind. She had chocolate, she said smiling, and the best time to enjoy it is when alone and in a good mood.

Someone bumped into her as Julian helped with her jacket and her breast touched the back of his hand. It was like an electric shock and it made her gasp. When her eyes met his it was obvious he experienced a similar reaction. Oblivious to people in the street she put her arms around his waist then stepped back, her eyes wide open.

"*Mon Dieu*, you are solid ..."

"To complement the lady's softness," Julian replied.

Ross greeted Julian without smiling. The day would be a difficult one. Not only had Brandt not reiterated support for Julian, he had instructed he should be cautioned about his behaviour before his next assignment. What was more, the security review was being monitored by the Central Intelligence Agency who were furious at having to come into the open with deaths in Amsterdam and Marseilles.

"There have been some developments in the last two days," he said soberly. "You're still off out-of-town assignments, at least those that might involve the CIA, though with the exception of Hamburg."

A smile passed across Julian's face.

"Well put, Ross. I am sure you also explained to head office, taking operatives off assignments means no assignments. And no assignments mean no Committee."

Ross decided to say nothing until Julian returned from

Hamburg. He was dismayed at Brandt's insensitivity. Friends' fingers do not arrive in the post every day.

He turned his attention to details of the Hamburg operation. Julian saw he would be attending a conference on Saturday morning and briefing on Sunday. He handed the air ticket back, saying he was motoring to Hamburg on Friday evening. Ross wrinkled his brow. Hamburg was half-a-day's drive from Brussels.

"I'm going on to Wiesbaden after the weekend to check on my nephew. He'll be convalescing there with friends."

Ross asked if he would go the usual way to Hamburg.

"No, I prefer the straight line up through Nordhorn to Bremen. I've been caught before with weekend traffic around Venlo."

Ross sat back in his chair as Julian went through the operation details. Different thoughts passed through his head. His Number One admitted no-one had seen Ann-Marie for almost two months and he, her father Count Maurice and their lawyers were concerned. He decided he would give Julian more time off the following week, assuming nothing untoward happened. It was time his holiday allocation was used up anyway.

Julian called at Daphne's apartment the following Friday afternoon on his way to Hamburg. Daphne knew it was him when her *Parlophone* buzzed. She was in the middle of drying her hair but pulled on an embroidered cotton top, gritted her teeth as she glanced in the mirror and bounced down the staircase.

"Hello!" she smiled.

"May I come in?"

He was there for her aunt and uncle's address in Wiesbaden and to say Thérèse would be telephoning. He had also brought a bag of clothes for Peter to save him going up to Rue Américaine and asked Daphne to mention the apartment would be locked. He did not want to worry them just then why the apartment was out of bounds.

Daphne set about making a pot of tea and Julian went onto the balcony. The afternoon sun fell across the profusion of tubs and potted plants he remembered from her party. He particularly liked the herbs in old jugs and bowls. Some of them were inside now, on jardinières and the combination of smells with those from the roses below was delightful.

"It's heaven to wake up to," she responded, "and as they're all happy at the moment, I am too!"

The rest of the apartment looked rather different without straw and the other trappings of her Provençal evening. Two computers now sat in the living room with books, files and printouts heaped around them. The bigger one was a word-processor 'on loan' from her father's office, she explained. Julian knew a little about it. There was one on Mlle. Arameau's desk.

"It does annoy me when people ask what I want, or even need a computer for. It's such a stupid question ..."

Daphne stopped in mid-sentence when she realised she was on her hobby-horse for no reason. Julian said he was glad he hadn't fallen into the trap. She excused herself and went into the kitchen to pour the tea.

He was sitting on the living room floor when she returned. She knelt before him and handed him a bowl with both hands in the way Japanese, and Chinese she had read, show respect to visitors. It was a vanilla tea from Mauritius, one Peter mentioned his uncle liked and which she had come across by chance. She drank it while trying not to screw up her face. Although pleasantly-flavoured it was too strong and she was grateful he said it was a nice treat.

She asked him what Mauritius was like, saying one of her dearest ambitions was to throw her arms open to a tropical sunrise across white coral sand and a blue lagoon. She didn't give him a chance to answer, following this up instead with the question,

"Didn't you meet your wife there, I think Peter said ..."

Julian looked at her.

"I would like to hear about, Ann-Marie, isn't it?"

As she spoke she realised what a dumb thing it was she was doing. The tea too, just because Peter said they drank a lot of it. She hoped now he would change the subject.

She watched him take a second walnut from the bowl she had put by him and crack it like the first, between thumb and forefinger. She put her tea down and moved closer.

"I can't believe what I'm seeing!" she exclaimed, trying to open his hand.

"A secret!" he said.

Curious now, she gripped his arm and demanded he open his hand. He smiled but said nothing. She lifted her skirt slightly, straddled him and tried with all her strength to prise his hand open. She was determined and nearly pushed him over. When she became aware of what she was doing she was unsure of what to do next. She closed her eyes and held her breath. His hands were on her waist and she felt herself being lifted gently. She desperately wanted to be held tightly but it didn't happen, not even an embrace. There was a delicate smile on his lips as her feet touched the floor. He said he looked forward to meeting her and her family and was gone.

"What are you doing, Daphne?" she asked herself, standing alone in her silent and darkening apartment. Cavorting with a man she hardly knew. Realising how clumsy she had been about everything she actually watched herself clenching her fist.

Thérèse telephoned later that evening and confirmed Peter was getting back to normal, the weather was wonderful and they didn't want to leave the Mediterranean but could she get the car and pick them up at Zaventem the following afternoon. Daphne told Thérèse everyone at Wiesbaden was looking forward to seeing them and her father was coming to Brussels to pick the three of them up. Thérèse was touched. He was such a kind man.

Peter was cheerful at the airport. His arm was in plaster, his chest was still strapped and he moved slowly but he was cheerful. He groaned when Daphne hugged him but told her it was only lack of practice between them. He also thanked her for the invite to Wiesbaden.

"It'll be good for you," Daphne said. "Several weeks there can cure anyone of anything, usually!"

"I have had a hard week in bed and need to relax a bit!"

Daphne was pleased at the prospect of them all being at Wiesbaden but seeing Peter limping about that afternoon reminded her the situation was by no means ideal. She had dreamt about Julian and asked herself what was going to happen, now she had made up her mind about this man.

5/3
Hamburg, Sunday 11 August

Julian paid an unofficial call on a Turk named Sadik on Sunday morning. The Turk, one of Germany's million *gastarbeiters* lived in an apartment building in St. Pauli in the west of Hamburg. The suburb felt damp and autumnal that morning. Turkish children stared from the doorways of the grey buildings, the VWs and Taunuses were that little more run-down. The Ferrari contrasted starkly with its surroundings.

Sadik did not smile when he saw Julian. He rubbed the sleep from his eyes and invited him in. He instructed his wife to prepare coffee and leave the kitchen. Sadik had just finished six months in prison when he and Julian last met. If it hadn't been for Julian's help and his co-operation with the American authorities on drugs and related matters it would have been years. There were many on Istanbul's waterfront after his blood, which explained the Americans' further assistance in securing him a job in the Federal Republic.

Julian looked around the flat. It was an improvement on his hovel in Atikali on the south shore of the Golden Horn but he was now suffering the indignity of unemployment and loss of face with his family. Julian came straight to the point.

"Do you know anything about criminal activity at Eurocargo?"

Sadik hesitated, then decided he would get this over with quickly.

"I tell you then you go. Okay?"

"Okay."

"Yeni and some Turks have big money now. They are Herr Hauptmann's boys. Eurocargo."

"Same racket?"

"Bigger here. They bring in number three and four heroin from Turkey, through Bulgaria and East Germany. An American army man buys. Big guy."

"And girls?"

"Plenty little girls."

Julian studied the man's countenance. His misfortune spanned more than twenty years, from when the *Agha* had bulldozed his village and ploughed the site over. He found a job in the big city on the ferries and was lured by the easy money of people-smuggling. The only reason he was talking now was because his own fourteen-year-old daughter had been abducted five years earlier. She was one of over three thousand females below the age of sixteen listed missing in Turkey that year.

It was a year in which Julian's office estimated upwards of forty thousand from across Europe taken into domestic or sexual slavery or traded on the international markets for

84

African and Middle-Eastern brothels. Istanbul is the main collecting place for Europe and Sadik had been at the heart of the business.

Two women began bickering beyond the door. The Turk looked sullenly over his shoulder.

"Who is the big man in the docks here?"

"Herr Hauptmann, I said. He bad news."

"One last question, my friend. Where are the goods held?"

Sadik thought for a moment.

"It is not the same as back home. Not in the Pleasure Houses. Too many tourists. Villas maybe and the docks. And the *Kornmarkt*. They take girls there. They make films."

He got up and turned the coffee off, wary of saying more. Julian took the two bottles of cognac in his bag and pushed them across the table. He also put the contents of his wallet into the man's hand and after checking the street was empty, uttered the words,

"*Allaha ısmarladık.*"

Sadik allowed himself a little smile. They never heard this from foreigners now.

"*Gülle, gülle,*" he retorted.

Julian drove back through St. Pauli to the Reeperbahn and Ost-West Strasse. It began to rain a tired city rain. He garaged the car again by the station near his hotel on Kirchenallee and decided to make time for a coffee before walking on to the consulate building.

Dozens of people were assembled to finalise the co-ordination of raids that began that night. The operation was concerned with drug-trafficking, illegal immigration and the abduction of minors and it had taken the German police, with the assistance of American agencies and the United Nations, months to plan. Julian was joining a small team of customs investigators. He had to be at a dockside warehouse on Zippelhaus, close to St. Katherine's church at Monday dawn.

There was a notably large American presence at the briefing, including five military personnel from an army base near Frankfurt and three embassy staff from Bonn. They were joined by officers from the German secret services anti-espionage in a separate briefing. The army base was the CIA's largest cover in the Federal Republic, the Bonn embassy the second. The American and West German governments took a dim view of hard drugs being dumped by Communist countries.

Julian did not know one of the CIA agents had been assigned a task not relevant to the Monday operation. The agent, 'Big' Joe Williams, would be watching Julian's activities over the weekend. He was a communications expert working with units in the army bases in Germany handling telephone tapping, mail-opening and surveillance. Before this he had spent years in Hong Kong in Army Intelligence and gained experience in Chinese communities all over South-East Asia since the early days of the Vietnam War. He spoke good Cantonese and was a first-rate exponent of *kung fu*.

More recently he had joined Walker's team, Section II, where he was known as the China Expert. He had now disappeared from the scrutiny of American government agencies, including the Tax Department, as Section II agents are protected by total anonymity identification. He was an untraceable national abroad and it suited his plans very well.

There was also an irony in his having been chosen for the Hamburg assignment, an irony that caused him to burst out laughing one evening in his house on a pleasant part of the Mosel near Koblenz. He knew more about de Lyon than Walker could imagine. He had been setting de Lyon up for some time. The weekend couldn't be going better. De Lyon's unscheduled visit to a small-time hood in St. Pauli that morning would seal his fate. The killing of two Company agents would shortly be pinned on this half-Chinese.

That Sunday evening, Julian prepared some simple weapons of his own design, needle-guns based on cheap refillable lighters with modified valve mechanism. Dart guns were a favourite weapon of CIA agents during the Fifties and Sixties and he had seen them used to great effect.

The herbal preparation incorporated was mixed for him during the afternoon by a Chinese herbalist. The family were friendly because he spoke their dialect, though they were cautious to begin with. The *Ah Kong*, another new and vicious Singaporean tong had recently begun muscling into the heroin business in a disciplined, military fashion in a city with the largest Chinese community in Germany.

He left his hotel at about nine o'clock and walked down to a deserted waterfront. He took a short-cut through a timber yard, scaled a five-metre fence and moved silently in the shadows of Nineteenth-century buildings on the cobbled quayside of the *Oberhafenkanal* until he reached the gable-end *Kornmarkt* Sadik had spoken of. Getting in was easy. He climbed the fire escape of the adjacent building, bridged the gap with a length of heavy timber and walked across. The wired glass of a skylight gave way with a kick.

The attic floor of the old building had been converted into a studio. The smell of photographic chemicals and photo-flood lighting was strong. Lighting equipment proliferated amidst a sea of black cable on the carpeted boards. Adjacent to the studio was a full commercial laboratory for the processing of 16 millimetre film and a paste-up operation for the production of a cheap magazine. Pornography here had not yet entered the video age.

The offices below were more interesting. He opened the one that was locked and had time for a quick look before turning his attention to the person who had entered the building on the ground floor and was making his way slowly up the wooden staircase at the end of the corridor.

Julian withdrew behind some boxes. When the figure appeared he saw by the flash of a navigation light through a window the man was American. He was large and sporting a baseball jacket and matching cap. He was light on his feet and he knew Julian was in the building. He was one of the Americans from the briefing, Williams.

Julian put his weight on a floorboard end and barely made it squeak.

"De Lyon?" the American whispered.

Julian asked him to identify himself.

"Williams, the Company. From the briefing this afternoon," came the unruffled reply. "We had a tip-off about this place."

There was no change in the man's disposition, in his aura. Julian could read it clearly in the darkness. Here was a man in control of himself. He also had a key to the front door.

"Sorry to creep in on you like this. I missed you at your hotel. We only got the tip this evening."

"From whom?" Julian asked, stepping into the corridor.

There was only one person who knew where he might have been that evening. Williams saw there was no point in lying and said he had called on Sadik. He admitted Julian was followed during the morning.

"This is a bad start. Just keep out of my way."

"Yeah, of course," Williams replied. "I'll take a look upstairs."

Julian watched Williams climb the staircase to the studio and returned to the room he had unlocked. The material here was not regular commercial pornography. Hand-written titles on stereo cassettes included Schoolgirl Walks Alone and Night Time is No Time for a *Jungfrau*. He ran part of a film in an editing machine and watched the frames jerk and dance their way silently to a final obscene conclusion.

On another, also of footage straight from a camera, he

flinched as a teenager was nailed to the floor by her hands. Yet another young female was suspended by her wrists from the beams of what looked like the studio above and was being whipped front and back by two masked men. Her blood was everywhere. The close-ups suggested strongly she did not survive.

There were eighteen snuff movie masters in the lab waiting to be copied, all more violent than those on file at the Place Madou office. Plastic bags under the cutting table bulged with scraps of film, some spilling onto the floor and Julian found himself stepping on the less interesting frames of these girls' final minutes edited out and discarded as easily as they. A strong stomach would be needed by those collecting evidence here.

He turned his attention to the filing cabinets and drawers and saw all records had been removed. He did find a small postage book that had slipped behind a cabinet. A glance showed regular entries for a *Schloss Belgien* and other places. All outgoing material was marked 'by courier'. The world's postal services are good enough for diamonds. It was a more exclusive merchandise in this little warehouse. The book was a good find.

He knew as Williams came down the staircase adjusting his shoulder holster he had been in the building too long. Cars had pulled up on the waterfront. There was the sound of breaking glass below. Voices could be heard on the roof.

"You've just blown this operation, Williams," he said coldly.

"Don't start on me, de Lyon, we're outa here."

The smell of kerosene reached Williams' nostrils. He turned to the window again. There was more happening than there should have been. Hauptmann's boys were on time but were hardly being discreet. De Lyon was on his way down the corridor when there was a boom from below and almost simultaneously from above. Both staircases lit up.

"Your office knows you are here ..."

"Nope," Williams replied.

"... so why did you follow me?" Julian asked, sitting casually on the edge of a table.

"Business, de Lyon. Me minding mine and you minding yours."

"Understand this, we will be talking again."

"So who was the tearaway who paid you a visit in Cannes?"

"You've got a nerve," Julian responded, "considering how ill-informed you're supposed to be."

"A bit more than coincidence, you being in the South of France at the same time as Jenny Lo. Old girlfriend?" Williams persisted.

There was a louder explosion beneath them, the distraction giving Julian a moment to weigh up the information. This was a name he had not heard for twenty years.

"Perhaps not so ill-informed. We know there was a Chinese woman involved. How is it you know her name – "

The American faltered.

" – You've got a big mouth, Williams."

Flames were now visible at the end of the corridor. The same soft red-yellow light was playing down the upper staircase. Williams turned to Julian, visibly angry and asked,

"What is it with you and the *sap sei kei*, Buddy?"

Julian didn't bother with a reply. Time was up on the trip-me-up game. He grabbed a hand towel and wet it under a tap. They swapped it at the end of the smoke-filled corridor. Williams pointed the way to the emergency exit. They went down the burning staircase and ran blindly between walls of blazing cartons.

"Jesus!" Williams exclaimed, at the steel exit door. The fire took a sudden vicious turn. The aisle they had come down erupted. Julian examined the push bar on the door.

The key was missing from the glass box. Williams dangled it in front of him.

"Full of fun, aren't you, Big Mouth – "

A solid wall of flame was creeping across the floor towards them, feeding on paint and chemicals. It was a searing translucent orange and yellow that reminded Julian of being behind a waterfall. A rack of plastic containers behind it exploded, doubling the intensity of the blaze. The floor above would be next. And then them.

Williams turned the key in the lock but did not push. They could not leave until the last possible moment. There was a chance the fire service would frighten off the waiting gang. Julian put his mouth to the edge of the door, eyes smarting, clothes scorching and lungs hurting from the acrid smoke. A section of floor came down, showering them with burning debris.

"Sitting duck, or roast duck ..." he said, leaning on the bar.

The stairs they had come down collapsed, followed by a section of floor. The quaintest of thoughts were passing through his head, such as the Japanese using 100-year-old pine to fire their best pottery, when Williams slipped the .45 from its holster. He moved to deflect the weapon but Williams moved with him.

Words, even gestures were lost in the following moments, in the blinding incandescence, in the roar of the collapse of the interior. A torrent of sparks snaked a terrible warning toward the two tiny figures in the corner of the conflagration, where Williams, instead of pulling the trigger was slipping into unconsciousness with his only thoughts being those of a fortune also slipping from his grasp.

Julian heard but did not see a great destructive ball of fire rise majestically into the night sky. He and Williams fell through the doorway. He dragged Williams clear with one hand, while shielding his face with the other. The door was sucked closed. Those seconds waiting for the herbal preparation of his needle gun to take effect were agony.

As his eyes and lungs adjusted to the shock of cold air he saw there was no-one at that end of the warehouse because the adjacent building was also burning fiercely. This was luck. He left Williams on the cobbles and peered around the corner along the quay. Cars had moved back but people were still running about. Tenacious bastards, he thought. The *feuerwehr* were taking their time. The fire must have been visible across the entire dock.

He returned for Williams, moving him just before a blazing spar came crashing from the roof. Muttering he didn't deserve such attention, he carried all two hundred and fifty pounds of the man to the corner of a building that had begun to crack. He swung him in two complete circles and let go. He had not attempted a Flying Wheel hold over four metres with such a weight but was not worried about so fine a point. Williams went through the night air and into the water with the dignity of a sack of potatoes. Julian followed.

When he surfaced, he turned the American over and pulled him along under cover of the granite quay. Faces did not appear over the edge and Julian was concerned he was having too much luck. Shielded now by the massive stonework from the agonies of a dying building he heard the thinner sounds of nearby cars and *polizei* sirens bouncing across the oily water. Blue lights were adding variation to the colours of a desert sunrise across the Hamburg waterfront.

A hundred metres away from the building he reached for a rusted iron ladder, transferred Williams' bulk across his shoulders and began the arduous task of raising them both out of the water. He dumped him on the quayside after considerable effort, gave mouth-to-mouth resuscitation and as his own strength returned, checked the postage book was still in his jacket.

Williams began coughing.

"Yes, my friend. Hell or High Water – "

This was a delivery Julian had been obliged to make. Three agents in a row would not have been good for his reputation.

CHAPTER SIX

Wiesbaden, Monday 12 August

Colours promising a fine day were creeping over the treetops when Julian pulled into a deserted *rastplatz* on the autobahn, fifty kilometres south of Hannover. He stretched his legs in the early morning air. The birch trees made a welcome change from the endless pine forests. An occasional truck howled past in the semi-darkness. He had left Hamburg early and still had three hundred kilometres more to drive. He had spent an hour only in hospital and was experiencing some discomfort.

It was a little after seven when he arrived at the village above Wiesbaden in which Daphne's uncle and aunt had their summer house. It was like a hunting lodge as Daphne had described it and lost, like the other houses, in the forest. The Rhine was visible in the distance.

"I'm so pleased you could come and visit us, Julian," Daphne's mother said in greeting. "I'm Margaret. You timed it perfectly to join me for breakfast."

"I didn't want to be so early I was an embarrassment," Julian replied.

She went out to the car to help fetch the flowers he had brought. Brushing his arm as they entered the house she felt him flinch. She started some fresh coffee, pulled her chair up to his and looked at his dressings

"You have burns on your arm as well as your face – "

"The very least I can expect, playing with fire. I must

apologise for arriving in such a state."

She invited him to help himself to the bread, cold meat and fruit conserves on the table. The dressings were clean but she would look at them again later.

"Well, I see why my daughter was so anxious last night," she said, moving her chair back and looking at him. "She was transfixed by the late news having mentioned you were in Hamburg. It showed several buildings blazing at the docks and much police activity. It was thought to be a terrorist act."

She paused discreetly.

"Oh, it was nothing as glamorous as that."

"I know now why she was worried – "

"If Daphne could have chosen her mother, she said recently, you would have no competition!"

The stirrings of others in the household began soon after Julian arrived. Margaret first introduced her sister-in-law who was immensely apologetic for having slept in. She had risen at five to see her husband and Daphne's father off on a morning's fishing and sneaked back to bed. She clasped her hands, thanking Julian for the flowers and arranged them as a dining table centrepiece. Thérèse said a pleasant hello and reported, smiling, Peter was almost back to normal. She set about preparing a breakfast tray.

"Three so far. Another four to come," Margaret said. "Perhaps we won't have another chance to talk until you visit us in Lille."

"I look forward to it," Julian replied.

Daphne's face lit up when she saw Julian and the flowers but clouded again when she noticed his burns.

"Julian, you're here," she said, clinging to his arm. She saw her mother grimace.

"My arm is a little tender, Daphne."

She apologised profusely for not being up to meet him and engineered him into the garden.

"I am fine," he said, reassuring her. "It was a small incident I got caught up in yesterday evening."

"Some small incident! It was no fun watching it on television," she began, "as I knew you would be in the thick of it. You're sure you're okay? Don't people get shock or delayed reaction to being burned?"

"The drive down was relaxing and I had a pleasant chat with your mother over breakfast."

Later that morning they took the car along the river as far as Lorch. They walked a little way along one of the many hiking trails in the forest before returning via Bad Schwalbach. It was a beautiful part of the Taunus and a spectacular section of the Rhine gorge. Daphne was really pleased at showing Julian places she had loved since she was a child. He was much less tense as the morning progressed but she was concerned and asked if they could stop at the *apotheke* on the High Street.

"I have some cream and a spray and I want no nonsense," she said, getting back in the car. "I've just worked out you've had no sleep, so I shall put this on you and make sure you rest after lunch. The pharmacist said infection is the danger with burns. And as you were probably in the harbour as well, I will also wash your clothes ..."

Julian laughed, actually too tired to contradict her. He had changed out of wet clothes and cleaned up as best he could before checking out of the hotel at one in the morning and must have looked a little crumpled.

"You are kind," he said, "and I won't argue. I expect your pupils don't dare either!"

Daphne apologised immediately for talking to him in this manner. Straight faces lasted until they reached the park when they both started laughing so much Julian thought it safer to stop the car.

Thérèse showed Julian up to Peter's room on their return

in an effort to get him out of bed for lunch. Julian had not seen his nephew since the clinic in Cannes and said the lie-in had done him good.

"It's more the attention I'm getting from these lovely girls!"

He winked as Thérèse walked into the room.

"And now you are taking advantage, *Chéri*, no?" she asked sternly in English. "Your uncle is here and you are not up."

"I'm tired," Peter complained.

"Splash your face with cold water," she suggested.

"That doesn't work."

"Then a little exercise?"

"That makes me more tired."

Thérèse put her hands on her hips and asked what he thought was the answer.

"More sleep is the only thing that wakes me up!"

She left the room shaking her head but her eyes met Julian's with a knowing smile on her lips.

Daphne's aunt relished the prospect of a big dinner for their new guest. The point of a summer retreat was to entertain family and friends and her idea of a hearty welcome was one with plenty of food. To this end she cooked and baked for most of the afternoon with help from Margaret and Thérèse and was satisfied a dinner of fresh river trout bartered from a neighbour and a good-sized pie was a suitable start.

Julian's eyes opened wide when the pie was brought to the table at dinner. It was beautifully decorated, contained game laced with cognac and peaches and was enormous. He had seen nothing like it.

"I have to admit, Julian," Daphne's uncle began in French, with a distinct German accent, "we are not eating the fruits of our endeavours. Charles and I are as successful hunting as we are fishing and as you know we caught nothing again this morning, this should say it all!"

He roared with laughter, slapped his brother on the back and refilled glasses all round from a barrel conveniently by him. He went on to say the pie was prepared from game the local priest caught and he did this better than anything else. This was also followed by gales of laughter.

After dinner, when the living room was being cleared for the evening's entertainment, Julian was alone on the verandah enjoying a rare feeling of well-being despite having drunk and eaten more than was good for him. The only sounds about him were crickets in the shrubbery and music and laughter from the house. Barbecue lights strung between the trees threw pools of colour down the garden. An occasional shaft of light swept the river far below. Having been put on the spot to make a speech at Daphne's Provençal evening he knew he would be called upon to do something in Wiesbaden. Story-telling and poetry recitation were a traditional part of this family's after-dinner entertainment.

When his turn came he first described the symbolism of cherry blossom throughout Asia. In China it represents feminine beauty. In Japan, it is a metaphor for brave warriors fallen in battle but nowhere is it more beautiful in Spring than on the Korean Peninsula. His tale was one of an inevitable tragic parting of a young *samurai* and his lover under Tokyo's *sakura*, its flowering cherry trees, one April long ago.

The story began, "If it pleases you, Miss ..." and Julian recited and part-enacted it in Japanese, translating into French as he went. Though he had to invent and adapt, the piece was received with cheers and whistles of approval. Daphne watched from the shadows then slipped away, her eyes brimming. She was taken completely by surprise.

When the house had quietened down, Charles joined Julian for a stroll in the garden. Daphne came out with her father but turned back. She didn't want Julian to see her with red eyes. Charles said how much he had enjoyed the charming return to Asia and its gentler side and asked Julian where he had learnt Japanese. Julian replied he was an undergraduate in Tokyo.

"So where do you consider your home to be now?"

"The notion of home is ever more elusive, I'm afraid."

"Even when you revisit, Hong Kong, isn't it?"

Julian watched the moon growing smaller. The pungent and not unpleasant aroma of the tobacco burning in Charles's elaborately carved pipe drifted about him. It was ten years since he had been to Hong Kong and fourteen since he had seen his mother, though they wrote to each other regularly. Now it was easier to travel in China he had little excuse not to return.

"I am overdue for a visit," he said at length. "Next time could be the decider."

Daphne reappeared, having sorted her face out and asked if they would like more beer, or tea perhaps. She overheard Julian but did not comment. When she had gone, Julian asked Charles about his time as an army engineer.

"I must warn you, I am a sucker for relating my army days. My age, I fear! When you're young and fall in love, the place where it happens remains in your heart also. In my case it was in a Saigon street I set eyes on the embodiment of a young man's dreams!"

Relating his first meeting with Margaret he said she stood head and shoulders above the Vietnamese women. She was slim but felt like an elephant. Julian laughed. Chinese women can be unkind about Western women, commenting, often out loud, on big noses and big feet. Charles chuckled at what his wife would think of this. He explained she had just started post-graduate work in Vietnam. He found it amazing she had managed such a thing in such unsettled times, the year before Dien Bien Phu.

Julian had tried to imagine the desperate, protracted fighting the expeditionary forces endured at this engagement, one of the great military blunders. He told Charles his memories were juvenile and comparatively jaundiced.

"Sadly, father's body was never found. The hope he had escaped to Laos was both a comfort and a trial. It was one of the worst periods in our lives."

Charles had checked through his old photographs and memorabilia, all of which he wanted to show Julian, and said he was sorry he could find no reference to *Capitaine* de Lyon. He promised he would enquire at their next reunion dinner and it would give them something new to jaw about.

"It was a large operation, with six battalions parachuting onto the jungle plateau to begin work on the advance base," he began. "It ended with a fifty-five-day battle for survival against, eventually, overwhelming *Viet Minh* forces. And do you know, Julian, I am as sad now about the greater loss of life sustained by the people whose country we were fighting in. It was unforgivable."

He sucked on his pipe in a sombre silence remembering the creeping despair and spectre of friends, dead and dying, sinking beneath the mud. Bodies lay everywhere.

"They entered the camp in the darkness in their large hats, grinning it seemed, on that night of May seventh," he recalled finally. "Shadows of Death, some called them. Ghosts, others. I had never known such fear but after so many weeks of fighting without let-up was too tired to care whether I fought or died. A crushing defeat for the Legion it was. As black a day as there will ever be in its history."

When Julian asked about the aftermath, he replied while it was thoughts of Margaret that kept him going through the fighting, worry about her safety during months of cruel internment almost finished him. A similar experience, he suggested, to one Julian, his brother and mother must have suffered.

"Happily, Margaret and I did meet again months later when I was skin and bone and I don't know if I would have survived without her," he said, his spirits lifting. "My army career ended but I am pleased to say my daughter carries on the military tradition ..."

Daphne came striding along the veranda on cue, with a large tray. She saw both men pretending to be serious and asked her father if he was not telling stories about his army days he shouldn't be. Charles commented on the difficulties of having two strong women in his life but made his daughter squeal by squeezing her waist.

She put the tray down, poured tea and coffee and whispered to Julian he would have to eat at least one each of the pastries. He looked on in disbelief at how she was piling his plate.

"Aunt made them specially because she thinks you're too thin. And you're not having it all your own way with the tea. This one is Alpine Tea and is especially good after one of our big dinners!"

She sat down, pleased to be in the cool and quiet of the garden. In the half-light she could see her father smiling and Julian looking at her. She asked if Julian had mentioned being in Saigon the year she was born. Her father replied he had not given him the chance. Julian said he was there when he was thirteen but it was not so interesting.

She was about to insist, when her father said she must respect Julian's wish not to be cross-examined. She attacked one of the pastries as her aunt came out to check there was enough to eat. Julian stood up to thank her and said the hospitality he had received that day was overwhelming.

"Well, young man," Charles resumed when his daughter had returned to the card game inside, "it is getting late but I would like to hear how the political and military meddling of the Western Powers affected your upbringing. You must have been chased just about everywhere in Asia in your youth!"

"It wasn't as bad as that," Julian replied. "The ones I remember are British policemen with big sticks!"

Daphne slept fitfully that night, eventually waking Thérèse in the spare bed next to her. Thérèse turned the light on and asked if she would like a drink of water.

"I think you know what I need," she said sleepily.

Thérèse told her she was saucy.

"I was having bad thoughts rather than bad dreams. Julian must see me as, well, as a child. I just wish I was older."

Thérèse did not reply immediately.

"You are very grown up, *Chérie*. You've always been a wise person. The man looks at you with a smile on his face. And it's not the sort of smile for a child ..."

"Wouldn't I be lucky."

"And I never thought I would see the day when you weren't absolutely sure of yourself!"

Thérèse giggled, then noticed the time. They had to be up soon for a trip down the river.

"I'm so pleased you and Peter came," Daphne said. "It's been good for both of you."

"I'm pleased to see you and Julian are friends. It's about time you found a man strong enough to keep you in order!"

Daphne giggled but said this was presumptuous. Thérèse went on to say she thought he was rather distant but had learnt a lot about him from Peter. He never had a family life, not one that could be described as good, and she understood this.

"Peter has certainly helped your English. He goes goosey over your accent, he says. I'm quite jealous!"

"I bought an English novel for him at the clinic, thinking it was about martial arts. Anyway, I started reading it to him and he translated bits I didn't understand. I liked the line 'to

103

tempt is but a woman's way; to be desired is but a woman's need' and I thought about it at his bedside ..."

"Now who is *méchante!*"

"Not naughty," Thérèse said, looking into Daphne's eyes, "it was lovely and I cried. Is that normal when making love?"

"It is lovely to be in love. Crying about it makes it special," Daphne said, hugging her friend tightly. She was really pleased. "*Naughty* is just one of my wish-words."

She couldn't tell Thérèse she had only just learnt this. She needed to work through it herself.

The whole family limbered up on the lawn the following afternoon for some *tai chi* instruction from Julian. They agreed Europeans and North Americans generally had neither the build nor the inclination towards this sort of calm reflection but were willing to have a go. Daphne's uncle did ask if a leisurely lunch on a river boat was an acceptable alternative.

Peter was not fit enough to demonstrate any *katas* as a follow-up and Julian thought he might do something entertaining, not knowing he was already booked. He should have guessed when Peter said he could borrow his *gi*. The entertainment was to throw apples at him as often and as quickly as possible. It was a game he had played with children where the apples disappeared, to be found magically in his *gi*. These adults showed no restraint, of course, even with a bandaged arm and they had a lot of fun.

It was unusual for Ross to telephone Julian. He wanted him in the office by ten o'clock the following morning as there had been developments. A concerted effort was made to get Julian to stay but Daphne saw the telephone call was final and said she would be ready to leave.

Margaret rose at dawn to prepare breakfast but decided while her daughter was dressing, to make coffee only and leave her and Julian alone. He had eaten enough for a month, he said, but took a slice of a bread that had been a particular treat. It was *holzofen* bread, wood-oven baked and a local speciality, Margaret said. Her daughter had bought it especially and would be pleased he liked it.

His visit had also been a treat, she said, reminding him he must come to Lille. She didn't feel the need to say her daughter was the most positive she had been for a long time. Her attention to him had been obvious enough.

"It's nice to see you more relaxed," Daphne said in the car, putting a touch of cream on Julian's face and wrists. "I knew you would like it here. You must have had a miserable time in Hamburg with those burns."

"Of several difficult days," he replied, "the hardest one was leaving Brussels."

Daphne did not know what to say.

6/2
Bonn, Wednesday 14 August

The morning before Julian left Wiesbaden, Major Walker was in his office early. There was a mountain of reports and correspondence to clear before meetings began. It was hot in the building and he loosened his tie. Parting the slatted blinds he looked at the river. Traffic was already passing to and fro in the half-light.

His bugbear of the past month had been a link between Company deaths in The Hague and Marseilles, a hospitalization, various operations since June and Bulgarian heroin popping up everywhere across Europe where the forces were based. His office was making little progress. He suspected the shootings of both Meredith in Amsterdam and Johnson in Marseilles occurred because they had discovered, or were on the verge of discovering, the Communist link. This was the closest he could get to the problem, a surmising.

The DEA Paris office managed to keep Meredith's

operative status secret but the press caught up with events in Marseilles. He was now under pressure from the Chief of Station in Berlin. Langley was also taking an interest.

Walker's only firm lead remained Julian de Lyon who had been paired with Meredith. Williams reported from Marseilles that de Lyon could also have been working with a Chinese girl there, a Red Pole of the very triad of old de Lyon had been a member of. Now Williams himself was hospitalized after being assigned to keep tabs on de Lyon. De Lyon this, de Lyon that. He was getting sick of the name.

He pressed his desk intercom and asked his aide if the coffee machine was broken.

The first correspondence and sheaf of photographs he picked up was information requested from the security liaison office of British Intelligence in Hong Kong. Referring to the European operations of the 14K triad, it confirmed their principal enforcer Jenny Lo had been making almost weekly trips to Europe since the beginning of July.

"Their top guy is certainly busy with the mess the various agencies on this side are making of their business," he muttered. "Amsterdam, Rotterdam, Marseilles, Hamburg, always the same places. Always the same names. We're missing their little get-togethers, their little deals. Someone else is in on this working damn hard to keep their liaisons a private affair."

He took the coffee from the lieutenant's hand and asked about Joe. The lieutenant said the hospital was releasing him that morning and he would be fit enough for office duty. Walker wandered over to the window and saw the mist had cleared across the river. It would be another fine day.

"I don't like the fact de Lyon was inside that two-bit packing operation when the Chinese torched it," he said eventually. "Joe thought they were trying to get rid of him as an embarrassment. Last week he said they were not working together. He can't have it both ways."

106

"Joe was their target and de Lyon just got caught up in it?"

"There is no way they knew Joe would be there. And de Lyon is with them, or he isn't. They don't get rid of their people in that way. Joe knows this."

"They put pressure on the Turk after Joe had been?"

The Turk was still in a clinic and Walker did not comment. He was thinking about the smart-assed journalist putting questions to the ambulance crew that transferred Joe to the army hospital. De Lyon had not hung about, burns or not. This character was altogether too slick.

"And, lieutenant put a note put through to the Directorate about those scum journalists on the press agency payroll. Tell them I'm asking what is the point of having an agency feeding trash to the media when one smart-assed outsider and his clever editor come up with a line the others follow instead."

"They got the terrorist story across on *Nord Deutsche* and *Hessische Rundfunk*. That killed the newspaper line."

"Ask them anyway. It's like I'm the only one awake around here sometimes."

Walker sat down again. He had never known anyone get the better of Joe. Then it occurred to him de Lyon might actually have saved Joe's life. He certainly would have been in a whole lot more trouble coming out of the fire alone.

"De Lyon would have been in big trouble if Joe hadn't come out," the lieutenant began.

"Yeah, I reached that conclusion," Walker replied tartly. "And don't forget, when something comes through from Hong Kong on de Lyon bring it straight in. If it doesn't, wire them and tell them to get off their butts. I asked for information days ago."

Walker opened the 14K file and spread the most recent photographs across his desk. They showed the woman, Jenny Lo, with five men in the departure lounge of Hong

Kong's Kai Tak airport two weeks earlier. She was slight in build and wearing a trouser suit, a *cheong sam* over trousers. She had no adornments about her other than a gold shoulder bag with a chain strap. The chain was steel and detachable and in her hands a dangerous weapon.

Walker was not surprised she made the local operators quiver. She had a reputation for being particularly cruel. A feminist, one wit in the office called her. She was a Red Pole with full 426 status, the enforcer who came most often to Europe if income from their main business, heroin, flagged.

The two youths with her had hair bristling on their upper lips and curling over their collars. Their slum origins was evident in their Ralph Lauren T-shirts and new jeans with turn-ups. Although ordinary 49s, they would be formidable fighters.

The other three in the photographs were from a different age and remained apart from the bully boys. The eldest of the three, a man in his seventies, was wearing traditional Chinese clothes with an incongruous black Homburg. He was Ma Lok Yu, the report said, the 14K's most senior 438, the Incense Master. With him was another veteran of the triad's beginnings in Guangdong, Hong Kong's chief 432, the Straw Sandal.

Of the third person, a man in his fifties, little was written. Hong Kong's OCTB who made the photographs available to the CIA had never known him travel. He was a 49, the Bureau reported, but no ordinary member. He and his family owned a butchers shop in North Point. Known by few in the triad and fewer outside, he was talked about by many. He was the Butcher.

Walker put the file away and looked at his watch. Such a high-ranking group flying out on that occasion meant something big but he could not see it relating to the deaths of two of his men. He doubted whether it was Jenny Lo, or one of her gorillas responsible for Johnson's and Meredith's deaths with a handgun. It wasn't their style. Whatever way he approached the problem it led back to de Lyon and it looked as though Joe would be right again.

Thoughts of Joe's sources crossed Walker's mind as he set about other business. Joe must have seen some of this information before anyone in the office. He approved of initiative but didn't always like it.

The information he had been waiting for from the Hong Kong Station arrived during the afternoon. He was thinking of going home for an evening with his wife but the idea went out of his head. He scanned the profile twice, allowed himself a smile of gratification and asked his aide to call the Geneva office of the Bureau of Social Affairs.

"This god-damn operative of yours went too far at the weekend again, Brandt," he began bluntly. "He has become a pain in my ass."

"You mean by saving the life of one of your men, Major?" the heavily-accented voice replied.

Walker drummed his fingertips.

"Herr Brandt, this is not the comment I expect. Goddamnit, we put up with your wonder Committee tagging along and then one of your men, your Golden Boy, assaults one of my staff. It is an intolerable situation. I want a satisfactory answer from your office."

"It would greatly assist our combined operations, Major Walker," Brandt began acidly, "if tighter instructions were issued to your field men and there was less of their egotistical intransigence. It is important work we do. May I remind you your men are not above the law. There is more than a suggestion your agent Williams is responsible for criminal damage and malicious assault in Hamburg."

Walker gritted his teeth. After all his years in Europe he was still exasperated by the quiet manner of these European civil servants who in his book were devious, evasive and supercilious.

"Then I think," he began quietly, "you will be interested in the report that should shake the dust off your desk in the morning. A very interesting report of one Julian de Lyon, alias – alias Christ Almighty for all I care – who from 1956 to 1963 at least, was a paid-up member of not one, but two of the triads that put the fear of God daily into my boys all over the Far East. And, Herr Brandt if he is still involved with these slant-eyed scum, and as far as I'm concerned if he is breathing he is involved, your office is due a major security shake-up – "

"That is enough – " Brandt retorted sharply. It took a moment for him to compose himself fully. "We are well aware of *Monsieur* de Lyon's background but I shall, of course, give any new information my fullest consideration and advise the director of the Committee whatever I feel appropriate. For the moment I bid you a good afternoon."

Walker put the receiver down and chuckled. He flipped open the lid of his cigar box and inspected three before choosing.

"That should start some ass-kicking around that mausoleum," he said to his aide. "I want that sonofabitch, Lieutenant. I want a trace on him and full surveillance. I want a team watching him as of yesterday. I want to know what he is doing every minute. If he scratches his ass, I want it reported. Understand?"

"Every minute, as of yesterday, Sir."

He then asked the young man to get McReedy in Brussels but was inclined to finish his cigar. It had been a long day and he was savouring the information in front of him.

CHAPTER SEVEN

Brussels, Thursday 15 August

Ross got the Geneva call he was expecting on Thursday morning, shortly before Julian's return from Wiesbaden. Brandt informed him Julian was to be suspended from all duties while head office assessed the Bonn embassy's report. Brandt also wanted an account of Julian's behaviour in Hamburg on his desk the following Monday morning.

Ross reached for his Harraps after putting the 'phone down. It translated one of Brandt's words as 'fudging.' He was not satisfied apparently with the recently completed review of security procedures and practices.

Mlle. Arameau brought coffee up and was surprised to find her boss so calm after the call. She was worried about the situation. It was a mystery why the American embassy was making such a fuss. She was no wiser after her boss's suggestion it was Section II, the most secretive of the CIA's special activities groups, putting pressure on head office.

Ross put his mind to a plan contingent on action being taken against his staff. After seeing Julian, he had meetings with his chief accountant and van Moolens, his legal adviser. Recent exchanges with Brandt left him with the impression funds would not be available to the Committee for a second five years. If this was so he had nothing to lose. Either way, he decided, he would back his Number One.

The thought of the cavalier dismissal of their work in Brussels angered him. He was impressed with Julian's recent work on the pattern of use of specialised containers used criminally for the transportation of live bodies. Half-height, side-loading and refrigerated containers are monitored individually around the world to optimise their use. Julian suggested enquiries should begin with the computer personnel of all container terminal companies, including Eurocargo in Hamburg.

At the same time, evidence of his Number One being involved in twilight activities was hard to ignore, even if the CIA deaths were coincidental. Photographs of the woman identified as Julian's wife taken in Port Louis in a compromising situation earlier that year remained unexplained. The CIA were now saying Julian was a member of the 14K and Shanghai Green Gang at least until the age of twenty-one. Financial searches also showed him to be a wealthy man.

Shortly before ten o'clock, Ross asked Mlle. Arameau to check on the availability of computer time early the following morning. He picked up the 'phone and dialled the number that bypassed the main switchboard at the NATO Base. It was time to look more closely at what Ann-Marie's family were all about. He wanted to establish finally if her disappearance had any bearing on Julian's other problems. American Intelligence would have everything he wanted to know about the Count, Maurice Courcy d'Arraques.

Ross walked to Place Madou early the following morning from his home in Rue Jenneval by the Berlaymont Building. The pale sky was smutted with clouds, sunlight hadn't yet penetrated the narrow streets. He normally had neither the time nor the inclination to dwell on anything other than the problems in hand but it was a pleasant enough start to the end of the week.

The stark neon environment of the computer room did not suit him. Messages in his day were scribbled on cigarette packets. Intelligence now spewed forth so voluminously one handled it with a mainframe and he was beyond being awed that in his lifetime, the entire human history would be stored on a device the size of a matchbox. He asked his assistant to fetch some coffee and was not even mildly amused at how fastidious she had become in locking her briefcase.

At a little after six-thirty the transmission from the NATO base was complete and the controller indicated he was ready to run it.

Ross knew a little about the family Julian had married into. He had met the Count's only daughter, Ann-Marie and found her rather cold and befitting a complexion akin to unglazed porcelain. She was also born with a sharp intelligence that did nothing to soften her personality. Her relationship with Julian was a strange one based on a contract from their meeting four years earlier.

He couldn't think of it as a marriage and neither apparently did Julian. He compared her with the Parian figure of the goddess Atalanta he kept in his study but said she would not be caught by the simple trick of dropping golden apples.

Ross was not surprised to learn Ann-Marie was the driving force behind a French business empire with roots in the Eighteenth Century. She personally controlled thirty-seven of the companies, many of which, in audio-visual entertainment and computer leisure activities she herself started, influenced by part of her education having been at the University of California.

The count himself was a recluse whose main residences were a château at Meaux and villa near Nice. His only close family was his daughter. He was surrounded by mementoes of the Twenties and Thirties, during which time he doubled and doubled again the income of a business at the time biased towards chemicals and heavy engineering. The figures illustrating the growth of the business since those days, which included many astute changes in direction, made absorbing reading to those who enjoy vicarious revelling in such wealth.

Ross was surprised to learn there was a Portuguese branch of the family and that the legal adviser to the business was Maurice's half-brother, Ferdinand. He was an international lawyer of considerable standing, the computer file said, who was now retired except for some honorary positions. He lived alone also, in a mediaeval castle on Portugal's Algarve coast.

The families were joined by Maurice's father marrying a titled aristocrat in Lisbon in the 1920s. She was his second wife and young Ferdinand was her son by her first marriage. It was not a universally approved union, as the Portuguese were considered notorious and *nouveau riche*. Ann-Marie once told Julian her father, Maurice, never forgave his father for remarrying. He never spoke to his Portuguese stepmother after his father's death.

The file suggested Ferdinand was also dismayed at his family's wealth being founded on opium trading in the Far East, although his mother removed the last vestiges of this business while he was still young. Ferdinand studied law at the university at Coimbra and attached himself to the French family only during the 1939-1945 War. The brothers' relationship remained merely cordial.

The datafile ran for thirty minutes at a rate of scroll that gave Ross a headache. Astonishingly quickly though the printer performed he was not looking forward to reading its spidery results. This he would leave to his assistant.

7/2
Hamburg, Friday 16 August
Later that Friday morning in the middle of August, in a suite in Hamburg's *Vier Jahreszeiten* Hotel, Chu Yuen Muk was dominating a meeting of the syndicate in his usual

aggressive style. He was battling with Kolmann over a highly incriminating postage records book that was missing, presumed destroyed in the burnt-out *Kornmarkt*.

Although there was the serious possibility of his dealers in specialised pornography in Holland being exposed, Chu was more concerned the *Kornmarkt* had burned to the ground without the desired results. Two bodies should have been consumed with it. He had arranged through Hauptmann for the American, Williams, to set a trap for the half-Chinese Committee operative but could not tell Hauptmann his plan was actually to do away with them both. The American failed with de Lyon. Both had got out. Stupidly, Hauptmann's men still fired the building.

"It is a bad mistake," Chu repeated, emphasising Kolmann's inefficiency in clearing the warehouse. "You cannot be sure the book was burned."

"Putting aside the questions of the loss of valuable stock, of an entire business," Kolmann countered angrily, "I want to know why you burnt the building and risked the life of one of the syndicate's best contact men."

"Your clumsy American," Chu threw back. "We would have done ourselves a service by removing him. It seems he lives through the wit of this Committee operative."

Kolmann seethed at Chu's contempt.

"And about the security of the château," Chu began, turning to Winkel, "you have records there. You have girls there at this moment. Is your security any more reassuring?"

The Belgian took exception to Chu's manner. He was not afraid of Chu because he thought the triad had no influence in Belgium. He was not remotely aware that in the previous twelve months more than two thousand kilos of heroin, refined and ready to cut had been brought into Holland by couriers arriving at Zaventem and that the 14K had an efficient little cell operating in Belgium to this end.

"Of course, we consider the château to be as safe as a

fortress," he said smirking. "The book didn't give address details but to be cautious we are moving sooner than planned."

Chu nodded.

"And the last batch of girls?"

"They will be kept until the weekend and dispatched through the route Herr Hauptmann has arranged."

Chu asked what other matters were to be discussed, pointedly ignoring Kolmann. The German-American was not satisfied with Chu's flagrant disregard for his property but would say nothing further just then.

The Chinese was correct in assuming Williams could ultimately de-stabilise the syndicate's operations. Kolmann and Hauptmann had known him as a friend before his posting to the Far East. The three of them had done business together for years supplying the US Bases in Germany with anything the boys wanted in the way of pornography. Williams had recently returned from Hong Kong hungry for big money. Unknown to these two he had begun to kill for it.

To Chu, it was an even more dangerous game Williams was playing with his government's secret service. He hadn't touched the child porn magazines and blue films since leaving the army. With wider contacts through the CIA he was now handling Middle-Eastern heroin, and Kolmann could not understand the CIA remaining blissfully unaware that the sizeable quantity coming in from Eastern Europe, to Chu's annoyance, was courtesy of the Bulgarian Secret Service and Williams.

Hauptmann wanted a further question answered before the meeting ended. He was concerned about the failure of the triad's warning to the Committee and asked Chu what further action he proposed. The senior operative they discussed at the previous meeting was not only alive and kicking, he had taken on a dramatically higher profile.

Winkel took Chu off the hook.

"We have the matter in hand, Herr Hauptmann. We continue to watch this operative and think we have the best way of disposing of him. It will be different from Herr Chu's rituals but we are confident we will succeed."

He relished briefly this oblique reference to the garish style and calculated public image of the Chinese gangster and knew the others would appreciate it also. Chu's predecessor was assassinated stepping into a bullet-proof Mercedes in an Amsterdam street, the very car waiting below.

"He is now under surveillance by American Intelligence and this has prevented us from acting. He knows about their crude surveillance but not ours. Herr Kolmann assures me this afternoon Williams could call off the Americans watching, long enough for us to move in."

Chu reasserted his authority.

"Do it. Kill him."

The Chinese checked out of the hotel after this meeting and stepped apprehensively into the Mercedes. The day had continued as badly as it had started. He was concerned now with his own well-being. His warning to the Committee on Slavery in Brussels, though dramatic, had apparently failed and might just have triggered a sequence of events that would lead to his own demise. He had just received formal notification from Hong Kong of a second visit by the Red Pole in a fortnight. He was not informed of the purpose of this visit.

He was worried it would be a repeat of her first call. Not until after the ritual disposal in Marseilles of the errant 49 operating in Hauptmann's company, Eurocargo, did he know the size of the group accompanying the Red Pole to Europe. They had telephoned from the Carlton in Cannes giving a day's notice they would be paying their respects before returning to Hong Kong.

It was under these embarrassing circumstances he learned of Williams' mistake with the de Lyon nephew in Cannes. De Lyon's assassination had been the second of the group's tasks. To make matters worse, Chu's struggle with the Singaporeans in Holland was not going well and there was a continuing loss of merchandise on the catalogue venture with the syndicate.

The group Chu was obliged to play host to at the beginning of that month was made up of the Incense Master, Straw Sandal and the Butcher. If the senior Ma Lok Yu travelled, it meant ritual. With the Butcher accompanying him it meant a full bloody ritual of a kind seldom seen among the triads and unknown to the newer gangs. Chu did not think the 49 in Eurocargo merited such attention and he remained a very worried man.

Although Chu was the *shan chu* in Europe, thereby having the highest status within the triad, he did not sit on the Council. Ma Lok Yu did. He was therefore obliged to respect Ma's seniority and was unable to ask why he was not informed a ritual killing was to take place. Hong Kong had caused him severe loss of face with the half-dozen branches and several sub-branches he was head of in Europe.

Chu's embarrassment was pushed to further extremes at his home with the discovery the Committee operative, de Lyon, was no ordinary man. The Butcher was listening idly to Chu's boasting about the attack on de Lyon's nephew in Cannes being a warning to his uncle when something sparked his memory. This de Lyon was the young foreigner calling himself 'the Lion', from more than twenty years back. Hong Kong confirmed this. De Lyon reached the rank of 426 then disappeared in South-East Asia. He was not dead. Neither should he have been active.

"A likeable young man," the Butcher recalled on Chu's veranda, looking across the dunes at a grey sea, a leaden sky and distant gas refinery.

"I have given him meat. He has seen me work ..."

Chu spent an uncomfortable afternoon with these three men, not knowing which had been worse, entertaining Ma, or the Butcher. He was on borrowed time.

7/3
Brussels, Friday 16 August

Julian began immediate and rigorous training at the beginning of his suspension, having suffered six months in taxis, trams and at an office desk. He also spent time in thought, his apartment quiet once more with his nephew in Germany. He didn't like leaving so many loose ends when the office was so close to exposing a syndicate but he would not concern himself with these things for a few days. He had learnt Ann-Marie had reappeared in France after ten weeks of isolation. She had resumed business but refused to contact anyone socially.

Later that Friday afternoon he decided to drive to Zeebrugge for some sea air. His burns were healing but he still needed sun and air. Though the holiday period was at its peak and the weather fair, only he and the two Americans who followed him from Brussels were on the beach. They were not so enamoured with a run. One, in a suit and ordinary shoes gave up in disgust and radioed his colleague to pick him up. They continued surveillance from the road beyond the dunes as best they could.

After a pleasant fish supper he returned to Brussels and called at the Hyatt to leave a message for Sophie. She was in the foyer in earnest conversation with a prospective client but excused herself for a few moments when she saw Julian. He was flattered, as the gentleman looked tired and she was probably at a delicate stage of the negotiations. She brushed aside his apology and understanding his visit had not been made lightly said she would drop by Rue Américaine.

He heard what could only be her car rumbling in the narrow street early the following evening. She didn't need to sound the horn but did anyway and the effect was shattering. She called up that she wouldn't come up because of the dog.

"I was not expecting you at this time of the day."

"My weekends are my own," Sophie answered coolly.

She was wearing a delicately printed silk blouse, tiny chamois leather waistcoat and matching skirt. Her hair was pinned up and she was wearing jewellery. She had told Julian she wore nothing around her neck with clients, this having once been a hard lesson. She extended her arm with a languorous smile and he kissed her hand.

"Good mood, new car!"

"Absolutely right!" Sophie replied, opening the passenger door for him.

Julian said hello to Brutus and strapped himself in. Seat belts would have been unusual but this car was equipped with safety harnesses. It had more muscle than her previous Corvette, sported ridiculous tyres and was marked L82 on the bonnet hump.

"I'm sorry about yesterday evening," she began. "I couldn't refuse a diplomat a dinner date and then a whole night with him, for companionship only, for the fifty thousand francs he was offering!"

A smile showed Julian was impressed.

Sophie turned into Rue de Facqz toward the Avenue Louise. The dog breathed down Julian's neck, the car purred along the street. They were only driving at thirty kilometres an hour but judging by the ease with which she handled the beast, Julian had a fair idea she could drive it to its limit. She asked if he minded them going for a stretch up the motorway and slipped into the tunnel towards the boulevard that would take them north and west around the city.

"But enough of the car. You have something on your mind?"

Sophie knew Julian worked for the United Nations. She expressed interest in his work and they had exchanged views on the causes of child exploitation and prostitution. Now he was after something positive.

"Last week," Julian replied, "I was accepted as a member of a club Daniel was keen to recommend. What followed in a château in the Ardennes was more positive for us. I am asking for your help with some information."

A taxi overtook them at speed on the blind left turn out of the tunnel and Sophie shook her head. They crossed Place Rogier and the Sheraton Hotel at the bottom of the Boulevard Botanique and motored onto the viaduct above the city lights. The sky was a darker blue and showing the remnants of dusk. Koekelberg lay ahead on the horizon. On the left were blocks of decaying tenements dressed in neon and on the right a great swathe of land cleared for development. Sophie glanced again in her mirror.

"So you want information about the château and Daniel?"

"Just the château and the organisation behind it."

"That's being a little too pushy," she said candidly. "Such questions could ruin a friendship before it starts."

A frown returned to her forehead. Julian did not turn around. He told her there was a temporary pair of Americans at his heels who were tolerably discreet.

"That may be," she muttered eventually. "These are Arabs."

As she spoke, she dropped a gear manually and the car roared but she was too late to prevent them being rammed. In one heart-stopping moment she jerked the car away from taking a trip into Quai de Commerce below and gave a belated demonstration of its startling acceleration. They left the road into the gloom at the end of the viaduct, contacting the ramp lower down with a bone-crushing jolt. The tyres squealed, the car twitched but the BMW remained hard behind them, its lights blazing.

Grimly, Sophie ignored two sets of red lights, cut in front of a tram clanging its bell and sliced through the road works before Place Simonis. The BMW fell back. She kicked down again and with the magnificent roar of a short-pistoned engine, accelerated viciously under the trees of the Parc Elisabeth on the north side of the cathedral. Traffic was light and she was seething over the damage to her car.

Julian glanced behind him and was curious to see there was indeed only one car following, criss-crossing lanes like Sophie. There was no sign of the Mercury and its occupants that had been following him everywhere that last week. His eyes also met those of the dog trying to stand.

At the cathedral's west end, with the tachometer needle on red, Sophie knew she would not make the bend. Julian braced himself as he saw Sophie toy with the idea. Instead she yanked the wheel with all her strength and cut across the traffic coming off the motorway. She stepped hard on the brake in the Avenue de l'Hôpital Français and stopped finally after a fifty-metre slide before another set of lights flashing night-time amber.

She glanced at the instruments before switching off. Tick-over was even, there was a satisfying smell of hot oil and heated paint work and they had long since lost the BMW. The car behind them now was a white Volvo, its blue lights flashing.

"I'm very sorry, officer," she began in Flemish, with an irresistible smile at the grim-faced police officer striding towards them. She knew Artur but did not know his name. "Two jerks pester me all evening then try and run me off the viaduct. I had to get away."

Artur nodded frostily to Julian, re-buttoned his holster and turned his attention to Sophie. She got out of the car without hiding the fact she was wearing stockings. He asked her curtly for her ID, taking the opportunity of seeing how old she was and handed the card back, impressed. The three of them inspected the damage to the rear of the car. One of the rubber strips serving as a bumper was missing, a lens was broken and there was a crack in the fibreglass. Sophie pursed her lips. The car was a day old.

"If you want to try out the car," Artur said putting his notebook away, "do it off my beat. You're lucky we didn't radio we'd begun a chase. Every car in Brussels would be here by now and you would be in big trouble."

"This, *monsieur*, is not good for my reputation," Sophie said, as they got back in the Corvette. She patted Brutus and whispered some calming words. "I must take you back to Ixelles."

Turning into the Chaussée de Gand on their way back to the Gare du Midi and the south part of the city, she said,

"The information you want, I cannot give you. I keep my nose clean but one of my friends might be able to help, if you can do her a favour in return."

"If I can."

"Then I will try to arrange a meeting for you on Monday. I'll leave a message with Bernard at the hotel tomorrow."

As the car rumbled over the cobbles of the canal road past the abattoirs on the grimmer side of town Sophie began smiling again. She asked Julian how he rated the car's performance. He replied he found her driving more impressive. She admitted the car was on the light side and she wouldn't want to try such manoeuvring on wet roads.

Julian invited her to test-drive his one weekend, saying she would find it better balanced, easier to handle and more finely tuned. Sophie laughed.

"That might be your character. It is certainly not mine!"

Her smile disappeared once again along the Avenue Louise, now quiet that Saturday evening.

"*Verdomme*," she muttered angrily, stamping on the throttle.

She turned the next block throwing the car sideways with the skill of a professional driver and swore again as she straightened up, still unable to lose the little car from a slower start. Its driver was determined to come alongside. A gun was levelled at them and she kicked down again. There was a bang, the bullet ricocheted off the roof. They roared past Rue de Facqz and Sophie whipped the car into Rue du Bailli. It bucked on the tramlines by the cinema and they slewed their way between the shops toward the old church, the BMW close behind them.

Julian raised his eyebrows at the sight of a baker's van trundling around the square to the right of the church. Sophie knew they wouldn't make it left or right and actually steered between the telephone booth and tram-halt, throwing the car sideways into Rue de l'Aquaduc, avoiding the cars parked on the corners.

Seconds later in Rue Américaine, almost outside Julian's apartment, she switched off the engine and lights and listened. There was only darkness and silence and her heart racing. She saw the BMW turn right at the church to head them off. Neither she nor Julian heard the squeal of tyres and shattering of plate glass but knew something had happened. The silence said it all.

Julian turned towards Sophie.

"You had better get out," she snapped.

"I enjoyed our evening," he said smiling broadly. "And I must pay for the damage to your car."

He reached into his pocket. Brutus growled until his mistress raised a hand. In no mood for further conversation she sent a shaft of light down the street and with a roar, disappeared.

Julian got the missing details of the incident from *Le Soir's* Monday morning edition. The *Gendarmerie* had sealed off an accident at the top end of Rue du Bailli in Ixelles on

Saturday night, the newspaper reported. A BMW turned a bread van over and crashed into a *pâtisserie*. Stale *baguettes* were scattered across the square and two Moroccans were charged with reckless driving. They had been arguing, the paper reported, over a football match.

7/4

The following evening Julian collected a note from Sophie from the night manager at the hotel. The next time they went out for target practice, she wrote, it would be in his car. It also read 'Royal Windsor Hotel, Monday midday'.

He found Sophie's friend in one of the alcoves of the hotel's English Bar. The young woman introduced herself as Ruth. The only other person there was a barman polishing glasses.

"This is a little early in the day for me," Ruth said in English "but I felt it important enough to come and tell you what I know."

Julian ascertained she was Israeli and asked what brought her so far from home. She was by no means professional like Sophie.

"I came here to study fashion design." She smiled quickly. "Surely no-one comes to this place without good reason. When I have saved enough money I shall return to Israel and start my own business. I don't do this kind of work usually, not hotel work, as they have their regular girls. This week though, the night manager asked if I would oblige at a conference of Arab Finance Ministers."

She fumbled in her bag for a cigarette lighter and made no comment.

"But I'm getting away from what I came here to say. Sophie tells me it is the trade in young girls you are concerned with. And you wanted to know about the château?"

Julian nodded.

"About three weeks ago, I was hostessing there with two other free-lancers. It was well-paid. I was upset when I realised the shows with the young girls were real. I've seen such things where models have been willing, sometimes drugged. This was *dégoutant*. The other two who had done it before wouldn't talk. I mean, there are different sexual needs and tastes but I draw the line at rape."

"Most of us do," Julian said.

He asked Ruth if she had been threatened.

"Yes, but I'm flexible. I could always leave this dump of a place and go to Paris. Then I got to thinking perhaps it wouldn't be so easy."

She glanced around the bar. There was one extra person in it.

"What made it worse, for me anyway, is them filming and recording the floor show. And I ended up with the man who had taken one of the little girls. God, he was revolting ... he hurt me."

Ruth stubbed the cigarette out nervously then slipped Julian a cassette tape she had found in one of the château offices. It should give him an idea of what went on there. Julian appreciated her confidence and asked if he could contact her again.

"Yes, through Sophie. Please don't implicate her in anything, though. She is a dear friend and I am also afraid of her. Angry, she is like a tiger."

He asked if it was possible the château was being sold. Ruth remembered many of the rooms being empty and boxes that could have been awaiting collection. Many of the rooms were locked also. She didn't know where the château was because she was chauffeured there in a car with black windows.

"Can I do something for you?" he asked finally.

Ruth did not respond immediately. She was deep in thought.

126

"Well, it is about my papers. My Identity Card needs renewing and the Commune will not do it because my passport is out-of-date. The Israeli consulate will not oblige because I have not done my military service."

He promised he would make enquiries.

The cab summoned by a yellow-liveried commissionaire dropped him outside the offices of Knight, Frank and Rutley in Place Louise. There was no sign of anyone following. The CIA had become either very good or especially sloppy over the last couple of days. Julian was shown up to the manager's office where he introduced himself, stating he wished to purchase a castle.

"Do you have a price range in mind?" the manager asked, inviting him to sit down.

Julian replied it was not a relevant factor. A faint smile appeared on the man's lips. He took a pile of folders from a cabinet beside the marble fireplace. Julian glanced at the photograph of the country house on the top and said,

"Something larger."

The manager opened the cabinet on the other side.

Most of one wall of the elegant panelled room was taken up with windows. There was a good view of Place Louise, its plane trees shimmering in the sunlight and gentle breeze. In that decade, the 1970s, many of the magnificent buildings along the Nineteenth-century boulevards had been razed to make way for modern office blocks. This suite was certainly a more pleasant place in which to spend a working day.

Julian was handed another photograph.

"A fine house, owned by the de Vries's, I believe."

"May I enquire the purpose of the castle?" the man asked, now blushing.

"For me to live in!" Julian replied with some incredulity. "I'm in the mood for something romantic. Something with a collection of towers, cloche-roofed perhaps, set in woodland with a kilometre of gravel drive. Something in the Ardennes. And isolated, of course ..."

"... of course."

Julian examined the next file carefully and a few minutes later thanked the gentleman for his attention. He walked out into the dappled sunlight under the plane trees with the feeling the first of a number of loose ends could soon be tied up.

CHAPTER EIGHT

Brussels, Sunday 25 August

Daphne hadn't heard from Julian a week and a half after returning from Wiesbaden and agonised again over taking the initiative. Her reason for returning to Brussels was to start a summer job but she couldn't put her mind to it with so much going on and quit after a week.

She had already called twice at his apartment. On her third attempt he didn't sound too friendly over the *Parlophone* but she raced up the stairs and greeted him with a smile like the Cheshire Cat's. It was a lovely Sunday morning and she would try and persuade him to take her for a drive.

She looked closely at his burns, said she was pleased they were healing and apologised for disturbing him. His costume must have had something to do with the shutters being closed. It was black and well-worn and quite unlike Peter's *gi*. A hood was folded into a pouch. The trousers were bound at the calves and a silk sash with red characters embroidered on it was wound around his waist.

"I have a little more to do, if you can be silent for a minute."

"I can try!" she prompted.

She asked diplomatically if he wore his *gi* out and about. Julian said he didn't think it very businesslike and she knew he was smiling even though she couldn't see his face.

He sat on the floor at one end of the living room and she sat on a chair but then also moved to the floor because she didn't want to be seen as sitting in judgement. Nothing happened except he sat with a grace that made her feel clumsy. This was how he was with all his physical movement, sparing and very graceful. He looked amazing when demonstrating *tai chi* on the lawn at Wiesbaden compared with how stiff and ungainly they all were.

He remained still as a statue for some minutes, breathing slowly and deeply and then stood up.

"That was the end of three hours of exercise," he said, seeing disappointment in her face.

"I know it's rude but I was hoping to see something Peter talks about. Breaking techniques, isn't it?"

"I was thinking more of a shower ..."

"Oh, please ..." she pleaded.

Julian succumbed and said he would show her a couple of things. It was honourable to his teaching, he explained, that ability and especially ultimate ability was revealed only if absolutely unavoidable. Although he was smiling, Daphne felt suitably subdued.

He fetched six bricks from his upstairs workroom and cleared the dining room table. He stacked the bricks neatly on a cloth and said the techniques Peter referred to were known in Japanese as *tameshi wari*. These were exercises to develop speed and strengthen limbs and were introduced into the *karate* Peter practised by Master Masutatsu in the 1950s.

"Does this mean they are not used in anger?"

"Certainly. But effective hitting requires more agility on the street. A stationary brick, for example, would be a very tame target. You might get a better idea by throwing one at me."

She stood up and took the brick offered, wondering if it was a good idea.

"I shall try and break it, assess what happens and attempt to break part of it again. If I don't hit it cleanly of course, it may shatter and I might end up just catching a piece. I don't do much of this kind of thing, by the way. Fingers and knuckles break easily."

She smiled weakly.

Julian was standing on the far side of the living room with his feet slightly apart and his arms by his sides. His limbs were loose but the intensity with which he stared at her was disconcerting. This was a man you could not ignore.

She lobbed the brick and brought her hand to her mouth. What happened was confusing. He let out a shriek that made her rigid. The ceiling light bulb shattered and there were bits of brick all over the floor. Now he was coming toward her in the gloom laughing and she was quivering like a jelly.

"That yell ..."

"An ordinary *ki ai*," he said modestly.

"I've never heard anything so potent. I didn't see you move ... how did the bulb break?"

"I broke the brick with a flat knuckle strike and helped a chunk of it on its way to the light shade, with a kick!"

Daphne stared in wonder. She saw him change position but didn't see his arm or his leg move. Even the sleeves of his *gi* didn't give movement away, as Peter's did when he did his *katas*.

"What would happen if you hit someone like that?"

"It might break teeth and lower jaw."

She could not see a funny side. It looked as though he could have broken someone's head then kicked it over a wall. What was more he was bare-foot.

"And the other bricks?"

"Well, didn't that unnerve you?"

"I've never seen anything so devastating but I wanted to know what it was all about."

As he cleared away the pieces of brick and broken glass she remembered a conversation with Peter and asked Julian if the family system meant everyone in a Chinese family from baby to grandfather practising martial arts.

"Well, it could be like that," he said grinning. "It's a common sight in the morning in open spaces in Chinese communities across Asia, people doing *tai chi* exercises, but the family system is quite specific. As a teacher, I am addressed *si fu*. When teaching someone else's students, I am *si bok*, 'older uncle'. Someone studying with a master for a long time who gives lessons to younger students is addressed *si hing*, which means 'older brother'. There are names for the very oldest to the very youngest."

He switched on a floor lamp, straightened the remaining five bricks on the table and asked her which she would like to see broken. She didn't understand as they were in a pile but pointed to the second from the bottom.

"This will give you an idea of something I have been studying for thirty years. It dispenses with brutal contact, utilising instead *chi* energy."

"The gathering and concentration of power, the power behind the power? We have books at home on this."

Julian nodded.

"Some of the most secret teachings in martial arts relate to this inner power," he went on. "*Ne gong*, as I know it in Korean, is the formalisation of breathing techniques and concentration of *chi* that can aid the physical body. Techniques exist whereby *chi* can also be extended beyond the body."

He said this was the power that enabled masters to heal by touch but whose energy could also be concentrated for it to help in the breaking of objects. He did not say it was also the power behind what was known in Korean as *dim muk*, the touch of death.

Looking at Daphne again he was getting used to being disarmed by her smiling whenever he looked at her. Whatever he was doing his concentration would slip. She reminded him of a Korean Spring and fine green tea and that he had spent his life in male company. She was kneeling on the floor again in a summer dress, her hands in her lap and he liked it. He liked her bright company, a pretty girl and the most caring person he had ever known. Was there ever a good reason to go on alone? It was not the first time thoughts of Hwagae and its Cherry Blossom Road came into his head.

Daphne watched Julian standing in front of the table. His breathing became deeper as he lined the flat of his hand and then its edge, with the top brick. He stood back, breathing more powerfully still. Then, exuding an energy she could feel, he brought the heel of his hand firmly down on the pile. She gasped. The brick she had pointed to was basically in two halves with fragments of it on the cloth as though hit with a heavy hammer. The others remained undamaged.

She took hold of his hand. It was heavy and muscular, as she noticed in her apartment when he was cracking walnuts. Now she knew he had been play-acting in Wiesbaden catching or deflecting the apples with astonishing speed but said nothing. What she did do, while avoiding looking into his eyes, was kiss his fist. Kissing it better, she called it. She might have seen in his eyes only she had ever done such a thing. She couldn't possibly admit to what it did to her.

She got her wish of a drive in the country. Julian was pleased she had called despite the house being watched and decided it was only a matter of making sure she got home unnoticed. They went out to Waterloo, to the *Butte du Lion* a few kilometres south of Brussels to see the monument cast by Wellington from Napoleon's cannons. She had taken groups of pupils there several times and was surprised he hadn't visited the site after four years in Brussels.

He had no reason until now, he replied and invited her to drive. She allowed herself a little smile, manoeuvring the car through the traffic out of town. It was like silk to drive and one of the secrets of a powerful car, as he said.

They spent an hour in the sunshine on the conical hill top, sitting on the limestone plinth beneath the great incongruous bronze beast. Maize stretched in all directions across the flat farmland, rippling and well-ripened. The air smelt dry and musty, like straw.

"The battle here in 1815 was probably lost and won at the gates of Hougoumont Farm, repeatedly attacked but never taken by Napoleon," she said, pointing to the farm a kilometre to the south-west in the direction the lion was facing. "Just East, there on the other side of the field, on the Charleroi road is the farm of La Haye Sante. That held also. These were Wellington's right and left flanks. His camp was at the crossroads we turned at."

She pointed to the road junction below them, 500 metres away and fell silent, conscious she was not talking to children now.

"Yes, yes ..." Julian said, coaxing her.

"Napoleon was further down the Charleroi road," she went on. "The battle raged for ten hours around these fields on June 18. He was finally out-flanked by the Prussians coming up from Plancenoit, the village we can just see on the south-east horizon."

She told Julian he had to imagine explosions, incessant musket fire, acrid smoke and cries of the wounded and saw in her own mind Napoleon's Old Guard, *les Chasseurs*, back and forth in the mud in their blue tunics with red trim, white waistcoats and helmets with black fur. There may even have been maize as tall as them in the fields at the start of the day.

"There were fifty thousand casualties from an engagement of a hundred and forty thousand troops in this quadrant," she said, indicating a generous south and east. "But Napoleon was considered so dangerous, seven hundred and fifty thousand Allied troops were available, with a million more across Europe in reserve. By nightfall it was over, though Napoleon's Old Guard Grenadiers were not beaten. They held ranks during the rout, enabling their general to escape and marched off the field in tight formation."

"Some piece of history ..." Julian said eventually, taking her hand as they descended the steep steps.

"... won on the playing fields of Eton, the English say!"

He asked if it was true that parties were thrown on the night before the battle and battlefield tours began immediately afterwards. She confirmed this was so.

"We could come again! Thérèse, Peter and I planned coming here looking for musket balls. With four of us, we could do a re-enactment!"

"The mind boggles, Daphne ..."

She knew they were out of vacation time. Her mother had dropped Thérèse and Peter off in Brussels on her way back to Lille and she remembered she was to pass on greetings.

"Julian, everything is all right between you and Peter?"

"Yes. Why do you ask?"

"I took the clothes over to Thérèse's yesterday. Peter's moved in, hasn't he?"

"He has, temporarily."

"He's sleeping under the stairs. The girls cleared out the cupboard and made him a nice little nest. They love having him there, he's such fun," she said, her mind following a different drift. Peter and her dear friend were at last getting on well together. It was the poem he slipped under their door in Cannes. And other things, of course.

"Thérèse was very gracious about it. I feel I have imposed my young nephew on them."

Daphne asked why he had moved in.

"We have learnt the identity of the Chinese woman who injured him," Julian began carefully, "and I must ask this be the last visit any of you make to my apartment. It is being watched."

"Surely you're safe in Brussels?" Daphne asked, telling herself she was silly thinking there was anything more to this remark.

Peter called at the apartment later that evening to pick up the rest of his stuff, having telephoned first to check with his uncle. He got the idea of what was going on from Daphne and was grateful his uncle met him at the end of the street. Though fitter now, the plaster had only just been removed from his arm.

He finished putting his things in a bag and began pacing around the room. When Julian asked what was troubling him he admitted Thérèse wanted to come over to say hello and help him back with the bag.

"You know what I said, Peter."

"She insisted – "

They both heard the scream from the courtyard. Peter turned ashen, knowing but not believing what had just happened. They descended the stairs and Julian sent Peter through the basement. He went via the street to the courtyard and dropped to his knees on the gravel to support Thérèse. A light came on in Mme. Grimeau's apartment showing the young woman bruised about her face and neck. She had been hit several times. Gently, Julian lowered her dress. She looked up at him, dazed, terror across her face.

As Peter tried to hold her stiff body close, all emotion drained from him. Until he saw her knickers on the other side of the courtyard. Then he cried.

It took a few minutes for Julian to circle the block, coming up the Chaussée de Charleroi and turning back into a deserted Rue Américaine. He looked down the side streets and began to concentrate. Children, young women, crushed. He had seen it many times and felt the violence of such an act linger. Yet there was no one in the shadows, in the streets, except for the two Americans on surveillance duty in their car a block down, pretending to be asleep. They were in a world of their own.

Thérèse was sobbing forgiveness when he returned, something he considered to be a nauseating mixture of the guilt caused by her Catholic upbringing and base instinct of submission still deep in many women. Mme. Grimeau had done her best to comfort the youngsters and was telephoning for an ambulance. Julian put his arms around his nephew's and Thérèse's shoulder. Peter was unable to whisper reassurance to the girl he loved. All life had drained from him also.

Later that night Julian worked through the principles of the *ne gong* he described to Daphne, in preparation for *shin gong*, the most advanced teachings of an ancient art. One of these mental power techniques edged into his consciousness. The man who had raped Thérèse was very close. He had been for weeks.

It was after two o'clock when he changed his clothes in the dark and picked up a lamp and long lead from his workroom. Still in darkness he went into the room Peter used and placed the lamp on the sill of the window looking over the street. He plugged the lead into a socket and took the ends of both cables with him through the skylight onto the rear pitch of the roof.

There was a good view over the empty street from behind the chimney. When he connected the leads, the houses opposite were bathed in light and he caught the briefest glint of glass from behind the net curtain of an attic room almost opposite. Disconnecting the leads, he slipped back into Peter's room, replaced the items in the workroom and made his way down the stairs.

The house on the other side of the street was a narrow

three-storey building unoccupied for a year. Its front door was made of hardwood and substantial, its paintwork still smudged by smoke from the fireball the previous month. Julian hit the door once above its middle rail with a vicious hammer-fisted blow, a *yup ju mok* in the best tradition of Korean temple boxing. His elbow sent the splintered spar and two panels into the hallway.

Very slowly in the darkness he mounted the stair treads, breathing evenly and precisely. With each step he could feel the crude animal power from the top of the house grow stronger. He could see the brilliant aura of a single being. He set foot on the second staircase. His breathing was deeper as he prepared himself for an encounter, for pain, for violence that would suck strength and energy if he allowed it. Above, waiting, was an extremely dangerous man.

He reached the top landing and attic door, silent now, and pushed it open with an almost painful slowness. Strong, brilliant reds and oranges bristled with yellow, the colours rife across the darkened room. He saw a chair and table with food on it. By the window was some photographic equipment and standing with his back to the wall a short, powerfully-built man.

Julian advanced with absolute caution. This man was on the edge of a pathologically violent outburst. He had no morals, no inhibitions. This was the man from the château who had given the star performance.

The man was transfixed by Julian's eyes, by his presence. He did not see the fingers come to his throat and wrist but felt the squeezing. He tried to retaliate. He tried and could not understand why he was unable to move a muscle. Julian gripped him until he slipped to the floor but did not carry through the *sa hyel*, a lethal pressure point technique.

Looking around the room he left a notebook and the partly-used roll of film in the camera undisturbed but took one exposed roll. Copies of *Lui* and Playboy and some hardcore pornography similar to material he saw in the *Kornmarkt* in Hamburg were lying about. There was some old sheeting material stained yellow with semen. A search of the man's pockets revealed three photographs of Thérèse naked in Peter's room opposite.

The man regained consciousness slumped on a chair in the middle of the room. His legs were apart, his body was numb and he had difficulty breathing. When he realised the figure was still there in the darkness he began sweating.

"You were not concerned with the terror a young woman experienced this evening while you were at your favourite recreation ..."

The voice behind him was calm, warm even.

"You represent lust and violence of a most insidious kind. It is therefore a mercy to all those vulnerable to this aggression that I will administer an appropriate justice."

Julian moved closer to the man who was staring uncomprehendingly at him and asked quietly,

"Do you understand if you live and behave in this manner you will die by the same laws?"

With these words, he kicked.

Such a kick is executed in less than three tenths of a second. Testes are highly mobile and usually escape serious damage from a frontal attack. Julian's kick gave him no chance. It broke the chair and smashed testicles and pubic bone. Slivers of bone punctured a femoral artery. The chair collapsed and the man began the slow death of haemorrhage and shock and Julian felt no compunction about it whatsoever.

The clinic would only allow Daphne to stay with Thérèse and told Peter to go home. He walked over to Daphne's apartment in despair in the early hours to find she had not returned and went back to Thérèse's apartment. It was four in the morning but Martine was still up. She put her arms around him once more. They took the tram to the clinic later but the doctor still would not let anyone else in. Daphne had stayed by her bed and knew this was the best thing while Peter was also suffering from shock. Thérèse was being kept in for minor surgery, the treatment of concussion, bruising and bites. When the sleeping tablets wore off her friend woke and was afraid and it broke Daphne's heart. She had to get a grip on herself to avoid a panic attack. She knew what Thérèse was going through.

When Peter and Daphne went up to Rue Américaine at midday they found the street barricaded by the *Gendarmerie* for the second time in a month. There was too much activity at the apartment building for comfort and Daphne stopped Peter telling the corporal at the barrier he lived in the building. Mme. Grimeau appeared from within the small crowd with a message for Peter. He was to stay away until Julian contacted him. About all the activity, she said, there was only the broadest rumour M. de Lyon was involved in the death of a man in the house opposite.

Julian had telephoned Ross in Rue Jenneval at daybreak and taken a taxi to the office. Ross, the Committee's legal adviser and assistant and two detectives from Police headquarters in Rue Marché-au-Charbon were waiting. The normally genial *notaire*, *Maître* van Moolens and Julian, had met. The detectives were stony-faced.

Legal wrangling over Julian's diplomatic status began immediately. In view of Julian's recent suspension the Public Prosecutor ordered his contract be minutely examined. He was outraged at such a barbarous crime and threatened to press for the maximum ten-year sentence for manslaughter.

The rape was of little consequence to him. His mood was not sweetened when van Moolens began counter-measures with an action for compensation for Thérèse against the Commissioner for Police for the rapist, a wanted criminal, having been issued with an Identity Card.

Ross had a bad moment listening to the official. He had heard all the platitudes, the high-handed chauvinism and once again could not understand how an otherwise intelligent man, a man who was probably married, perhaps with a sister or daughter, could remain in a position carrying a supposedly high moral responsibility when his judgement was patently lacking. The least that one of the most trying weeks of his career brought him was a royal temper to match his king-size headache.

Charges were not brought and after fifty-six hours in custody Julian was released. The victim was indeed wanted by the French and Belgian police after escaping from the notorious Ste-Ann asylum in Paris.

Using details of the château, including its location Julian had worked out from information obtained from the estate agent's file, the police and five Committee operatives raided it while Julian was still in custody. Initial evidence pointed to the place being frequented by many powerful people from the judiciary, *Gendarmerie*, government, Belgium's financial oligarchy, it's conglomerates and by members of the aristocracy.

Ross gained some satisfaction from his operatives' work with the discovery of other specialisms at the château apart from rape. It had rooms with sado-masochism facilities including whips, gags and chains. There was a pseudo operating theatre with an obstetrics table and instruments including knives, needles and razor blades. A film studio in the cellars had evidence of children being processed through the château.

The press picked up on the police operation but articles were buried within a week, an editorial practice long observed by the Committee in Holland and especially in Belgium.

The press did not get details of the Rue Américaine incident and even Brandt calmed down. The Americans finished their investigations and presented Brandt with a letter saying they were satisfied there was no evidence Julian de Lyon was still connected with the triads with which he was associated in his youth. They made it clear he was not considered a threat as long as he was not engaged on such sensitive field work as he had been previously and Brandt had no option but to suspend him formally for an unspecified period.

In Brussels there was admiration from the CIA's surveillance team over how the Spook had dealt with the rapist. Among jibes about it being unsafe to be on the streets at night, several of them felt sorry for the girl they knew as 'the Blonde'. She had walked past them and turned into the alley. They heard her scream but thought nothing of it.

As professionals, they were disenchanted with not having spotted something going on above their heads for weeks. Neither had they appreciated de Lyon evading them at will. He was one of their strangest. The activity of that evening put them on their toes, yet they completely missed him in the early hours crossing to the house opposite and breaking down the door.

When the Bonn Station confirmed the subject had been neutralised they moved on to other work.

8/2

Van Moolens was waiting in Rue Marché-au-Charbon for Julian on his release. He drove him to Rue Américaine, then on to the Berlaymont Building to see Ross who had cut short a meeting with one of his sub-committees. Ross greeted Julian in the foyer and they sat in adjacent black leather armchairs as part of a hushed murmur of a multitude of sober-suited Eurocrats hurrying a drink before lunch. Ross asked Julian how he felt. He was okay, he said. Just stiff from a brutally air-conditioned cell.

They took their place in a queue in the noisy basement

dining area. The food was subsidised and bland but it was a place in which they could talk. Many of the bureaucrats brought their families along, making lunch-time colourful, almost festive. Ross put a modest meal on his tray and Julian limited his lunch to fruit even though his breakfast in the police cell had been the perfunctory slice of bread and margarine and bowl of warm coffee.

"I appreciate the meeting, Ross. I'm pleased to hear of the progress you've been making in my absence."

"I can't apologise for what is going on, Julian. Van Moolens brought you here because I feel I can make suggestions on how you might restore your name since your job is seriously compromised."

"I also appreciate your concern. But might our meeting prejudice your own career?"

Ross was not surprised at Julian's response.

"The first point is that Ann-Marie's low profile of the past months has more to do with the work of the Committee than I'm comfortable with. If you didn't know already, the château is owned by one of your father-in-law's companies. None of this has gone into my report as we still need hard evidence. Telephone numbers on the PTT printout match many addresses linked with the syndicate."

"I don't recommend these plums," Julian said.

"This is the discussion I was hoping for," Ross said, relieved Julian had not reacted adversely to the slight against his wife and her family.

"The second point is Geneva have known for eighteen months it was Ann-Marie talking to the captain of the freighter in Port Louis in photographs I have been holding. You may remember the ship tracked from France to the Indian Ocean with a dozen youngsters in confinement? It seems to me the only way of discovering what is going on with the family is to sound out the old man himself, Maurice. Perhaps better, the half-brother, Ferdinand down in

143

Portugal. I would lay odds on him being the neutral party."

Ross looked furtively about him. He was almost sure there was a detective watching them. They usually gave themselves away by wearing policemen's trousers. He searched his Number One's face.

"I am thinking about what you are saying, Ross. This is certainly not the place to hand over incriminating documents," Julian replied.

"So, as you perceive, I will make available what material I have. If you want it, that is. The report on the château raid for starters. I'm uncomfortable even suggesting a link with you father-in-law's companies but we might both regain a little gloss if you can come up with something. God knows, it's been hard enough dragging anything together this last four years."

"Anything that might clarify my own suspicions would be welcome, Ross."

"So the problem is how to get information to you."

Ross laughed briefly. It was thirty years since he had been up to such things. It was ridiculous he couldn't get anything out of his office because of procedures he initiated. There were also a pair of auditors from Geneva busy in the office.

As Ross lapsed into silence, Julian thought about Daphne's computer. She had neither modem nor acoustic coupler, she explained. No telephone in fact, except the one in the hall. This was a pity. Hers was the kind of brain that could tap into a mainframe computer somewhere down the line.

"Could you put something on the discs Mademoiselle Arameau uses?" Julian asked.

Ross shook his head again.

"She has a head for this sort of thing. I'll see what she can do. I must say, Julian I don't know if I'm enjoying playing spies with my Number One, even if it has an ironic humour."

CHAPTER NINE

Brussels, Thursday 29 August

Julian walked through the dismal streets of Schaerbeek to Mlle. Arameau's house by the Parc du Cinquantenaire the following night. Ross's secretary was tired and didn't smile for the minutes he was there. He absorbed everything she said about the two discs she had prepared at the office but would leave its comprehension to Daphne.

Walking to Daphne's apartment in Etterbeek on the south side of the park he thought twice about calling in. He was no longer being followed by American intelligence but was acutely aware the threat to Daphne, to everyone associated with him, was growing. Other methods of surveillance, including the tapping of his telephone were still going on.

Of most concern was another attempt by the 14K to 'wash his face' without them blundering as they had in Cannes. As their prime target he had three to six days' grace from the time of the château raid and consequent serious disruption of the syndicate's operation in Belgium, Holland, Germany and France. This was the time it would take a pair of 426s to fly out from Hong Kong. The danger period had begun.

Daphne was relieved when Julian came in through the door, his first smile dispelling her anxiety. She knew what had been going on because Peter had called the office at

Place Madou and spoken personally to the director. Considering everything she was amazed at how calm Julian was. She was suffering heartache over both her cousin and the man before her and was sure it was putting lines on her face. She wanted desperately to talk about what had happened but it became clear Julian did not and she had to accept this. His note said he needed help on a computer problem and that was how the night started. It was fortunate it was computers. She would never have been able to concentrate otherwise.

They sat together over a cup of a new tea from the local Chinese emporium and Julian explained what he was looking for on the discs. The tea was a *pu-erh*, reddish in colour and pleasant to taste, if rather musty. She hadn't boiled the water enough but said nothing about it and slotted the first floppy disc into her word processor.

"You must pull up a chair too," she said looking at the huge directory of files. "It looks like this might take a while."

She asked Julian if he did much computer work. He said he always handed such work to someone more clever. She could have replied but turned her attention to the first group of files.

"Perhaps we could just read it through?"

Daphne looked at him casually.

"Each of these discs holds about two hundred and forty pages. It'll be a long night if you want to read all of it. Like reading three novels ..."

She went on to demonstrate the commands for moving about within files and said she would leave him to it and prepare something to eat. She said it ought to be safe for him to eat, then realised this was not a tactful remark. She asked if he was hungry – another stupid question – and was relieved he said he would eat everything put in front of him.

Knowing his nephew was staying with Daphne, Julian asked where he was that evening.

146

"He's at the girls' flat tonight," Daphne answered from the kitchen. "Martine's taken him to a film she wanted to see. My idea, so you, or we, could get on with this."

"Is he okay?"

"He's okay."

Daphne closed her eyes. She was still going hot and cold about Thérèse, who was still in the clinic under observation. Only Julian's presence and his painfully slow clicking on the keyboard cast her unhappiness aside.

She made him come away from the screen at midnight to eat and they talked about what he had done. He admitted he was not finding it easy holding the information in his head and had resorted to pencilled notes. She told him this was not the way. The computer held the information and the idea was to use the computer to manipulate it.

"These pages, for example. The PTT listing."

Julian sat down again wearily with Daphne leaning over him flicking around the screen pages.

"The operator has put all the calls from the château, wherever this is, into a database. I can bring to the screen a list of the volume of calls in destination order. See, Belgium is at the top and Portugal, with only a handful in August is at the bottom. I can also show exchange codes alphabetically. Easy!"

"How many calls does a business make a month!" Julian exclaimed, momentarily daunted by the prospect of looking for patterns in pages of listings.

"ITT's estimate of the number of calls world-wide for 1980 is a hundred thousand million."

He took the cup of coffee Daphne offered and apologised for being somewhat reticent about the contents of the disc.

"I still feel I can help," Daphne said, her mind now on the task in hand. "The datafile looks quite good. The operator has gone to town with the telephone calls."

They exchanged seats.

"Take these Marseilles numbers ..."

Telephone numbers filled the screen.

"They're now listed from the most, to the least dialled. It shows the last number was dialled six times in five months, on the first of each month, except on the last occasion. Why don't you dream up lists and I'll try and put them on the screen."

Julian was impressed with the speed with which Daphne assimilated numerical data. She was more than clever she said. She was special, one in a million in her age group in Belgium doing computer studies. Even more special in France, one in five million.

Julian stretched his limbs and laughed. He was slowing down. Daphne was speeding up but he was beginning to think this sort of work was best left to the office so it didn't waste her time. Then he remembered this was no longer an option. The office had done a stint cataloguing and in some cases, re-dialling numbers. He reminded himself Ross's primary reasons for passing the information was for him to look for further connections, apart from the ownership of the château, between the abduction of minors and Count Maurice's business.

"You're not too tired to go on?"

"No," she replied patiently. "It's great having something to actually work on. At least ..."

"Okay, something specific. List the calls made out of the château from the last, backwards."

One of the Marseilles numbers appeared as the very last and an idea came to Julian. He asked Daphne to find the Château Report file and look for the time it was raided. She did this at lightning speed and he saw the call was important enough for the person to have been caught red-handed by the *Gendarmerie*. Daphne brought the details of the number to the screen.

It was an accommodation address in the Old Port used only by shipping brokers. Mlle. Arameau noted the French police later visited the run-down building and apprehended an employee who said she was only doing her usual job of re-directing mail and telephone messages for two of the clients. The third picked up their own mail. A second telephone line into the building, the *Gendarmerie* discovered, had its own answer phone and all she did was make sure the tape was ready to start each morning.

Julian considered the fact the call was made at dawn. Daphne said it was probably received by an answering machine and it only needs a simple gadget, one that whistles down the line, to instruct the machine to play back messages to whoever is using the gadget anywhere in the world.

He asked Daphne one more question about how a computer might work out a probability. How, recently, more children from wealthier families were going missing. She listened to the figures and said,

"It sounds like a trend rather than a growing business."

"It does, doesn't it?"

An idea came to him, abduction to order. Why not, he concluded. Somewhere in Europe an organisation touting exclusive merchandise, supplying a particular child for prostitution, or personal use. Mail order even, with a ceiling on the number of children available because of logistical problems. It would have to be an organisation with accurate information on the movements of people on that social level.

Julian turned his attention again to the screen and to Daphne sitting by it watching him. Mlle. Arameau's second disc contained case files received from Interpol and other sources in the three weeks he had been out of the office. These were what he would now concentrate on.

It was almost six when he saw enough had been done for one night. Daphne was resting her head on her arms on the table before the printer, asleep. He switched off the machines and began some gentle *shiatsu* on her neck and shoulders. She moaned softly and a smile of pleasure showed on her lips when she realised what was happening. He did not wake her too much. She listened to him thank her for her help and her company.

"You can come again," she said sleepily at the door and offered her lips.

He kissed her, to her surprise. His lips were cold, the effect turned her to ice. She tried not to react but knew every part of her was offering no resistance. Her hand between them prevented her doing or saying anything foolish.

Standing alone in her bathroom a few minutes later, shivering a little from being up so long, she asked herself if she really knew what was going on. She had spent the whole night with this man, helping, talking, smiling a lot. The sun was shining, birds were singing and tears were running gently down her cheeks.

All she could think about was his passing remark about his wife. AM to her friends, *Madame* to everyone else, though sometimes *comptesse*, to amuse her. She couldn't compete with this.

9/2

Julian carried on through the day summarising the areas he considered the Committee should be concentrating its resources in. The report was for Ross's appraisal and was his final gesture to the Committee. Nothing had turned up that had a direct link with Ann-Marie. He walked to Schaerbeek again late that evening after taking evasive action and delivered it to Mlle. Arameau.

He went on to the Hyatt after this. Ruth had not telephoned the office and he wanted to talk to both her and

Sophie once more. The night manager's smile disappeared. He said in a low voice Sophie was in hospital and he could answer no more questions. Julian posted a note to both Peter and Daphne after leaving the hotel and returned finally to Rue Américaine to sleep.

At first light that Saturday morning he took a local train to Charleroi, where he changed to the Paris Express. Ann-Marie's father was waiting at the Savoy Hotel in Place Vendôme. It was a meeting arranged with a single telephone call with both parties attempting to get to grips with quite different problems.

Count Maurice was in the lounge sitting stiffly on a low leather settee that suited neither his age nor his mood. Dressed as distinctly as ever, his concession to the oppressive heat ushering in September was a white suit and red carnation. His fedora and cane were beside him. He was openly smoking a custom-made Turkish and marijuana cigarette.

They did not greet each other, not even with an icy formality. Maurice reviled Julian and he was a man who had never had to compromise in his behaviour in his life.

"This tiresome *mésalliance*," he began, without preamble. "You are doubtless aware of my daughter's intentions of discontinuing this contractual association she has with you. I wish it to be settled this morning."

"Your views are clear. Perhaps Ann-Marie would prefer to speak for herself," Julian replied.

"When I speak on such matters it is my prerogative. And when I speak it is with considerable influence ..."

The old man manipulated his words with a moment's silence. Julian looked at Maurice's bodyguard sitting at a discreet distance across the foyer smoothing his kid leather gloves. The gloves and uniform matched the colour of the vintage Rolls Royce parked in the square. He would be

151

carrying the statutory Beretta in his shoulder holster and he was nervous.

"Of course, there is a need for discretion and to facilitate this I am prepared to furnish you with what you will no doubt agree is a considerable sum of money. A deposit of twenty-five million French Francs could be effected into your Swiss account within the hour. What I require is your immediate return of the contract."

Julian watched the Count impassively. There is a fine line between intrigue and melodrama, between the cunning and the predictable. The old man had just crossed it.

"We are wasting time, Maurice. I will point out once more my interest in your interest in our contractual relationship, is nil."

The old man's eyes flickered as though he had not quite heard.

"And as of this morning I will no longer tolerate your rudeness."

"How dare you ..."

"... If I may finish," Julian went on quietly. "This meeting may relate to Ann-Marie. It is a question of vice, of ascertaining whether you are aware that a corner of your business is being used as an umbrella for an extensive vice operation in Europe."

The Count's bodyguard stood up, concerned with the reaction of his employer to a conversation he could not quite hear. The Count made a move to rise from the settee but Julian willed him to sit. The pale, rather frail figure was a little confused. His aura had been bold and expanding and very clear in a deep red velvet lounge lit only by crystal chandeliers. People nearby were touched by it, not knowing why they felt uncomfortable. Now Maurice was floundering.

"This is gross impertinence ..."

"Let me not be misunderstood. I am talking of abduction, prostitution, paedophilia, trafficking ..."

" ... and I will not listen further," Maurice said asserting himself finally. "I will not forget this meeting."

"Of course not," Julian responded. He was not being facetious. The old man would now be searching his conscience. He might even begin enquiries.

The Count placed his hat on his head and with his bodyguard steadying him left the hotel, waving off the salutations of the manager. The bodyguard did not turn. He was thankful to be leaving.

Julian did not finish the bourbon brought as a courtesy. He ordered another with fresh ice then decided he had no time to drink it. He took a taxi to Orly and boarded a flight to Marseilles.

Also on Thursday morning of that week, Thérèse left the clinic. Daphne took her back to her apartment in Rue Louis Hap where Martine, having taken time off work was waiting to cuddle her. Thérèse hardly spoke in the tram and was tense in the street and Daphne saw signs of agoraphobia. She wanted to be alone for a while and Daphne helped her unpack her bag before helping Martine prepare lunch.

Daphne's parents were shocked at the violence against Thérèse and wanted her to come and stay with them in Lille, at least until the autumn term started. It was her final year at university. She wasn't close to her stepfather in Paris – she would tell him nothing about the attack – and therefore accepted their invitation. Charles was driving to Brussels to pick her up. Both he and Peter were expected for lunch.

Daphne walked with Peter across town to her apartment when her father and Thérèse had gone. Peter had barely been able to speak over lunch. Daphne understood this. She also hurt mentally and physically. She too loved Thérèse.

"It's very kind of you to put up with me this week. I'll remember you in my will."

"Not a good joke," Daphne said. "Anyway, I've been glad of your company."

"I have to say it again," Peter went on bitterly. "The most upsetting thing was the premeditation. The bastard. The fact it was going to happen and I could do nothing about it. And the fact he might even have photographed Thérèse in my room. Girls can be so stupid about such things."

"It is innocence, not stupidity and you mustn't brood," Daphne said gently. "You've got to be positive. She needs love and affection. She will respond to this."

"If I ever see her again."

Peter was wrestling with the prospect of returning to university. Bloody bio-chemistry, he thought. There seemed little point to anything now, yet he did not know what else to do. He was also struggling with the morality of his uncle having killed the man.

"Now don't be ridiculous. Don't go cold." Daphne put her arm through his. "She needs our strength and support to get over this."

"Thanks, Kid. I'm not my best. You are right, nothing compares with the psychological beating she must be enduring. But I feel so bloody useless. I couldn't get it together in a fight and now the girl I love, I couldn't even protect her."

"Whatever you do, you mustn't give up. She can't."

Daphne clung to Peter's arm and squeezed when she saw the sadness and pain in his eyes. It had been like this all week and there was nothing more she could do.

9/3
Friday 30 August

Peter walked from Daphne's place to his uncle's apartment in Rue Américaine early the next morning for a change of clothes. He had been there only ten minutes when there was a tap on the door. He was both surprised and relieved it was Daphne. She must have followed him.

"You're not supposed to be here," he said, drawing her inside.

"Neither of us are," she corrected. "Madame Grimeau let me in round the back!"

"You came through the courtyard ..."

"With this in my hand," Daphne replied, showing Peter a CS Gas spray she had bought in her local hardware store. "It's a dark corner even during the day but I needed to do it for Thérèse's sake. For mine to. We can't live in fear."

Sitting on the edge of a chair without taking her jacket off she asked Peter if he had any idea why his uncle had gone to Lisbon. Julian had written in his note to Peter he would be away until after the weekend and under no circumstances was he to go near the apartment.

Peter had wondered.

"The only person I know of who lives in Portugal is Ann-Marie's uncle."

The uncle's name was something like 'Cavaillos', she recalled. He was Ann-Marie's uncle, her father's half-brother and legal adviser to the family business. She couldn't remember the details on the disks Julian brought over. If Julian was away for several days she would miss him. After the weekend she was returning home to Lille for the remainder of the vacation to keep Thérèse company. It was the least she could do.

Her feeling Julian would not be around much longer worried her deeply. It was a foreboding. He could not have been happy about what he had done. The prison cell must have been awful too. She should not have held back from cuddling him.

Brightening up she said to Peter,

"I've decided. I'll take a chance and see if I can meet him in Lisbon."

"You're bonkers, Daphne," Peter responded. "We don't

155

know what he's doing, where he is or even if he'll be there. Isn't it a bit dumb, popping down to Portugal on the off-chance?"

Daphne was not listening. Julian mentioned to Peter he would be in Marseilles for a couple of days before going on to Lisbon at the weekend. It was the morning of day two, Friday and he would surely still be in France. She could see nothing wrong with the idea. She began kicking herself mentally for having bought a pair of boots the day before with money her father had sported.

"The problem is my bank account's at zero."

"You could always hitch," Peter replied, working through the possibilities.

Then he remembered the cash card.

"You can do it, girl! All we have to do is walk down the road. We can use my *funny-money card*!"

"*Funny-money card*?" Daphne mimicked in English.

"A *Bankomat*. We can get nine thousand francs in one go from the Banque Bruxelles Lambert machine in the Gallery Louise. That should do it"

Daphne was about to protest.

"It's all right, it's uncle's money. He gave me the card for emergencies!"

"Then I'm going to find out if I can do it."

It took her twenty minutes to discover there were two flights that day between Marseilles and Lisbon, the first via Madrid, the second direct. She also found out she could get a Sabena flight from Zaventem directly to Lisbon at eleven that morning and be there before both of these flights. She counted the money in her purse. There was more than she thought. "Good old Dad," she said.

Peter purloined the groceries money from the kitchen. He was sure there would be more cash in his uncle's study but it was locked. He could see Daphne needed money in reserve. Thinking about the situation, if they hadn't been able to scrape enough for a return flight he would not have let her go.

He looked carefully up and down Rue Américaine before leaving the apartment with Daphne. They walked down the Chaussée de Charleroi, crossing at the Sieman's offices into the sun. Daphne had her arm through his and was holding tightly. She had been wonderful that week, the least selfish person he had ever known. He would miss her when she left.

"Are you going back to your place first?"

Daphne looked at her watch.

"I have to go as I am, with this little bag. Just girlie stuff. Anyway, if I'm to keep up with your uncle, I need to be more practical."

Only then did Peter realise Daphne and his uncle had become friends. He had recently compared her to a bottle of champagne just uncorked and his uncle's silence spoke volumes. Many things fell into place and for the first time in a week he felt himself smiling.

"The Dynamic Duo!" he said with an American accent.

Daphne understood and running through the marble passageways of the Gallery Louise they began a spontaneous,

"*Da-da da-da, da-da da-da, Ju-lien,*" finally bursting into laughter.

There were others interested in Daphne's telephone call to the airport that morning. Major Walker's humour soured on learning in Bonn the day before that Julian de Lyon had slipped out of Belgium, being seen at Paris's North station only by an agent on leave. The imbecile had not thought to let his office know immediately. Only the phone tap that morning yielded the first positive thing on de Lyon in weeks.

All the huge communications centre in Brussels told him was mail and telephone intercepts to the Rue Américaine apartment revealed nothing. De Lyon hadn't used any plastic for weeks. His bank balance was on the high side but had been for years. He wasn't earning excessively and he wasn't spending. The withdrawal in the last hour from a machine in the south of Brussels would have been one of the kids, air-fare money probably.

The man was certainly an exceptional operative. Watch anyone's home for a couple of days and you learn where the men keep their socks and the women their underwear. Even professionals have habits. Not this one. The team christened him the Spook. He heard this around his own corridors and noted with irritation, rumour and gossip were more potent than the Agency's most sophisticated electronics.

When his aide came in with a coffee, Walker asked him to place a call to Cascais. The Deputy Chief of Station in Lisbon was a personal friend and would be at his villa above the old harbour for an early lunch before his Friday afternoon golf.

"Get Joe on the 'phone as well, lieutenant."

"He's still on leave, sir, down in the Black Forest spa he likes, Bad Wildbad."

"Then get him on the 'phone there. I want him in Portugal, by nightfall. Fix it with the Air Force if necessary and give him anything he wants."

In view of the intelligence on de Lyon and continuing flow of heroin in to Germany, he would hit him that weekend in Portugal, where they were less likely to draw attention. The latest information from Hong Kong was the *sap sei kei* were also on his tail. He wanted de Lyon first. It was time for some hard talking.

9/4
Lisbon

A glance around the arrivals hall at Lisbon airport late that Friday afternoon showed Julian two parties interested in his appearance. Daphne he was genuinely surprised to see. She flung her arms around him.

"Please don't be cross with me," she whispered, "I really wanted to see you."

She gripped the leather strap of his shoulder bag with both hands as though afraid he would break free. He took her hands in his.

"How can I be cross with someone who is an exasperation and a delight!"

The other party interested in his arrival folded his newspaper and walked to the telephones. Julian told Daphne to stay where she was and followed the man to an adjacent booth. He could not avoid eye contact with Julian and knew he must leave the hall. Returning with the keys of a hired car, Julian listened to Daphne tell him of a man with military haircut and rolled up sleeves sitting nearby all afternoon also checking incoming flights.

"I am expecting trouble, Daphne."

"And I am a liability," she replied.

"You are a treasure."

"Which is even more a liability ..."

She could see Julian was not pleased and it had to come into the open. There needed to be this level of understanding between them. He stopped by the car and began a little too severely,

"I am responsible for your safety and must ask you to consider very carefully if you feel able to cope with trouble, any kind of trouble?"

Daphne faced him squarely and replied she was confident of anything in his company. When he opened the car door for her it was with relief she got in.

As they set off from the airport he said more gently they may get through the weekend smiling. He really didn't know what to expect. She thought carefully before saying the only way of getting to know him was by getting into the thick of things with him. She had the feeling, she said, there wasn't much time.

He passed over her remarks but there were things she would have to know. Beside him was a trusting and caring young woman, caring enough for her to have made a long and for all she knew, fruitless journey. He asked if she was aware they were on their way south to the Algarve, to Ann-Marie's uncle, Count Ferdinand da Cavaleiro. She might have remembered he was legal advisor to the French family's business.

Daphne thought about her lack of clothes, of everything.

"I won't be an embarrassment, will I?"

"I'm sure he'll find you absolutely delightful," he said, more relaxed at the prospect of her company. Remembering she had come with nothing he turned off the ring road towards the city centre.

"We'll make a detour through Baixa, Lisbon's main shopping area and get anything you need."

"Thank you, Julian. I really appreciate that."

"We'll have to be quick. It's quite a drive to the Algarve. But it will give me a chance to tell you what I know about the family. The *castelo* on the cliff-top should be interesting too."

Daphne's eyes lit up. She had forgotten about the castle.

CHAPTER TEN

Costa Vicentina, **Algarve, Friday 30 August**

The first toast that evening was to Daphne.

Though somewhat subdued because of the surroundings, Daphne knew she had gone too far in asking Count Ferdinand about the family's wealth, the family Julian had married in to. It just dropped from her lips. She followed this with a question about their notorious past and was amazed at how tactless she could be. Both Julian's and the Count's face creased into smiles and Ferdinand said they must refill their glasses for his favourite story.

More than once, Daphne reached unconsciously for Julian's arm. The three of them were seated at an oak table before a white stone fireplace in the castle's great hall. The walls were of a sombre pink and grey granite and decorated with tapestry, heraldry and weaponry. The ceiling was supported by beams the thickness of tree trunks. The floor was made of flagstones that made them look like chess pieces at supper.

Fire-light danced across the old Count's face as he offered the toast, that youth and beauty remain in them all.

"As recently as the early Nineteenth Century my family were pirates and adventurers, Daphne," Ferdinand began, a playful smile on his lips. "They migrated from a country laid waste by Napoleon's armies to seek a fortune in the colonies and were to become the scourge of the China Seas. These gentlemen, black-bearded and wild-eyed who hang around us, to my housekeeper's consternation. I must say, in deference to a line going back to the Dukes of Braganza, we have not always been involved in such things. It was in the 1920s my mother removed all such nefarious elements from the business, if not from the minds of local people."

"Has the castle always belonged to the family?" Daphne asked, unabashed. The dark-haired septuagenarian was conversing in a most elegant French and had gone out of his way that evening to make her feel at home.

"Actually, no," he continued. "It was given to us in 1834. Those more spirited members of the family who had sailed off to the Far East returned in three ships laden with booty early in the civil war being fought between the Crown Princes Pedro and Miguel. They chose to support the winning side and the estate, sequestered from the church, was presented by Pedro as a gift for their services. The lands were run down and the house derelict and it was to remain this way until a bigger fortune was amassed trading Indian opium for Chinese silver. My father completed the restoration of house and estate when he returned home from Macao in 1897."

"What did he do then?"

"He certainly married my mother!" came the reply. "But the lure of the Orient was strong. His last visit here was in 1910, when he planned to settle but he felt he must leave once again when an anti-Royalist Republic was established. A relatively young man, he succumbed in 1917 to the last pandemic of the Black Death. My mother married again in about 1920, a Frenchman this time, another widower and the reason, Julian, that you and Daphne, are here today."

Helen, the woman the Count had introduced as his housekeeper, appeared at the end of their supper of *bacalhau*, traditional salt cod neither Julian nor Daphne had tasted before. Thanking everyone for their compliments she gently reminded Ferdinand topics such as plague were hardly

162

appropriate over dinner.

When she had gone, with a promise she would join them a little later, Daphne asked the Count impishly if he could tell her about the pandemic. Ferdinand poured a liqueur for Daphne and port for Julian and himself and told how the last great outbreak of bubonic plague broke out in Hong Kong in 1894 and touched every part of the globe over a twenty-five-year period. By 1917, he said, it had claimed more than ten million lives in India alone including those of his father, grandfather and an uncle.

"And if it hadn't been the plague, it would have been the even more virulent flu pandemic shortly after. These were days of adventure and adventurers, Daphne. Julian will, I'm sure, concur that for those who spend a lifetime flirting with danger, a commensurate death is but the final blossoming of that love affair."

He added,

"My father's epitaph reads: 'I receive just desserts. But I have lived.'"

Daphne excused herself at ten-thirty and left the two men and Helen in the great hall. The maid accompanied her to her rooms. They walked along the south and east corridors, up a spiral staircase and back to the south side. Although the castle was eerie because of a faulty generator, her bedroom, bathroom and dressing room were lit by candle light and lovely. The maid ran a bath and asked in broken French if there was anything else she could do. Daphne apologised for keeping her up and the girl, blushing, left with a curtsy.

The moment the door closed there was perfect peace. Candles and a dying log fire, sputtering occasionally, cast a soft glow about the bedroom. Daphne opened a window and sniffed a delicious mixture of sea air and the fragrance of early autumn. She had walked with Julian along the battlements soon after they had arrived, wondering if a mediaeval European castle evoked romantic feelings in him. He hadn't put his arm around her as she hoped. He picked her up and lifted her over a parapet as though she was a flower. She was still tingling from the sensation.

By the time Daphne fell asleep, Helen had retired and Ferdinand and Julian had moved to the Count's sitting room and study by the lower terrace. The old man liked to take a last stroll under the pergola and enjoy the scent of the vines and the garden. He poured two glasses of cognac and apologised for being unable to resist lighting a Davidoff.

"I am immensely pleased to have the company of you two young people," he said, "but I must ask of the things that trouble you enough for you to come all this way and why other parties have gathered nearby also."

Julian asked Ferdinand how he knew of such things.

"Since retiring from private practice I enjoy many occupations," he went on, unsmiling. "One is that of chairman of the district *câmara* and there is little here about which I am not informed. Yesterday afternoon our *Guarda* Captain called here enquiring if it was you who was to be my guest. Only after some cajoling would he admit he was under pressure from the American Embassy that want to interview you. Perhaps you could explain this?"

Julian was thoughtful, not least about the sudden efficiency of the CIA in knowing his movements from Brussels. He asked Ferdinand if he was familiar with his contract with the United Nations.

"You are aware it was I, four years ago who made the enquiries into your background on Maurice's behalf with regard to Ann-Marie?"

"Then I must say I have been implicated in the deaths of two US intelligence agents in recent operations. Since drugs and triads seem to be involved the CIA will no doubt again be concerned about my past association with drug-trafficking in South-East Asia."

"And you do not feel you need assistance!"

"Not yet, thank you, Count."

Ferdinand fell silent. He liked Julian and differed from his brother Maurice in feeling Julian could have been a modifying influence on Ann-Marie's sometimes queer behaviour. Her liaison with him would only have been for gain with regard to his United Nations connections. Their relationship soured when it became clear this would not bear dividends.

"So now, your questions. About Ann-Marie?"

"About her health, her mental health," Julian replied.

Ferdinand nodded. He poured himself another cognac and stood motionless beneath the yellowing vines. He was not searching for answers, he was remembering precious moments.

"Such a tough little girl, her childhood spent in the shadows of the quest for wealth and status. In recent years, with her more proactive role in the business it has been a challenge keeping pace with her innovatory ideas. I have frequently advised she cannot do things that she has done anyway, sometimes with spectacular results. It is a tragedy this last year she has become the child she never was. One now with power, responsibilities and a rapacious intellectual capacity – "

He broke off suddenly.

"I will not speculate further. Ann-Marie is your wife and you are consort this weekend to a charming young lady. But forgive me again."

Julian brushed the apology aside. It did not trouble him Ferdinand knew more about the situation with Ann-Marie than he would reveal. His fears were confirmed.

"You have one specific request, I believe?"

Julian handed Ferdinand the report he had compiled with

Daphne's assistance. The Count turned several pages and said gravely,

"This meeting was inevitable. I am prepared to add details on the extent of this type of vice that, shamefully, carries on with Maurice's, perhaps tacet, approval and I will do this before you leave."

He closed the folder and led Julian back inside the study. After securing the shutters and French windows he suggested he and Daphne might like to browse the various collections in the castle for the remainder of their stay. He also recommended a picnic, a speciality of Helen's, though reservations about Julian and the young woman leaving the castle he kept to himself.

"And you must not miss the dungeons."

"I will enjoy Daphne's company on that walk!"

Both men chuckled.

"Ah, it is not fair. But the world would be a grimmer place if we did not think we had the upper hand in teasing the fair sex!"

Ferdinand took a last sip of cognac and placed the remains of his cigar in an ashtray.

"Now it is midnight and I am taking liberties with the day, or it with me. I must show you the staircase and bid you a pleasant night."

Daphne had no idea what time it was when she woke with Julian's words at the airport taking over her dreams. She held her breath and listened but there was a deep silence punctuated only by the mournful lament of a restless sea. The heavy door made a hideous noise as she closed it behind her and she felt wicked indeed in the darkness in a strange house wearing only a short silk wrap. She stepped barefoot along the corridor, felt her way cautiously up the spiral staircase in pitch black to the floor above, drew a deep breath and began the walk past the line of forbidding armoured knights.

The twelve figures along Julian's corridor glinted in the starlight, their empty eyes watching her every move. She felt goose pimples under her wrap but on reaching the room flanked by the fifth and sixth of these silent warriors she was no longer afraid. She reached for the iron door handle but was overwhelmed with a desire to embrace the figure by her, though she dared not in case it fell over, or worse, on her.

The impulse grew stronger until absorbed by thoughts of bloody battles and brave men she opened her wrap and pressed herself against the iron figure. Its cold hardness, the roughness of the chain mail made her gasp and she stepped back, flushed in her face, telling herself she should not be so naughty.

She had difficulty orienting herself in Julian's room until she saw the outline of the four-poster by starlight and the embers in the fireplace. A warm hand touched hers. Her wrap slipped to the floor and she was drawn into his bed.

"Sorry to disturb you!"

"Just as well a ghost didn't get you," Julian whispered in her ear. "Such extraordinary things you were doing outside the door."

Daphne did not reply. His arms were around her. He was also naked.

"You saved me from ghosts, mediaeval knights and myself, I think!" she said giggling.

"Sleep, Monkey," he whispered.

She was aware of asking if his evening was pleasant but was suddenly overcome by the need to sleep.

10/2

At seven, Julian was standing on the lower terrace drinking tea Helen had prepared. The grey sky was flecked with crimson by a sun about to peep over the distant mountains. The south wall of the castle stood starkly above him. The west wall rose straight out of the cliff. Below, down a scarred face of crystalline rock, the sea pounded relentlessly, hypnotically, along a ragged shoreline softened only by touches of sand. There was no sign of human habitation in any direction. As far north and south as he could see, the honey-coloured rock of this south-west corner of Europe – the edge of the known world when the castle was built – stood defiantly to the Atlantic Ocean.

Eastwards and just below him the unmade road dropped steeply away from the castle towards a dry river course. It followed this for several kilometres through woodland and farmland to the road proper. It was a bleak and beautiful place with spectacular views of a deserted and unspoilt coast and the *Serra de Monchique* inland. Goats and sheep grazed in the tight scrub that survived dry summer heat and a sometimes ferocious winter battering from the sea. Trees and bushes were established in vales further back from the cliff.

Around the castle's immediate grounds there was also woodland, including cork oak, giving the house some privacy. There was no sound other than that of birds singing and the sea. Julian knew it would not remain like this for long.

Opting for a picnic and a day's sightseeing, he left the castle with Daphne after breakfast and knew before reaching the small town of Aljezur they were being followed. He had erred in his judgement of the situation, including allowing Daphne to remain with him.

"Daphne, there is something we must talk about."

Daphne turned pale.

"I have been under surveillance by the CIA for some weeks and we are being followed at this moment. If trouble develops you do exactly as I say. Do you understand?"

168

Daphne nodded.

Seeing a sign *Castelo de Aljezur*, he pulled off the main road suddenly and up a steep hill through an old village. The car he was talking about followed but slowed between the houses. From the Moorish ruins above they saw it turn and stop under trees. Daphne tensed, wondering if the two men would get out. Julian brought a box out of the glove compartment.

"Cigarette lighters?"

"No, they are needle guns."

Each one had a needle in the tube below the valve, Julian explained. It was ejected by pressing the trigger, pressing harder than usual to break the safety seal.

Daphne studied one, intrigued.

"The needles are large and hollow and contain a preparation that will paralyse within twenty seconds. They will penetrate light clothing on contact. I must also show you points where entry can be fatal."

"Is it a stupid question to ask if you made these?"

Julian put the box away without replying and started the engine. He didn't go back down through the village, turning instead into the hills. When he stopped on the dirt road a few minutes later and got out of the car, she thought it was because they were lost. There was only silence and he said now they could enjoy some sightseeing and their picnic.

Daphne smiled briefly, uneasy about other things, not the least of which was her and Peter's last visit to Julian's apartment and why he had given explicit instructions not to go near it.

"I'm sorry, Julian, but I have to ask how Americans can be doing these things so blatantly in Europe?"

"It's up to me whether they get away with it."

She fell silent with this answer. She thought she was getting somewhere with Julian but knew now she was not. One question she could not ask was why all this was happening. She didn't know if she could bear the answer.

They both cheered up on the drive through the hills, charmed by the spa town of Caldas de Monchique, unspoilt villages, deserted countryside and gentle woodland. After Helen's picnic lunch in a grove of eucalyptus trees, Julian did as Daphne suggested and stretched out on the bank of a stream. Below them were fig, almond and orange groves and a view of the coast forty kilometres away. It was a perfectly peaceful spot with the sound of bubbling water, a welcome breeze whispering through the trees and the soporific smell of eucalyptus heavy in the air.

Julian opened his eyes with a start when he realised he had not heard his young companion for a while. She was just below him, sitting on a rock with her toes in the water. The trousers of the cotton suit she had bought in Lisbon were tied loosely around her shoulders. Her head and hair were thrown back and she was absorbing the afternoon sun dappling through the trees. Her legs were long, slim and brown against the pink of the tunic. She no longer looked like the stick of peppermint rock her father said when she last wore that colour.

She brought the bottle of *vinho verde* cooling in the water and lay beside him with her head on his shoulder and hand on his chest. She smelt of spring water, eucalyptus oil, wild flowers and of herself.

It was almost eight o'clock when they turned off the coast road to the cliffs. They were a kilometre away from the castle and its copse silhouetted against an indigo sky when Julian pulled up, turned lights and engine off and said sharply,

"The road is blocked in front and behind. Lock the doors and keep low. I'll be back in a moment."

He disappeared into the gloom and Daphne was calm

until headlights were turned on up the road. A figure crossed the beams. Ducking, she broke into a cold sweat and opened the glove compartment. A great hulk of a man loomed by her window and tried the door handle. She shifted to the driver's seat. The man grunted, the window popped and she was showered with cubes of glass. His hand reached in and opened the door and with a reflexive action she grabbed the CS canister from her bag and let it off in his face.

As the man backed away muttering a stream of expletives, his hands to his eyes, she swivelled in the seat and kicked the door hard with both feet. The frame caught his chin and he fell backwards.

There was no further sound in the darkness other than her breathing and her heart thumping until Julian reappeared. He walked around the car before getting in.

"Well done," he said. "You laid Mister Big out cold, with your own armoury."

"I didn't have twenty seconds," she replied, laughing, crying and shaking at the same time.

He turned her face towards him and said,

"I can still take you back to the airport, or to a hotel."

"No, no," she said, recovering her composure, "I want to stay with you."

Julian reversed the car a couple of metres and turned the steering wheel.

"No, you can't ..." she began, horrified.

He took a deep breath and steered past Williams. Daphne did not comment on the other man lying in the road by the jeep wearing a black *gi* and sash. If he had done what he intended to the American it might hastened a conclusion in their favour. Now only her strength of character would get her through the night.

Ferdinand himself opened the main gate wide enough for them to drive straight into the courtyard. Daphne was relieved to be behind strapped oak doors and the only iron portcullis she had seen working but still didn't want Julian to leave her on her own.

"I must apologise, Daphne. I know more about what is going on than I have led you to believe," he said as Julian was making a telephone call. "I have some things to discuss with Julian when he is finished but I suggest we all get together in half an hour."

Ross had just arrived home from the office that Saturday evening and knew as his phone rang there was no point in taking his coat off. He did not pretend the CIA could not have attempted such an abduction and said he would return to the office immediately, contact the base at SHAPE and play hell. Julian told him to ask Cummings why there should be Chinese with this surveillance team. He didn't feel it necessary to say they were dressed to kill.

Daphne joined Julian and the Count in the great hall half an hour later and kissed Julian's cheek without reservation. She had gone straight to the kitchen to seek Helen's advice. The situation was looking serious as Julian hinted it might. Whatever was going on outside, Helen said, their men would deal with it and they might yet manage dinner. Daphne appreciated Helen putting her arm around her advising she must keep a level head, do what was asked and keep smiling.

"As Julian is going up to the battlements and we have a little time before Helen serves dinner, perhaps you would care to accompany me on a little tour, Daphne?" Ferdinand asked. "To assist with the now occasional ceremony of the lighting of the candles."

He said power lines were down on the main road, his generator man was away and the equipment was not recharging the emergency lighting batteries. Daphne touched Julian's hand in a gesture he take care.

She put aside her anxieties as she and the Count made their way up the main staircase. She had noticed immediately on their arrival the weathering of the stone inside the great hall and impressed Ferdinand by guessing the hall must originally have been the *enceinte*. The keep now served as the main staircase, he said and she dated the castle correctly as not later than middle-Twelfth Century. She asked about the seemingly arbitrary use of left- and right-hand spiral staircases, defensive sometimes from above, sometimes below. The Count admitted he did not know why this was.

Her interest, she said, was made up of history, engineering and romance and she made him chuckle by saying these professions were represented individually in her family.

At the north-west corner of the castle above the great hall, they entered a ballroom floored in elm. It was in such good condition it looked new. They crossed to the staircase to inspect the musicians gallery and walked back along the line of windows on the west side. On the very edge of two hundred metres of cliff they faced a vista of ocean, now luminescent in the starlight. A stiff wind was blowing, whipping up spindrift far below and pushing it in lines inshore.

The west side was his favourite, Ferdinand said with pride. He was often the only audience to a private showing of the sun setting over an entire ocean.

"My father was both proud of and disappointed with this addition," he said. "I do not believe it was ever used."

"Why ever not?" Daphne asked.

"The castle was never a home to him. I think the ballroom was a desperate attempt at being accepted into the bosom of the society of the day."

"How sad. Could he have been disappointed because the castle was not big enough? Is it possible because his life was played on so large a stage across the world he could not come back to Portugal? That to settle here would have been a slow death?"

She cleared her throat self-consciously.

"Very perceptive for one so young," the Count said smiling. "Showing you around this evening has been a joy. You have a presence missing from this house since my mother was a young woman."

Daphne blushed deeply and looked at her watch. She was worrying about Julian and wondering if he would have to rescue her. Twenty minutes had passed and the Count agreed they must see he was safe.

"And about your consort, it is a pleasure to see such strength of feeling between you."

"I have known such a man all my life," Daphne said, subdueing the emotion in her voice, "but don't have the experience to complement him."

"May I suggest it is not lack of experience. Neither is it sunshine that melts ice. It is but a breath of warm air."

"Oh, thank you," Daphne said putting her arms around the old man's shoulders, "thank you for being so kind to me."

"We have an *entry situation*, as one American has unwittingly informed me in this clear night air."

Daphne jumped at hearing Julian and at his appearance in the gloom dressed in his *gi*. She was amazed he was smiling and smiled back, as recommended.

"We must escort Daphne to her rooms and move on to my communications room," Ferdinand responded with more urgency.

He thanked Julian for making sure Helen and the maid were safe and made sure Daphne also locked herself in. One floor below he turned a light on in the room leading off his study. Here was everything he needed for international business, he said; telex, facsimile, video recording equipment and a mini-computer. There was also closed-circuit television.

"I might be isolated, Julian but I am in touch."

"You have back-up power."

"There is battery reserve in these rooms and for emergency lighting throughout the castle, now on its fourth and last day. We have the telephone. If there was power we would have this also, as both come underground from ten kilometres away. I did not think it prudent to have a fortification that could be isolated by the snipping of a wire."

Ferdinand pressed a button on the console and one of eight monitors began to glow.

"Gadgetry has always been a hobby in my family," he went on. "Because of the battery situation we can only operate one camera at a time. It was quite by chance I witnessed the incident by the river on your return, doing my rounds with the cameras. And let me affirm my duty to you as guests. It is my house and my estate. I have a responsibility to help you to the best of my ability."

Julian's attention was now wholly on the monitors as Ferdinand switched between them. The old man then sat back in his chair.

"I must also tell you I have known for some months what has been going on with you, with Ann-Marie and certain members of the CIA. Tonight, a determined group of men have come to avail themselves of the family silver, Julian, the inheritance. I cannot explain in two minutes. Suffice it to say, you are closer than you know to losing a fortune."

Julian almost understood. Ann-Marie's delicate mental state undoubtedly laid her open to manipulation but he regarded their contract as tenuous, even whimsical. There was also the triad seeking final retribution for his early breaking from them and recently, inflicting serious damage on their business in North-West Europe. His attention re-focused on the matter of survival.

"And survival it is," the Count said reading him well. "I am not in the rudest of health but will help as I can."

Looking at each monitor in turn they counted half-a-dozen men about the gardens with more grouped beneath the east wall. These included Chinese, two of whom were skulking under the pergola on the terrace beyond the study windows.

"Unlikely bed-fellows," Ferdinand commented.

"How secure are the shutters?" Julian asked.

"They are a weak point. They are oak and the glass is ten millimetre armoured, to hold back the ravages of the Atlantic you understand. The shutters should withstand the shock of a grenade and the glass is, of course, bullet-proof even from a light machine-gun. If they look like failing we could go above and pour boiling oil."

"Let's hope we don't have to go to the trouble," Julian responded.

"So what do you wish of me?"

Julian asked how long it would take the police to reach the castle. Ferdinand said it would be their *Guarda Nacional Republicana* officer, if he or his men could be located on a Saturday night. Julian saw Williams again, on the screen, recovered from his brush with Daphne and no doubt very sore. This was the CIA involvement, though with Williams surely working on his own. He asked Ferdinand for the study extension number, saw it was nine-thirty and said he would ring.

10/3

He was in a room close to Daphne's, high on the south side within seconds. He opened the window a fraction and heard a huff of exertion in the darkness. A steel claw hooked onto the casement and pulled it open further. The claw, a hand and an arm appeared. Julian stood aside, let the intruder haul himself in and administered a sharp blow. The man was wearing the sash of a teacher and should have known better. Julian pushed the figure back out, picked up

176

the room 'phone and dialled 10.

"What are they doing on the east wall?"

"They seem to have secured a line to the top, half-way along. They used a rocket!" came Ferdinand's incredulous reply. "What number are you at?"

"32."

"Daphne is 35."

"Hi Daphne!" Julian said moments later.

"Where are you ... what's going on ... are you all right?"

"I'm all right. Bar your windows. I'll call again."

He moved swiftly along the south and east corridors and up the spiral staircase snuffing candles as he went. He doubled back to the small staircase by the bathroom at the end of the corridor and went on up to the battlements. Slipping the bolts of the narrow oak door he tuned his senses to the darkness.

Warm air was pouring from the mountains, sighing like a harmonica through the mellow stonework. There was a tang of saltpetre, a cry from a gannet on the cliff and a shape leaning through the crenellation busy signalling below. Julian almost reached him without being seen. The hooded figure turned, nostrils and eyes flaring. The *shuriken* he threw missed. The second, Julian also avoided.

"Holiday?" he asked quietly in Cantonese.

The youth thought about running then changed his mind. The indecision cost him a broken neck. The other figure hauling himself up the wall on the knotted nylon line did not make it to the battlements. He was pulled up a metre then dropped suddenly. He hung on gasping. The line had slipped off his glove and tightened around his wrist. He was yanked upward and dropped again this time the line cutting through to the bone with the sound of a zip being fastened. Blood squirted into his face. He blacked out and floated silently off the wall.

Julian tossed the line over the inner edge of the terrace,

onto the lead-covered roof of the ballroom. He caught the sound of tinkling glass from the north side and ran back to the tower. On the corridor of knights he relieved the figure nearest the stairs of its axe and the lanyard holding the heavy iron sword. The sword he discarded. The belt and steel buckle was a more potent weapon.

A floor lower he heard steps in the ballroom and broke into a run. The figure he met at the corner, a white face in denims, he hit in the throat with his elbow without slowing. He stopped at the edge of the polished wooden floor, saw a shadow pass a distant window and sent the axe spinning through the darkness. It was beautifully balanced. There was a soft moan and the figure pitched headlong across the boards. Julian could only guess the axe, blunt as it was, had sliced the back of the man's thigh above the knee and that he was trying desperately to stem the bleeding.

He turned his attention to the room on the north side, through which these two had entered. Peering cautiously out of the broken window he saw and heard only the waves breaking far below at the cliff base. He picked up the telephone, dialled 10 again and whispered,

"Speak to me."

"Watch the north side, Julian. The batteries are exhausted but Helen rang through to warn about the front also. What number are you?"

"41."

"Yes, yes. Be careful."

"How many on the ground below me?"

"Four or five. Gendarmes will be here soon. Good luck."

Julian picked up the leather gloves dropped by the American he had collided with and looked around the storeroom. He was above the kitchens near the maid. They lived in opposite corners of the castle, this little family. The maid's room overlooked the ocean. Ferdinand preferred to wake to the garden. Helen occupied a suite below Daphne, where the sun shone in all day long and from where she could also see the sea. Julian looked out of the window again and decided he should see what was going on below.

Two Americans trotted up to him as he came down the line.

"What the f..." one of them began.

A kick broke his jaw. The second man Julian felled with a blow to the head. Borrowing the combat jacket of one and cap of the other he stepped over some box hedging into flower beds. Here in a patch of *nicotiana alata* Daphne said smelt their best at night, luck deserted him. Three shots from a small-calibre pistol spat out from the darkness. One bullet missed but one embedded itself in his thigh and the other tore across his hip. He rolled across the mass of pink and white flowers and jerked the belt twice at the shadowy figure. The two-inch buckle scythed back and forth across the man's face.

Julian had no time to dwell on his own wounds. He picked up a walkie-talkie, limped back along the grass at the foot of the north wall and hauled himself up the line he had come down. He listened to the sounds around him as he regained control of his breathing and dialled 10 once again on the room telephone.

"What's the latest?"

"Helen thinks they have succeeded in climbing the south wall. I can be of no more help now."

"Any word from your maid?"

"She is not replying. Probably too frightened."

"Do you have a first-aid kit to hand?"

There was a pause.

"The infirmary is on this side, by Helen. First floor south."

Julian replaced the handset and made his way cautiously to the far side of the castle, making sure he did not trail blood. His senses caught the presence of intruders but he

179

could do nothing further for the moment.

Joe Williams and the remaining three members of his team were in urgent discussion in the safety of one of the outbuildings, waiting for word through their radios. Huang-lin was not far away. He was angry. Two of his men were dead, one was dying from having fallen twenty metres and one man was missing. Williams had been told three of the team had sustained serious injuries and Pete inside had not reported back. De Lyon had more than halved the odds against him and they were urging Williams to call the operation off.

Going along with Joe on an operation with no official brief was one thing. Working with a gang of grim and silent Chinese, with the likelihood the whole operation would collapse, was another.

"There is also the question of the telephone line, Mister Wirriams," the Chinese said coldly. "We must finish now."

Williams ground his teeth.

"For Christ's sake, Joe. The Spook is dangerous enough without this bastard of a place."

"That's enough," Williams snapped. "Bronski and the Indian just got over the top at the front. We're in. De Lyon can't have got to three groups at once. He's likely taken a bullet as well. We're in. We wait."

"Wirriams," the Chinese began again, this time in Cantonese. "We are here two hours. This is more than a lifetime. We have seen what 'the Lion' can do. He is good."

Williams glowered at the Red Pole, one of the triad's most experienced 426s. He was suspicious of the wizened little bastard, Brother or not. He spat on the ground, reminding him the GNR were taken care of. They would stay on the job until dawn if they had to.

The walkie-talkie crackled. Williams was expecting the Indian but the voice asked,

180

"Is there something you wanted, Williams?"

"You sonofabitch ..."

"I would have broken your legs, Williams but a goddess smiled on you. Walk, while you can."

Daphne was sprinkling surgical spirit over Julian's wounds. She didn't quite understood what he said but there was no mistaking the American's response.

He put the handset down on the bed and looked at what she was doing. He had grabbed a medical bag from the infirmary and slipped into her room. She propped him up on the bed and using scissors from the bag cut around the bloody patches in his *gi*. Dabbing the wounds with a wad of gauze and surgical spirit, she said,

"My beginner's certificate didn't cover bullet wounds."

Julian raised her chin.

"I feel better already. These things are never as bad as they appear."

"I'm just feeling so useless, again," she replied.

"All you have to do is extract a small lump of lead from my thigh. There's nothing to it."

Daphne saw he was serious. He pointed to the instruments and said he couldn't twist around enough to do it himself. She said the lower part of his *gi* would have to come off but didn't wait for a response. She cut down from waist to ankle and pulled it off. She made him turn on his side, brought the candle closer and was about to say it would hurt her more, when he remarked she must be firm. The bullet was not in deep but she had to concentrate on getting a firm hold on it.

She saw it but found it surprisingly difficult to grasp, even with a second instrument stretching the wound open. After managing to remove the piece of metal she reluctantly splashed more surgical spirit into the gash.

"Good girl," he said gritting his teeth.

The walkie-talkie crackled into life.

"So you are still here," Julian responded to Williams' prompt.

There was a moment's silence, a few words of Chinese and a strangled scream. Daphne stiffened at hearing Julian's reply. She had heard him speak several languages but not Chinese. The high-pitched, sing-song sound delivered with such aggression took her by surprise.

"What was that?"

"They have the maid."

There was a moment's silence. She dared not speak, thanking God she didn't have to make the decisions.

"I am going out again," he said calmly.

"You can't go out without trousers," she found herself saying. It was not that he was undressed. She saw them as protection.

Julian actually laughed.

"Have you anything I can borrow?"

"Only the pink cotton thing I was wearing today."

She retrieved the trousers from her bag and he put them on, securing them with the belt from the suit of armour. He spent a couple of minutes in the bathroom washing in cold water. When he reappeared he was stripped to the waist. His deep brown eyes flashed in the darkness. Daphne stared in awe.

"Aren't you afraid ..." she asked, trembling.

"This is a determined group," he replied, "but they know I am not finished with them. You must face your enemy. The alternative is fear and that can be worse."

He listened at the door, told her to blow the candle out and keep the door locked until he said otherwise. She brought her wrist near the candle flame and saw it was after eleven. She blew the flame out as he had asked and curled up on the bed in darkness. A sudden and immense sense of loss came over her. It would get worse. She would not hear, see or know anything more until dawn.

CHAPTER ELEVEN

Sunday, 03 September

A thrush trilled insistently and flew. The damp September morning was fluid with bird song and heavy with the scent of the sea. A cock crowed down the valley. Sheep on the cliff top made sheep noises. The scene was pretty, like a page from a child's pop-up book.

Julian focused his eyes on the maid lying next to him in the dry river bed. He aimed a hand at her heart but pain shot across his chest and he found her breast instead, cool and damp with the dew. He had received a shock in the generator outbuilding from a dart with an electrode attached. He had also been injected from a distance with a tranquilliser, like an animal. The maid was similarly subdued and they had been dumped unceremoniously from the jeep. He estimated from the position of the sun they had been in the gulley for three hours.

He grimaced as he rolled over. He vaguely remembered the argument in the outbuilding and Huang-lin out-manoeuvring Williams and putting his own gun to his temple. The American's baseball boots and battledress trousers were visible under pine trees further along. Plainly, he was dead.

Julian's thoughts were interrupted by the sound of the hired car approaching and he dragged himself to a better position up the bank. The car was being driven by a *Guarda* officer with a very concerned Daphne next to him. She threw her arms around Julian, pink trousers, someone else's jacket and all, paying no heed to his groans. She then fetched a rug for him but he wrapped it around the maid and the corporal laid her limp figure on the back seat. Daphne explained on their way back to the castle she knew it was all over at dawn when engines started up. There was an argument, a gunshot and the sound of vehicles driving away at speed. She ventured out of her room to find the Count only when she was sure the grounds were deserted. The soldiers arrived soon after. They were holding a wounded American they came across on the road but said they saw no-one else. She persuaded them to go out again.

"I am happy to see you, Daphne. It wouldn't have been the same, just the corporal."

"And if I hadn't known you for a couple of months, *monsieur*," she replied soberly, "I would have asked what you were doing on the river bank with the maid."

Julian knew if he laughed he would suffer.

When they reached the castle, Daphne insisted he have a hot bath after Helen had checked him over in her apartment, rather than the infirmary. Thankfully, he did not argue. A nurse in a bygone age Helen admitted, she was tending four injured American military personnel in the infirmary. They were polite, if unsmiling, she said and had taken her threat seriously about being put in the dungeons if they misbehaved. The Chinese had taken their dead and wounded away.

Daphne went upstairs and began filling the sunken copper bath in the tower bathroom, perfuming it with attar of roses from one of the crystal bottles by the dolphin tap. The curved windows in the tower gave a spectacular view of the ocean. It was quiet that morning, gunmetal grey in colour with banks of mist lingering under a clouding sky. When the bath was ready she went to fetch Julian.

184

He closed his eyes as he lay back in the hot water and Daphne asked if he did not feel better. He did not want to talk or think and waited for her to decide what she was doing. She was standing above him wearing only her wrap, studying the console by the masseur's couch. There was a telephone on it and switches which altered the lighting. Julian opened his eyes and closed them again, a gentle smile on his lips. When she knelt on a rug on the stone floor and began washing his shoulders he smiled again, this time at the pleasure of her touch.

"You have endured much and I am entirely to blame," he said at last. "I must not delay an explanation any longer."

Daphne said she was listening, if this was what he wanted. She had been prepared to lock them in the bathroom to find out what was going on. Now she was just thankful he was alive. If he was going to explain, this was a bonus.

"This Chinese business, my involvement with triads that is, began when I was fourteen years old," he said quietly. "I go back now to 1956, two years after my father's death. It was a very difficult time for my mother, my brother and myself in Hong Kong. It hadn't been so bad for me that Summer in Korea in a place I had known for years and where I received instruction in martial arts. This was because my father was an expert in *savate*, by the way. He'd served in Korea in 1951 and become interested in a new style called *tang soo do*. It is mainly kicking techniques, as are most Korean styles. The point is he was impressed with a monastery he visited on Jin-do, an island off Korea's south-west coast and thought it a suitable place for me to receive some schooling. It is a wilder, more dramatic place than Hong Kong, with a much older culture.

"Back in the colony, I worked in markets and building sites and continued my martial arts with a man called Yeung Lai-yin. I actually spent more time at his home on Cheung

Chau island than I did at my own. I was fortunate again as Cheung-Chau is 'Old China' compared with where I grew up on North Point. Unfortunately, with a growing confidence and surrounded by grinding poverty and great wealth Hong Kong style, I developed big ideas, mostly about money.

"My troubles really began after carousing one night with friends in a market in Mong Kok on Kowloon."

"At fourteen?" Daphne interrupted.

"Fourteen or fifteen. Anyway, we stumbled on a gang fight in an alleyway. My friends escaped but I witnessed a stabbing. The gang tried to beat me up as a warning not to talk. Some of them were good fighters. Eventually I was clubbed and woke up on Hong Kong Island in a farmhouse at Shek-O on the east side. Because I was half-foreigner they didn't know what to do with me except take me to their Red Pole."

"Red Pole?" Daphne asked.

"*Soeng faa hung gwan*," Julian said absently, "is the leader of triad enforcers. I'll explain in a moment."

"That particular gang," he went on, "were enforcers of the *sap sei kei*, the 14K triad. They had been fighting the Wo Shing Wo, one of the New Territories triads. All us kids knew of the gangs. We used to watch the toughs swagger around the markets and admired the respect they commanded. Anyway, one thing led to another and I was soon leading a double existence, learning from a gracious old man during the day and living the ways of the street at night. They had power, they were on top and I wanted to join them."

Julian went on to describe the gang's routine around the shops and markets of North Point and Wanchai. It included the protecting of property, of bosses and their houses and the collecting of squeeze, and flower money, the cut pimps take from the girls they run.

186

"About the 14K," he went on again. "Its origins are not in the Seventeenth Century, as those triads founded for the purpose of bringing down the Manchu Dynasty. This was an anti-Communist organisation formed a couple of years before the People's Republic. It was forced to relocate to Hong Kong and during the Fifties became the most ruthless triad ever seen there. It was checked by law enforcement but was expanding again when I joined."

"You actually joined? Isn't that a secret ritual, with oaths?" Daphne asked. She had forgotten her tiredness now.

"I went through the ritual and became a 49," Julian affirmed.

He pulled the plug and began topping up the bath. Daphne reached for the rose oil and checked the time on the console. It was half-past seven. Cloud was rolling in from the Atlantic and the ocean was stirring.

As Julian fell silent, perhaps even asleep, she smoothed her hand over his chest and abdomen avoiding the waterproof dressings, just enjoying touching and looking. She didn't know a man could be so beautiful. His hand stopped her going further. The bath was big enough to take both of them but she knew it would be inappropriate.

"Just imagine I'm a *geisha*," she whispered, pleased he had responded to her touch.

"Geisha's behave," he said with the faintest of grins.

When the bath was full again Daphne stopped the dolphin gurgling, smoothed his hair across his forehead and asked him to go on.

"The ceremony involved the beheading of a chicken and the mixing of its blood with wine, which we drank," he said. "This was our acceptance of a similar fate were we to cross the organisation. It was compounded by other threats and the ceremony in my day was intimidating and uncomfortable. It ended with the swearing of the oaths.

"And don't think I took all this lightly, Daphne," Julian

went on, looking up at her. "Tradition and superstition are an important part of the Chinese way of life. Entering a brotherhood takes this to the extreme and you know what you're doing.

"The oaths, thirty-six by tradition, are the swearing of secrecy about membership, from one's family even. There are promises to accord all hospitality to brothers in need, promises not to steal triad property and so on. Such a charter doesn't need much imagination. The important thing is the breaking of any of the oaths is on fear of death. I should also say the relationship of brother is fundamentally more important to a Chinese than is that of spouse."

They were both silent for a while until Daphne asked again how a triad operated. He described the hierarchy from the common 49 to the big boss 489, *daai lou jyun seoi* or 'top of the mountain', telling her something of the functions of the offices. He also said he had not been involved in such things for twenty years and understood the bigger triads were now global in scale and operating like multi-national companies.

"Are you still a member?" Daphne asked.

"Yes," Julian replied. "You are a member to your grave, though I like to think my membership is in abeyance. After three years with the 14K, by which time I had reached the rank of Red Pole, I walked out. I turned my back on it and returned to Korea."

"A Red Pole at seventeen?"

"I was certainly mouthy," Julian said without smiling.

Daphne raised her eyebrows. She realised the Chinese woman who hurt Peter in Cannes must have been a Red Pole. The situation was becoming clearer.

"Let me finish by saying that from 1957, I was into profitable deals of my own and was giving a great deal of money to my mother. Unfortunately, I saw her grow sadder. Master Yueng also knew what was going on and it was on my sixteenth birthday he confronted me about the gang. I was so full of myself he had no alternative but to ask me to renounce my association with him until such time as I thought myself ready to return. Confident at the time and humble not, it was still a moment of great sorrow."

He fell silent again and looked across a cold blue Atlantic. The swell was heavier, showing white water. Gulls, sharp-eyed, were riding the air currents almost within reach of the window. His thoughts were in the South China Sea, with Yueng Lai-yin and happier times at the villa on Cheung Chau. It was a peaceful place, decorated in pink and white mosaic stones with potted geraniums in the courtyard and a view down a tiered garden to North Foreland. He no longer asked himself if he was ready for the final counsel. His chance was gone. The old man was dead.

He was also remembering wilder days and his girlfriend Mai Lo, whom the gang nicknamed Street-fighter. He couldn't forget one of their friendly fights in which she knocked out one of his teeth. It was the only one missing in his mouth and not much to remember her by. She lived in a hut on the west slope of Hong Kong and was killed, ironically considering the company she kept, in Typhoon Gloria in September of 1957. The bank had collapsed during the rainstorms and much of the shanty town disappeared into the sea.

"Also in that week of my sixteenth birthday," he went on suddenly, "I left home. My excuse was that several of us were needed urgently in Vietnam to protect a 'trade' route from the border of northern Laos to the Gulf of Tonkin. I could speak reasonable Vietnamese and within a month was in the jungles I remembered as a child from my father's tour of duty in Hanoi. For three years I trekked back and forth across that part of South-East Asia, until the Americans came."

He paused, then quite unexpectedly took her hand and

189

kissed it.

"At least, that is the official version. If ever you had cause to look closely at my early years – and I expect you would be as thorough as the CIA – I also want to tell you that, from the beginning, I was playing a very dangerous game."

"From the age of fourteen?" Daphne asked again, desperately concerned why he was telling her these things. All she wanted to do was put her arms around him.

"Going back again to 1956, there was some serious rioting in Kowloon and Tsuen Wan over the annual celebration of the 1911 October Revolution in China. The trouble was stirred for days by triads affiliated to the Kuomintang. The army and police were involved and many of the rioters and other people in the streets were killed. As you know, the Kuomintang were the Nationalists who withdrew either to Formosa or north to Burma when the communists took control of China.

"Anyway, almost all triad activity in Hong Kong ceased over the following year. Thousands of members were arrested or deported and others, including myself carried on with a more normal daily routine.

"Then someone in the 14K had a bright idea about me. Since I was a new boy, not yet initiated, it was decided I should join one of the Nationalist triads for the sole purpose of gathering intelligence and taking away its business. And so I became a member of a rival, the Green Gang. Only when things began stirring again was I also formally initiated into the 14K as I described.

"Things got worse when my treachery, as it became known, was discovered, even though there was a historical link between the two gangs with both of them anti-Communist. The original reasons were forgotten and I had to disappear. At sixteen my best reasoning led me back to the fold of the last remnants of the Kuomintang and drug-trafficking from the Burmese highlands to Thailand. The

14K were not involved in opium or heroin refining in the Golden Triangle there, only in its marketing to the outside world. And I tell you all this, Daphne, because I would not want you to hear it somewhere else first."

Without giving her time to comment he finished by saying he returned to Korea for almost three years before leaving for Japan at the age of 20 to begin formal academic studies. He looked up at her, feeling tired but happier, never having spoken to anyone about those difficult years. She remained silent.

"So there is the story of my escaping the 14K, so I thought. It caught up with me last night. With Williams, too. He was involved in some way with the 14K, probably drugs and possibly as a member.

"I'm alive because of sentimentality from the leader of the Chinese, Huang-lin. He was a mentor and friend from those early days. Williams would not release the maid even though they had me and the argument you heard developed because Huang-lin would not accept this. I can only think he decided Williams was a greater evil than was not carrying out the assassination order against me. Sadly, that probably means his end.

"Put simply, it was a mercy I was not shot dead at dawn, Daphne. Huang-lin lived in the same house as Master Yeung. He was my *si bok*. I learnt many skills from him. Today I was also reminded of compassion. The most important thing now is that I take you home. It's unforgivable I continue exposing you, and friends, to such danger, such evil.

"But, Daphne," he said suddenly, taking hold of her hand again, "all this is only one facet of my life. As a Chinese, French, British and American, is how I've lived. How I should behave is Korean, according to the way of the art I've devoted a large part of my life to. I do have responsibilities on Jin-do, to my students, to an ancient art known there as *Hwarang*. I have failed in my duties there over the years and can no longer ignore it. Whichever way I look at it, I have to return to the Far East and face my past. If I don't, I have no future. All I've done in the last few hours is delay the inevitable."

Daphne stood up and reached for the towel she had laid on the solarium. When she turned again Julian was also standing and she put her arms around his chest. He gasped and she transferred her arm to his waist in an effort to help him up the steps. He was heavy. If he collapsed she would never be able to hold him.

"Would anyone mind if I missed breakfast?" she asked eventually. "I think I really need to sleep."

She was sitting on her bed twenty minutes later, desperately tired. It was with great difficulty she pulled on a pair of jeans, realising then she was supposed to be getting into bed. The situation had hit her hard. It was the worst night she had ever known. She thought Julian had been killed. She had seen dead people. She had heard things she didn't want to hear. Now he was saying this was the end of anything that might have been between them. Her heart was fluttering and she just wanted to sleep. She had tried. She had really tried.

Naked except for the jeans, she lay on her side and felt her eyes closing. The next thing she knew was a quilt being drawn over her and Julian whispering sleep peacefully.

"You're not going out again, are you?" she asked tensely.

Sitting on the edge of the bed full of admiration he caressed her hair, assuring her he was not. Sensing he was looking at her, she opened her eyes. Then, sitting up bare-breasted, she put her arms around him.

"This has been a very hard day for me, Julian," she whispered, "but I want to tell you, I love you. I have never loved anyone so much."

"This is important to me, Daphne," he responded. "I appreciate your caring very much and hope we will know

192

better days."

"And how are you feeling now, young man?" Ferdinand asked. He had invited Julian to his sitting room, saying he preferred not to eat breakfast alone. Julian replied, without putting much thought to the remark, that he was well.

"You must first forgive my under-estimation of the facility the CIA still have in this country, though the *Guarda* say our 'prisoners' in the infirmary insist they are regular army. To clarify the situation regarding this rather lacklustre five-strong squad I am just about to begin legal proceedings against the American embassy in Lisbon for assault, damages and anything else I can think of. This will bring them here in force, by helicopter probably, within the hour. Of more consequence to you Julian, Ann-Marie is my daughter."

Julian was suddenly wide awake.

"The circumstances need no elaborating beyond the fact it was a time of war. What is important is that for the last two years Ann-Marie has been planning a decentralisation of the management of the family business. She has wanted the income and responsibilities divided more fairly between members of the family, fairness being her word. I've stalled on these plans because I have the gravest doubts and let these be known, of course.

"At the same time I know she has been suspicious of who her father really is. She did not approach me directly, when I would have been the ideal person to make the search."

"Are you saying she knows now?"

"On her last visit, five weeks ago, she presented me with an even more complex plan for taking direct control of the business on Maurice's death. In this she was side-stepping his wish that the bulk of its assets and income remain in trust. I could not permit her to force my hand. Under French law, control of the business comes upon my shoulders as I am Maurice's closest relative.

"What is more, Ann-Marie would not even have been second in line. I have been married for some time to Helen. And along with considerations of my family comes the question of your contract with Ann-Marie."

He broke off to let Julian digest what he had said.

"Daphne knew Helen was your wife," Julian commented. "She remarked she is every inch a lady."

"A compliment I shall pass on," the Count said with a smile.

"And Ann-Marie's reaction?"

"She went to pieces," Ferdinand resumed soberly. "It was most distressing to see a hitherto formidable young woman break down. I tried to placate her by saying I was prepared to let the larger part of the fortune remain in trust with access to both families but she would not accept this. For a day the household was under much duress. She departed late in the evening and I heard nothing until I received a note from Maurice's housekeeper at Meaux."

Julian poured more coffee but did not drink it.

"Unfortunately, Julian, this information is not as private as it ought to be. There were others who knew of Ann-Marie's mental instability and who tried hard this weekend to force events in their favour. Both you and I were to be 'removed'."

"And so we come to Williams ..."

"And I have to tell you," Ferdinand went on, "Ann-Marie also had a contractual arrangement with Williams, one drawn up before yours. Not by myself, I must add. She knew Williams from her university days in California. A very interesting legal point it would have been too, had he lived and she inherited."

"Contractual bigamy," Julian muttered. He was stunned.

Ferdinand saw no point in disclosing Ann-Marie had taken two other consorts whose discretion Maurice had secured in exchange for the contracts. He was sure it would only hurt Julian further.

"And on this question of your contract with Ann-Marie," Ferdinand went on, "I believe it is still central to your well-being. It is a truly sad admission of one's daughter that greed is destroying her but this is what is happening. On this day, Helen and I are indebted to you for our lives. Williams may have gone but we three are still in danger and with an element urgency. Maurice is dying of cancer."

It was after ten when they had finished talking. Helen knocked to say the *Guarda's* senior officer had arrived with more men and two ambulances. They were searching the area for two other American military personnel who had left the scene. Ferdinand asked her to show the captain to his study. He wanted an explanation of why, under obvious dire circumstances, only a post of four men commanded by the corporal had been dispatched and why they had tarried until breakfast.

He told Julian their indolence would now be to his advantage. None of his guests, of course, would need to be detained over the matter of several Americans, dead and seriously injured.

Daphne was tired and disorientated when Julian woke her but asked how the maid was. The girl had not stopped crying and been taken home, he said. Daphne felt for her.

Shortly before their departure, Ferdinand walked around the garden with Julian. They were surveying the damage to the castle. It was superficial but Ferdinand was thoughtful about the way in which the impenetrable was penetrated. Those who managed it used techniques centuries old and he was impressed. If it hadn't been for Julian they would have swarmed all over the castle within minutes. He also remembered Daphne's comment, of a mediaeval fortification being a place of both sanctuary and vulnerability.

"Do you know," he said watching Daphne putting bags into the car, "the Braganzas practised the custom of marrying their daughters to their uncles – "

He stopped abruptly.

"Oh, I would be mortified if you thought this an improper suggestion."

"Not at all," Julian replied.

"One understands in those difficult times it would have strengthened the family considerably. But it is, of course, inherently weak. It is surely plainer a union with a positive partner, of a different culture even, when the affinity is a strong one, can be highly beneficial during difficult times ..."

Julian and Daphne arrived in Brussels late that Sunday evening after a protracted return via Faro and Barcelona. Daphne returned to her apartment and her bed, once more exhausted from trying to keep up. Julian went on to Ross's home. Ferdinand had provided two more folders of material implicating Maurice and Ann-Marie and a small segment of the family business having ties with a known international vice and torture ring.

Ross, the Committee, were without his assistance from that moment.

11/2

Brussels, Wednesday 11 September

A week had passed when Julian telephoned Daphne to ask if she would meet him at the restaurant in the Grand Place where they first had lunch together. She should have been in Lille but wanted to see him one last time.

He was waiting in the alcove on the first floor, staring across the square. Although he was almost facing the stairs she knew he had not seen her. It was almost as if he was without defences.

"It is very kind of you to come," he said with disconcerting formality.

"I would have been cross if you hadn't asked me," she replied as cheerfully as she could. There was a lull as a waiter asked if she would like something to drink. Not knowing how long she would be there, she declined.

"Daphne, I will be leaving on Friday," Julian went on without warning. "I shall be flying out to the Far East."

Daphne had known this was coming and was able to retain her composure, until she realised it would be Friday the thirteenth. She put her hand to her face in a desperate attempt at holding back tears. She did have the grace to ask if she could be of help to him, having planned to say this at least. She also managed to say that despite everything, Portugal, the castle, would always be special to her. He put his hand on hers.

"It will be special to us," he responded. "You have been more help than you know and you must not take this decision in a personal sense. A past I wanted to forget has caught up with me. As I said in Portugal, if I don't face it, there is no future."

Daphne put his hand to her cheek and whispered the words, "I shall always be with you."

Julian watched her walk across the Grand Place. Her tears were on his hand and it saddened him greatly. From wherever she came, this young woman with a smile like blossom itself, a face of summer and hair the colour of autumn leaves, she was now gone.

197

TRIAD – PART TWO

CHAPTER TWELVE

Hong Kong, Wednesday 05 March, 1980

Fog was the talking point in the colony at the beginning of March. A container ship had run aground on the eastern approach to the harbour and aircraft had been diverted. Vietnamese refugees, known now around the world as 'boat-people', continued to arrive. More than 68,000 had been allowed in to the colony over the previous year.

Mrs Lee was not concerned with these things as she hurried through the marble halls of the Ocean Centre complex at Tsimshatsui. Two officers of the Royal Hong Kong Police stood aside for the little party, Mrs Lee and her daughter Su-Mai in matching fur coats, bodyguard Fong and driver Max. This was one of the most civilised places in the whole of Asia in which to shop and Mrs Lee was pleased to be back after a winter break in Hawaii.

She had done the rounds with Su-Mai since early that morning looking for a welcome-home present for her son, Teng, who was due to join them from Korea. They visited Lane Crawford in Central and the China Fleet Club in Wanchai, mingling with the diplomats' wives whose leathery faces and acrid smiles Mrs Lee knew well. They lunched at *Yung Kee*, browsed in the Japanese Daimaru store in Causeway Bay and alternated between a clammy cold and the excessive air-conditioning of innumerable boutiques before crossing under the harbour to Kowloon. It was past four o'clock and she did not want to be late for the last ritual of the afternoon, tea at the Peninsula Hotel.

As they squeezed into the Mercedes for their return to the Peak, Mrs Lee looked pensively at the glossy bags and gift-wrapped boxes acquired during the day. A shopping expedition with her soon-teenage daughter was important but she had nothing for her son. She directed Max to take them along Gloucester Road but the traffic was heavy and fog thicker. The neon signs, stacked high, were charging the dank, polluted air with a sickly glare and Mrs Lee decided she would resume in the morning.

More relaxed, she turned her attention to her young daughter idly inspecting the tissue-wrapped contents of one of the bags. Mrs Lee hoped her efforts during the day had cheered Su-Mai up. She was a different girl after her trip to Europe the previous summer and Mrs Lee was grateful for any occasion that might bring the girl out of her depression since her return.

William Lee was in his study in the west wing of the house on the Peak when the Mercedes came in through the gate. He stood by a window between a pair of K'ang Hsi *famille noire* porcelain vases and watched with satisfaction the two Great Danes offer their paws to his daughter. South-west, beyond the lawn and ornamental trees of the garden and almost within touching distance was Lamma Island, though this had been shrouded in fog for days. To the west was the distant bulk of Lantau showing above the mist, brooding beneath a rapidly darkening sky. This was one of the better views in the colony.

A small, greying and hugely energetic man in his sixties, Lee was unusually subdued that afternoon. Immaculately dressed for formal business with a silk handkerchief flowing from his breast pocket, he had been alone for an hour with his thoughts. This was the period of the third moon and the most important meeting of the 14K council. Lee was the *shan chu*, Hong Kong's 489 and therefore head of the triad's

200

world-wide business operations.

Among several problems brought back to the Peak from an early meeting of the council at Tai Tam Bay on the south side of Hong Kong was an assassination order to which he was obliged to apply his seal. This was an unusual second request. After Ma Lok Yu's realisation it was a former Red Pole, Julian de Lyon, who had been the curse of several 14K European cells, Lee had taken a personal interest in events in Europe. With reports of de Lyon's reappearance in Asia he could no longer remain silent over the young man evading his destiny at the hands of their most experienced enforcer.

He told himself recent meetings of the council no longer had the edge, the smell of blood, the taste of the old days. It was in reality a matter of him having the stomach. This order was one he could not sanction without regret.

When Teng wrote home during his winter vacation on Jin-do saying how pleased the monastery was Julian had returned after a long absence, Lee knew clouds were gathering. He had met Julian's mother and helped her return to China in the late 1950s under difficult circumstances. He had watched Julian grow up a member of the brotherhood and for a while flourish under its guidance. Both he and his son had spent time at their beach house as pupils in meditation and martial arts of this gifted young man. Su-Mai had spent part of the previous summer holiday in France and been a guest of Julian's wife in Paris.

An unusually high-ranking gathering of three 489s from around the world and two 432s representing North American branches had attended the morning meeting at Tai Tam Bay. Their relationship with the mainland had been discussed and Lee had been advised that high-level meetings between de Lyon and DEA personnel at the American embassy in Seoul may have repercussions with the triad's negotiations with the Beijing government.

It was because of this a further stay of execution of one

month for Julian de Lyon was grudgingly agreed despite him having twice evaded his destiny in Europe and his imminent and brazen return to Hong Kong.

Lee, acutely aware his authority was being questioned, was again obliged to explain Julian de Lyon's association with son Teng in Korea, beyond the man's long-standing association with the family. Such extraordinary events involving this errant 426 were being tolerated only because of Lee's status as senior *shan chu*. Until the situation with his liaising with the Americans was clarified, de Lyon would be watched twenty-four hours a day.

The ignominy continued with their insistence the family bodyguard, Fong, start immediate duties with his son and report directly to them. Lee's situation was about to become difficult. Julian was flying in to the colony that evening from Seoul. Teng was due in the morning. The three of them would be dining together.

Lee made his mark in red on the document relating to Julian, laid the antique jade chop in its box and locked it away before calling his secretary. It was his wife who walked in. She picked up his desk diary, made an entry in her fine calligraphy and reminded him the entire coming Saturday evening should be given over to Teng's party.

"We must make Julian feel comfortable while he's here," Lee said, gazing through the window. "We see him rarely now."

"Julian de Lyon? Do we know he is coming?"

Mrs Lee looked impassively at her husband watching the evening sky claim Lantau. When asked if their afternoon shopping had been successful she replied in response to the signal it had been tiring but a small penalty for having sufficient for their needs. Her husband was well aware how difficult their daughter had been in recent months and she did not feel it appropriate to concern him further just then.

Lee glanced at his wife as she left the room. It was his

turn to appreciate his wife knowing what was required in all domestic matters with no apparent effort. This woman who wore silks like a mannequin and who was still the sexy teenager he rescued from humiliation in Korea after the Japanese withdrawal. Since she was seventeen years old she had applied her energies to their marriage as if it were a game of chess. Privately and occasionally in front of close friends, he acknowledged her as the stronger player.

12/2
Thursday 06 March

Julian stood at the water's edge behind the Hong Kong Hotel on Tsimshatsui, watching the ferry making its way across the harbour in the darkness and heavy mist. Fog the previous evening caused his flight from Seoul to be diverted to Guangzhou where he had a restless night. He arrived at Kai Tak on the early flight, checked in to his hotel and was waiting casually in the gloom for the Star Ferry to Hong Kong Island for a meeting at the American consulate.

Knowing how dangerous his presence in the colony was, this first visit would be short. He was reasonably sure he had been seen at the airport. Showing his face for one day only was his opening gambit.

He glanced at the first copy of the South China Morning Post he had bought in ten years and binned it before embarking with some tight-faced office workers and a group of schoolgirls at Central. Rickshaws were lined up without their pullers. Though the business district was deserted at six that morning it was not so quiet elsewhere. The older folk were concentrating on their *tai chi* and the younger ones on their jogging. Bars were still open in Wanchai. The market in Western would have been trading for hours.

He felt good about being back, despite the hair on the back of his neck prickling. He liked Hong Kong, its islands and the early morning.

He was shown into a conference room in the consulate building on Garden Road by Larry Peterson who introduced himself as his CIA contact in the colony. There were two others at the meeting, Colonel Jim Andrews from Naval Intelligence and Anthony Wong, a China specialist on the consulate's permanent staff in Hong Kong. Julian remembered Jim Andrews from a brief spell in Manila seven years before in a BNDD operation under Andrews' command.

Peterson apologised for the early hour as the best they could do in view of the short notice of Julian's request from Seoul and said he wanted first to confirm what the Korea station had forwarded.

"Your main interest is the 14K here in Hong Kong and putting pressure on its council to quash a particular activity that's tying up a lot of manpower in Europe. Is this a fair summary?"

Julian said this was correct and that he had long considered a direct hit on the 14K council with a small team was the most likely way of achieving results. He was not talking assassination, rather self-incrimination. He did not want several years' work of many good people in the Brussels office of the Bureau of Social Affairs thrown away through want of a final effort.

"I'm here this morning," he went on, "because I would prefer it to be underpinned by some larger action. Something under the auspices of the American government. The triad will take this seriously and it will give me more leverage."

"But you would go it alone," Anthony Wong suggested grimly. "We are aware the triad's European base is not strong and they could be hurt if a little more sustained effort was put into interrupting their operations. We are talking of formidable organized crime. What makes you so confident of successful infiltration, let alone achieving your goal?"

"That extra effort is not being made, Anthony," Julian replied. "I will go ahead, though not alone and not in any event. I have a team, some very able young Koreans. Most are students of mine with unacceptable political views in Korea who feel they have nothing to lose on a sortie in Hong Kong."

"And you don't worry either about the ethics of using students for something that is clearly a problem with you," the China specialist went on.

"Let me put it another way. There is no guarantee my approach will yield results. But you have something going, I can fit in and we could be of help to each other."

For the next half-hour Julian showed details of his planned operation, its goals and likely repercussions. Blank spaces in his diagrams indicated the need for a safe area in Hong Kong for at least two weeks and information on 14K structure, its council and when and where the council met.

There were seven members by tradition at any one meeting, he said, admitting his information would be well out-of-date. He didn't know if these meetings were by invitation or merely a quorum at which decisions by the Hong Kong *shan chu* were rubber-stamped. The real business might even be done elsewhere. He would find out eventually but time was not on his side because of political tension in Korea and the unresolved issue of a 14K contract against him.

Peterson and his colleagues spent a few moments in close discussion before Peterson said,

"Well, there doesn't seem to be a problem in us working together, Julian. We are concerned about the contract these people have on you but according to Seoul, you have this in hand Your requirements are modest and we are happy to have your expertise along.

"The only change to the summer operation here in the colony since you were briefed has been a one-month postponement to coincide with some new legislation. Jim will tell you about this.

"We certainly have a base from which you can work and any non-military equipment you might need. Some uniformed personnel is also a possibility. A Navy chopper is also available as no-one has yet put in a request for it. A carrier will be in the harbour at the time and they were keen to contribute to the British operation as part of its goodwill visit. All this hangs on whether you can wait until July."

When Julian said the delay was perfect and offer of personnel and *matèriel* generous, Peterson invited Jim Andrews to continue with the briefing.

"The July operation along the Chinese border will be a big one, Julian, involving almost every department of Hong Kong's law enforcement agencies. It will be backed up by units of the Royal Air Force, the Auxiliary Air Force, the Volunteers and Gurkah Signals and Transport. The Royal Navy are involved too, as are mainland Chinese border police. Thirty thousand or so would-be immigrants were stopped last month but at least five thousand made it into Hong Kong.

"The British are particularly interested in 14K and King Yee involvement in bringing in these 'Ils', they call them and are trying to get some new legislation ready by July. This will change the 'leave them alone if they make it to base' policy and stiffen up penalties for those in on the racket.

"Our part in this is one of intelligence-gathering on organised crime in China and will be our biggest effort on the problem to date. It will make a change for us using a British operation as cover," Andrews went on. "As before with the Bureau of Social Affairs, if we can help, so much the better. Your work in Europe, including that on triad infiltration of the military in Germany was appreciated and some liaison with you is in order at this time."

Julian acknowledged their appreciation.

"On your intelligence requirements," he said, "the Immigration Department are keeping track of business people visiting China in recent months. Some of this is known to be triad business and your surveillance input would be useful."

"I say again, the nub of American Intelligence interest at this moment," Anthony Wong went on, "is not the immigration racket, or triads *per se*. Our concern is the stark possibility of the Beijing government colluding with the bigger triads in their absorption of the colony in 1997 and ultimately more devastating, the re-establishing of powerful Hong Kong triads on the mainland. It is actually our most pressing medium-term economic intelligence requirement in the region."

"Thankfully," Julian responded, "my view of the whole thing is relatively innocent."

After agreeing a further meeting the following month, Julian asked if there was anything more they would like to know about him. His requesting a meeting in Hong Kong was without consulate personnel knowing his standing there and Joe Williams would have been well-known. Peterson said the issues between the Bonn Station and Geneva during his time in Europe were resolved and there was a copy of his *CV* somewhere in the building.

Julian proffered his thanks to all three men.

"We owe you one," Peterson replied.

Julian grinned when told of the name of the American operation, Snow White. He had planned his as Operation Seven Dwarfs.

It was still cool and misty when he left the consulate building. The car at the Peak Tram terminus, the first of the day, was emptying of a few Europeans and Chinese in three-piece suits on their way to work and Julian decided on a whim he would ride it back to the top.

As the wooden car creaked its way up the mountain he looked at the extent of new building on the island and on Kowloon peninsula. A construction blight at North Point where he had lived as a teenager was clearly visible, poking up through the thin mist. Nearer, Causeway Bay and Wanchai had edged into the harbour and up the hillside. Central below him had spawned a dense cluster of rectangular blocks. There was virtually nothing left of the mellow white colonial architecture he thought had some style. Urban Hong Kong had taken on the hard edge of glass, steel and fiscal nerve.

At the upper terminus he set out along Middle Road and was heartened that peace still prevailed along the leafy lanes, dappled now by sunlight. The view to Aberdeen and Lamma Island was unchanged except for a crop of tower blocks by the town's power station. He decided he would walk down the old Pok Fu Lam Reservoir Road to Aberdeen. Winding his way down the mountain pleasantly shaded by bamboo and spruce, he knew he was not being followed.

In thick, unspoilt woodland on the side of the mountain he found a knoll overlooking the reservoir. The busy shipping lanes of the East Lamma Channel reminded him this was a place of doing, not of idling. To the north lay the New Territories and mainland China. In front of him were two smaller islands, Hei Ling Chau and Sunshine, with Lantau beyond. To the south beyond Lamma was open sea, except for an occasional rock, all the way to Malaysia, the eastern Philippines and Australia. The mist was clearing. Freighters were moving infinitesimally slowly through the milky green waters in the far distance.

His attention turned to the birds in the trees as he stretched out on a grassy bank and he thought how nice it would be to see a native parrot. This was not to be, for in the quiet and warmth of the mid-morning sunshine he fell asleep.

Early that evening he walked the short distance to the Peninsula Hotel on Tsimshatsui to join an old friend, William Lee and his son for dinner at Gaddi's. Lee was one of the colony's leading business figures and Julian had known him and Mrs Lee, a notable beauty from a Korean family with royal Japanese blood, since he was a young teenager. He had not seen the couple for years and would need to be discreet about seeing their son, Teng, regularly through the winter as his teacher.

Teng, tall and slim, with a slight stoop, square-faced with sparkling eyes and a fashionable cropped haircut was still one of Julian's best martial arts students. He was nearing the end of his academic studies in Korea when Julian had returned to Jin-do from Europe the year before. Teng had kept up his formal meditation and training as best he could and was pleased to be under instruction again from his long-time master.

The Lees had a holiday home on the island, Korea's third largest, off its south-west tip but had not crossed paths with Julian there for a decade. The island and a monastery on its rugged southern coast with views of the Korean archipelago had been Julian's home often since the age of ten. It was certainly his spiritual home.

Over the winter, Teng had been living at the family holiday home and occasionally the monastery, preparing for his second degree exams in business and economics while helping Julian with an unexpected request. This had involved the selection and training of a group of friends for an operation in Hong Kong which, Julian emphasised, would involve conflict with one of its most vicious triads.

Teng had needed little time in which to decide if he could join the team. He wanted to do something exciting before formally joining the family firm at its Hong Kong headquarters. The political situation in Korea was deteriorating and many of his friends had been forced to abandon their degrees, go into hiding, or leave the country.

The team of ten Teng chose had been training with Julian on Jin-do since January, with Teng suffering the six-hour bus journey from Seoul as often as he could during semesters. Julian had got to know them well in the quiet of the countryside and on deserted beaches and saw a group that had been depressed over their various problems with the authorities now charged with a new confidence and purpose. After this mission in Hong Kong, some hoped to return to their studies, while others were planning to see the world, particularly America.

Teng had been concerned about such activity on his parent's doorstep. He was less worried about the danger than the possibility of having to lie to his father and agreed with Julian there must be no mention of politics, Korea or criminal organizations over dinner that evening. Teng felt under pressure enough from his father over which division of the business he would join. Similarly, Julian insisted there was to be no mention of anything they were doing on Jin-do apart from continuing formal instruction and training.

Lee greeted Julian loudly in the restaurant with his customary flamboyance, waving a large silk handkerchief and requesting the immediate presence of the head waiter. Julian responded cheerily to Lee's greeting and said it was beyond doubt, the secret of his youthful looks was Mrs Lee.

A beaming Lee re-introduced his son and said graciously Teng must call half-time should they be found guilty of slipping into more reminiscing of more innocent days than was good for them.

Very much the successful Chinese with regard to food, Lee liked to be seen to be enjoying it. Waiters fussed throughout the meal, addressing him as *tai-gor*, 'big brother', knowing him as the most successful of a line of Cantonese merchants prosperous in Guangzhou and Hong Kong for more than a century. Despite the strange choice of restaurant in a city renowned for its food, Julian also enjoyed the dinner and was pleased he had accepted the invitation.

He had side-stepped Lee's questions on what he was doing in the colony but had been unable to avoid some wrangling. Julian knew father and son as political animals and was warned their differences might show at the table. Lee's affability slipped once with his pointed remark that political disruptives had no place in a world business community.

Teng had the good sense to remain tight-lipped on his first day back in Hong Kong. He might have guessed his father was in contact with a government minister in the Korean capital and been warned his son would be detained if the student situation worsened. In business and politics, his father reigned supreme.

Dinner was rounded off with the appearance of a beaming pastry chef who set about the preparation of a *Bombe Surprise*. This, with an appropriate flourish from the pianist, delighted Lee but caused disdain in his son. Teng inherited the intelligence of both his parents but had his mother's quiet dignity. More than a little irritated by a particularly brash paternal, even parental, ego he was respectful of his father if only because, at the age of twenty-five, he was still living on an allowance.

When the head waiter appeared, asking if the evening was to their liking, Lee pulled several notes from a gold clip in his wallet. He looked at his watch, even though he couldn't see the time without spectacles, tossed his napkin onto the table and expressed his regrets that he and his son were obliged to round off their evening with Japanese clients anxious to sample some Wanchai night life.

He reminded Julian of Teng's party at the weekend at the Peak and asked if he would be able to stay over for one of Mrs Lee's Sunday roast beefs. Julian said he could not refuse.

"Are you comfortable here? Good hotel?"

He didn't wait for a reply. A grinning manager and waiter helped him with his coat.

"But how thoughtless of me. You would surely prefer our apartment on Cheung Chau. It's empty at the moment and I know you're fond of the island. It has everything you need. My son will arrange it."

"Wonderful idea *si fu*," Teng said, almost willing Julian to comply with his father's wish. "I could come over at nine tomorrow morning and pick you up, if this is okay."

12/3

Julian also thought of crossing over to Wanchai that night for a quiet drink in a tea room, rather than in one of the new topless bars. It might have been his age – he was forty now – but he rejected the thought. His priority was with another old friend he heard could be found in Yaumatei.

Shortly after leaving the Lees to their Japanese clients, he emerged from the deserted shopping area beneath his hotel and the adjacent Ocean Centre and wrapped himself against the night air. Looking about him briefly he walked by the seedy tenements of Ferry Street into an altogether bleaker district, that of the typhoon shelter's floating community.

There was little activity in the waterfront warehouses or the market around Temple Street, perhaps because of the chilly night. He had raised his collar to hide his face. Almost immediately on his return to Korea and Hong Kong after years in America and Europe, he realized he was no longer Chinese. He didn't act like one and he wasn't treated like one. The fact he was not a Westerner either did not bother him. He was content that moment with being a tourist.

This part of the Kowloon Peninsula had changed completely since his last visit. The shelter was more claustrophobic, especially in the dark. There were no longer open hillsides around the Laichikok Amusement Park up the coast, only more housing estates and manufacturing centres in what was now New Kowloon. The lights of Kwai Chung's container terminals further on showed it still to be a twenty-four hour operation.

The boats laid out across the shelter were linked in endless rows moving with the rhythm of the harbour waters. This floating community also demonstrated unity in its noise. There was a hum of generators and hissing oil lamps lighting card and *mah-jong* games. Radios and television sets played, channels cutting across each other. People could be heard in anguish, in laughter and in love in the mist. There was some movement of smaller sampans and junks around the shadows of bigger craft. It was not yet nine o'clock.

Julian offered \$20 then settled for an exorbitant \$50 for a ride through the shelter. The boat chugged through the darkness and filthy water past creaking wooden craft looming high above him. Three times the man called out for the Yeungs Julian was seeking before delivering him to the correct junk.

Yeung the younger, known as Tan, Julian recognised instantly. Now in his forties with lines on his face that come from making a living at sea, Tan was leaning over a deck rail with a beer can in his hand.

When Julian appeared beneath him Tan stood upright in surprise. Hardly believing who it was coming out of the mist, he shouted excitedly to his wife and others in the adjacent junk an old friend had come to visit. An old friend of many years. When he jogged his wife's memory she did remember Julian at Tan's parents' house on Cheung Chau before she and Tan were married.

As soon as he was aboard, Julian asked Tan of his mother. He was shown into living quarters smelling of fish, food, lamp oil and stale cigarette smoke. Countering this was the aroma of jasmine tea and sharper smell of incense. Sitting in a rocking chair and lit by the glare of a television set, a frail old woman looked up at Julian.

"It's thirteen years since you visited us," she said smiling, recognising him immediately. She accepted his gift and went on, "You bring memories of happier days with you."

This was a hospitable family, Julian recalled, when Master Yeung ran the school where Julian learned much of his fighting skills.

His protestations he had already eaten well were ignored. Tan decided they would also make a party of his visit. With a clap of his hands he raised the cushioned seats of two chests that were evidently someone's bed and showed Julian his immediate store of refreshment. He didn't fish any more, he said. He and his brothers ran beer and spirits sampans. His wife and other members of the family looked after customers who came to the junk and he could not remember when he had last taken it out of the shelter fishing.

By midnight, Julian could hardly remember what town he was in. Neither was he sure if it was himself laughing so heartily with old friends.

Peterson was also burning the midnight oil in his apartment in Bowen Road close to the Peak Tramway stop. It was a leafy part of the lower slopes with a view over Central, Wanchai and across to Kowloon that was pleasant enough to make him feel his Hong Kong posting was not a bad one. After meeting Julian that morning he looked through the man's 'CV'. Brussels told him the previous Fall they expected him to surface in Hong Kong. This was shortly before Julian resigned his employment and left Europe and the Williams story broke.

Peterson had worked with Joe in the China Department in Army Intelligence and thought he knew him well. The exposure of Joe's criminal connections, his colluding with the Communists and triad supplying heroin to the armed forces had shaken the whole Far East department. As of that morning Peterson was gratified his office might make amends to Julian for harassment by his European intelligence colleagues.

Before leaving his office for the day he asked the librarian's help on the martial art referred to in Julian's file. The book she came up with suggested a commitment quite different from early morning *tai chi* and the more specialised *kung fu* classes some of his colleagues went down to Causeway Bay for. Julian's concern over the triad's operations in Europe were obvious. The reasons compelling him to such action were puzzling.

Korean *Hwarangdo*, Peterson read, was a military art almost two thousand years old. For 1,300 years it was practised by the elite guard of the nobility, these *Hwarang do* being from noble families themselves. The physical prowess of the young men, along with their cultured manner and the strict ethical code by which they lived meant they were feared and respected by warriors across Asia. They were known never to retreat in the face of the enemy, or take life without cause.

With dynastic changes in Korea in the Fourteenth Century, the art survived in remote monasteries. It came through the Japanese occupation of the peninsula in the first half of the Twentieth Century, despite all such arts and practices being banned and was seen outside the temple in the 1960s for the first time in 500 years. One branch of the art had established itself in America and copyrighted the name but this was not where Julian's affiliations lay.

The power of this ancient martial art, Peterson learned, was divided into outer, inner, mental and weapons, *we gong*, *ne gong*, *shin gong* and *moo gi gong*. The outer was about physical combat. The inner formalised breath control and the harnessing of *chi* energy. About this, the book said, masters attained skills ranging from healing by touch to killing by the same.

215

The six mental power techniques Peterson found most interesting. These drew on *chi* and the power generated by others. They included *gun shin pup*, the equivalent of Japanese *ninjutsu* concealment and deception, and *cheum yan sul* that could induce sleep. Training in weaponry gave masters the ability to use whatever was to hand as the situation required.

An essential part of the ethos of *Hwarangdo* and how they conducted themselves was showing courtesy, kindness, a sense of justice and filial duty. Also expected by tradition was accomplishment in archery, horsemanship, music and good manners among other things. Medical and healing skills to balance the injury they could inflict were also important and included *yak bang bop*, the use of herbs as medicine, and *chi ap sool*, a knowledge of acupressure.

Peterson was absorbed by what he read and well aware it was a special type of person who was a master of this venerable art, this late in the Twentieth Century. One description of *Hwarang* was 'the way of the flowering knight'. It was a code followed by the *Hwarang do* comparable with, but pre-dating the *Bushido* of the Samurai warrior and chivalry of the knights of feudal Europe.

"Must be some guy," Peterson muttered, when he saw it was time he got to bed.

Julian was woken by Tan's wife placing a bowl of noodles and some tea by his bunk. She told him it was after eight and his escort was waiting. His head was not functioning well. Only when she returned to customers on the deck beyond the canvas flap did he think to pull a sheet over himself with more modesty.

He propped himself up on one elbow, shielded his eyes from the glare of the morning and caught the scent of cheap perfume from a young woman sitting in the chair Madame Yeung had occupied during the evening. With bright red shoes, short leather skirt, skimpy top and red lips this youngster was at the wrong end of the day.

The girl introduced herself as cousin Millie and said she would take him across the harbour when he was ready.

Julian looked at his watch.

"Don't worry," the girl said. "Tan left a message at your hotel this morning for your friend. He will be at the Outlying Islands Pier at Central at nine."

Julian got out of the bunk holding the sheet around him with one hand and his head with the other.

"Great night, eh!"

The living area had been tidied but there was still evidence of some hard drinking. Julian remembered he and Tan taking on a bottle of cognac each for starters and was embarrassed when he realised the young woman, now smoking, was gazing not at the empty bottles and cans but at him. Millie with the red lips would wait outside.

Twenty minutes later he stepped gingerly off a slippery wooden ladder into a sampan, having all but forgotten the small ones were as reassuring as dustbin lids on open water. Millie rolled back the canvas canopy and tied it neatly against its arched metal frame. She buttoned up her padded cotton *mien lap* against the morning mist, pushed off from the junk and started the motor.

Julian waved weakly at Tan's wife but out of the shelter all confidence left him, not least because the water was deep. Millie was unconcerned about riding across the harbour in sling-backs and mini-skirt. No doubt brought up on the water, she handled the little craft well both times they were pitched over the wake of large vessels passing too close for comfort.

Only with the sanctuary of high-rise Central visible through the mist after some fifteen minutes of open water, floating garbage and a heavy swell did Julian feel the trip might have been worth it for the fresh air.

His thanks for the lift and offer of money brought a lusty

smile from Millie.

"Free for family," she replied in broken English. "Look me up any time ..."

Julian gave her the money anyway and said her invitation had made his day.

Teng was waiting anxiously at the pier in his car.

"*Si fu* ... you were not at your hotel ... are we not crossing to Cheung Chau?" he began, surprised at Julian's appearance from an unexpected quarter, without luggage. Too polite to say anything, the question 'master in a one-girl sampan?' was all over his face.

Missing the implication Julian replied absently he could handle a ferry trip after his excursion across the harbour and changed the subject to the young man's car.

"I haven't driven her for months," Teng said brightening up. "I have a place for her in the underground car park on Connaught Road. The ferry will wait while I park."

He took his bag off the boot rack, left it at Julian's feet and joined the traffic on the main road. Heads turned as they always did at the white XK120 Roadster with single personal number.

Julian looked around him, took the bag on board the ferry and found a place on the outside deck from where he could see the gangway. Messages at hotel desks, a classic Jaguar and sampan across the harbour were so obvious even the simplest lookout could not have missed him. Announcing his presence in the colony was one thing, flaunting it another.

A handful of tourists came aboard followed finally by a breathless Teng. He found Julian and went into the saloon for two cups of stewed, scalding tea with condensed milk. Julian had forgotten this particular treatment of tea but did not find it unpalatable. Teng said he was sorry about the difficult dinner. He and his father would surely see eye-to-eye on politics one day, he said grinning.

He ventured to ask if Julian had a good night. His wits sharpening with continued sea air in his face, Julian came straight to the point of their improvised meeting on the ferry.

"I was with an old friend in Kowloon, having a quiet drink. The 14K will know of my presence now and if we get through the next hour without confrontation the quiet drink was a risk worth taking," Julian said with a glimmer of a smile. "This means secrecy over this operation is ever more vital. As we agreed, no friends, girlfriends and above all no family involvement. Neither can we make contact after this ferry ride in the way we planned. You are clear on all this?"

Teng said he was and asked Julian if he would be staying at all on Cheung Chau.

"No. We are doing a round trip and I shall be leaving. This is our first briefing."

Teng nodded again and asked if he had achieved what he wanted at the American consulate.

"Everything and a little more," Julian replied. "There are some minor changes we'll talk about when I return with the team."

It was almost a year earlier in the South of France, at the beginning of a summer vacation, he brought misfortune on his nephew and his nephew's girlfriend. He was mindful the affair in Hong Kong would be altogether more bloody. He told Teng he would take over all the arrangements on returning to Seoul. Teng understood. It would be unwise for him to try and return secretly to Korea. With the authorities' continuing disregard for democratic rights, of the opposition leader Kim Dae Jung in particular, many of the team knew they were marked men.

"It would be doubly difficult, *si fu*, as Dad dropped on me this morning he wants Fong, our bodyguard, to accompany me around Hong Kong all the time I'm here. I

219

don't know where he gets these ideas. I didn't have time to argue. I'm afraid I left Fong at the gate."

"Whatever your father's reasons you should go along with him for the moment. He could be right about the protection. Regard Fong as your saviour, excuse, alibi, anything. You must have a social life to catch up on. You talked at length about Cecilia over the winter!"

"I suppose when you start sounding like Dad," Teng muttered, "there must be something in it."

"A compliment, I'm sure." Julian replied.

Teng studied the shoreline around the west end of Hong Kong. The sky was overcast but the mist was clearing and it promised to be a warm day. Half of the team in Korea were friends he had grown up with. All of them were fighters, three of them formidable and all were interested in broadening their horizons. Several were activists, their most seasoned campaigner being a veteran of the demonstrations of the previous year when eleven students were killed in the streets of Seoul. Most of the team had foregone their education and probably their careers as a consequence of their political stand.

Student trouble had come to a head again that week in Seoul. The army was in the streets and his master was probably right about the possibility of team members being arrested on sight in the capital. It was just as well he had means and there were places on Jin-do where they could hide, including, at a push, the seaside villa. Although the Myeongnyang Strait separating the island was narrow, the boat negotiates treacherous currents and a whirlpool. It gave the illusion of sanctuary from the mainland. Here, in a more optimistic moment over the winter, they had warmed to the idea they were like the characters in one of their favourite movies, The Dirty Dozen.

The ferry edged its way into the harbour on the isthmus linking the north and south parts of Cheung Chau. Sampans bobbed, barefooted women seated in them fishing, some carrying babies on their backs. Traders on the narrow quay with baskets of seafood were busy with vigorous verbal exchanges with Chinese wives. Julian and Teng watched quietly as a handful of tourists boarded and disembarked.

"Remember too, Teng, when I'm back here with the gang," Julian said as the ferry set off for Silver Mine Bay on Lantau before its return to Hong Kong, "attention drawn to us could be fatal."

Teng apologised for the highly public pick-up. He asked thoughtfully if Julian was not worried at having to look over his shoulder because there might be triad behind him.

"No it doesn't, young friend. You make sure it is the *tong* looking over its shoulder, worried about you. Treat this next couple of months as an introduction to something you may have to face in your business."

Julian was unable and at that moment unwilling to tell Teng of what he had learned during the night about his father being a senior triad boss. If he was the 14K's most senior member, then he controlled its operations world-wide. It was something he needed urgent and absolute proof of before he decided how far the operation could go with Teng and Teng's friends.

When Julian mentioned he had dined with Lee and his son, Tan asked, "William Lee, the tycoon? The one who waves the handkerchief about, the one with the twitching eye?"

He asked Julian if he was serious, being seen with a 14K *gong wu daai lou*, then showing his face in the shelter. At least he was reassured about Tan when Teng said no message was left at the hotel desk. A stranger stepped in front of him in the foyer, delivered the message without making eye contact and walked away.

Julian didn't need reminding of the friction between Tan's brotherhood and the 14K. Seeking support against the 14K was one of the reasons he had made the visit. Perhaps the alcohol had dulled his senses on learning of Teng's father's pact with the Devil. Then, perhaps he was not so surprised. Tan said with even more urgency on breaking the seal of a final bottle that morning, he would need help. A major feud was developing between their two gangs over the immigration racket. More bloody fighting was expected.

The last words Julian remembered before opening his eyes to Millie were if there was to be a triad feud, why not turn it to his advantage?

As the ferry moved gracefully alongside the Outlying Islands Pier, completing its first round-trip of the day, Julian asked Teng to thank his father for the offer of the apartment. He also offered his regrets at missing the weekend party. By lunch-time and little more than twenty-four hours after flying in to Hong Kong he was on his way out again.

12/4
Monday 10 March

The weekend passed and an urgent meeting of enforcers of a Hong Kong 14K cell was called in the basement area of an apartment block in North Point. Six young men were standing in line heads bowed, their arms by their sides before a women in her early thirties. Twenty or so 49s and several other enforcers of the same cell watched grimly the humiliation their brothers were enduring at their failure in tracking a contract into, around and out of Hong Kong.

The woman's voice rose to screaming pitch at each youth in turn. After delivering her invective she administered a single blow to each from behind. Because the woman was slight in build the baseball bat she was holding looked both heavier and longer in her slender hands. She took her time before swinging it to bring the point home to everyone present.

One of the six youths in a grubby white cap and apron from the restaurant from which he was summoned collapsed howling from the blow he received on the side of his knee. There was a second loud crack as the woman hit him again for his inappropriate response. He received the broken elbow in silence except for a gurgling in his throat.

The woman was the cell's senior 426, Jenny Lo. Their contract was Julian de Lyon and they had been notified of his arrival in Hong Kong and chosen hotel. He was followed to the American consulate but evaded them the rest of the day until his arrival at the restaurant on the top floor of the Peninsula Hotel. He vanished again, though it might have been him at Kai Tak. Her seniors were furious. Jenny Lo's frustration at being grounded in Hong Kong because of her failure on the same contract in Europe nine months earlier was also plain to see.

Information 432, the Straw Sandal, had not passed to Jenny Lo at dawn was that their target had returned to Seoul and probably Jin-do by bus and boat. The problem was now a different one, the isolation and mountainous terrain of this island and Straw Sandal decided a specialist was needed to complete the contract on de Lyon's return.

A coded radio-telegram had gone out to an ordinary seaman on a cargo vessel in the East China Sea on its way to Nagoya in Japan. On the vessel's arrival in the middle of that week the man would contact Hong Kong for further instructions. This seaman was one of their best enforcers, a man who had never failed on a contract. Coincidentally, he and Julian de Lyon had known each other from the earliest days.

CHAPTER THIRTEEN

Hong Kong, Friday 04 July

Three months after a brief private Easter visit to the colony, Julian returned. Travelling on the same aircraft in the guise of a table tennis team were his chosen Koreans. It was a good deal hotter in Hong Kong than in Seoul and approved of heartily by all ten young men outside the arrivals building. They were met in glaring sunshine by three American embassy staff, two of the men's wives and two teenage boys. The boys helped load the team's kit into a mini-bus and two private cars.

Julian remained separate and was met in a secure area by Peterson's wife, Gillian. She had a similar position to her husband in the Far Eastern Intelligence office at the consulate and Julian had met her there in April. She could see the team through one-way glass and was impressed with their ping-pong look.

"I bet they play!"

"Like a national team, if they had to," Julian replied in response to her cheery demeanour. The contrast could not have been greater between Americans, who are particularly friendly, and Hong Kong people who are not.

"We take our Independence Day holiday seriously wherever we are," Mrs Peterson said as they left the airport's service area in her car, "and thought this meeting and greeting was plausible. They will certainly be well-fed tonight!"

"An auspicious start for them!"

She asked where he would like to be dropped, needing to refer to her map for the best way across Kowloon to the Castle Peak Road. She didn't ask why he wanted to be taken to the far side of the New Territories.

"We were concerned about absorbing your team," she said easing the big car through heavy morning traffic around the industrial estates and factories of Sanpokong, "but staff response was generous. Hosting is as needed, since the facility is not quite ready. By tomorrow evening, hopefully, supplies will have been air-lifted to the compound and the boys will be taken to Lantau individually.

"There is indecision over your accommodation, Julian. We thought you might have made your own arrangements."

"You are very kind and absolutely right," Julian replied. "I'd like to go straight to the facility, ready or not, later this afternoon."

Their base was an unmanned radar facility on a bleak hill top at the south-west end of Lantau Island. Mrs Peterson said someone would be there all that day with keys for the disused compound and buildings adjacent. Two maintenance engineers made Monday morning visits to the part that was operational and could be there all morning. They were Ghurka Signals people.

"It's still all go for Snow White on the twenty-second?"

"It certainly is. I guess with the political troubles breaking, Seoul didn't get the message to you yesterday?"

We were in a hurry to get away," Julian replied.

"I can confirm there will be a full 14K council meeting on the twenty-second at the villa over Tai Tam Bay. So far there's no reason why it should not be at six in the morning like the last three. The main British anti-illegal immigration operation in the New Territories has been put forward one hour to coincide with your six o'clock rendezvous at Tai Tam. They were not well-suited to an hour's delay in their

226

round-up operation but appreciated you not wanting their activity frightening off any Big Guys."

After passing the container terminal and new town of Tsuen Wan, Mrs Peterson pulled off the old Castle Peak Road. The fields around them were deserted except for a few animals. The hills rose steeply inland, the coastal highway was just visible a couple of kilometres away. She kept the engine and air-conditioning running.

"With the information you passed to us two months ago," she said pulling out some notes, "we are sure we now have the names of seven probable members of the council in this list of candidates. Seven ticked and four with question marks. The Hong Kong 489, and therefore top man, we believe, is William Lee. The CIA wanted to know why he often has more guards around him than the President! He's also backwards and forwards to Beijing."

She showed Julian the details of the eleven names, the list reading like a Who's Who of eminent Chinese in the colony. Here was confirmation from American Intelligence that cast serious doubt about Teng and even the team taking part in the operation.

"Any problems here?" she asked.

"William Lee, Mrs Peterson. Ironically, an old family friend and one-time esteemed pupil."

"Please call me Gillian," she said searching for the latest on Lee. She pondered the ramifications of discovering a personal friend to be a triad boss then decided Julian was adult enough to sort it.

"Yes, here it is. A 'black and white' named Ah-Lien was placed in the Lee mansion two weeks ago, an address on the Peak you must know, as a replacement for a servant in China for a bereavement. Contact is made at Aberdeen market. Nothing reported except the Lees are big buyers. The woman is brought down to the market every day by the driver. She was concerned only that Lee is paying her too much attention."

"Quite a feat," Julian remarked. Black and whites are a powerful servant class and a particularly difficult sisterhood to infiltrate. His thoughts returned to Tan's warning of how dangerous the Lees were to him. He had cautioned that whatever it was Julian was up to in Hong Kong, the son should not be involved.

"That's it for the moment," Mrs Peterson concluded. "It'll be Larry coming over to the island at the weekend to check you have everything you need. I'm afraid I can't get along with small boats."

Julian said he knew what she meant. He looked at the time and decided for the last part of his journey to Tuen Mun he would catch the bus they had overtaken. Mrs Peterson did not look surprised. The family car could not be described as discreet.

"Normally, I would ask visitors to drop by, Julian," she began, as he stepped out into the midday heat.

"I know," Julian responded, "but bad news travels fast!"

Peterson's wife burst out laughing. She wished him good luck on his operation if they didn't meet again.

Late the following afternoon almost the entire team of Koreans were assembled in the mess hut of the disused military compound on the hill top on Lantau. The only person missing from the team was Teng. He sent his apologies to Julian via Kim and Kim's younger brother Kim Pyong who had stayed the night with a nearby family on the Peak.

The view of a deep green sea dotted with islands was compensation for the compound's brick buildings with their steel windows and wired glass. There were three of these blocks; a dormitory, wash-house and Nissen hut containing stores and mess area. A covered area for vehicles formed a small yard sheltered from South-Westerlies. The stores were piled high with an assortment of foodstuffs evidently got together at speed. They had been air-lifted from Sek Kong airfield by the Royal Air Force and were mostly American branded goods. The adjacent radar site was newer and automatic and visited weekly for a maintenance inspection.

The grassy slope fell away in three directions to the sea. There was a welcome breeze coming up from the sea. The team agreed it was a fine spot but its exposure meant they should have contingency defence plans. Rosters for watch, mess and cleaning had been worked out in Korea and begun on arrival. Julian was finalising security arrangements that included a dawn reconnaissance of that end of the island. Fine weather on a Sunday morning meant plenty of pleasure craft, one of which would be bringing visitors.

By the time they had finished eating that evening, Julian had heard a range of good-natured complaints, from the steepness of the hillside to the exceptionally hot weather. He knew the ten-strong team well after nine months of intense physical and mental activity, albeit on a part-time basis for some because of their studies.

Kim and Kim Pyong were student activists in their late twenties. They had been the first to journey to Jin-do with Teng in November, looking for a refuge from the authorities. They were the eldest members of the team and had been voted lieutenants in Teng's absence. The ebullient So Song-san had courted similar trouble with the Korean military and had no desire to return to his home country. Similarly, his friend Bill had adopted what he thought was a good American name ready for the day he would be joining cousins in California.

Kim, Teng and 23-year old Ah Yong were formidable fighters. Ah Yong particularly, Julian considered to be a worthy opponent who could, if he wanted, achieve the highest physical prowess. Completing the team were Ah Kwan, Li-an and the unrelated Kwan I and Kwan II.

Later while kicking a ball around idly outside the compound by the light of the mess hut, several of the team saw Julian coming and fell in line. Each bowed graciously addressing him 'master', thanking him for the chance to do something useful. Julian said he didn't want to hear this again. As it would soon be the end of several year's work for him he had brought out a case of Colt 45, thoughtfully provided by the Americans. It was warm but accepted enthusiastically.

Sunday 06 July

The following morning at seven, it was clear to Kim Pyong and Song-san the pleasure junk they were watching from the old fort above Fan Lau would land. Song-san made his way down to the cove where Julian and most of the rest of the group were exercising. Bill and Ah Yong were dispatched to follow the two Westerners making their way up the hillside from the jetty.

The radar station was not visible from some distance out to sea but the two men, dressed in lightweight zip jackets with peaked caps knew where they were going. They had landed on the bleak and rocky southern tip of Lantau and were not comfortable with the long, steep climb. Although Julian knew it was Peterson and a colleague, he left Song-san and two others below and led the rest of the group back up to the compound to meet them. An impromptu game of volleyball began in the weedy, rutted yard while they waited.

"Sorry to come in on you unawares," Peterson said breathing hard. "We couldn't resist a trip out today with the sea as calm as this."

"It must be for your wife to be on board," Julian replied, grinning. "And just as well you didn't try bringing one of the Aberdeen Boat Club's new junks off either beach north of Fan Lau. The currents are tricky."

"We thought we could slip in as weekend admirals, rather

than thunder across in one of the Navy's power boats. I see you're on the ball."

Peterson introduced his shipmate, Al. They watched the group for a moment and commented they looked a good bunch, like acrobats. When they had drunk the bottled water Kim offered, they looked around briefly and said the neatness of kit bags and bed rolls would have been a credit to the Navy.

Peterson asked Julian if he could come down to the boat to look over some paperwork. He warned him the kids were anxious for a picnic on the remotest lump of rock of the nearby Soko Islands and he might be kidnapped for a short while if they had to sail over and drop them ashore.

Julian said hello to Gillian, Alan's wife and three children. The children were dressed as pirates and looking for adventure.

"You see I can brave the High Seas, Julian," Peterson's wife began, "when I can see my reflection!"

Al took over the wheel and turned the craft towards their destination, visible on a crinkly horizon. Peterson took Julian below.

"It is definite, Julian. A full gathering of 14K mandarins on the twenty-second. There have been meetings between individuals on the list which could be regular business."

"Do we know how many will meet?"

"That's a tough one – does any corporation know these days, with global offices, flight cancellations and the rest?"

Julian was thoughtful for a moment. The more at the meeting the better. This was damning evidence. Without it, members might survive.

"And your final requests?"

"We don't need much, Larry," Julian said soberly. "A small oil tanker, or water carrier. It must be full of kerosene or a mixture of petrol and oil. A couple of detonators and timers. Two power boats crewed and three, or better, four ordinary-looking cars."

"A big bang and good blaze!"

"With plenty of smoke."

"We have a few more details here on the candidates, including Lee," Peterson said. "Arrest warrants will be prepared for all of them, just in case. And here are the three US visas you asked for."

Julian nodded his thanks and scanned the information on Lee. There was nothing new from the 'black and white'.

"If the chopper is still available I'd like to drop in on Lee, at 05.00, I thought, before he leaves for Tai Tam. It will be less dangerous getting him out of bed than getting in to a slanging match at the villa when he's surrounded by guards. He could also be a bargaining tool."

"You mean drop the chopper in his back garden in darkness?"

"I've been up there with a tape measure," Julian replied without smiling.

"You don't need to catch him seated at a table with triad business in his hand?"

Julian said there looked to be enough against him.

"You will need muscle then, with due respect to your boys. I'll arrange a unit that, hopefully, will not need to fire a shot at the Lee mansion, though, as you say, the bodyguard lives in and some of his guards could be on their round at the time."

"I'm grateful for the use of the helicopter and back-up on that first stage," Julian said looking again at the photographs in the Lee file. There were several good close-ups of the family, without Teng, taken at a civic function earlier in the year.

"Pretty girl," said Peterson, seeing Julian's interest in the Lee daughter.

"Described only this week as in training as an appendage for some wealthy Chinese male," Julian replied without

232

smiling.

"Sounds like a good idea to me," Peterson muttered with a grin. "We have one back home who is sure hard to handle."

"Mrs Lee should know better," Julian responded.

"I'm sure she knows best, in this part of the world," countered Peterson's wife who appeared with a tray of drinks.

There were two visitors at the camp after the Americans. Sagumi, whom Julian had known as a teenager at the monastery on Jin-do and from whom he learnt much of his Japanese, arrived the following afternoon. Sagumi owned a health and leisure complex in Tokyo and it was years since they had last met. He had promised himself some time away from his family and business that summer and Julian's request for assistance came at a good time.

He spent Sunday night in comfort at the Peninsula Hotel and was met after lunch by two of the team at Tuen Mun in the New Territories. Already charmed by the small ferry that hops along Lantau's north coast, the Japanese was delighted by the dwellings on stilts over the creek at Tai O. Such sights have all but passed into history in Japan, he said.

The three of them set off under the ferocious afternoon sun along the coastal path towards Fan Lau with Sagumi insisting on carrying his heavy bag. After five kilometres of walking and running and a straight climb up the bare hillside to the camp, he was exhausted. Pleased to see Julian, he confessed immediately his condition was not what it should be.

He spent the next two nights on the dormitory floor. A gentler fifteen-kilometre run around the west end of the island before dawn, breakfast on the beach and football and volleyball were also to his liking.

He had a long discussion with Julian on his third night and said his summer of reflection was clearly a romantic notion and he must return home. It was a sad realisation he had become too much like his clients. He was positive however, about introducing a new regime at his complex for those who thought they could handle it. He would name it Camp Lantau. He had fallen in love with the island and made everyone laugh with his plans to tow it back with him and anchor it off Tokyo.

Of the entire group, he said he would welcome them as his sons should they honour him with a visit. Much liked, especially because he tried hard with his few words of Korean, he was given a good send-off from the compound before being escorted quietly back to Silver Mine Bay for the early ferry to Central.

Julian's second visitor was a former colleague, Eric Chan, to whom Julian had written from Korea. They had not met since working together as narcotics agents in the Philippines. Eric, who was also part-Chinese, arrived in a squall looking thread-bare and tired. It was only after several beers on his first night, with rain and wind howling around the camp, he admitted he had welcomed the opportunity of coming across the Pacific to mull over marital problems.

His week on Lantau with several young men working hard at re-organising their start in life made Eric ashamed of the self-pity he was wallowing in over his divorce. He realised he had to return to America and pick up the pieces of his own life.

As an under-cover agent Eric was highly professional. He had considerable all-round skills and Julian and the team learnt much about the commercial teaching of *kung fu* in America. At how styles were pared down with extreme efficiency so they could be learned relatively quickly.

Eric in turn was fascinated by the discipline of the young men in the camp that showed the dignity, the real teaching of the fighting arts, was not lost. Many of his students back home, he admitted, suffered from an attitude problem which he called simply 'being American'.

Of Julian's ability and fighting style Eric remained reverent, regarding him as a latter-day warrior. He did not mince his words on the dangers of taking on a triad with such meagre resources but paid Julian the compliment the world would suffer a great loss if he miscalculated. Julian would have been happy working again with Eric. This was not to be and he paid Eric's return fare to Los Angeles.

Willy's arrival on Lantau on the day Eric left was unexpected. Julian and half the group were returning from a trek around Lantau Peak under a brilliant blue sky. Having heard the old bus stop briefly at the monastery turn-off after straining around the reservoir, they waited. Julian recognised immediately the rolling gait of the lone figure on the hillside even after twenty years. His destination was the radar installation.

Willy Djan Tong was a merchant seaman, the classic hard-drinking barrel-chested seaman. Willy himself did not know his exact parentage but thought it was Malay-Chinese. He did not know his true age either but admitted to being older than Julian.

"Well, I'll be ..." he began, confronted by a group appearing from nowhere.

He dropped his kit-bag on a rock, heard the half-bottle of whisky break and was forced into an immediate defensive posture by Julian's crouching tiger stance. He began to chuckle. His faded T-shirt expanded, his biceps bulged. One forearm was tattooed with an anchor and the Chinese sailor's equivalent of 'Mother', the other with the name of a long-forgotten sweetheart.

Willy was an expert in an Indonesian style Julian had long ago teased was one that could scratch the boys' eyes out. Willy had never forgiven him. At first he didn't believe his old friend would embarrass himself in front of several youngsters, though he looked good, as though he could handle a fight. They circled each other on the grass then Julian clapped his hands and went to embrace Willy. Though Willy had an answer to this ploy Julian was quicker. His forearm brushed Willy's neck and the Malay-Chinese staggered for several seconds as though drunk. There was a murmur from the group who had moved a respectful distance away on the grassy slope.

"I was going to ask how that Korean mumbo-jumbo of yours was coming," Willy said when he came to, rubbing the back of his neck, "but you're in good form!"

"Easy, when ageing friend becomes soft and heavy."

Willy would not normally have tolerated such a comment but remembering what had just happened he began chuckling again.

"I have time off, Julian," he said retrieving his bag. "Tell me what you're doing, introduce me to the guys. Is there something going on down here you can use an old war-horse for?"

An hour before sundown, while food was being prepared, Julian went out alone with Willy. They ran along the grass-covered cliff top then took the steep path by the old fort down to Fan Lau. Before reaching the fishermen's huts they turned north and made their own way over the rocks at the water's edge. Picking up the unmade road to the main road they went on up to the reservoir. Here in the heat and humidity of late afternoon, Willy called for a rest.

"I could do with a cold beer," he said sitting heavily on a rock. "On second thoughts looking at you, Old Mate, it should be a rye."

After slapping Willy on the shoulder, Julian moved a short distance away. When he spoke, Willy knew the pleasantries were over.

"What are you doing here, Willy?"

236

Willy, easing muscles in his legs not used for a while, did not answer.

"Willy ..." Julian prompted.

"Oh, things I just heard, Old Mate," he began quietly, keeping Julian in his peripheral vision. "You know how news travels around the Seamen's Missions. I was in Shanghai last week having a beer in the *He Ping* opposite the Mission there, when a Brit and a feisty American girl sat at the next table. Most unusual to see Westerners, so I joined them and we got talking. They had come all the way up from Hong Kong and said some half-Chinese with a French name was doing something extraordinary. The next day I heard a couple of other things, dangerous things about taking on triads – "

He detected Julian moving closer to him and went on cautiously,

" – and decided to see if it was you."

The sky was darkening rapidly, the sea behind Julian was turning black. His impatience was clear.

"And they know you're here, Old Chum. If you swim across the bay to Ping Chau, they know. They're not the simple street gangs you and I were weaned on. You're still 'the Lion' here, even after twenty-odd years."

Julian backed away and Willy stood up slowly.

"And if a couple of deck-hands in my, er, union are talking, then the rest of them must be very worried you're back in the colony with these kids and some powerful friends, because maybe you're after something of theirs ..."

"... So I ask you once more, Willy boy," Julian interrupted, "what are you doing here?"

Willy began chuckling again, at having put himself on the spot. He repeated he was offering his services. He also said he was giving the advice of someone a bit older and a bit wiser. Julian sat on a rock again and so did Willy. They were both silent for a moment until Willy asked if Julian was serious about the team.

"They are a decoy, Willy," Julian began, knowing at that moment the operation had reached maturity before even starting. "But don't think you won't be feeling your age after a few days with them."

"The odds are not in your favour on this one, Boss. And I'm a bit worried about it."

"So, I'll tell you what," Julian began quietly, "I'll think on it and we'll talk some more. In the meantime *daai lou*, I shall treat you as an old guest ..."

Julian crossed to Aberdeen before dawn charging Kim with looking after the day's activities and introducing Willy to the routine. Huge changes had taken place in the colony in ten years and Julian had a lot to catch up on. A forecast storm developed with vengeance during the day and he was forced to disembark on Cheung Chau with other passengers on his return late in the afternoon. The ferry skipper wouldn't risk calling at Silver Mine Bay. Julian and two other Europeans had no choice but to negotiate a junk to take them across to Chi Ma Wan, the nearest point on Lantau.

He could have done without the last fifteen minutes of wind and sea kicking the old boat along. It came alongside the rickety jetty with difficulty and he was glad to be on solid ground. His humour was further stretched at the main road when, soaking wet under an angry tropical sky he was told by a local resident the Tai O bus was out of service. The last two hours would be a real uphill battle.

He took his time on the final three kilometres along the hill top to the camp, feeling more relaxed. This was the second storm in a week and warm rain on his face still felt good after a long time away.

His thoughts returned to the cold weather at the beginning of May and the *Ching Ming* Festival. Having been honoured with an invitation by Madame Yeung and Tan to join them on Easter Sunday at Master Yeung's burial place in the north cemetery he was glad he had flown back in to the colony from Seoul.

The cemetery is a peaceful place of tiered rows curving around the hillside facing the West Lamma Channel. He did not stay through the weekend, when families pay homage to their ancestors and turn the occasion into a picnic. Yeung's family had done the old man proud with the siting of the grave. Its *fung shui* was good and having made an offering of willow branches, Julian felt better about aspects of his past.

He managed a quick visit to Yeung's house on North Foreland, passing the luxurious apartment block where Lee had invited Julian to stay. Master Yeung's house had been abandoned to make way for a similar development Tan said had made no progress in five years. What was once a delightful villa with tiled courtyards and carefully terraced garden was abandoned and overgrown.

The sight of the radar station with rain driving up the hillside and scattering against the grey metal structure, brought Julian's thoughts back to his meeting with Teng. He had lost Fong again but meetings were becoming more difficult with the rows he was having with his father. He had managed only two visits to the camp. The bodyguard had seen Teng with Kim and his brother on the Peak on their first night in Hong Kong. Teng had told his parents four of his university friends were in the colony and that he was spending as much time as he could with them. Of course, they wanted him to invite his student friends to the mansion.

At his suggestion he bow out because of this increasing complexity, Julian insisted he support the team as best he could, for as long as he could. Julian couldn't consider cutting him loose at that critical time.

Frustration moved close to anger as he approached the camp. No-one heard him rattle the wire gate. There was no watch, no-one in the yard. Joviality and guffawing rang from the rain-lashed buildings. Willy had taken upon himself the opening of a couple of cases of beer after the evening meal.

13/2
Saturday 19 July

Willy chose not to cross Julian after the incident and did what he was told over their final three days on Lantau. Reconnaissance trips by small groups continued. Julian was aware the isolation on an otherwise disciplined and motivated group would get to them. None of them, including Willy, knew the precise date, or purpose of his operation against the triad.

It was a low point when Julian caught himself pondering the folly of it all. It was also on that sunny afternoon of 19 July that a concerted assault on the camp by an unknown rabble began. The afternoon watch was waiting for the return of Kwan II and Ah Yong when a car pulled off the road at the bus stop at the top of the pass and five Hong Kong youths got out, their loud voices and brash manners destroying the afternoon tranquillity of the island. They removed hold-alls from the car's boot and set off along the grassy hillside to the radar installation.

At the same time, the hillside watch over the western approach settled themselves between boulders on the rocky cliff top watching two power boats. They were not Marine Police boats. These they had seen around Aberdeen. Willy thought they were more the type used for running drugs or immigrants between Hong Kong and Macao, or from the mainland to the outer islands of the colony. Seemingly unsure about landing on the island's rugged south-western tip, both launches eventually cruised around the headland to the jetty at Fan Lau.

Julian called a hasty meeting in the dormitory to make the point confrontation must be avoided. Five of the team were on watch around the camp. Two had taken the early ferry to Tsimshatsui to meet Teng in the New Territories.

This left Willy and three of the team to agree tactics. Likely attack from both east and south-west was confirmed by Bill and Song-san in advance of the five youths on their way over the hill. Kim Pyong also warned of guns. All evidence of the team's presence was stowed in the loft area. Julian grabbed the flare gun and flares, the camp was evacuated and gate padlocked. An empty cardboard box flung onto the roof of the main hut was a signal to those out on watch. Julian, Willy and the three remaining Koreans retreated to the cover of rocks on the windswept hill top two hundred metres along the ridge. There were bushes and trees behind them.

"What is this all about, Willy?" Julian asked, seeing the first of the city youths appear cautiously around the east side of the radar compound.

"Search me, Boss," Willy replied without looking up, "as I don't know what you're up to ..."

"Curious, Willy, this operation has become event-driven in the last couple of days."

Willy did not answer. Fighters had circled the camp and radar installation and two shinned over the wire gate. An argument over why there should be stores in a disused camp reached Julian on the wind. He instructed Kim Pyong and Ah Kwan to take the flare gun and form a flank fifty metres to the left. Two of the fighters were moving steadily in their direction peering carefully at the scrub. Julian looked at his own team crawling into position. All of them, including Willy and himself were wearing light-coloured T-shirts.

"We're as visible as sheep on this hill top," he muttered.

Willy began to chuckle.

"There sure are a lot of us sheep in Hong Kong!"

Julian nudged him. The two fighters spotted others of their group coming up from Fan Lau and turned to meet them.

Eight other youths, moaning about the steepness of the

hillside joined the five looking around the compound. They broke the padlock on the gate and all of them entered this time and began tipping foodstuffs from the mess into the yard. Their momentary interest in some packets of marshmallows was curtailed with a sharp command and they turned their attention to the empty offices of the radar installation. Having ascertained no-one was about and concerned they were on government property the group began arguing vigorously again before leaving the site.

While Julian, Willy and the team were watching events on the hillside, Teng, Ah Yong and Kwan II were on their way back to Hong Kong after a drive along the Chinese border to Sha Tau Kok and Starling Inlet. A turn in the Jaguar was not what they should have been doing that afternoon.

Pulling cheekily into the bus station by the ferry pier at Central in a hurry to catch the four o'clock ferry, Teng's heart began racing when he realised the two other cars keeping up with him through the harbour tunnel were not aiming for the same ferry. Several men piled out of the vehicles and were on their way over, pushing people roughly out of the way. Teng chastised himself for having failed in his promise over shiny white sports cars before gathering his wits.

"No mistaking trouble," he said to Ah Yong and Kwan II. "Disappear but stay together. I'll meet you in an hour at the Peak Tram terminus."

Teng's thoughts got as far as planning to drive them later to Aberdeen and the back way to Lantau, when he saw an opportunity to use one of the double-decker buses as cover. He put his foot down on the throttle but frustratingly got nowhere on the patch of oil he was parked over. There was a scream as the car slewed. He thought he had hit someone in the queue but saw out of the corner of his eye a gorilla in a suit lunge at the car. He put his foot down hard again and the man fell flat on his face into the same patch of oil. He skidded wildly around the bus and out into Connaught Road, glimpsing at least one car in pursuit.

Ah Yong and Kwan II sprinted across the concrete and up the stairway of one of the covered walkways around the bus station. They watched the Jaguar careering about, miraculously hitting no-one and decided they should use the cover of traffic and people in the main street on their way to the Peak Tram Terminus. Ah Yong had no answers if they were forced into a confrontation. They were not on home ground, though they knew how to get back to Lantau if Teng did not make it.

Like Teng, Ah Yong also went cold at the thought of their stupidity zooming about waving at the girls. If he did not concentrate on their survival, the whole operation might go down. To make matters worse, Kwan II's fighting was better suited to chequers.

Seeing several other men running to head them off, Ah Yong knew they must get off the walkway. They sprinted into the post office and out the other side. Once in the street they walked around the Connaught Building as casually as they could but were spotted again and forced to run across the road to the Mandarin Hotel and up Ice House Street. It seemed to the pair of them gang members were everywhere. The feeling of being hunted in a busy street was not pleasant.

Resting in the doorway of an expensive boutique on Des Vouex Road at the top of the steep steps, the two Koreans discussed their next move. It was useless trying to hide in buildings they did not know. A high-rise is a dead-end. Ah Yong decided they must stay in the open until they found a shopping complex they could slip in to.

He did not believe there would be confrontation with so many people around. The pavements were bustling with people. There were plenty of cars and a dozen trams down the long, straight road. There were also queues of people on little islands. When they needed one, if only to hide behind, there was not a policeman in sight.

While Ah Yong was checking his pockets for a dollar with which they could make a spectacular escape by tram, Kwan II, with admirable wit kicked the shin of the fighter who stepped unwittingly into the doorway. Ah Yong assisted with a kick to the head and was not slow in dealing with the second man who came at them from the other direction. He hit him with a devastating punch to the kidneys and made sure both men stayed down by banging their heads together.

Out of the corner of his eye, Kwan II noticed a young Chinese beauty in a tight skirt come tottering out of the shop and promptly fall over the bodies. With no time for gallantry they turned their backs on the incident and hurried into the street.

Alerted by a shout from across the road and a woman sent sprawling over the pavement as two more fighters started towards them, the two Koreans cut in front of a tram about to move off and tried to get in it. Kwan II got his fingers in the door, forcing the driver to stop. Proffering a polite thanks in his mother tongue he dropped all the coins in his pocket in the box, most of them Korean. The driver looked suspiciously at the perspex box, stuffed full of coins at that time of the afternoon and Kwan II realised they shouldn't have spent their day's expenses on fripperies either.

As the tram moved off, three fighters broke into a trot, keeping alongside it to the next island. It took only a hundred metres and the supercilious grin of the leading fighter for Ah Yong to understand their predicament. Keeping his eyes fixed on this individual in a suit and tie with tie-clip leading the other two, he made his way to the rear of the tram.

As it squealed gently to a halt, Kwan II knew what his friend had decided and mustered confidence to match. They stepped calmly out of the door onto an island packed with people. The leader slowed down and his companions caught up with him, breathing hard. The leader brazenly pulled an automatic pistol from his belt and holding it loosely at his side started walking towards the island.

Teng, meanwhile was spiralling up the Peak Road at speed and thought it typical a China Motor Bus Company vehicle had broken down outside the gate to his house. He had changed his mind anyway about trying to get in. The electronic gate took an age to open and the occupants of the car chasing him would not watch and jeer.

"And what would Mother think," he said aloud, dropping into second gear to overtake a dustcart pulling out to pass the bus.

On reaching the bridge near the top of the Peak, he knew in his exhilaration he should not have gone that way. The new road simply went in a loop by the tram terminus. The old roads off it were barred to traffic and he had no time to get out and try raising barriers. Realising his only options were Peel Rise or returning to Central, he stopped at the No Entry sign, squinting at the sunlight reflecting off the thick foliage of the mountainside.

Before him was a track hacked out of the rock for palanquins. On foot it was a pleasant way down to Aberdeen. In a car, unthinkable. There was nobody about, birds were twittering. The only other sounds were the gentle pulse of a 3.8-litre engine and coming up the hill behind him, the hoarse clattering of a well-driven Toyota.

Teng took a deep breath, let the clutch out and approached the first hairpin on Peel Rise with only faith the car would not go airborne. Not wanting to rely entirely on vintage Jaguar engineering he got a grip on himself and quickly fell into a pattern of shifting between first and second gear, discovering a touch on the hand brake helped flick the car into a tight enough position to take each bend in one. By the fifth hairpin he had got into the rhythm of shift, throttle and hand brake. He glanced at the Toyota above him. They were falling back, guiding the car around the bends as though it were a cow.

Pleased at his progress, between grim concentration and dissatisfaction at his stupidity, Teng didn't like it thought Asians were poor drivers. He once had an Italian girlfriend who drove well but didn't consider Jaguars real cars. Her favourite car in her father's collection was a Bugatti Type 57 Coupé, the Atlantic.

His concentration slipped on the final bend in the thick woodland and he missed a gear. His heart was beating wildly. His luck at staying on the track was not without a tree laying the most unforgiving marks along the pristine white coachwork. It wasn't a sudden yearning for that volatile European beauty. The tranquillity of the lower Peak and its blanket of suffocating heat were interrupted briefly. Trees and foliage strained with an unexpected visitor, birds scattered squawking. It wasn't a mighty parrot he saw flying through the air in his mirror, it was a metallic green Corolla.

Teng threw his fist into the air, let out a full-throated *ki ai* and took off down the long gradient toward the shanty town in the valley and Aberdeen. In his moment of triumph he only heard terrible noises and himself gasping for breath after taking evasive action.

Several pairs of hands helped him out of the car and onto a concrete bank. He had not expected an old truck to be lumbering up the same track and been forced to take a hard right at sixty kilometres per hour. His car, minus sump and rear suspension was nose first in water at the junction of three storm-water drains he last played in as a kid.

"My car ..." he began in English, clutching his aching chest. Several workmen looked at him in surprise. "I'll have to get another, even if I have to go back to Britain ..."

Julian met Peterson under the trees at the end of a deserted Bowen Road much later that night. With no-one about they slipped into the garage area beneath the apartment block. When the kids were home, Peterson said, the car was sometimes the only place he could get his paperwork done. Julian actually laughed and said perhaps he would give children a miss.

Peterson knew how the incident with two of Julian's Koreans ended that afternoon. There had been a Wild West-style shoot-out on main street at the beginning of the rush hour. Two cars had rammed lamp posts and several people had gunshot wounds, including four suspected triad enforcers. The police brought in reinforcements for what they thought was a gang disturbance. They had no idea it was two Koreans harrying 14K fighters.

Ah Yong had relieved their leader of the shiny semi-automatic he felt very big with, shot him in the foot as punishment and told Kwan II it was their turn to hunt. The tables were turned but eventually seeing the Stars and Stripes over the consulate building in Garden Road they ducked in. One of Peterson's colleagues in the foyer understood immediately their *no speak American*. Fortunately, no-one saw them seeking refuge there and they were escorted quietly to Aberdeen.

Peterson admired their courage and fortitude; Julian had an idea how it had come about and was not amused. He was now concerned about the extent of exposure of the operation against the 14K and asked again if there had been comment from the 'black and white' at the Lee house.

"She is worried but about different things now," Peterson replied. "A note today mentions a chop in Lee's desk bearing the mark of the turtle. She is deeply afraid. Learning something every day about these people, I find this is the seal of the highest authority of a triad. Anthony Wong is considering bringing her out before the operation begins."

"If it is a turtle, he is ours," Julian said. "And I want to get some timings of the operation to her. She will be most useful remaining in the house."

"She's recently been accompanied around the market by the driver, as the Lees are prodigious socialisers. But we will get a message to her through one of the traders."

"Anthony wishes me to pass on his thanks for the reciprocal information about the 14K, by the way. He knew Joe Williams well and is still sore. He admires your single-mindedness on this issue. He's been on the receiving end of triad brutality."

Tan's triad had provided Julian with enough evidence to commit several high-ranking 14K members, including Lee, to trial. 'Playing dirty with the rival triad', Julian would have described it had Peterson been indelicate enough to ask his source.

Peterson handed Julian the latest file updates, including that on Lee, saying it included the note from Julian about Lee's guard and layout of the mansion. He said he would make a flask of coffee. The kids would be in bed by now but he didn't want to disturb Gillian working in the study. They just needed a bigger place, he said, like everyone else in the colony.

Julian began reading the file.

William Lee, a member of the original 14 Association in Guangzhou brought business expertise into an organisation set up in 1947 to counter Communist infiltration into the Nationalist Army. When the association was forced into exile in Hong Kong in 1949, Lee provided the framework for the association's growth with investment in property and real estate alongside the more traditional triad lines of drugs, prostitution, protection and smuggling.

After the death of its founder in 1953, Nationalist

Chinese ambitions became irrelevant. The 'k', for karat was added and the association became known as the 14K (*sap sei kei*). Expansion of the new triad throughout the colony began with a regime of extortion and intimidation never seen before. With efficient organisation they rose above the infighting characteristic of the smaller triads and ousted their main rivals, the Green Gang (*Ch'ing Pang*), originally from Shanghai and also exiled into the colony after 1949.

Lee's business affairs became inextricably bound up with those of the brotherhood. He was promoted immediately, at the age of 30 in 1948, from a 49 (*zi tai jau*) to the local 415 or White Paper Fan (*pak tze sin*), an adviser in administration and finance. As his own business prospered and he began to travel extensively he was promoted to 432, Straw Sandal (*chou hai*). With this rank he was entrusted with carrying information and messages between branches of the expanding triad.

By 1970 he was the mother organization's 438, Deputy Mountain Master (*fu shan chu*). He saw the triad through its difficult years from 1974 and establishment of the Independent Commission Against Corruption (ICAC) that signalled the end of the cosy relationship between the triads, police and, to an extent, judiciary.

In 1980 under his guidance as senior 489 or Mountain Master (*shan chu*), the 14K has weathered the re-emergence of the Triad Bureau in 1978 and its integration with the heavyweight office now known as the Organized Crime and Triad Bureau (OCTB). By allowing some independence to branches, the triad has taken control of criminal activity in almost every overseas Chinese community from Canada to New Zealand. The triad situation generally in Hong Kong is looking to reach a *status quo* with law enforcement agencies once again by 1983. Lee has become one of the colony's wealthiest men ...

As Julian read the notes by the interior light of the car a chill came over him. It was a run-down of his own youth and his unforgivable part in the triad's development.

When Peterson returned with coffee and a hip flask, Julian said he would appreciate information on the outcome of any trial they might secure of Lee and other high-ranking officials caught in the operation. He did not want to underestimate co-operation between the colony and Beijing government with regard to bad publicity affecting both sides. If there was a possibility of justice being overpowered by politics he wanted to know. Peterson said he would pass on the request.

"How are you getting on with the Lee son with all this? He does know, doesn't he?"

"He knows as of this evening," Julian replied. "He is shocked but bore it with maturity. His questions were pragmatic. Would media be present at the arrest and how should he behave toward his father? He has thought about triad infiltration of the business and how shareholders might react. He's deeply concerned about his mother's role. She must know what has been going on since the beginning, he said, with some distress."

Peterson also asked Julian about Willy and as he spoke he realised Julian had not mentioned the Malay-Chinese. Both men looked at each other.

"That's curious, Julian," he began thoughtfully. "I know the name but can't remember where I've heard or seen it relative to your operation. There's been such a stream of intelligence this way in the last two weeks, I just can't remember."

Julian said it was getting late and he did not want to spend another night in the open.

"It makes me tired, Larry," he said smiling, "and more suspicious than ever of everyone about me. If you see the name Willy Djan Tong again it should be associated with the

14K. If not, let me know."

"I'd make it a priority," Peterson said grimly.

Julian did watch the sun rise once more above the mist from a crude hut in the woods on the south side of Mount Collinson. Of the many things he considered during the night, the principal one concerned the monastery on Jin-do. He could not accept the responsibility of becoming the senior master of that Buddhist order. It meant the last secrets of the art of the *Hwarang* as it had been taught in the monastery for centuries would be passed to him. Only the Old One, Buddhist monk and friend, had a higher status and greater knowledge, of course.

To be accorded such a senior status was a hitherto unknown honour since he was young and neither Korean nor a Buddhist. It would mean residence at the monastery, celibacy, relative poverty and total commitment.

He knew also the planned bridge to Jin-do would change it for ever. History belongs in the past, he found himself saying. He had to move on. His mind was made up on other matters also, once his contract with the Bureau of Social Affairs was concluded to his satisfaction.

Which left Willy, the snake, who had made no attempt to feed information on the preparations on Lantau back to the 14K. In any case he would be unable to stop the operation against the council and he did not know of the direct assault on its boss's house. Julian doubted he would try passing messages to his masters during the next twenty-four hours. He was Willy's ultimate target.

CHAPTER FOURTEEN

Hong Kong, Tuesday 22 July

Peterson went in to work early on Tuesday morning and had an unsatisfactory shave while catching up on the latest from the teleprinter in the consulate's Operations Room. It was not yet four o'clock, the tropical cyclone warning signal had moved from three to four and the Royal Observatory's new computer facility predicted the newly-named Typhoon Joe would pass three hundred kilometres to the south-west during the day.

He couldn't hear what was going on outside but could see what the rain was doing across the car park. He was concerned. A colleague, just arrived, said the wipers on his car had not cleared the water from the wind shield and the wind had pushed him all over the road, all the way from Aberdeen. "This should have been Operation Joe," Peterson said to himself. Poetic justice Julian would have liked.

The same weather information was being assessed by Naval Operations on board the US aircraft carrier lying with its escort inside the Western Quarantine Anchorage. This was the second day of a planned four-day courtesy visit to the colony and the ship was alive after a reception, dinner and drinks that had gone ahead for Hong Kong notables despite the weather closing in.

Several tugs were on standby, as was the carrier's entire crew. All engines were running and anchors weighed. The carrier and its escort vessels were about to set out for the relative safety of open sea, as two Royal Navy vessels had done. A United States Navy ship would normally have dropped storm anchors but in view of the severity of this one they were leaving also.

At 04.40 the signal moved to storm eight. Minutes later a message came through from the commander of the Carrier Air Wing asking Peterson if he was serious about a fully-laden chopper lifting off the carrier with forty-odd vessels around them, skimming oil storage, a typhoon anchorage and crossing high-rise Central to land in someone's back garden on a mountain top in a full-blooded typhoon, in the dark. Peterson considered it a rhetorical question and did not reply.

The important thing was the unarmed Black Hawk, its two-man crew and eight navy commandos were on stand-by. The UH-60 helicopter had just come into service and this one, code-named Seahawk, was undergoing modification for Navy use. Operations were interested in its capability, fully-laden, in a tropical storm but had specified they wanted it back in one piece.

Operations' next message said the carrier was on its way down the West Lamma Channel. The chopper had been forced to take off several minutes earlier than scheduled and was also out in the channel. It would return for a westerly approach to the Peak, thereby minimising flying time over land. The chopper did not have flight clearance, they stressed and they were concerned about British reaction, particularly with an armed unit on board. Peterson replied he would handle it, though he couldn't think how.

All aircraft had been grounded at midnight. This aircraft and special operations unit, one of three direct actions involving US personnel, was vital to the US operation and the British hopefully would understand. It was go on all fronts for Operation Snow White. The helicopter ride would be a roller-coaster.

A few hours earlier, as Peterson was getting into bed for some sleep, Julian was briefing Willy, Teng and the Koreans. It wasn't yet raining at midnight on Lantau but the buildings were being battered by a wind passing through the compound like an express train.

Once the objectives of the main group were understood and details absorbed, Teng voiced his concern again privately to Julian about the smaller operation at his parents' house in the morning. He wanted Julian's reassurance his sister and his mother would be safe if there was a forced entry to arrest his father. He assumed it would be the Hong Kong police making the raid. Julian did not tell him otherwise. Teng was in charge of the main group with Willy advising and Julian repeated he would be nowhere near his home during the raid and should not be concerned with it.

"If they are not granted access, they will not go away, Teng," he went on with some irritation. Willy was wandering over. "They won't wipe their feet either before going in. But no-one in your family will be harmed. It is hoped your father will be taken out of the house within minutes so stress is minimised."

"And I trust there won't be damage to the furnishings, or porcelain in father's study," Teng persisted. "There's enough in that room alone to put a down-payment on Taiwan."

Willy found this funny, Julian did not. There had been only a rudimentary briefing with the Special Operations commander and Julian knew the damage a unit could do. The bodyguard would use his weapon and would be the first casualty. Julian was concerned about Teng's nerve holding out. His watching Willy's every move should be the diversion needed. The young man was struggling too with the fact it was his sister's thirteenth birthday, though he had not mentioned this to anyone.

The main group were to leave the compound early, pick

up their vehicles at a country club in Deep Water Bay and head east along Island Road. In view of the weather they agreed they should do it then, at midnight, to be sure of getting across forty kilometres of open sea. Julian saw them off down a treacherous hillside path to a waiting power boat at Fan Lau. Kim Pyong, Song-san and he would take the second boat, also to Deep Water Bay and head north for their rendezvous on the Peak at 05.00.

Julian radioed Operations at half-past midnight to say his briefing on Lantau was complete. He didn't ask about the helicopter or talk of deteriorating weather. This little operation was going ahead, whatever. The other certainty of the night was that the crossing of the Lamma Channel in small boats and several hours in vehicles in storm conditions would not be pleasant.

Something woke Su-Mai just before five. She looked across the rear garden. The security lights had come on in the storm and she could just about make out the trees around the perimeter swaying in silence. She couldn't see further than the gate because of the spray bouncing off the lawn and was not happy because she would obviously not be going to the race track with her father. She had absolutely fallen in love with a young racehorse there and he agreed if it performed well that afternoon in trials it would be hers.

She was concentrating on what she should wear for her birthday when there was a tap on the door. The servant put her head around with a little bow. Tight-faced, she said her father was asking for her on his private telephone.

Su-Mai followed Ah-Lien downstairs into the study. As she entered the room she could hear the roar of an engine over that of wind and rain. It grew louder. She saw the telephone off its cradle on the desk, detected movement in the garden and screamed as Ah-Lien lunged at her. She remembered nothing until she was being sick on the carpet.

256

Her unpleasant experience did not end there. When she turned over, deaf and coughing in the smoke-filled study she looked up at Julian and gasped.

Julian was almost as surprised.

"'Suzy Wong'," he mouthed, relaxing his grip on the disoriented young girl. "No harm will come to any of you here, Su-Mai. Trust me again. It is your father we must speak to. He is not in the house. Do you know where he is?"

Half an hour before the helicopter landed, Julian had ascertained none of Lee's guards were on the streets. Lee had a guard of six to eight 14K enforcers around him at all times. They occupied an apartment in a block a little way down the road. Behind this was a covered yard for their cars. Security around the mansion was a problem. Peak Road is the only good road up and down but there are a dozen other ways for vehicles and walkers to come and go around the mountain.

The rear garden of Lee's house backed on to the road and was the most difficult section to protect, especially with the road being narrow and on a bend. Lee had been unable to prevent a double yellow line painted around him. On the other hand, the Hong Kong police could do nothing about its constant violation.

The absence of guards on the road was hardly surprising that morning with the road running like a river. Julian was wearing Navy waterproofs but was still soaked through. It was twenty minutes to five when he saw a light come on in the apartment block. Unsure if it related to Lee he ran for a closer look.

On his return minutes later he found his look-outs Kim Pyong and Song-san in the entrance of the apartment block across the road from the mansion asleep, exhausted. They should have been watching the gate. He sent them back to the car parked further up in Mount Kellett Road and told them to stay out of trouble.

The gate had been used and was not quite closed. Vehicles had to go up Peak Road before coming down and it was fortunate he was hidden by the apartment block staircase as the Mercedes passed. There were five occupants, one of whom he assumed was Lee. It was possible he was leaving early for Tai Tam because of the storm. This would surely not have been in one car, with only two guards. He didn't have time to dwell on the alternatives.

The helicopter arrived over the rear garden on schedule and Julian guided it down with his own flashlight and improvised orange and green filters. He knew the flight deck wands he had been given would not be powerful enough for the weather conditions.

It was fortunate he had one hand free. While signalling the aircraft into position directly above him in the centre of the lawn, both Great Danes appeared. Though afraid of the descending helicopter, they were dangerous and he pointed a borrowed M16 at them while watching the buffeted helicopter's descent. The red laser sight did the trick and the dogs retreated.

As he backed away to the side of the house, only just avoiding being hit by an external fuel tank he saw Ah-Lien with Su-Mai as planned, in the ground floor study. She dived on top of the girl as one of the commandos broke a window with his rifle butt and lobbed a stun grenade in. While he was there by the window, Julian cut the telephone line into the house.

Neither Ah-Lien nor the girl heard four more grenades go off on the ground and first floors. The six commandos had gained access to the house within seconds and were on a room-by-room search for their target. The girl and servant struggled to regain their wits in the smoke-filled room. Mrs Lee was out cold in her first-floor bedroom, a grenade having landed on her bed. There was no-one else in the house.

The servant confirmed that Lee made a telephone call at four-thirty and shortly afterwards was joined by two of his men. He left with them, the driver and bodyguard in the Mercedes at four fifty.

Su-Mai shrank at seeing armed men in black running about. The roar of engines, the sickly smell of exhaust and pulsating of the helicopter's rotor blades made it difficult to breath. To Julian's repeated question about her father's whereabouts she said he might have gone to Happy Valley to see the horse. Julian heard the words 'one minute' from the hallway above the mechanical din driven through broken windows by a howling wind and spattering rain.

Taking a chance with the girl's feelings, he said,

"Your father knows of your suffering in Europe last August. He wants to talk about it. We can see him together."

The colour drained from the youngster's face. She held the key to Lee's movements and would have to go with them.

The commandos, Julian and Su-Mai took off in the helicopter in almost zero visibility within two minutes of it having dropped in over the garden wall. In the event of Lee not being at the house the re-scheduled drop was the Shek O Road on the mountainside overlooking Tai Tam Bay on the lower east end of Hong Kong Island.

Ah-Lien was left to her own devices, her seat taken by Su-Mai. She would need to make her escape before an enraged Mrs Lee broke out of the closet. Her bag was already packed. She was working out the best way of leaving without running into a pack of guards who would surely have worked out what was going on.

Su-Mai felt ill again almost immediately the helicopter lifted off the lawn and lurched over the garden wall. As it pitched and yawed its way south down the mountain bludgeoned by the wind, she succumbed to the terror of tree tops whistling by and passed out. Julian did not find it easy reviving her. When she came to, she saw Julian smiling and heard him ask if her father had gone to buy a racehorse.

Several pairs of eyes watched him and the girl in a nightdress impassively through the eye holes of their balaclavas.

"It's my birthday," Su-Mai responded. "We were going to see it running around the race track this afternoon."

"Is the horse at Happy Valley now?" Julian asked, dispensing with salutations.

"It's been there a week. But it won't be running today."

Her voice tailed off and afraid once again of the violent movements, she buried her face into Julian's jacket.

Julian, now convinced of Lee's intentions, signalled to the unit leader their destination was not Tai Tam. They had a new rendezvous at Happy Valley, the Hong Kong Jockey Club Headquarters on Sports Road, the north end of the race track. He changed channels on his headset and asked Peterson to get the police to Sports Road, seeking confirmation from the co-pilot of their ETA as six minutes. He also asked that the Mercedes and possibly a green Corolla with up to six men in it be intercepted on the Peak Road down, on their way to Tai Tam or Happy Valley.

Lee knew about horses and grand gestures and this was his little girl's thirteenth birthday. Julian guessed a pot of money was about to be handed over for a racehorse at Happy Valley. Lee was securing the deal before his morning meeting.

As the Seahawk passed north of Aberdeen it was slammed sideways in a particularly violent gust and trees sixty metres below on the mountainside came uncomfortably close a second time. The pilot was battling with the worst wind shear he had experienced. Passing over Aberdeen's Upper Reservoir his co-pilot advised their tail wind was a steady 60 knots gusting to 100. The only way of avoiding the massively built-up residential Happy Valley, they agreed, was to go straight over Mount Nicholson, pick up the Aberdeen Tunnel road, skim the apartment blocks on Wong Nai Chung Road by the racecourse and position the aircraft over a patch of grass the size of a quarter. The warning of extreme turbulence came seconds before they dipped into the lee side of the mountain.

Julian hadn't expected to hear from the pilot this was a piece of cake and he was impressed.

"Racing, this early?" the commando next to him asked, his knuckles white from gripping the poles on either side of him.

"Ten to one we make it, guys!" another piped up. Several of the unit began an audible laughter over the throbbing of the rotors and roaring of rain.

Lee's white Mercedes and accompanying vehicle were just visible inside the Member's Enclosure as the helicopter passed twenty metres above the Racing Museum building, perilously close to the lamp standards around the collection of pitches at the track's north end. Drifting a little towards the road the pilot put landing lights on and dipped towards the middle of the top left-hand bend. The aircraft wobbled to within a metre of the ground. Julian would have to jump with Su-Mai and make a dash to the enclosure offices, trusting Lee was in the building, or at least not realising what the helicopter signified.

The Naval Operations commander on the carrier, now clear of Lamma Island had categorically forbidden the helicopter to land again and ordered its direct return to the safety of the airfield at Sek Kong. Happy Valley was not quite on the flight path but the pilot decided he wouldn't be a spoilsport.

"Sorry to dump you," the unit leader shouted.

"It's been fun … nice aircraft … good luck!" Julian shouted back. A thumbs-up was returned from the flight deck.

Julian half-carried and half-dragged Su-Mai away from

the helicopter, with down draft, rain and wind almost bringing them to their knees on the waterlogged turf. Lee's driver was out of the car, his jacket over his head, peering in disbelief. Within seconds the aircraft could neither be seen, nor the dull thudding of its rotors heard. Their timing was better this time around. Half-a-dozen police cars had blocked off Sports Road and entered the enclosure as they landed. Two ATV World television vehicles slipped in cheekily with them.

Lee, his driver, Fong and two other bodyguards were arrested immediately. One of the bodyguards was relieved of his weapon but would not part with an attaché case packed with banknotes. It took some time before the senior police officer at the scene was satisfied the two other men and a secretary and two officials of the Hong Kong Jockey Club were not involved in anything other than the sale of a racehorse.

Peterson and several other American intelligence agents were also on the scene. Jim Andrews had taken over operations at the Consulate for the rest of the morning.

When Peterson saw Su-Mai, shivering and dazed at Julian's side he called for a blanket, a hot drink and some female support. He congratulated Julian on his timing and advised him they probably had only a few minutes in which to interview Lee before his lawyer arrived. Lee, predictably furious, had told the police inspector, heads – his head – would roll, even though he had been formally arrested. The inspector, fully briefed by the Triad Bureau, stood his ground.

"And when the lawyer does arrive, he will secure Lee's immediate release from the station on bail?" Julian asked.

The inspector, a Scotland Yard veteran, nodded.

"But he can't be sure of this, even with the best lawyer in the colony?"

"The best team of lawyers in the colony."

"Then make sure no lawyers get through for as long as possible and we'll bargain while he's vulnerable," Julian replied.

Returning to the main entrance hall of the enclosure building, Julian was appalled to find the television news crew bombarding a bewildered Su-Mai with questions about 'the kidnapping'. They had been out early seeking storm pictures for the lunch-time news and coming out of the tunnel from Aberdeen could not believe a US Navy helicopter was directly over them. They didn't have to chase it far.

All Su-Mai could do was shield her eyes from the lights and intrusion of a camera and microphone. On the edge of bad temper, Julian stepped between her and the crew. They would get their story, he told the director but it did not include pictures of the girl.

He moved Su-Mai's hair away from her eyes and steered her towards the racehorse owner's secretary and a policewoman who had appeared with a blanket. It was then he remembered where he had seen pictures of her naked, probably just prior to her abduction in Paris. The last piece of the jigsaw fell into place. Lee, shortly, would be taken to task.

At twenty minutes past five, Julian was also concerned how the operation at Tai Tam was faring. The weather was preventing radio communications with Teng and Willy. He did not know if the enforcers at the Peak apartment block had seen the helicopter. *Shan chu* should still be at the race track. No 'phone calls had been made from the race track by Lee or his men. Julian needed to get over to Tai Tam as quickly as possible. They were in with a chance.

Seeing the array of equipment the television crew brought into the offices, he re-introduced himself to the director, Graham Wu, his assistant, his sound engineer and cameraman and said he would like to exchange a favour.

"No problem, Mister de Lyon," the youthful director replied with a fulsome grin on hearing the proposition. "We have a facsimile machine in the Jeep. Sam will get it."

The assistant plugged the machine into sockets at the reception desk and stood back. Seeing Julian had no idea how to use it but sensing the urgency he handed him a biro and sheet of paper and said,

"Write your fax. I'll send it ."

The director's assistant reminded Julian they were hanging on a story. If it was about William Lee as a gang boss, it was imperative they got it in the can and back to the studio inside an hour and a half to make the mid-morning news. Julian promised they would get their story and repeated absolutely no footage of the girl should be used.

"This is a long shot," he said to Peterson, putting his signature to an urgent request to Mlle. Arameau for the last notes and pictures of the Chinese girl he filed before leaving Brussels. "I didn't have a nameplate on my door when I was there."

"Probably because your name was already on it in blood," the American replied.

Mlle. Arameau's reply from the Place Madou office came eleven minutes later. It seemed she was now working late as well as early. European time was twenty past ten. She must have run around the records room and back. Sam, the director's assistant handed the two-page fax, two pictures, to Julian without expression. The prim, middle-aged secretary who had accompanied the horse's owner to the track and who was now comforting Su-Mai, caught sight of the first page. She was shocked at how the morning had progressed from the sale of a fine horse, to a huge police operation, to the comforting of a victim of child pornography.

Julian sat next to Su-Mai and explained quietly amidst the continuing hubbub there was evidence her father was responsible for the organisation and abduction of girls like herself throughout Europe and this operation was to bring him and his associates to justice. Her abduction in Paris had been part of this trade.

"With you it must have been an error," he said trying to ease the girl's pain. "I want you to ask your father."

Lee's jaw dropped as Julian and his daughter appeared at the door wet and dishevelled. Julian closed it quietly behind him and thrust the faxed pages at Lee in stony silence. The photographs showed his young daughter waist upwards looking at herself in a two-way bathroom mirror and an elegant full-length of her stepping out of a round marble bathtub. That she had just reached puberty was clear. There was a third picture, also close-up from another hidden camera Mlle. Arameau chose not to send.

Julian had realised only minutes before, these professional pictures of Su-Mai, albeit poorly represented by the fax machine, were taken in the guest bedroom with the onyx bathroom at his father-in-law's château. It was Ann-Marie's favourite bathroom. The pictures were given to him by the journalist Jean-Phillipe in Marseilles because the subject was Chinese. Julian had filed them under the heading Catalogue. It was just about the last thing he did at the office at Place Madou.

Lee was red, his face twitching. He reached for the handkerchief in his inside suit pocket and began flicking it. He turned to Julian, letting go of the waxy sheets at the same time. When Su-Mai caught sight of herself for the first time, new lines appeared on her face.

"Why did they take pictures of me there?" she blurted, sobbing from this degradation anew. "The family I stayed with in Paris. Why?"

"Is this what happens when my young daughter visits your home?" Lee began, addressing Julian but hopelessly wrong-footed.

"What page of the catalogue was your daughter on, Lee?

What was her asking price ..." Julian responded.

Lee did not hear his almost hysterical daughter repeat her question. He didn't hear her ask if he thought she had come home early because she was tired of France. He had no idea she was missing for a week in Europe. He simply did not know what his daughter was talking about. He tried to interrupt again but Su-Mai, now shaking, would not be placated.

"They took me away from the château. I was put in a cage in a warehouse. I had a friend holding my hand while those men were on me. We cried together."

Lee stepped forward but his daughter took a deliberate step back.

"This man rescued me. He brought me here to see you now. He says it is part of your business."

Lee's response was to lunge angrily at Julian. A policeman tried to intervene while unbuttoning the holster of his pistol but Julian immobilised Lee by gripping his testicles.

"You are disgrace, Lee," he began. "You are finished. Now we start picking up some pieces."

Su-Mai didn't hear anything of what Julian whispered in her father's ear, his deal with regard to his wife, his son and daughter in exchange for absolute co-operation with the authorities. Lee heard it and came down from the tips of his toes only after nodding agreement. Gasping for breath, he didn't notice Julian leave the room. All he saw was his child staring at him, wild, her shoulders hunched, her fingers outstretched at her side. He dropped slowly to his knees.

Julian looked at the time again and saw there were thirty minutes only before the main operation in the colony began and Teng and the team closed in on the villa. He was now more concerned about unnecessary casualties than losing the rest of the triad's top hierarchy at Tai Tam. The team had weapons but no firearms. It might yet be a job for the

266

police and even the detachment of Volunteers on an operation in Big Wave Bay across the Dragon's Back from the villa. The storm was worsening. The police would not risk a patrol car on the exposed road around Repulse Bay to the Stanley Gap but had called for a Land Rover.

"Would either of your vehicles stay on the Shek O road in these conditions?" Julian asked Wu.

"They're both heavy with equipment, especially the four-wheel drive. We've been out since before five shooting storm damage. Had no trouble with them so far, though trees are coming down."

"You've got Lee. The story's now shifted to Tai Tam."

"Just lead us to it," Wu grinned, glancing at his crew. His gut feeling from what had occurred in the past half-hour, with a snatched shot of Lee through a partly-open door, was they were on their biggest story since the Red Guards had crossed the border.

"I'll have to hitch a ride ..." Julian added.

Peterson stood in the doorway shielding his face from the spray, watching Julian and the four-man television crew struggle across the car park. He didn't see Wu's assistant flip a coin, lose it in the wind then decide anyway they would go north and then south, as North Point to Chai Wan would be deserted and the roads marginally better.

Detritus was streaming through the air; hordings, tree branches and the occasional piece of corrugated sheet metal. He instructed the police road block to let the tv cars out and the ambulance and Lee's lawyer in with an apology for the misunderstanding that had delayed his access to the race track. The tv cars disappeared into the gloom and Peterson had no doubt the crew also would be put to good use.

14/2

At the time of Lee's arrest the storm was coming straight in off the sea on the south side of Hong Kong Island.

267

Aberdeen's floating city was battened down but an emergency was developing, the junks being battered so much some were in danger of sinking. Smaller buildings, including the *Hung Shing* shrine on Apleichau Island on the other side of the harbour were being well and truly rattled. *Hung Shing* is the local god and a revered weather forecaster. Roads were deserted across the colony.

Teng, Willy and the others had long been in position in the wild countryside straddling the Dragon's Back. As Julian left Happy Valley, Willy and Teng in the tanker emerged from their hiding place and joined the Shek O Road south. The vehicle laboured for a couple of kilometres in torrential rain before stopping at the Cape D'Aguilar turning. Ah Kong, waiting there with three of the team, sped off down the steep road. A few minutes later, Willy followed with the big vehicle at a more sedate pace and came to a halt directly outside the gates of a large white villa halfway down a cove above the bay.

Opening the cab doors was not easy with the wind against them and the rain stinging their faces. Teng set a timer underneath the tank to twenty seconds and they ran. They slipped and slid a little way down the hillside by the walled villa to the safety of a rock outcrop and covered their heads. The tanker blew in a massive eruption of orange flame and filthy smoke. Teng's heart was in his mouth at the sight of the smoke being carried back inland, away from the villa. Seconds later he was coughing as it changed direction, whipped by the wind and spray into an oily pancake that engulfed villa and gardens.

As the second group began climbing the wall into the front garden, Teng and Willy closed in on the rear of the villa. All but one of guards at the back sheltering under a porch had vacated their positions to find out what the explosion was.

Willy now took over the second stage, the more

dangerous task of entering the villa. They had carried out Julian's instructions to the letter and thus far everything had gone well. Willy hurried across the rear courtyard with a cape over his head straight to the look-see at the kitchen entrance also too busy looking down the corridor to the burning tanker to notice him. Willy stuck a knife in him, simultaneously lifting him off his feet to a position under the stairs. He couldn't believe his luck finding two Bren guns on a rack and a pile of magazines. He grabbed one, banged a clip in and pointed it at the guard who had foolishly left his position inside the cellar door. The man jerked backwards into the cellar.

There were urgent shouts from an upstairs landing about securing the cellar and Willy knew their objective. He stepped back under the stairs, his eyes following the neat line of bullet holes across the mosaic floor where he had stood. He pointed the Bren gun up and squeezed the trigger. There was a muffled cry and a body tumbled down the staircase. Moving brazenly into the corridor, Willy flicked his hand for the rest of the team to come through.

Ah Yong, Bill, Kim and the others moved quickly into the empty upper cellar. Teng hesitated and was thankful Willy gestured he take the other Bren gun from the rack, showing him with exaggerated movements across the hall how to use it. Teng had long got the idea of why Julian wanted him watched, knowing also he was no match for this wily Malay-Chinese, twice his age and with a lifetime's more experience.

When they were all inside, Teng signalled from the cellar door but there was no response. He couldn't see Willy jammed stoically under the staircase at the end of the passage, exposed to whoever might poke his head around the front door and fire. One slip in concentration, where he did not fire first, he was finished. Three triad men lay sprawled across the floor as a warning.

The team were eight minutes into the infiltration and for several more tense minutes, Willy and Teng kept the enforcers away from the cellar door. Ah Yong, meanwhile, leading the rest of the group had progressed to the lower cellar, disarming three other guards on the way. There they remained, their way blocked by a heavy steel door.

It was the attempt at putting this problem to Willy that caused an almost fatal lapse of concentration. He caught sight of two bedraggled figures taking up positions by a garage at the front at the same moment as earnest whispering from the cellar door and was not quick enough to avoid a spray of machine gun bullets through the open front door. A searing pain went up his arm, blood spattered against the wall and he yelled for cover. The cellar door flew open, there was a wild burst of fire from Teng over his head down the corridor to the front and back of the villa where other guards were also advancing. Willy dived through the door and was caught on the steps by several pairs of hands.

Teng pulled the flimsy door shut and stuck the Bren gun through a chink, his heart racing. He could not see what was going on but every few seconds squeezed the trigger, knowing they were safe as long as the clip lasted. He had not expected *kamikaze* tactics from rank and file 49s. Neither was he happy at exercising such a weapon of destruction he held in his hands.

He checked on Willy's condition and saw four of the team bunched with nothing particular to do. Not wanting a frightened group to contend with he gave several orders, including one for a casualty report. The team split between the two empty cellars. The lower group he ordered stay put for a final assault on the steel door. On the other hand, he said, if the door opened they were to come straight back up.

The gun's vicious kicking stopped and Teng put his ear to the door knowing they had ground to a halt. They were trapped, council members in the house had probably bolted, or, if in the cellar, left the back way. A mass retaliatory attack was probably being planned at that moment. The team was too stretched to cover exits and their skills were no match for the automatic weapons confronting them.

His watch showed five minutes to seven. Never had he wanted to see Julian more. Even with the support of all the gods on the island, he did not think Julian would reach them at the appointed time with the elements stacking up against him. He had no idea how the operation had gone at the Peak. He also wondered about their timing and indeed, if the meeting had been cancelled in the last hour because of the weather conditions. Some may even have seen the blazing tanker and turned back. The only shred of comfort was that, in his father's business at least, top directors did not miss meetings.

Willy bound his wounded arm with a strip of cloth. Spying a bottle of Suntory Whisky in a locker, he poured some of it on his makeshift bandage and a good measure down his throat. There was shuffling in the corridor and heated orders being given, then silence. He and Teng heard the clunk and something roll across the tiled floor to the cellar door. Teng had an idea what it was and looked to Willy.

"Grenade ..." Willy hissed.

Teng jumped sideways off the top of the steps. The door followed him with an ear-splitting bang. In the acrid smoke and sudden darkness, bullets bounced off the cellar walls. Several enforcers then piled in. There was a frenzy of activity with cleavers, bare fists and butterfly knives wielded in the confinement of the cellar.

Willy, having no time to reload his automatic smashed the whisky bottle on the edge of the step. He stuck it so firmly into someone's face it was wrenched out of his hand as the recipient fell. The rest of the team, including those who had come racing up from below, held their own.

It was Teng who brought the proceedings to a sudden

standstill in a moment of both desperation and inspiration. Looking at his watch he screamed, "stop fighting ..."

Julian did arrive, at that moment, on six o'clock with dawn attempting to break through heavy blue-black clouds. Instantly soaked again stepping out of the car he moved cautiously through the garden in the gloom and blinding rain. The television crew followed, their equipment primed. When their lights blazed suddenly on Wu's nervous order at seeing movement by the house, Julian dropped, rolling out of the line of fire. He had not wanted to see enforcers.

Only when he saw the three youths throw their weapons away and scramble over the wall into the woods did he realise the power of television. He stood up and chuckled at his unorthodox troop with its armoury of lights, camera, battery packs, sound equipment and tripod.

"You'd be wise keeping your distance," he suggested, as they entered the house.

"We have no intention of upstaging you ..." Wu replied.

Kwan II stationed in the doorway of the first cellar told Julian how pleased he was to see him and would they be on the news? He reported Bill and younger Kim were dead. Willy was wounded and about ten enforcers were down. There were six to ten left around the villa but they may have gone. He described the situation below as a stalemate of seven against eight. Willy held the casting vote, with an empty clip.

Julian asked the lighting technician and cameraman to hold back until he was halfway down the steps and with several thousand watts of photo flood lighting behind him, descended slowly into the lower cellar. His lengthening shadow went before him and as the light grew stronger the effect in the darkness was immediate. Everyone backed away, shielding their eyes. A nervous Wu stifled a laugh as he slipped into the cellar with the camera, directorial mode conquering fear of a room full of angry young men. With claws, Julian's entrance could have been off a Bela Lugosi set.

Julian did not like what he saw. Five bodies lay on the brick floor, including those of Bill and Kim II. Teng called out urgently in Korean from the other side of the vaulted cavern.

"The door, master, what do we do about the door?"

"They don't know who we are," Julian replied in the same language with a demonic grin, "so first, we ask nicely."

He indicated the enforcers standing about, almost mesmerized, drop their weapons. He pointed to another of the guards and invited him, in Cantonese, to open the door. The fraught youth reached for the call button on the intercom by his head and whispered into it. Nothing happened. Julian repeated his request more slowly. The youth pressed the button again and said more urgently,

"Open the door, open the fucking door – "

There was a gasp from some of the Koreans at the sound of bolts drawn and hinges squeaking. Wu was beside himself when, with tape rolling and perfect lighting a young woman emerged from the tunnel. With hand on hip, a black beret with red star, neatly pressed khaki shirt and rifle slung across her back, the only things missing were cigar and beard.

Shielding her eyes she shrieked,

"What theatre is this?"

Willy lowered his gun and turned to Julian, grinning.

"Just in time for a costume party, Boss. Great idea, the film crew. Just the thing for a pair of old show-offs!"

"Speak for yourself," Julian responded without taking his eyes off Jenny Lo.

He knew the woman, though slightly-built, possessed formidable fighting skills. She was also at her most unpredictable. It was one of her men who ran at him from the shadows with a knife. The man sank to his knees, unable to breath and unsure exactly how he had been stopped. A second fighter also tried his luck and Julian concentrated a different force. Ah Yong had stepped in the way and was perplexed at seeing the man totter, his eyes rolling in his head. He fell, apparently asleep.

The Red Pole opened her mouth. She knew of only one master of *cheum yan sul*, one of *Hwarangdo's* mental power techniques.

"*Si hing ...*" she muttered, shielding her eyes again, this time looking for Julian.

"It has been twenty-three years, *si mui*," Julian responded.

Her eyes searched Julian's face. Before her was a man she had not seen since she was a girl. He had loved her sister but then joined the caravans in South-East Asia. She cast her mind back to the previous Summer, to her aborted contract in Europe, the trip that had put her on house duty in Hong Kong. She remembered the likeness of the boy in the hotel room to 'the Lion' she had known.

"So your death is but a formality, *si hing*," she began, her voice hardening. "The punishment you accept for breaking the vows ..."

"If you try, *si mui*," Julian replied, barely able to conceal his displeasure at the young woman's unbending nerve, "you will forfeit your life."

Jenny Lo took Julian at his word. Her cold eyes did not leave his but she had respect enough to fall silent before her teacher.

A burst of machine gun fire broke the tension, causing several people to jump. Willy, also taken aback at the gun unjamming itself while he was absently fiddling with the trigger, began cackling.

"Get us out of here, Boss. Doesn't anyone else need a cold beer?"

Having ordered the collection of all weapons, Julian sent

three of the team back into the house. He gave Kwan II his walkie-talkie and told him to take cover at the front and co-ordinate reporting on all outside movement. He then invited Jenny Lo to lead them into the tunnel.

The room at the end was also brick-lined, vaulted and lit temporarily by oil lamps. In the centre was an incongruous stainless steel boardroom table with glass top. Around it were seven comfortable chairs. There was an eighth against the wall. A second steel doorway on the far side of the vault was open a fraction to daylight and howling wind. Teng pulled the door open further then leant on it to try and stop water streaming in. Mud, boulders and a tree had blocked the exit to the cove and jetty below.

Around the table sat five trapped men. As a dozen strangers and camera crew entered the room, all five hastily slipped black hoods with eye holes in them over their heads. Apart from this covering each was casually dressed that Sunday morning, as if on his way to a round of golf. They were, however, clearly in distress.

The young Koreans looked on in awe. None of them knew the power of the ritual and oaths, or understood the wealth, the status and expertise of the men before them. They certainly sensed it was a place no ordinary people should be.

While Kim, with the camera crew at his shoulder checked each for weapons, Teng approached Julian grimly and said it was absolutely essential these people were immediately unmasked. He and a lot of others needed to see who these triad people were and public humiliation was surely the most direct way of helping him in difficult days to come. Julian saw Wu look at his watch again and invited Teng to step forward.

Teng walked slowly around the table searching each pair of eyes. He stopped behind the figure wearing golfing slacks and tartan jersey with leather elbow patches. Two things were missing from this small man's weekend wear, studded shoes and the string gloves normally hanging from his hip pocket. Teng removed the hood so quickly the Japanese gasped. So angry was the young man at this confirmation of his senior and one of his father's golfing partners seated at the table he almost struck him. Julian was watching but his mind was on the three empty seats in the room. The television crew had taken over the scene. If he had a final card to play, he could not have played it so publicly.

"Mister Moto ... *bucho-san*. The firm's shipping director," Teng began in Cantonese. "After the supreme disappointment of learning my father has operated in a sewer for years and two of my friends lay dead outside, I find our senior director has been working the same sewer."

He repeated himself in Mandarin and with panache, English, for the benefit of the World Channel.

"Be careful, *Teng-kun*," the Japanese responded, returning the honorific, also with a hint of sarcasm. "I am still your boss."

Teng screwed up his face and thundered,

"You are a rat in a sewer, Moto. Do you seriously think as of today, in front of us, in front of the whole of Hong Kong, you are still my boss ..."

Highly agitated now, Teng walked once more around the table. As he did so the other five removed their hoods in a final act of submission. Two others he also knew and was shocked. As he walked around the table Wu indicated to Sam to get their gear together. They were out of time and almost out of tape. Having missed the fighting he was praying now for one more incident to complete the spectacle.

His prayer was answered when Teng came up behind Moto again and in a state of extreme exasperation began slapping him in a curiously feminine manner. Only his nostrils flaring prevented tears. One of his friends pulled him away, telling him to be calm. This was the moment Julian knew would save the family name.

Teng quickly regained his dignity and addressing the five triad bosses and television crew hanging on his every word, announced that from the moment he joined the business he would work to remove every trace of gang activity. It would be his mission, he went on in the same uncompromising tone, to restore the century-old good name of family and firm.

Peterson, above, in the garden with several colleagues was a few minutes too late to hear Teng first hand. He could only have guessed he would grow heartily sick of hearing the speech over the next few days. A star was born. Young, good-looking, educated and able to communicate in perfect Korean, Cantonese, Mandarin and English, the media would not be letting him go awhile.

There was a change of wind direction to the South-East later in the morning but the serious storm category remained. One of Peterson's men at the cove from where council members would have departed had the risky task of checking the boat house. A fallen tree had all but demolished it and the motor-launch inside sunk. The recess in the cliff face into which the cellar entrance was set had collapsed after being hit by a torrent of water from an unexpected direction. It was a black rain situation and he was mindful of being flushed into the sea.

Blue lights flashed in the mist all around the villa. A huge police presence had begun processing the remaining triad members. Their bosses had been taken away under tight security. An array of sober-suited gentlemen were in earnest discussions around the villa filling boxes with papers and other items. Cars were back and forth under heavy skies. The television crew and nine Koreans who had survived the operation were gone.

14/3

Lantau Island, Thursday 24 July

Julian's last debriefing, two days after the operation was with the Triad Society Bureau. He was somewhat guarded even after reassurance from Peterson this was not the lax police office of his youth. It had re-appeared as a law enforcement organization in 1978 then merged with a far more potent new office, the OCTB, the Organized Crime and Triad Bureau.

That evening he was walking on a grassy hillside on Lantau. It was fresh and cool after the rain and oppressive heat of recent weeks. The wind was still brisk, a moon was rising. Typhoon Joe had raged for twenty-four hours causing loss of life and considerable damage in Hong Kong and neighbouring Guangdong province.

Beyond the peace of a summer night in the hills, distant Hong Kong may have picked up speed again. Julian had no sense of it, far away on the south-western corner of Lantau overlooking the small island of Peaked Hill. Just the week before they had swum out to the scrub-covered rock and back as an excursion. He still had the sickening feeling the empty chair next to Lee's was for the triad's *fan shan chu*, Lee's right hand man and the person who really ran the organisation. The chair against the wall would have been for his scribe. These men had escaped by the grace of the weather gods.

The consequences of the break-up and arrest of all but the most important member of the Hong Kong council did not bear thinking about. There was also the question of an unknown number of other 14K *shan chu* in the larger Chinese communities around the world. The triad would already be undergoing urgent, radical and thorough restructuring. A rebirth. Then Julian remembered his own advice to his nephew in Cannes a year earlier and knew he had to let it go. It was while looking at the moon he saw cycle, inevitability and fate. He had done what he could in that phase of his life.

Reaching the cliff-top track he realized there was a presence in the darkness some way from him in that quiet place. The sweet, gentle breeze playing through the grass and around the craggy rocks offered nothing. Nonetheless the darkness of the hillside was playing host to someone other than himself. He caught the reflection of a pair of eyes in the moonlight and walked towards them. The figure began to glow.

"Thought I'd join you for some air!" Willy said, his teeth flashing.

While calculating the distance between them, Julian found himself on his back, telling himself he must respect a snake with a powerful bite. He wasn't sure why he was lying on his back and why everything before him was turning gently over and around. A tree cartwheeled by him into the darkness. He heard Willy's laugh from one direction, then another. Willy, whom no-one had seen since Tai Tam Bay.

"You are the one getting soft, Old Man!"

He felt himself being handled and heard Willy whisper,

"I'm neither sorry, nor happy at catching you out, Julian. I am a committed brother, like yourself but not a wanderer. I've had no trouble over the years doing what I am told, no conscience, no searching for who I am. I do what I'm told and even get paid ..."

Julian could not get his brain to function properly. This was the time he dreaded, the dream of how his end would be. When dreaming it, there was no panic, just a supreme effort to no avail. Now he only felt pathetic. This was not the waking in a sweat to a silent city or throbbing jungle. This time he was in trouble. Willy had blown a stream of toxic powder into his face from several metres, with the breeze, with devastating accuracy. All he could grasp on that hillside were harsh echoes and a darkness shot with lurid colours.

"Yes, it was a surprise in New York in '69 discovering you were still alive. The *sap sei kei* has changed a lot Julian, since you were with us. You were dismissed after Vietnam. That was luck. But then you got busy when we were trying to strengthen our business in the States. We lost you again, also luck. But you were a good boy over the years, until this week. This week you have been very bad ..."

Willy began in his own dialect but finished in Cantonese to chilling effect. Because Willy talked, Julian had been able to orientate himself, his position on the cliff and where Willy stood.

"... And all this business, this worry of recent weeks," Willy went on. "You can't imagine what pain you've caused, bringing me along to stick a knife in my own people. In your own people, Julian, *zi gei jau*. The girl, Jenny Lo was just sloppy. Huang-lin paid for his sentimentality when he came after you. Now you are not getting away ..."

To Julian's astonishment Willy then began quoting the initiation ceremony they had undergone many years earlier. If Willy was stupid enough to run through the entire thing Julian knew he would survive and once again he began the supreme effort of his dreams. His brain was functioning well, except for the colours.

"Who do you go with ... stranger, why come you here?" he heard Willy ask. "We come to enlist in the army of the brothers of the Hung family ..."

Willy's recitation floated about them.

"Then you will suffer many hardships. Your rations will consist of seven parts sand to three of rice ..."

Julian was counting his fingers with his thumb and feeling down his leg. He stood up and saw Willy staring strangely at him. His legs buckled but he willed himself to stand. More importantly he saw a black hole by the path, a gulley on the cliff and rolled down it knowing sand, the beach, was not far below. He didn't feel anything apart from winded and stood slowly in a routine that would tell him if any bones were broken. He had to be quick, rocks and Willy, were tumbling after him.

His breathing was steadier and through his mouth only. Some of the substance was still in his nose. He blew it. He was lucky his mouth hadn't been open. His eyes were no longer swimming. He saw Willy but needed a few seconds more. Then, almost liberated from his dream he began floating away over the shore. Two people passed, like spirits on the air and a hand reaching for his shoulder stopped his flight.

"*Si bok* ..."

These words were uttered by Teng.

"Be very careful," Julian found himself saying, jolted into reality and pushing both Teng and Cecilia behind him. He could only marvel at the appearance of his best student on so remote a spot, just as his time had come to an end.

Willy came upon Julian again, almost out of the cliff, like an apparition and Cecilia gasped. He was silent and more cautious with the younger man to watch also. As he edged forward, so Julian retreated to the waves breaking a brilliant white, drawing Willy away from the cliff into moonlight. And just as Willy realised he should have dealt with Julian's student, Teng attacked.

Teng would have done better stalling, allowing time for his inexperience to assess the odds. He might just have held Willy off with a combination of strength and luck. Instead he tried a flying kick. Willy reversed himself, caught Teng's leading leg between his own and twisted his body in an amazing display of agility. It was Teng's friend who screamed at the sound of cracking bone. Teng landed in a heap, unconscious.

Willy turned again to Julian but as he moved forward this time, Julian stood his ground. Willy understood the taunt and knew, even with the advantage the placing of a final blow would not be easy. He heard the girl gasp again but this time it wasn't fear, it was through effort.

Cecilia was not rushing at him in anger, she was incensed. Lifting to her chest a rock she would normally have been unable to move, her hands bleeding from the effort, she was propelled by her own demons. Willy's final tactical error was thinking he would step aside and follow the girl through to his target but the rock caught his bandaged arm. He stood no chance as Julian hit him at the same instant, square to the heart. The Malay-Chinese sailor sank to his knees and pitched forward into the sand. Julian rolled him over.

It was a blow that would have killed most outright, a linear punch developed to break through wooden armour and bones. This was Willy. Within minutes he was dark blue from abdomen to neck and upper arms. It was twenty minutes before his breathing faltered and his heart stopped. It was a difficult decision but Julian began resuscitation through Willy's mouth. There was too much internal damage for him to touch his chest.

Cecilia was kneeling at Teng's side. He was moaning but having recovered from the shock of what she had done to Willy, she was calm and reassuring. Here was everything her finishing school had taught her and a little more.

Julian looked at the damage to Teng's leg.

"We must call for an ambulance. The 'phone at the installation is probably the nearest."

"I'll go," Cecilia said. "My car is not far away, at the end of the track at Fan Lau. I'll drive round. I couldn't cope again if that monster woke up."

Julian assured her he would not regain consciousness for a couple of days and his chances of survival were slim, if they got him to a hospital quickly. She looked at Julian's bruises and bloody patches on his clothes and asked if he was feeling better.

"I am, Miss. I am in your debt."

She started off along the beach to the path back to Fan Lau and the old fort. She stopped to take off her shoes, threw the silk scarf flapping in her face into the sea in disgust and disappeared into the gloom, running for all she was worth.

Julian made Teng comfortable, treating him with acupressure to keep blood flowing through his leg. He also searched the rocks for a particular herb and gave it to the young man to chew. When Teng's pain was sufficiently dulled Julian advised him to yell at the moment his knee was being straightened.

Teng, with tears on his cheek, apologised for crying like a baby as Julian made up a temporary splint from pieces of driftwood. He was very tired, he said, with family concerns, interviews and preparation for meetings with the firm's directors. Cecilia and he were there that evening because he wanted to escape the media circus for a while and show her the beautiful beach opposite Peaked Hill.

The moon cast a look of death over Willy nearby. When Teng's pain had subsided again he asked Julian why he had revived an old enemy. Willy showed no mercy. Of everything to do with triad activity Teng had witnessed in recent weeks, the most telling had been the killing. Now his master had shown compassion.

Julian watched the tiny pinpoints of light on a solitary cargo vessel far to the south at the beginning of another long journey.

"Life is too short already," he said. "Even Willy has a journey ahead and things to do. He might now even reflect on his past."

Cecilia returned within the hour with Song-san, Kim and Ah Yong, having run and driven like a maniac on the dirt roads around the southern peaks. The three Koreans were horrified at what they saw. They had asked if they could remain in Hong Kong as Julian's bodyguard until he left for China. Their failure to protect him subdued them greatly when they realised how close was his demise. It was those minutes on the hillside that matured them, rather than the traumatic events of recent weeks.

They also reaffirmed their support for Teng at a difficult time. His father, they learned from their pocket radio, had been removed from prison and was under guard in a private hospital in Kowloon after a suspected heart attack. Teng, his mother and sister were still the subject of a media frenzy, with television crews from around Asia camped on Peak Road, to the frustration of the police. Other members of the team had returned to Korea with American help, taking with them the body of the younger Kim. As was his last wish, Bill would be going on to his cousins in California.

Julian and his remaining students put Teng and Willy onto stretchers for the steep climb over the ridge and around the old monastery to the Tai O road. Julian asked Cecilia if she had a lipstick and could he borrow it. She produced one from her shoulder bag with some embarrassment. He wrote a little note and placed it in Willy's pocket and to the astonishment of all of them drew a pair of lips on the man's cheek. As they lifted the stretchers he smiled, then laughed. The others laughed too and Julian felt better than he had done for a very long time.

The note read,

Goodbye, Old Fruit. Goodbye for ever.

CHAPTER FIFTEEN

Guangdong, September 1980

A few days after the activity in Hong Kong Julian focussed on his visit to China. Picking up his visa as he checked out of his hotel, he took the express train to the border, went without fuss through the white marble customs hall reserved for foreign visitors and passed from a tiny British colony into the vastness of China. From the railway station at Guangzhou he had no option but to walk to the nearby bus station. Taxis had not yet come to this part of the world.

The bus journey south to Zhaoqing took five hours. The monotony of green paddy-fields on a September morning was relieved only by the occasional village, a ferry crossing of the West River and a stop for an early lunch at a dusty roadside restaurant. Once again he was obliged to walk from the bus station to the traffic circle at the top of Tianning Lu. He would have to carry his bundles on his back to his destination.

Cherry trees offered welcome shade from the wooden arch at the entrance of the Park of the Seven Star Crags to the river. Everywhere in the midday sunshine people were shopping or trading on the pavements or from the fronts of tenements. A policeman in a white jacket directed the mass of bicycles by the town's largest hotel, the Zhaoqing Mansions. The sound of bicycle bells and hawkers, the roar of an occasional bus, the smell of food and the sight of all manner of livestock on hand carts and handlebars accompanied Julian all the way.

He turned into a quieter tree-lined street by the river and found the Tung household without difficulty. Two children skipping in the garden stared as he pushed the iron gate open and ran inside when he said "*hello*". Chi-ling appeared. She smiled broadly at her nephew, extending her arms. Julian put his bundles down. He had not expected this un-Chinese greeting.

"It is a great honour to have you visit us, Favourite Sister's son," she said.

"And how ashamed I am not making the journey frequently when I have such an aunt as you," Julian replied.

This was Julian's first stop in China on a lengthy round-trip meeting and revisiting family on his mother's side. He had indeed reproached himself for having met his aunt once only, in Hong Kong in 1955 when she had come to visit after his father's death. She made an extraordinary journey leaving China and returning illegally, at great cost. She was then Younger Sister. Now she was near fifty with two grown-up daughters of her own.

Her husband, Te-wen, appeared with a bag of carpenter's tools. He was a tough, wiry man with several gold teeth his smile showed to the full. Chi-ling introduced Julian as "the little Lion grown so tall". He grasped Julian's hand and apologised for having to return to work. A truck pulled up at the gate and hooted. He said he looked forward to returning that evening.

Behind Te-wen was younger daughter, Li-min. She was a pretty girl of nineteen years who looked much as Julian remembered her mother. She held out her arm stiffly, knowing Westerners shook hands and said they were honoured. She in turn introduced the children playing in the front. They belonged to Elder Sister who was shopping in the town. Julian removed his shoes, was presented with a pair of sandals because he was a special guest and was welcomed inside.

He was shown around the house after taking tea and marvelled at how spacious it was. His observation it was two dwellings was confirmed by his aunt who said it was only possible because of his generosity. He was not aware that money he sent every New Year went in to a communal fund that had paid for the adjoining property.

He complimented his aunt also on how fresh everything was and she said Te-wen had painted inside and out and white-washed the garden walls for his visit. She also pointed proudly to one of the power points and Julian remembered his mother writing that electricity was a recent improvement.

"It is a fine house," he proffered, walking through the kitchen into the rear courtyard. "The facilities are good."

"We are grateful not having to wash everything in the river any more," she replied.

After the tour Chi-ling insisted on preparing him a proper midday meal. He tried to hold her off, replying with traditional good manners she must not trouble herself on his account. It was to no avail and after his second lunch of the day he could do little but chat to his aunt, two cousins and their neighbours and children under the shade of a plum tree with the extraordinary smells and sounds of China about him.

Later, at a gathering of the immediate family he gave out the small presents he had collected in recent months in Korea and in recent weeks in Hong Kong. He came fully laden, his mother advising that at least fifteen people would congregate for his visit.

His main burden, brought on public transport and on his back, was a colour television set. The dealer tuned it for both Guangzhou and Hong Kong television and the quality of the picture brought a gasp around the room. Such sets did exist in the town he was told but none of them had seen one.

Jade TV's offering was a soap opera. The Hong Kong studio set two hundred kilometres away was in marked contrast to the room receiving it and they understood well, Julian saying perhaps it was unwise to introduce such a demon into the house. Te-wen said they would not let it become master but Li-min and a neighbour's son admitted they were not so sure. It was soon switched off, however, and the entire gathering broke into applause.

Later, after the evening meal, Li-min contrived to walk with Julian to the Zhaoqing Mansions where he had booked a room for two nights. Her mother said it was past eight o'clock and too late for her to be out but Julian said he would welcome her company. They set off at a brisk pace along Tajiao Lu past the boarded-up pagoda and up Gongnong Lu, walking in the road.

There was little activity in the town now. A naked light bulb at each intersection lit their way to the main street. They passed a snack vendor chatting to his last customers, his glowing brazier showing the gaunt faces of the young men on the kerb sharing a bottle of beer and cheap cigarettes. A cyclist appeared in the gloom. He rang his bell idly but on seeing Julian and Li-min he was so fascinated he kept pace with them, causing a cyclist coming the other way to swerve and words to be exchanged.

Li-min was embarrassed. She also liked to look at the foreign tourists but it was different being with one. She asked Older Cousin if he found this rude and he said this was only his first day in China.

They called in at a soda shop at the top of Tianning Lu by the hotel after a polite request from Li-min. Here, trying not to look too pleased with herself, she introduced Julian to several teenagers who had apparently known of his visit since his letter was received in the Tung household.

The boys stared unabashed, uncomfortable at Julian's obvious physical strength. He was certainly Chinese, he spoke Cantonese but he had dark brown hair and the look and stature of a European. He was also wearing clothes of a quality they had not seen. Li-min's girlfriends were most interested in his looks.

Using new *Renmin* notes given to hard-currency tourists and unseen by most traders, including this soda shop owner, Julian treated them all to imported Cokes and stayed for a little polite conversation. Cream and lime green paint was flaking from the walls. The floor was littered with cigarette butts, brightly-coloured cartons and other rubbish and a ceiling fan flicking above his head did nothing to soothe the neon glare. He made sure his young cousin would be escorted home and excused himself. He needed to sleep.

That night, when noise from the street and from other residents in the hotel abated, Julian reflected on the previous autumn and winter in Korea. Only through the monastery, the peace of the mountains of Jin-do, its magnificent sunsets, meditation and physical training had he succeeded in regaining strength lost in a seemingly interminable struggle against triad power. For the knowledge passed on to him and the unstinting support from his teachers in Korea, Hong Kong and Japan over decades, he would be eternally grateful.

The Hong Kong operation had also reminded him how important family was. His second call in China would be a lengthier stay with his mother in Xian, where she was engaged in the excavation of the *Qin* Emperor's tomb and terracotta army. After these obligations he would decide his next move. He knew only that it would be back to Europe.

He woke at seven the following morning, refreshed after his first proper sleep in days. There was no time for breakfast. Li-min and two friends, including one of the girls from the soda shop, were already waiting to take him around the Seven Star Crags. It was cool and sunny and all three, Li-min, Yu-liang and the boy, Ken-lang were dressed in light quilted jackets, grey trousers and sandals. They were pleased Julian greeted them with a smile saying he had been looking forward to seeing one of Guangdong province's great attractions.

The crags rise almost vertically above a series of artificial lakes ringed by a causeway several kilometres in length. The narrow limestone formations with trees clinging to them form shapes known by individual names since the *T'ang* period. There are also extensive caves where painters and poets have inscribed praises in verse for centuries and it was one of these systems Julian and his companions explored first.

When they emerged again into the sunshine they climbed to the top of one of the pinnacles up a winding pathway more fitting for mountain goats. The view from the small pavilion was worth the effort. A tree rooted in the rotting limestone was decorated with empty soft drinks cans on strings. The lakes lay far below. Zhaoqing was spread across the middle distance amidst a patchwork of fields and beyond this, the silver ribbon of the West River, showing like fine silk slit occasionally, lay delicately around the mountains.

While they were resting, Julian brought out photographs of his nephew taken in Belgium and France. Li-min's relationship to Peter as second cousin was highly pertinent and she and her friends were very interested. They studied a grinning Peter posing with Thérèse and Daphne before the *Arc de Triomphe* and no-less-impressive *Atomium* in Brussels. There were other shots of them including one by Julian's car in front of the hotel in Cannes.

"He looks tall," Li-min said eventually.

"And he doesn't have a big nose," Ken-lang said absently.

Li-min nudged him but Julian laughed. He remembered

Thérèse annoying Peter in Paris by saying his nose was sweet. If there was evidence of Chinese in him, it was in his nose.

They examined the pictures for a long time. Li-min touched her hair unconsciously and Julian guessed it was because she had not seen hair as blonde and fine as Thérèse's. She was also looking carefully at Daphne, noticing Peter did not have his arm around her in most of the pictures.

"This lady is strong, Older Cousin," she said looking up at Julian. "She is lovely and I think you must like her?"

Ken-lang volunteered to take a group photograph, first studying Julian's Japanese camera, then eliciting a promise they receive copies of all pictures. Julian was now to be photographed with two girls younger even than Daphne and Thérèse. Wherever Peter was in the world, and he did not know where at that moment, he would surely have offered some comment.

On their return that afternoon, Chi-ling begged Julian's indulgence in her carrying on with preparations for the evening celebration while they talked.

"Everything is in hand here and Te-wen is not due back for an hour," she said looking at her new watch with pride. "He is on some construction work for a brigade in a nearby village. A team of skilled workers was loaned by the town to help them build a rice-milling plant."

She asked Julian if he would like some steamed dumplings to keep him going. Li-min placed four newly-prepared *dim-sum* into a basket over water boiling on the coke stove. She intended to have one. Her mother would surely say nothing. She also prepared the tea using their best cups, the turquoise blue ones from Shanghai with red and gold dragons and gold rims.

"So, you enjoyed our local attraction?" Chi-ling asked. "We think it every bit as good as the scenery around Guilin!"

Julian agreed the Park was impressive and he felt the distance they had walked was well worth the effort. The caves, with the lighting and commentary on the rock carvings, were especially memorable.

"Older Sister is well-known for her work on the project," she said proudly. "They started when I was still a girl. She began – she was put to work, I should say – on the landscaping of the park in the second winter, that of 1956 when she returned here. She soon proved herself, with her extra work on a catalogue of the cave drawings and bits and pieces they found and was made leader of the women of the Brigade."

Chi-ling went on to explain the local people toiled for three winters on the creation of the new park before turning their attention to the irrigation scheme and increase of food for the famine years, by which time Older Sister had won an award for her work and been accepted at Lingnan University.

She excused herself briefly to take a tray of finished pastries into the kitchen. Julian heard her issue further instructions to her daughters. She returned with a refilled thermos flask of boiled water and Julian took the opportunity of their being alone to ask of things he had thought about for many years. How his mother, how the family, had re-adjusted to her returning to China from Hong Kong.

"We did suffer a little at the beginning of the Cultural Revolution," Chi-ling admitted, topping up the tea pot a third time and jumping ten years to 1966. "She was lucky to escape re-education in the fields, there's no doubt about that. There weren't too many hooligans here. We did have a local cadre take a vigorous interest in what we were doing as a family. But we survived."

Julian listened intently. This was not something his mother had written about. Neither had they spoken since the end of those difficult times.

"The posters were the most upsetting thing," Chi-ling went on. "They put them up on the wall at the gate and they were aimed, of course, at your mother. Some townspeople were quick to bring up the fact she was an 'individual'. They remembered when she left as a young girl in the late 1930s, wanting to emigrate, like many others, to the West Coast of America. Walking as far as Guangzhou, she hid on a train, from the *kuo min tang* some say, from the Communists say others, and after days in a freight car reached Shanghai. To add to her problems it was not long afterwards the Japanese entered the city."

She paused for a moment before returning to Zhaoqing and more recent times.

"It got very bad here when the PLA came in 1967 and accused us of being capitalist-roaders. This was not fair because we have never owned land, or even knew about Western ways. In fact that was the worst year," she said her voice faltering. "Older Sister endured more than twenty denunciation meetings. Those hooligans came to conduct study of the works of Chairman Mao at the school Li-min had just started at. The Revolutionary Committee was the beginning of the end of what I call a traditional education and it got worse when the workers began giving the classes.

"But we must not talk about the past. Li-min had a lot of catching up to do and has won a college place. She's clever, like her aunt, and a good girl! Times are changing for us again, for the better we hope."

Li-min accompanied Julian from the hotel to the bus station at dawn for the next stage of his long journey north. He was tired and a little hung-over from feasting past midnight. Thankfully, his request for low-key celebrations over his two-day visit had been largely respected, otherwise he would not have slept at all. Li-min was bright and fresh and a little self-conscious as they walked in matching track

293

suits. His was pastel blue. Hers was pink and would certainly stand out in a crowd. It was decided again only she had the character to wear it.

Workmen huddled in a little group in the unpaved yard of the long-distance bus station stared at them. A motorised trailer transporting pigs bound in rattan came noisily by on the main road. Once passed, the mist settled again and the only sound in the half-light was of cocks crowing. People were already at work in the fields.

Li-min said she was very sad Older Cousin was unable to stay longer. She had enjoyed their conversation and photographs of faraway places. Julian knew she watched Hong Kong television, seeing young Chinese women expensively dressed, immaculately made-up and living Western lifestyles. Americans and Europeans were also coming to the Park in little buses from Guangzhou and it was quite an achievement for her to have spoken to one of them about foreign lands.

"There are beautiful places to see in China first," Julian said. "Many envy you here."

A smile returned to the girl's face.

"But will you take me somewhere foreign before I am old and married?" She blushed as she spoke. Her mother would have beaten her for such a remark.

Julian watched her from the back of the bus, standing in the dusty road in the early morning sunshine as the bus gathered speed. He raised his hand in a final parting wave. She reciprocated and as she smiled, it was as though the whole of China smiled also.

CHAPTER SIXTEEN

Brussels, 1980

As Summer approached, Daphne became more dissatisfied with her course. The offer of a teaching post at a *lycée* near Dijon gave her the incentive for a last effort and she was rather pleased to learn at the end of August she had acquired her masters degree. Looking forward to teaching again, she knew it could have been somewhere worse. She would not be living at home and did not think it was a good idea anyway. On the whole, she felt pleased she had a direction in her life at last.

It had not all been so certain. In the autumn of the previous year, soon after Julian had gone, she slipped into depression and did not eat properly for months. Weeping in her mother's arms, the depth of despair she reached frightened her and she knew for the second time in her life she had to take control. With counselling and love and affection from her parents and friends, particularly Martine, she gradually began smiling again.

She saw Peter briefly at Christmas when he stayed in her apartment. He was full of energy and she liked him very much. Unfortunately, his relationship with Thérèse had not survived and there was nothing she could do. He had written and talked a lot about Thérèse, admitting finally on Christmas Day he could not cope with what had happened. The attack on the girl he loved affected him deeply. He did not stay to welcome in the New Year, the new decade, and said he would never return to Brussels.

She went skiing in Switzerland in January with her parents, sad she had been unable to persuade Peter to come with them. She enjoyed the holiday and began to understand what it meant to be at peace with oneself. Her mother insisted she continue seeing a psychiatrist until the avuncular figure was sure of what it was troubling her daughter and advised her not to spend money on further visits.

She was happier at Easter and went on a sun-seeking holiday in Spain with some friends. She found herself alone most of the time walking along the beach or taking the bus inland to an old country hitherto unknown. Drink and discos had never been an interest and the trip was a last gesture to her student days.

Throughout the Spring she spent a great deal of time alone, reading and just thinking. She remembered Julian saying to have time, to make time to think is essential in one's life. It should not be a luxury. Finishing her Spring and Summer terms only with difficulty she made up her mind there were more important things to do than brood.

Deciding to stay in Brussels over the summer holiday before beginning teaching she took a temporary job with an accountancy firm in Place de la Monnaie. She had managed to keep up her evening classes in Mandarin at the Ixelles Institute where she had enrolled the previous Autumn. It was a gruelling course but she persevered and had learned much about the language and Chinese culture over the nine months from a Cantonese-speaking classmate. They had many long conversations over tea and the girl, Jenny, who was from Hong Kong, looked forward to meeting Julian.

Only occasionally did she see Thérèse and other friends socially, although she accompanied Thérèse to yoga classes until she returned to Paris after her graduation. Her dearest friend never again spoke of the rape but caused Daphne to cry one night after saying coldly she would never marry.

With her formal studies finished at the beginning of the summer, Daphne had more time to read about Chinese culture and arts and the martial arts. She also discovered *fung shui*, the I-Ching and Chinese astrology and was charmed to learn that being born in the Year of the Fire Monkey must have been the reason Julian occasionally called her 'Monkey'. She was not surprised he was a Metal Dragon, a warrior, the strongest-willed of all the Dragons. It gave her a new insight into his character and motivation.

She also decided that to become more cosmopolitan she should master English. She did this by watching British and American films in their original language and doing what Thérèse had done, read lighter novels. It was a good feeling she was succeeding in a basic understanding of the two most widely-spoken languages in the world, that she would eventually speak the three languages of three thousand million people. Julian was fluent in several tongues and she saw no reason why she couldn't be either. It was clear life was as big and fulfilling as one wished to make it.

There were many nights however, when she was desperately lonely. One of her greatest regrets was their relationship not being consummated sexually. Thankfully, she had told him at his lowest ebb she loved him. But she had also asked herself countless times if he had left Europe to find completeness elsewhere.

That she had not comforted this man at the times he must have needed her was one of the biggest traumas of their parting. He had always held back emotionally and physically and yet she knew in those few short months what he was feeling and what he needed. She resigned herself to thinking she had done something wrong, or his feelings were just not strong enough for him to take her. This is how it went around in her head. Only her psychiatrist knew.

Her plan now after saving as much of her salary as she could from two years of teaching was to travel. She wanted to see the world, to meet people. It was time, she decided. She was almost twenty-seven years old. She left Belgium for her new flat in Dijon at the beginning of September and was ready for a new challenge.

Lille, October 1980

Five weeks into a hectic first term at the school she made time to visit home, arriving late on a Friday night and almost falling in to bed with tiredness. She got up early the next morning and hurried to the local shops in a drizzle for some *brioches* and the newspapers. It was the 19th of October. It had been a year and five weeks since Julian had gone and a year since she had last walked the considerable distance from her apartment in Brussels to the Chaussée de Charleroi to buy the newspapers from the shop on the corner of Rue Faider. She had done this only to walk back down Rue Américaine.

She was wet through when she reached the end of her parents' street and was pleased to see her father out with the dog to meet her. He greeted his daughter with a kiss and they returned arm-in-arm admiring the yellows and browns of the plane trees along the avenue.

Inside the house, her mother passed her a note she had been looking after. Daphne's heart missed several beats. The envelope, postmarked in the People's Republic of China, was in Julian's hand. The note began,

Dear Margaret,

I hope you and Charles and Daphne are well. If you consider it expedient, I would consider it very kind of you to let Daphne know I shall be returning to Europe at the end of October. I hope she will understand and perhaps even forgive my writing to you ...

"I sent a reply to the Hong Kong address he gave," her

298

mother said. "I wrote that we, that you especially, will be very happy to see him again."

Daphne arranged three days off from her teaching and took the train to Brussels the day before Julian was due back in Belgium. She went to see Mme. Grimeau in Rue Américaine and was flattered the concierge recognised her and pleased she asked after both Thérèse and Peter. Mme. Grimeau knew Julian was returning from Hong Kong. She thought it a wonderful idea that Daphne bring flowers, agreeing it was not right for a gentleman to return to an empty apartment.

"You must, of course, arrange them yourself *Madame*. He will know it was you and I think it will please him."

Daphne kissed and thanked the woman. This was not the first time recently she had been addressed as *madame*, rather than *mademoiselle*. She was *mademoiselle* in class and to senior colleagues and was still unsure how to respond to her elevated status in public. It suggested she was more adult and it gave her a certain satisfaction.

She was not afraid, apprehensive certainly, as she waited for Julian's flight to come through from Luxembourg. She was worried she no longer knew her true feelings towards him. She was also deeply concerned about his feelings for her. But she was truly pleased to see him.

"Welcome home!" she said in Cantonese, her arms outstretched.

Julian smiled broadly.

"The world is my home, when it is you who greet me," he replied slowly and clearly. It was to the delight of them both her translation showed she had understood.

Only then, when they embraced, did he remember her femininity, her hair against his cheek. She was too choked to do anything but hold him tightly.

He was touched she had gone to the trouble of meeting

him and of arranging flowers with a little note in his apartment. He had much to do that afternoon but sat contemplating the return compliment of a bouquet of mixed lilies and the grown-up young woman who had brought them. He made tea, changed into warmer clothes and picked up the telephone.

Daphne had got out of the cab in town and wandered around until early in the afternoon. Julian had asked that they have dinner together. It all seemed so inevitable but what puzzled her most was she almost said no. How could she be so fickle, almost dismissing a year of pain and longing with a single 'no'? She pulled herself together when she saw the time, took a tram back to Martine's and began getting ready for the evening.

With guidance from her friend she decided on a short black dress and heels. Martine insisted she wear stockings.

"Your legs look great in them. You'll be more lady-like in them. He'll know straight away you're wearing them!"

"And every little helps ..." Daphne said smiling.

When the cab arrived, Martine gave her friend a final appraisal, telling her she looked absolutely stunning. Being dressed completely in black showed her hair and figure off perfectly. She was nervous but Martine said her man would relax her.

"Go, Girl and take no prisoners!"

Neither of them spoke much over dinner. Daphne had read once about the Language of Silence but only then knew its power. She could not help looking at Julian. He had not changed except he looked happier, more peaceful than she remembered. There were many things she had forgotten and she realised she hardly knew the man.

When they were ready to leave, he helped her with her coat and she remembered the time by the *Bourse* his hand accidentally touched her. She put her arms around him in the cool night air and he responded with a gentleness she had forgotten. She had forgotten too, how strong he was. She closed her eyes to stop tears from rising but the agonies and frustrations of more than a year finally cascaded down her cheeks.

"I missed you Julian, I missed you so much," she whispered, looking into his eyes.

"You were always with me, as you promised," he responded. "I had to wait. I didn't know if I would survive."

" ... but you would have been inside me."

The old market square was deserted and discreetly floodlit. The sound of live music from a nearby club and laughter from one of the beer cellars drifted by them. The cobbles were wet from a cold October drizzle. Daphne didn't notice these things. Her arms were inside Julian's coat and he was warm.

It was dawn when she focussed on the bedside clock. She couldn't quite believe how long they had made love. She brushed his hair across his forehead and got out of bed with some difficulty. She ached all over. As she crossed the bedroom floor she caught sight of herself in the mirror in the harsh morning light and was horrified she looked so wretched. She tried to do something with her face in the bathroom but gave up and returned to the bedside with a bowl of warm water.

Asking him if he could stand in the bowl, she bathed him from head to foot with sandalwood soap and a sea sponge. She dried him with a warm towel, arranged the duvet over him then washed herself. She had first washed in this way when the plumbing went wrong in her apartment and found it so sensuous she dreamed of sharing this one day with him as her lover.

Thérèse would not have been disappointed in her putting these items in his bathroom, she thought, with a little smile. She cradled his head against her breasts until he was asleep and was sure of his need of her. She had absorbed his soul, his whole being and could only think how beautiful he was.

When she woke later her heart sank at being alone in the bed. She turned over to see him appear from the kitchen with fresh coffee and a leisurely smile on his face.

"I didn't want to wake you. I didn't want to leave either, which means coffee but no *croissants!*"

Standing by his bed with autumn sunlight playing across her body she was acutely conscious of him looking at her naked in daylight. She tried to cover herself and thought how ridiculous this was. She closed her eyes and sustained a deep pleasure as he turned her slowly, kissing her body until he was kneeling in front of her. Feeling the need to examine herself carefully, she said with a wry smile,

"So this is how it really feels to be a woman ..."

"I'm sorry I took you quite so hard."

"Oh, I shall get used to it," she said, ruffling his hair.

When he had gone she wandered around his apartment. She admired herself in the mirror in the heavy embroidered silk dressing gown from Hong Kong. She took the remains of the breakfast they had shared into the kitchen and found there a small and beautifully-wrapped package with her name on it. Inside was a most exquisite ring and a note in Chinese.

Suddenly wide awake she sat with pencil, paper and dictionary. Julian began the note very simply, saying she was clever indeed if she understood half the characters. The ring was a tiger's eye carved into the head of a lion-dog and set in a heavy gold mount. It was a present to her from his mother. The lion-dog symbolised power, courage and victory and originated in Indian Buddhism, he wrote. They were how the Chinese thought lions looked and by tradition guarded temples and palaces. He had smuggled the ring out of China, as export of antiques is forbidden, so one day it should go back, with her wearing it.

Daphne set about scripting a reply in Chinese to Julian's

mother. This was hard but that single note, she knew, was the reason she had persevered with her studies and with her belief she should not let the memory of, or her feelings for this man go.

Eventually she ran a hot and luxurious bath and lay in the soapy bubbles until it was dark again outside. Her aches and pains disappeared. In fact she felt quite extraordinary she thought, as she caught sight of herself again in the mirror, smiling this time. Like a cat that has had all the cream.

16/2
Brussels, Thursday 30 October

Ross greeted Julian that Thursday afternoon with all his personal charm. He had heard nothing from his Number One since his resignation the year before and was pleased he called at Place Madou, whatever his reasons for returning to Europe. The only official mention of Julian was in a routine report from the Hong Kong police several months earlier. They commended his part in a highly successful Operation Snow White and suggested the Committee's work in Europe would be easier by the end of the year.

They were certainly pleased with the outcome in the colony, the custodial sentencing of several top triad members. Ross cross-checked the item with Cummings and found the Americans were also satisfied with the results of an operation that had enhanced their relations with the People's Republic. Julian had evidently caused quite a stir.

As they talked, thoughts of re-offering Julian his job crossed Ross's mind. He knew though, it would be sentimentality and perhaps a touch of conscience on behalf of those who had patently misjudged the man's ways. It was clear they had kept abreast of the problems laid on them by Common Market member governments mainly through Julian's calm professionalism.

Re-appointment would have been possible because a second five-year term for the Committee, with considerably increased funding, had just been secured. Seeing Julian smiling and fitter than ever, he knew such an offer was wholly inappropriate.

Julian accepted a cup of coffee from Mlle. Arameau and listened to Ross struggle with words and sentiments. The charges built up against him had been good ones, if somewhat engineered by Williams. His principle thoughts in that office however, were on how Ross had aged. He felt no compassion for the director, the job or for the city that had taken four years of his life. He had learnt the simple lesson that we are all dispensable, that the world will carry on without us. Others, possibly more suited, would be doing a perfectly good job in his place.

Descending in the lift, Julian heard the adjacent one activate and waited. It was an anxious Mlle. Arameau who emerged. She handed him a sheaf of United Nations brochures, saying he had forgotten them in her office. Julian guessed he would get the information he had returned to Europe for. He opened the first brochure on his way down to the Metro and saw she had scribbled her new home address and the time, '8 tonight.'

Two days after calling in on Ross's assistant, Julian took a flight to Marseilles and checked into a small hotel on Rue Paradis by the Prefecture Building. He did not have to wait long in the afternoon for two Committee field men, one of them Marc, to check in also.

"Julian, Old Fellow. I can hardly believe my eyes! How the devil are you?"

"I'm well," Julian replied, stepping inside Marc's room. "I'm delighted to see you in one piece again!"

Marc picked up the telephone and asked the hotelier's wife if she could bring wine and sandwiches to his room.

He turned again to Julian and said he assumed he was there unofficially and they should not be seen together. He laughed at Julian's reply. A dull operation might about to be livened up.

"I was surprised to learn you were on this operation," Julian said. "The last time I saw you, you were in quite a state."

"I had to carry on," Marc replied. "It was my nurse who, one day, ordered me to get up and get dressed. And, *mon Dieu*, on that very day she took me to a squash match! Not to play, of course. Just to make me see other people with worse disabilities not feeling sorry for themselves. I mean, what's in losing a finger, diabetes, being a bit deaf and a bit slower! Anyway, she also made me ask for my job back, to give me something to kick against and the Boss granted it. As she was obviously good for my health I brought her back to Brussels with me!"

Julian said he was very pleased life was going his way at last.

"And about you, Julian. It was a bad business, the pressure put on you last year. I was sad you found it necessary to resign. We heard reports on what you were doing in Hong Kong. Sounds extraordinary. You must tell all when we have the time. We threw a party for you, by the way, all seven of us. Four months after your departure, this was, because it took me that long to get back to work. We thought it was a good idea and wanted to wish you well, one way or another."

"That was thoughtful," Julian said. "Thank the rest of the team for me."

When the wine arrived they drank each other's health. Marc went on to say he was pleased Mlle. Arameau passed on his message they should meet in the event of his turning up in Europe. It seemed Julian had appeared at just the right time, before an operation where there could be a break. He chuckled at the thought of the Boss's reaction if he knew Julian was in Marseilles again with them. If he hadn't been able to do Julian a personal favour he thought he should at least let him in on the Committee's latest bit of business, whatever Julian's reasons for turning up.

He related the details of the operation of the following Monday morning. He was working for the first time with a new Number Ten, who, he said was a bit of a plodder. There were DEA people involved, some specialists from the *Deuxième Bureau*, the French Narcotics Bureau and a representative from the WHO, not to mention back-up from the *Gendarmerie*. They would be converging on several addresses in Marseilles and other points along the coast in the early hours. It was an attempt at picking up suspected heads of a syndicate involved in slaving and raiding buildings that might be holding abductees for transit to North Africa.

The Committee were, as ever, short of vital information but results in recent months showed they were edging in the right direction. A very small criminal group, perhaps even a single Mister Big, was handling a large number of adolescent girls through French ports.

The catalogue business had been squashed, Marc said, but the French authorities were concerned the South Coast had become a centre of operations for a trade that still seemed to feature youngsters from society backgrounds.

When Marc left the hotel for his evening briefing, Julian took a taxi to the address of an aunt of Jean-Pierre. He knew the young journalist was dead, learning this the day he arrived in Brussels. He spoke to the editor of Jean-Pierre's newspaper in Marseilles and was told of the young man's death from a car accident six months earlier in the mountains north-east of the city. The wreck had burned, suspiciously perhaps, and his body identified from dental records.

The editor was proud to tell Julian that Jean-Pierre came

up with the story he always knew he would, a story about triads controlling abduction, slavery and so on along the coast. It was a long run, the editor said, with muck stirred to such an extent it touched nerves in the government.

There were repercussions, not the least of which was the Minister of Trade's cancellation of a visit to China because of strong public opinion against unacceptable Chinese ways, even though it didn't relate to the People's Republic. The Palace tried to suppress the story because an arms deal was involved and this, the editor said, was when sales of the newspaper really took off.

The year before, on his way to Portugal to see Ferdinand, Julian spent an afternoon in Marseilles with Jean-Pierre. He gave the young journalist substantial information on triad crime and methods of operation in exchange for some leg work. He also warned the young journalist if he became involved in anything the triad was operating his life was at risk. It seemed he was unable to resist following the story to the death.

Jean-Pierre's aunt read Julian's letter of introduction, invited him in and went searching for the tin box her nephew referred to. Though he put things in it regularly it took her a moment to remember it was behind the kitchen stove. Julian thanked the woman for her trouble and returned with the box to the hotel.

It contained little. There was a letter addressed to him, a scrap book and a large plastic bag. In the letter was written:

> ... as for your advice about my head being on the block if a story broke, well, you see by the scrapbook it happened and after four months I'm still here! I have been careful but can't afford to move away. Marseilles is my home, though I dream of travel and the South Seas now I am almost famous!

And the story. I made it a big one, right up to the President himself! That put a few noses out of joint in my office and with those snobs in *Le Monde*, I can tell you ...

So, for the favour, I am watching the accommodation address. Apart from an employee going in a couple of times a week to pick up mail, activity is usually only at the beginning of the month. I have seen a secretary, two men (one with hat and cane) and a rather chic woman go into the building. I got the wind up one night when I think I was spotted in my car down the alley and so hit on a better idea I hope is of some use, although if you will excuse the pun it is garbage to me!

In the plastic bag are all the golf-ball typewriter ribbons from the *poubelles* sacks of the building. Every Thursday night, and I haven't missed any, I search through the bags. There are five ribbons at the moment. They are easy to read and of course everything typed on the machine is on them. Pretty clever!

So, my thanks once again for the break and I hope I will be around to have a drink with you again ...

Julian spent that Sunday evening reading the correspondence recorded on the ribbons. It would require cross-referencing but it was clearly an important source of information, the addresses and dates in particular. He held on to one of the carbon film cartridges and left the others in the hotel safe for Marc to take back to Brussels. When Marc returned from his briefing he saw Julian's note under his door and arranged with him over the telephone to meet in a café along the street.

Marc listened to what Julian planned to do the following morning and said he could join him at seven. They were to look over the office building the cartridge ribbons had come from and wait. He cast his mind back sixteen months. The building was only a couple of streets away from where he was attacked by the little banshee and left for dead. That was also on the first of the month, the beginning of a holiday he never saw. Neither he nor Julian would say there was no coincidence here.

After a couple of glasses of well-watered Ricard and a limp salad, Marc looked at his watch and suggested ten o'clock was a suitable time for a pair of elderly gentlemen to retire in view of the morning's activities.

At a little after seven on the morning of Monday the 3rd of November, Julian heard footsteps and some bottles accidentally kicked in the alley below him. It was still dark, the old harbour was silent, its yachts tightly packed and well-wrapped for the winter. He dropped silently to the ground from the fire escape directly in front of Marc.

"Nice to be working with a professional again," Marc said when he had regained his composure.

"How have things been this morning?" Julian enquired. Marc had been up since four and looked pale.

"A few fish," he replied, his voice low, "stunned by the dirty great sledge hammer of the French police. You must have heard the three sirens in chorus. They startled some Sicilian in his luxury apartment and chased him up and down. I could have throttled them. There's been mayhem and bad temper in the last couple of hours. I don't yet know what has been happening along the coast. But yes, we have a few fish."

They checked the quay at the front of the building and the alleys around. There was not a sound, save the odd gull, the lapping of water against glass fibre hulls and the faintest clacking of rigging.

"I hope something happens soon," Marc said. "I'm tired and I could do with some breakfast."

"The best I can do is a shot of this," Julian said, proffering a hip flask. "Vintage Armagnac for a change. We'll do breakfast later."

Julian saw the colour return to his colleague's face and decided how they would get into the building. Marc was not as quick as when they had last worked together, although they must have saved his lung, otherwise he would not have been on active duty. He said he would shin up the pipe to the toilet window on the second floor and open one lower down.

"Very considerate of you, Old Man. Just get on with it. I'll be right behind you."

Julian was up the soil pipe and in the upper window with a speed that made Marc raise his eyebrows. When he reached the lower window breathing hard he pulled himself in, with help, and stood in the gloomy wash-room wiping sweat from his forehead. Julian let him catch his breath.

The upper two floors were empty. The ground floor was stacked high with packing cases they had no time to inspect. There was also a workshop and garage with a wreck of a car under an old dust sheet. Four rooms made up offices on the first floor. These were spartan and unswept but magazines and journals relevant to the shipping and cargo container business were up-to-date and showed it to be a shipping broker's office.

Marc looked through a desk and filing cabinets in the room with the typewriter while Julian looked through desks and cupboards. Finding nothing of immediate interest they decided they would wait on either side of a partition wall from where they could see the top of the staircase and from where they could cover each other.

The port basin was visible through the grimy window in the stairwell. The mist was clearing across the water, white lights were still shining in single file down either side of the basin and they made themselves comfortable. They would wait, they agreed, for the morning at least.

Three-quarters of an hour only had passed when a car pulled up on the quay in front of the building. Julian managed a quick look from the stairwell window before the lock and the padlock at the entrance were undone. It was a black Citroën waiting, with condensation coming from its exhaust. He thought quickly as footsteps came up the staircase. It was important he did not miss whoever was in the car.

He signalled to Marc he was going out through the window to the alley. Unfortunately the debonair individual, complete with hat and cane chose to run up the staircase and Marc had no option but to step in his way to cover Julian. He aimed his pistol at the man's head with the warning he should not make a sound. The man shouted, nevertheless.

Julian lost time looking at the face under the rim of the hat. It was 'The Frenchman' and he asked himself what this arch-criminal was doing there. The delay meant he had to take the quick way down. He opened the landing window dropped six metres to the alley, sprinted around the corner and dived onto the roof of the car.

He was lucky, as the car surged forward, the passenger window was open. It gave him something to hang on to. He hit the windscreen with a closed fist and a small hand responded by punching a hole through the milky glass. Julian reached for the passenger door handle. The car slewed left, the door flew open and he rolled, gasping as he became wedged between door and car. He removed the rest of the windscreen with two more blows, caught hold of the steering wheel and turned the car back to the water.

The choice was simple. The woman driving was unable to break his grip and it was stop, or go over the quay. She braked sharply and with venom in her eyes started clawing and kicking at Julian. He lifted her bodily out of the car and held her face downwards on the cobbles, it needing all his strength to do this. Then in a moment of compassion he let go and stood back. She sat up and spat at him.

"So we catch up at last," she began with a theatrical laugh. "What took you so long – "

Julian stared into Ann-Marie's eyes and went numb as she began a low hysterical laugh and continuous mutter. It was an animal beneath the expensive furs. He could only stare at a woman he had once loved and held in his arms.

"So you find me at last ..." she repeated, " ... you who lost us millions with your moral crusade. Never had we such trouble until you appeared. Oh you, so clever, loosing us millions ..."

Julian now felt only her laughter cracking his bones. He heard Marc ask the question and heard him repeat it,

"Who is she? Who the hell is she?"

"She is my wife," Julian replied.

The sharp-eyed crew of a *Gendarmerie Maritime* inflatable in the Old Port as part of the morning operation, pulled alongside. The *sous-lieutenant* was on the radio to his boss even before climbing the ladder to the quay. The Frenchman, still holding his cane, was handcuffed to the passenger door of the Palais. Marc flashed his ID and asked the officer if he could be patched through to his operations *contrôle*.

The woman on the other side of the car had begun an astonishing monologue of obscenity. She was still sitting on the cobblestones and could not be approached. The gendarmes tried but she became vicious and they were so engrossed in a spectacle they would talk about for months they did not notice the stranger disappear in the morning mist.

She was screaming as Julian left but he did not look back. Marc's words hung in his ears.

"I'm so sorry, Julian. I'm so sorry."

EPILOGUE

To be for one day entirely at
leisure is to be for one day
an Immortal.

Seychelle Islands, April 1981

"Once on a tropical island and gorged with coconut my
next wish was to eat great piles of tropical fruits for
breakfast," Daphne said, "but there's no doubt it is too much
day after day!"

As she spoke, she was scraping the seeds out of a papaya
fruit. Neither of them could face another pineapple. Julian
was lounging in a cane chair near her. He was wearing a
white T-shirt, cut-offs fixed with a piece of rope from the
beach and was bare-foot. A battered straw hat was on the
table ready for a stroll after breakfast. Daphne put fresh
bread and coffee by him, began feeding him pieces of
papaya and asked,

"Is it because I have flesh like a peach and a heart of
stone you sometimes call me a peach?"

"It's because you are like *P'an-T'ao*," he replied, "Peaches
of the Orchard of Heaven that ripen only every three
thousand years and which bestow immortality on those who
eat them."

Daphne's eyes danced. Yet despite Julian's gentleness she
knew he was thinking about what they would be doing after
their extended Indian Ocean trip. She smoothed his hair and
asked if she could help. He said he was organising his

313

thoughts and was sorry his concern was showing.

"Are you planning something like the job you had in Brussels?"

"No, but I, we, could soon be short of money."

He leaned further back in the chair smiling.

"It is curious. For the first time in my life I have no income yet it is only a secondary consideration. But we have to be practical."

Daphne flexed her muscles.

"We have great talent between us – we're both masters of our art for a start!" she said gleefully.

Julian's gaze lingered over this adorable young woman half-naked in the cabin in her strong-arm pose. The early morning sun prickled its way through the palm leaf screen across the window. Beyond the doorway was an abundance of foliage all but swallowing heaped boulders of granite. The view gave way to a softer one of frangipani and palms, of white sand, a blue lagoon and the deep green of the Indian Ocean.

Daphne's tanned body glistened in the stray sunlight. She was wearing only a *sarong* about her waist. Julian stood and kissed her neck and shoulders and she tried to save the piece of material from slipping until she realised it was being removed.

"I was so under-utilised this time last year ..." she began, looking up at him, "... especially my body!"

She broke free and whooping with delight raced naked under the palms and down the beach, splashing into the lagoon. Julian caught up with her, this time holding her more firmly.

"We don't want the gods turning you into a laurel again!"

"Must I be less naughty or more ..."

She wrapped her legs around his waist and held him tightly as they glided about in the water. Small, brightly-coloured fish darted around them. The gentle swell lapped sensuously around her. The sun burned her shoulders but she was cool in the breeze. She had no intention of letting go.

"You are happy, aren't you!"

"I love it here. I love you."

Their weeks together in so perfect a setting was a dream realised for Daphne and she had told Julian a thousand times she loved him. He shielded her head from the sun with his hat and turning her face saw sadness in her eyes. She had waited a long time.

"I am also very happy to be here with you. And I love you."

Daphne relinquished her grip. Her legs slid down his and she stood on his feet in the warm water to gain more height. This was the first time he said he loved her and she kissed him and kissed him and kissed him.

The rain roared tumultuously around them after sunset and they dined by the light of an oil-lamp, sharing a lobster and a fish caught an hour earlier. Later in the evening the sound of one of the cooks strumming a guitar and singing came floating up from the beach and they walked arm-in-arm toward the driftwood fire bringing with them wine and fruit. Three other people welcomed them to the impromptu beach party.

They had hardly shown their faces in weeks at Choppy's Bungalows. Most of the island is taken up with a coconut plantation and there were never more than twenty people on it. It was easy for them to be alone, to explore, to swim and get to know each other. This was their third month together. They had gone looking for animals in East Africa, moved on to Mauritius, taken a boat to Reunion and were now lingering in their favourite to-date, the Seychelle Islands.

If she wanted to return to teaching, Julian said, he was sure they would find something somewhere in the world where they would be together. She replied she had much more to learn first and would follow his lead.

They walked along the beach early the following morning, Daphne with a bag over her shoulder. After three weeks of isolation on La Deigue she volunteered to venture out on the three-and-a-half-hour ferry journey to Mahé for some shopping and to see if there was any mail. The ferry would not be back until the middle of the week and although she would miss Julian she would at least see a little of the capital, Victoria.

He watched the ferry slip away beyond the distant islands and walked for the rest of the morning along the shore. After a siesta he took a boat out and cruised to a group of tiny islands between Praslin and Round Island for some spear fishing. Round Island lay peaceful and silent and crinkled in the fierce heat across a couple of kilometres of calm green water.

A smile came to his face. They were about to explore it the previous week when Daphne had noticed a derelict shelter. He mentioned it had once been a male leper colony and fifty metres was as close as they got.

He manoeuvred into the lagoon of an island just big enough to sustain a few palms and pulled the boat up on a narrow bank of sand. He swam for a while and late in the afternoon collected driftwood. He watched the sunset from the highest point of the atoll, about three metres he thought and after the evening rain made a fire in a hollow in the coarse white coral sand. After cooking a small fish and tasting the soft flesh of a coconut he lay on his side and thought the island as good a place as any to decide he would take Daphne on to the Far East, to Hong Kong and China if she wished. Perhaps even to Korea.

His thoughts drifted back to his travelling in China the year before. He could not think of a greater contrast with the intimacy of a sunset beyond the lagoon of this Indian

Ocean paradise than with the vast anonymity, the greyness, the basic level of existence in the world's most populous country.

He was very pleased to see his mother again after so many years, although meeting her at Xian airport was not the occasion he thought it would be. He was obliged to spend the evening with the delegation she had returned from Beijing with. This had included her assistant, three other archaeologists and two directors of the *Qin Shi Huang* Excavation Project.

It was only later that night he was able to put his arm around her shoulder and whisper happy birthday. It was the right day, he had remembered and she did not conceal her pleasure.

His most memorable tour was of the excavations of the Emperor's Pottery Army his mother and the other archaeologists were working on. He was quite unprepared for the effect of rows of life-size terracotta soldiers. A wooden building had been erected over them and the first one or two were uncovered. The rows behind showed them in stages appearing from the ground, so the fifth and sixth revealed heads only. There they stood, staring and silent and seen again for the first time in two thousand years.

A greater pleasure was seeing his mother once more using her arms in the most elegant of gesticulation, as a woman used to explaining things. Her facial expression too, showed how gracious she was. He was always surprised hearing Westerners say they could not read anything in an Oriental face. The human face expresses everything. Daphne had a rare perception in this way. She would have appreciated that day.

Lying in the sand on his little island watching the flames dancing before the waning colours of a tropical evening sky, he had almost forgotten how tired he became travelling in a country where travel was not an everyday occurrence.

From Guangzhou he journeyed by bus and train to Guilin, Xian, Beijing and Shanghai. In Beijing he did what all Chinese must do once in their lives, stand in the square of Tian an men. The occasion did prompt the question why, with a giant portrait of Chairman Mao looking over one end and grim Soviet-style government buildings dominating the other. Wandering through the silent and empty Forbidden City palace complex, the seat of twenty-four of China's celestial emperors to 1911 was more evocative of China's past.

He had also sympathised on many occasions with other foreigners frustrated with the difficulties they had endured because he at least knew the language. China was huge and as a host for tourists, not yet prepared.

Meeting his family in his middle life was a turning point. He saw people still cautious in how they expressed themselves, taking care not to re-open wounds caused by political ideology. He also discovered his family and their friends and neighbours had the same hopes and aspirations as people anywhere in the world. His most profound realisation was that he had crossed a racial and cultural divide and it was while shopping as a tourist in Shanghai's Friendship Store on the *Bund* he knew it was time to return to Europe.

He put more wood on his fire and lay back again in the sand. No words could express his contentment at the Milky Way looking like smoke from a dragon's nostrils. He thought he would shut his eyes eventually and abandon himself to the heavens and surrounding ocean but quite unexpectedly began to sing,

"Sleep, little brother, softly bye bye ..."

He listened to the sounds of the darkening island, the incessant noise of the cicadas, the crackling of the fire, the surf cascading almost luminous over the reef and on the rocks along the little shore. Pleased he was remembering a song his mother taught him, he began singing again until he fell asleep.

He was waiting on the beach with a small group of people on the morning of Daphne's return. They watched the changeover from the ferry to the whale-boat. Only the smaller craft had a draft shallow enough to cross into the lagoon. Daphne jumped out of the boat before it even landed and threw her arms around him, nearly knocking him over. The two other Europeans on the boat and the island people employed at the Bungalows smiled happily.

"I nearly missed the ferry, Julian! Wouldn't it have been awful, trying to catch a ride in the helicopter to the plantation."

"You would have managed it!"

"One of those colonial-looking policemen in knee socks drove me to the pier in a Mini Moke, leaning on the horn all the way. I told him my lover might desert me for a beautiful island girl, or worse, for a mermaid if I stayed any longer in Victoria!"

Julian took Daphne and the parcels she was laden with to the cabin. She put everything on the wicker table and presented him with a bottle of the bourbon he liked. She had bought copies of The Nation and Coastweek but neither of them were interested in reading. She produced two packets of vanilla tea, one red, the other blue.

Julian saying he was getting used to the way she made tea made her even more determined to do it properly. She wanted to be able to tell the difference between the two types. The last item was a cotton dress. She held it up for his approval, twirling with it pressed against her.

"I feel very beautiful with nothing on when it's you looking at me," she said carefully, "but sometimes I think being naked all the time is not very dignified."

"You have a natural dignity, Daphne," he said appraising

319

his vivacious young friend. "With or without clothes, I win!"

She poured him a whisky before lunch and out of sheer exuberance ran in the merciless heat for some ice, only to find there was no water again. When she returned she retrieved the two letters she had in her bag. The first was from Thérèse and addressed to both of them and she thought she had exercised commendable restraint in not opening it until then.

Julian lay back as she read and was pleased Thérèse wrote she was well and finding her job in a commercial design studio in Paris satisfying. She wished them both happiness. She also mentioned receiving a letter from Peter. He had been in Japan for some time and found a job and thought he would be staying a while. Having lost track of his uncle he asked that love and best wishes be passed on.

"That's lovely," Daphne said, "but it means he did drop out of university."

"He will go on to bigger things," Julian replied.

"And the other one looks very formal. It's also from Paris."

It was addressed to 'Daphne and Julian de Lyon', which looked nice Daphne thought, if a little premature. It was from Count Ferdinand and it began,

My Dear Julian,

I am writing to advise you that the legal problems remaining over title to the estate, its assets and gross income, of the late Count Maurice Courcy d'Arraques, are now resolved ...

It is with great sadness, however, I am able to write this has been done only because Ann-Marie has been sectioned under the mental health act and is likely to remain in confinement indefinitely ...

Julian looked up from the letter, mulling over Ferdinand's words that at least she had not suffered the humiliation of it becoming public the late count was not her father. Maurice knew Ann-Marie was not his child and understood the extent of her instability.

Daphne watched Julian carefully. She was sitting by him drinking from a coconut. She had managed to cut the soft yellow husk with four strokes of a machete and lift the square out, as even the children could do. Seeing his thoughts were many and his sadness great, she moved closer and put her hand on his chest. He began reading again.

> ... but on a happier and indeed enjoyable note, I am also letting you know that, as trustee to the French estate, I am able to make a bequest to you in the manner set out below.
>
> I have appreciated your integrity in the matter of your contract of marriage with Ann-Marie. You are a man of honour and I could find no other way of arranging that you benefit from Ann-Marie's substantial inheritance, as set out in Maurice's will, in the way I believe you should, whilst not going against your wishes. I sincerely hope, therefore, you find the following arrangements satisfactory ...

Curiosity now gripped Daphne and she asked Julian if he would finish reading it. He got out of the hammock and kissed her forehead. She took the letter and her eyes opened wide. When it came to the size of the bequest, the conditions and income to Julian set up as another trust, her mouth opened in astonishment. The last paragraphs read,

> It now remains only for me to tell you of my retirement. My good fortune at having a woman as wonderful as Helen as my wife continues. Our retirement has resumed at her family's estate in the north of Portugal where we have a delightful and rather more manageable *quinta*. It also looks

out to the New World, which has been one of our most cherished privileges over the years.

We will welcome a visit, Julian, from both you and Daphne. Helen and I were delighted to meet with your young lady and you must indulge our parental inclinations when we say we approved of her grace, her care for you and your association with her. It is for you therefore, Daphne, that, as well as expecting you will be sharing the income of the trust with Julian, this bequest includes the castle and estate.

Helen and I will in the future, be your guests. Our home now belongs to both of you.

Daphne turned toward the sea and the brilliance of another afternoon over a tropical paradise. When she looked at Julian eventually, tears were rolling down her cheeks. He took her hand and kissed it.

"I would say this day belongs to you."

"I loved that house," she responded. "I really loved it. But why me? Why me?"

16989721R00171

Made in the USA
Charleston, SC
20 January 2013